Published in the United States and Canada by Whisk(e)y Tit: www.whiskeytit.com. If you wish to use or reproduce all or part of this book for any means, please let the author and publisher know. You're pretty much required to, legally.

ISBN 978-1-952600-53-1

Cover painting by the author. Cover design by Olivia Hammerman.

ADVANCE PRAISE

Part stoner road journal, part coming-of-age narrative set in the apocalyptic wasteland of the 1990s American West. Dunne's language is at times reflective and at others vividly concrete. The detritus of post-industrial life remains in the forefront: the fully fleshed-out characters navigate a labyrinth of decaying vehicles, forgotten suburban ravines, scrub-desert vistas, spiritual anxiety, and an increasingly complex network of migratory road people. While taking seriously the concerns of a teenager set loose in the world, this story manages not to get lost in or fetishize those concerns. The result is a sober meditation on freedom and responsibility that at the same time manages to stay ridiculously high most of the time.

— Patrick Tonks, PhD, wine store clerk

This debut author has effortlessly picked you up from the side of the road and brought you along for the ride. And what a ride it is! From the very first chapter, the reader is brought through the emotional and practical highs and lows of life on the road as a young person finding their way. This is a time capsule of life before technology took over and is a gem of what life was like in that void. A page turner for the adventure reader, hop on in and come along for the trip!!

— Sarah Lupinacci

Western Starlands is a special book, a tautly lyrical account of traversing the United States in the early 1990s. It belongs to the tradition of American travel narratives, and it's there, in the stars around names like Kerouac and Pirsig, that Dunne carves his initials with wry humor and a lasting sweetness and lucidity. Here are friends like the ones you had, or like the ones you wished for. Here are places you used to know and dream about. Here's the journey you longed to make, here's a chance you should have taken.

— Hugh Sheehy, author of *Design Flaw* and *The Invisibles*

Recklessly abandoning societal norms and hitting the road in search of a deeper experience Toby's narrator rolls with hitchhikers, spare changers, punk rockers, hippies, addicts, and drifters, all living in the moment and going with the flow. Time on the road is a great adventure, a thrill, and often a humbling spiritual human awakening. Toby speaks the language of this experience in sublime heart-wrenching passion and accuracy.

— Cassandra St. Peter, Traveler, Taoist Educator and Poet.

CHAPTER 1

I didn't know what I was supposed to be doing with my young life. I was nineteen, deeply spiritually conflicted, and had recently flunked out of a state vocational school. I had only made it halfway through the second semester, returning to my hometown in failure after having rashly sworn an oath before Jesus that'd I'd never return. Instead, I was back living in the attic of my parents' house, my brief launch already arrested, spending the summer working and trying to figure out how to be a good young Christian man while simultaneously being a stoner metalhead, a tough balance to make since I had failed the drug test where I worked in the first couple weeks on the job. I had been working as a deck hand on one of the ferry boat companies that offered the only means of escape from my isolated island town and was owned by one of the church elders. My dad worked there too, as did many of the adults in my life. The owner in his benevolence had allowed me to continue working there only if I passed a weekly piss test to prove my sobriety, this after having had to stand before the congregation one Sunday morning and confess the wretched sin of weed burning, a sin I knew well and loved. I hadn't wanted to piss off Jesus any more than I figured I was already doing, so I played my part, and meant it. Jehovah God with his furious wrath was a constant background hum then, looming over every action, over every underage beer, over every lusty teenage thought. There was no escape from this unblinking eye, no escape from the ever-present guilt of my teenage sins.

By midsummer, I had somehow hooked up with my first legit girlfriend and had myself a soul-shattering breakup about a month later. I was so sure God had assigned this girl to me in some way as an answer to my virginal prayers and eager teenage fantasies. For what other reason would she have come to someone so unattractive as me, I reasoned, chubby and awkward as I was. Emerging as she did like an angel from the inky darkness of a local teen beach party, catching me as I stumbled drunkenly on the sand through the empty beer cans and solo cups to press her lips against mine. Not surprisingly, this fundamentalist born-again church I had grown up in heavily influenced my adolescent sexuality, animating me with completely ignorant ideas of what love and sex were supposed be. Being terrified of an angry Jesus, I came out to her with a full-on bended knee marriage proposal during the first week of the relationship, eager as I was to know sex with someone besides myself. It was surely because of this ridiculously preemptive proposition, driven by the fundamentalist position on premarital sexual abstinence I held as totally non-negotiable that this "love of my life" dropped my ass after a mere four weeks together. Her rejection devastated me, leaving my faith shaken to its core, and shattered the shaky confidence in my attractiveness she had briefly emboldened me with. I had failed God somehow, again, and blown my blessed chance at intimate relations. I felt like such a loser, my chances at life failed at every turn.

It was hard to not let these thoughts dominate my head space given the rote nature of my work on this boat, back and forth across the short channel dozens of times a day. But there were those times when distracted by one of those impossibly colored August sunrises over the bay, or the whirling cries of the terns working the bait fish, mingled with the dull thumping of briny swell gently smacking against the boat's hollow steel hull that I would have a clear moment free of my regrets and guilt. Then, in earnest I would yearn for a release from this place. Away from the failings I felt I had built around my life. Away from the self-perceived shame and guilt I had taken upon myself. Away from the expectations of the various authority figures who loomed over my daily life. I would look out over the side of the ferry at the dazzling light of the sun glittering off the surface of the water and think that there simply had to be more to life than this.

That summer, a young couple I knew from that state school I had dropped out of were regularly commuting over the ferry to work in a fancy restaurant off island. I would often have them on my boat and would look forward to the distraction they afforded me from my troubles.

Pete and Jen were not from my island town, or anywhere near the area. Pete was an Afro-Borinquen punker kid from Brooklyn, topped with a mop of multicolored dreadlocks and a buoyant indifference to life's troubles that always seemed to brighten my mood. His girlfriend, Jen, was a rebellious country girl from an area outside the upstate town of Ithaca, with a fiery temper, long straight mousy brown hair, pale complexion, and a rail-thin, bird-like physique.

The two had come to the island for the summer to work the seasonal restaurant shifts. They had heard that easy money was to be made in these high-end restaurants during the summer months. Yet as I got to know them, they lamented to me that this plan was not really working out as well as they had hoped. Pete's skin tone, not to mention his green and purple dreads, had put him on the radar of the local police pretty much straight away. There were only maybe a dozen residents of various shades of brown on the island at the time, and Pete with his bright style stood out everywhere he went. He had already been harassed by a few vocal locals several times while out walking his gold-colored mutt dog, Dylan, and had been threatened with a trespassing charge by the local cops for flying a kite in an unfenced unposted open field. So, take all that hassle, and what had turned out to be long thankless hours serving rich snobs for little pay, and they were also looking to get out.

We had hung out a bunch of times over the summer and gotten to know each other well enough that they felt they could let me in on their plans. On one morning trip across the channel, they confided in me that they were not long for this town, and since they knew I was of a similar mind, said that I should join them on a road trip to the west coast. Instantly the fog of doubt and gloom which had so clouded the preceding weeks blew away.

"Hell yeah!" I exclaimed. "Where are you guys gonna go?"

"Seattle," Pete answered. "We've heard the rents are cheap, and the scene is awesome. Local bands playing shows all the time, coffee houses, cool people. It'll be great there. We can all go in on a place, get jobs and shit, and just live well."

"I am so down, man," I said as the boat neared the dock. "So, when are we leaving?"

"In about a month, probably," Jen replied, leaning over Pete from the passenger side, her eyes squinting in the swirling smoke of her cigarette.

"Oh, man, This is exactly what I need! I've been feeling completely hopeless these past few weeks, and this just, just. This just totally made my fucking day!" as a smile grew across Pete's sparsely bearded face.

"Stop by the shack tonight after work. We'll talk details," Pete said, as the landing ferry's steel lip slammed against the dock ramp.

"Fuckin a, man. You know I will."

"Hey! Come on!" shouted the captain from up in the pilot house window. "Get moving! Open up the gate and let these cars off, come on!"

"Ok, man, I'll see you guys tonight," I said as I hustled with the thick bow rope, looping the knot over the heavy steel cleat at speed by muscle memory alone. "So fuckin stoked, dude!"

I directed each car off the boat with what I'm sure was the stupidest grin splashed across my face, and gave a big high-five wave to Pete and Jen as they rolled up off the boat. Holy shit, man. This is it, I thought. All the despair over that girl, all that self-doubt. Man, it was the past. God had heard my pitiful cries, I was sure and had offered me an out. And just like that the world with all the endless possibilities of youth began unfolding in front of me like some ridiculously painted flower. Holy fucking shit, man. This is it!

I spent the rest of my shift with a spring in my step like I hadn't felt in weeks, and the hours flew by. I had gone in to work the first boat, like an hour before sunrise, so I was cut loose by midafternoon. I knew Pete and Jen wouldn't be done with their restaurant jobs till much later, like well after dark, so I had some time to kill. I was totally amped up with the thought of this now impending road trip, so much so that my hands shook. I rode my bike back towards my parent's place taking the longest way I could without doubling back, just to burn off the excess energy raging inside me.

The cool evening air felt good as it rushed over my sun-tanned skin, cutting through my unkempt scraggly hair and patchy juvenile beard. I eventually made my way out to a secluded beach on the east side of the island: an area bordered by an environmentally protected strip of sandy flatland populated by tall rustling grasses, native cacti, and dwarfed fragrant junipers. It was one of the few places left untouched by residential development on the island where one could almost guarantee some degree of solitude. This place we called Starlands.

Back in high school, my friends and I would often head out to this beach at night, light a small driftwood fire, and get hammered by moonlight. It was on this beach in fact, one autumn night a few years earlier while in the throes of a particularly intense acid trip, where my friend Donut and I discovered that the secrets of the universe were written in the patterns we saw in the starlit expanse above us. In the way the juniper branches intertwined and twirled fractal like with the darkness. In the way the polished beach stones churned like perfectly placed bubbles at our feet. In the way the stars swirled over our heads with quiet intensity. It all was alive and sentient, animated with forces both strange and wonderful. It all fit together so perfectly and made so much sense to us in that moment that it just had to be true. It couldn't not be true. We spent that night stomping around the sand with our heavy knobbed boots kneading the dough of a new earth where we were an integral part of this cosmic carnival, the masters of our own reality, the lords of our own destiny. That night we reverently gave the place its name. Later, when the sharp light of dawn lit up the beach, we found that what we thought were the answers to the riddles of the cosmos were merely our chemically enhanced propensity to spot patterns where none were present, our glittering epiphanies draining away like sand through our fingers as the accelerants left our systems.

Nevertheless, I would often return to this place when my head was running hot, for I viewed the place as something of an anchoring point when some important issue or event was weighing heavy on my mind. This coming road trip was obviously such an event.

I laid the bike onto those polished, bubbly beach stones and dropped my ass down next to it, pulling my knees up to my chest. A tickling feeling rose from my core as I sat looking out over the bay in the fading afternoon light. Ripples of tingling energy radiated throughout my being, so much so that I began to laugh out loud. It was freedom I was feeling, raw ecstatic freedom, and it felt fucking great.

CHAPTER 2

I rode around aimlessly 'til long after the sun went down attempting to burn off the abundance of excitement that coursed through me like a strong drug. Eventually I gave up trying to quell my anticipation and headed to the shack, even though I still had some time to kill before they came home. I spent over an hour there in a dark field across the street from where they were living, my back on the shaggy grass, looking up at the stars, dreaming of those unseen and unknown western lands and wishing I was stoned. It was damn near midnight by the time my friends finally arrived.

The dead-end street they lived on was a quiet one with only a couple of other houses. There hadn't been any cars until they came around the corner. I knew it was them instantly by the sound of that old jalopy car they drove around in. This car was a beat up old two door 1969 Oldsmobile Cutlass, then about 25 years old. Older than any of us. A mutual friend on the island had given the wreck to Pete in exchange for an eighth of weed. It had been in pretty rough shape, having been abandoned for years along the overgrown property line of an unkempt yard overtaken with brambles and brush. It was also left with the windows rolled down for some reason, so the front seat became home to a host of woodland creatures. Pete had pulled it from its leafy decay and nursed it back to health with a few used parts harvested from other junkers down at the town dump and the help of a local shade-tree mechanic.

Despite its run-down condition, it was still a sharp-looking car. Sporting the sleek lines of Detroit's glory days, it was fitted with recessed double headlights and designed with a sloping "fast back" finish that gave the car a somewhat sinister look. Time had ravaged the exterior though, blistering its original hunter green finish and leaving its sheet metal skin faded, cracked, and rusted. So once Pete had the car out of the weeds, and running well, he gave the car a rattle can army green paint job topped off with two flat black perpendicular stripes running up the hood from the grill to the windshield. And with its oversized knobby snow tires lifting the ride height in the rear, the car looked bad ass. It suddenly struck me that this would be the ride we would be taking out west.

"Yeah, man! This just keeps getting better and better," I said aloud to no one as I rose from the grass and mounted my bike once more.

I rolled up behind them just as they were shutting those heavy steel doors, the solid "Ka-chunk!" sound masking my initial meekly pronounced hello. They were unaware of my presence there in the dark.

"Jesus Christ!" exclaimed Jen as I materialized beside her. "You scared the ever-living shit out of me!"

"Sorry," I muttered sheepishly.

Instantly I felt the panic of displeasing the opposite sex that so often interjected whenever I was trying to look cool or whatever. No damn it, not when everything was coming together so well, I scolded myself. Me and my stupid, stupid… I don't know. Damn it, man, don't blow it already! Fuck! Now they are going to think I'm some kind of weirdo creeping up on girls in the dark, and who knows what else. Damn it! Fuck!

"Come on inside, bro. We got a couple six packs here." Pete said, obliviously indifferent to my unspoken concerns. "Let's crack open a couple cans, and we can talk about this road trip."

"Oh, yeah, awesome, cool, thanks." I bumbled out in a way that made Pete chuckle audibly in the dark.

He handed me one of the six packs he was carrying and put his free arm around my shoulder as we walked. Man, I have got to chill the fuck out, I told myself. These kids are not going to think I'm some weirdo or anything. We've been hanging out off and on this whole summer: they know me; think I'm cool or whatever. They invited me to travel with them and their dog in a small car across America for fucks sake. It's all good, man. No worries.

So we three picked our way through the darkness up to the front door of the shack using the barking of their dog, Dylan, as a guide. Pete and Jen had been living in this place all summer, and it had been at times a little rough. It wasn't really a shack so much as an addition to a much older house owned by the lady they were renting from. The whole place was really run down, and the yard was mostly choked with mats of bittersweet vines draped over dying trees and bushy overgrown shrubs.

This "shack" was basically just a room. It had one electrical outlet, no bathroom or kitchen facilities, and the far side leaked considerably when it rained on account of a failing union with yet another addition that was so rotted it was uninhabitable. This other addition was a little aluminum travel trailer from the 1950s completely obscured from the outside by a blanket of vines. I hadn't even known this little immobile camper trailer was back there until Pete let me in on the secret one evening after a few beers. He had forced opened the door at the back of the room with his shoulder earlier in the day and just had to show somebody what he found. There, a few feet from where they slept, the decomposing remains of this little forgotten mid-century camper festered in musty darkness, its moldy interior wet, covered in gray slimy mushrooms, and smelling of raccoon shit.

The rest of the house wasn't much better. A series of bright blue tarps had been laid across the roof to slow the leaks into the main house. The splashes of color from these multiple layers of half assed roofing were the only part of the place you could see through the brush from the road. The whole scene had an air of advanced decay: if you didn't know any better, you'd think the place was straight up abandoned.

Their landlady, Annie, had grown up in the house with her grandmother and inherited it while she was still quite young. There had probably never been any kind of real maintenance done to the place in the years before her grandmother died, and certainly none after. Throughout the house you could still spot vintage appliances and furnishings of this now long-dead grandmother which had remained in place since the time before the neglect of the house became Annie's responsibility.

Annie also kept cats. Lots of cats. She had a reputation around town for taking in strays, so people not surprisingly called her "the cat lady." I'm sure a lot of towns have one of these ladies who for whatever reason takes on this archetypal role as keeper of the cats, and our town was no exception. Most of the cats lived in a big fenced in area that wrapped around the side of the house and into the back yard, encompassing several dilapidated little sheds and clusters of boldly colored plastic totes with cat sized holes cut into them.

But some of the cats, the oldest and sickest ones, lived in the main house with her. It smelled vaguely of cat piss inside, of course, but not as bad as you might expect. She loved those cats and took care of them as best she could, seeing them in a sense as her children, no doubt. She had a lot of love for the animals in her care, and was a very friendly, kindly person to all who crossed her path. But she carried the weight of a desperate loneliness that lurched out of every interaction I had with her. It was a dark spider hole of a life she lived there, basically alone with her cats and decay. I felt for her and would often stop by to visit her and her feline roommates even when Pete and Jen were not around.

When we opened the door of their shack, the smell of mold punched me right in the nose.

"Whoa, shit!" Pete exclaimed, as Dylan bolted out of the door at us like a rocket. "It wasn't that bad this morning."

At the back of the room, a one-foot square piece of moist sheet rock had let go from the ceiling exposing a mass of damp insulation that hung in the air like a moldy pink cloud.

"Let's take this to Annie's side of the house," I said rather loudly, attempting to overcome the barrage of barking Dylan was unloading on me. "I'm pretty allergic to mold, I don't think I can hang out in here and still breathe."

"But it stinks like cat piss on Annie's side," Jen cried, as she attempted to get Dylan to chill the fuck out.

Jen was not too fond of Annie and had been pressing Pete to do something about the moldy room they were paying for the privilege of sleeping in. Pete was inclined to just ride it out for the remainder of the season, mainly because there was no place cheaper to rent, but that didn't stop Jen from bringing it up again whenever the stink presented itself. I can only imagine the arguments the two of them had in that room as they lay down to rest. They were both very headstrong, and the place sure smelled hard of mold that night.

"Well, cat piss smells better than this." Pete decided "Take these six packs next door. We'll be right behind you." And he held out the rings of cans with both arms.

I went around the side of the house with the beer, and through the wire mesh gate of the cat pen to the back door. The front door was pretty much swollen shut with rot, so this was the only way in. But you had to be quick about passing through the gate because some of those cats were crafty and would shoot out between your legs if given the chance. Then Annie would spend the next hour or so calling out to the escaped animal in the night, as if a half feral cat would answer to its name anyway.

I stepped up the mossy cinder block steps and gave a quick rap on the faded aluminum frame of the screen door. Annie looked happy to see me when she opened the inner door and invited me in. We each took a seat at her cluttered kitchen table, and I cracked her open a beer.

"So, how are you doing this evening, Annie?" I asked.

Before she could respond, a tortoise shell cat with one eye leapt up on the table scattering some loose papers and damn near knocking over my freshly opened beer.

"Grab her!" She asked me. "I have to put ointment on her eye."

That was a task easy enough to accomplish because that's really what the crusty looking creature wanted anyway and began to purr like a little motor as soon as I put my hands on her. "What eye?" I sarcastically asked, as the cat attempted to rub my face with the eyeless side of its head.

"Don't be mean. She has been very sick. She needs all the positive energy she can get," She said as she got up and left the room for the ointment.

The cat's eye hole was oozing a clear liquid, but she didn't appear to be in any pain. The purring now was reaching a fevered pace, and I could feel the vibrations in my chest whenever she passed over my lap and rubbed her thin bony body against my stomach. Other old and infirm cats were beginning to come into the room now and approach me, perhaps attracted by the rumbling purr emanating from this mangy little motor.

About this time, I became aware of the sound of Jen's raised voice muffled through the walls. They were arguing again, surely about the moldy room they had to sleep in. I finished the first beer quickly and reached over the cat to grab another. Jen's voice was getting louder now, and Dylan was barking as loud as ever. I still couldn't make out what she was saying, but I could tell from the inflection of her voice that she was pissed. Annie had come back into the room with the cat's eye ointment when a significant thud sounded through the wall.

"Do they always fight like this?" I asked.

"They're all bark and no bite. It usually doesn't last long. Jen yells, then Pete slams the door, and goes for a walk, and that's the end of it for a while."

Just then the back door swung open and Pete stepped in, silently pulled a beer from the ring, and drank it all down in one shot. Wiping the foam from his mouth he declared: "Two weeks. We're leaving in two weeks."

CHAPTER 3

Those next two weeks progressed at a frustratingly slow pace. I gave my notice down at the ferry and spent my off time attempting to wrap up the loose ends of my life at home.

My folks were not really into my sudden desire to drop everything and head off into the sunset, but I think they understood why I felt I had to go. When my father was about my age, he had lived in his VW bus during the restaurant off season and traveled around the southeast, stopping in to party with his buddies at various universities and college towns. I could see his mixed emotions when I told him of my intention to take this road trip. I'm sure he felt a combination of fatherly anxiety for my safety on the road, knowing full well the trials I might run up against, and an admiration of my desire to make this trip at all. He was also probably a bit envious of the idea too, remembering the wild times he surely had out on the road of his youth. My mom was pretty much all worry and did not think this trip was such a good idea, figuring it might be better for me if I just went back to college. But all the same she made no attempt to forbid it. Instead, they wished me the best, assuring me we all would be in their prayers, and advised me to turn the savings I had accumulated over the summer into traveler's checks, so I wouldn't get ripped off by any shady characters we might cross paths with out on the road.

As for my gear, I followed Pete's instruction and kept it as light as I could. When I had graduated high school, my parents surprised me with a quality backpacking setup complete with a sleeping bag and a little tent. They figured I would use the stuff on weekend camping trips while at the upstate school that I ended up dropping out of. I took the gear into the woods maybe a half dozen times or so while I was up there, but really spent most of my free time at school getting fucked up and trying to find my "soul mate," or any girl for that matter who wouldn't recoil at my awkward virginal advances. Along with some clothes and other small sundries, this gear was to form the core of my worldly possessions for the duration of the trip. I didn't yet know what Pete and Jen were planning on bringing, but I assumed it would be a lot of stuff since it was their car. I knew I had to keep it basic.

Saying goodbye to my island friends was unpleasant and at times pretty difficult because I was vocally of a mindset that I was never coming back, and these next weeks might be the last times we could all be together. Some of my friends were still in high school at the time, so the idea of me blowing out of town forever hit them kind of hard, I guess. One of these nights, while we were all shitfaced at a party down some dead end cul-de-sac, one of my friends got verbally resentful of me for leaving them all behind to languish in their high school misery.

"Fuck you, man!" he said to me. "How could you just leave us here like this to rot? I thought we were friends, man. I thought we were like brothers. We were all gonna stick together forever, man."

"I'm sorry," I sighed. "But I have got to do this."

I think deep down he understood why I was leaving, and I think he would have done the same had our places been switched, but it was still a sad way to leave off after all we had been through together. He ended up getting especially hammered that night and took a shit right on the front seat of somebody's unlocked pick-up truck on his drunken walk home. He was kind of a dick like that.

My last day on the job was exhilarating though mind-numbingly slow, and it seemed like no matter how many times that old rumbling boat crossed the channel the clock just never moved ahead. But once my shift was finally over, walking off the boat and punching out one last time was absolutely exhilarating.

I had a couple buddies pick me up from work in their beat-up old Jeep, and we four-wheeled it out onto Starlands beach for the evening, lit up a little driftwood fire, and burned down a shit ton of weed they had rolled up into huge spliffs. I had not taken a single puff in months. What better way to break a prolonged marijuana fast than to consume comically copious amounts of the herb with friends.

I couldn't help feeling a little sad to be leaving these friends and familiar places behind, and now that I was rip-roaring high for the first time in months an acute sense of nostalgia began to wash over me. I wanted to just hug my buddies.

"I love you guys," I said randomly after a sizable stretch of silence was spent staring into the fire. "I am really going to miss you all."

They both laughed aloud and agreed. They would miss me too. But that's the way life goes, you know. We each follow the path laid out before us, and when opportunity knocks, it's best to answer. All my island friends had told me they wished they could either join me or at least have a road trip of their own, but for whatever reason -be it work, family, laziness, or fear of the unknown- they all either couldn't or wouldn't follow my lead. I hoped that someday they could also find this freedom I was feeling now, if at least for a little while, but I knew for some of them this would never happen.

Fear of the unknown for a lot of people just froze them up solid. So many of the people I knew were stuck like this. Stuck in a dead-end existence, wishing they could just go out and do something for themselves. Instead, they all would just bitch about some local grievance and deal with the ominous spirit of the unknown by numbing the pain with drink and drug or just being a dick.

This unknown road ahead did not present itself as something to be feared to me at all, but rather as an adventure of the noblest kind, for it would be God's work I did as I traveled, living by example. It would be God's work when I faced trials and adversity and leaned on Jesus for support. And it would be God's work when I would finally penetrate the mysterious membrane of sex with my unknown future bride, whoever she might be. I felt confident the angels would walk with me and guide me as I traveled. Yea, even though I might walk through the valley in the shadow of my very own death, still I knew I would be protected on my mission. I felt almost indestructible in my blessed youth. I could do anything, and nothing could stand in my way. I began to pray a silent prayer of praise and thanks that felt all the more intense because I was so God damn high.

Lord, God, I thank you, I prayed silently to the fire. I thank you for all this you have given to me despite my wretched unworthiness. All praises be unto you! The fire danced higher into the night as if responding to my unspoken words, throwing sparks into the sky, swirling and mingling with the stars. All was right with the world, and my soul was right with God.

It was late, and my buddies wanted to go to their beds, but I was really grooving on this moment I was having. I told them I would be staying; I could walk back to my parent's from here, or maybe just spend the night under the stars. It was a late summer night and was still warm enough to sleep outdoors without a blanket, so I decided then I would do exactly that, even as I spoke with them. They again had a chuckle at my out-of-doors inclinations, left me with a couple fat roaches to share with the fire, and rumbled off down the beach leaving me alone with my thoughts.

As I puffed on one of those roaches and watched their taillights crawl away along the shoreline a thought came to my mind. What would I do about church while I was out on the road? I understood it was forbidden to forsake the assembly and miss the communion ritual. How was I to reconcile this aspect of my faith with the realities of traveling about with non-believers? I would have to find a church every Sunday. And it would have to be one of my denomination, or it might not count. That would be a pain in the ass.

Again, I took a deep drag off the smoldering stump of spliff I clutched vice like between my fingers. As I exhaled a thick dank cloud into the fire an obvious solution sprang into mind. If God is everywhere, and everything, then why do I need to go to a building built by men? All the world could be his church. Of course! I could find his house of worship anywhere in nature. I might as well be before the altar in his house even now.

But what of communion, the partaking of the body and the blood of Christ? I could not just cop out on that. It was like the most important part, right? I would have to carry the matzo crackers and the grape juice with me. Okay, so no big deal, I could do that.

I took another big puff and pulled the hot cherry closer to my fingers. Yeah, I could do this. Every Sunday I can retreat to some private place, preferably in some natural setting, and perform the ritual of communion on my own. I don't need a preacher man to walk me through it, I can figure out how to pull this off in a way God would find pleasing. I'm sure he would understand and find my offering acceptable in his sight, right?

Just then the pain of that red hot cherry burning into my finger snapped me out of my focus, and I automatically flung the smoldering roach into the darkness. Damn it! There was still a puff or two in that thing, I grumbled to myself. I reached beyond the firelight to find another piece of driftwood to drop on the fire. It was getting a little colder now as the night leaned into the early morning hours, but not so cold as to dissuade me from laying out by the fire. I stretched out on the sand, set my sights to the heavens above, and slowly drifted off in the presence of this glorious cosmos, confident all would be well with my soul.

As the dawn approached, I was haunted by troubling dreams while I slept there in the sand. I found myself alone in a vast dark room, piled high with thick dusty books as far as I could see. Some of the book stacks climbed up and out of sight into the darkness above like thick threads. I was attempting to find something, something in a book not surprisingly, but every book I opened was blank.

I was beginning to panic in my fruitless searching and moved about the piles frantically, looking for this unknown thing, bumping into these precariously piled tomes and making them sway dangerously. Soon these tall stacks were all swaying around like crazy, throwing off clouds of dust. Then they all began to move in unison and in an instant it became apparent that these moving piles of books were in fact the flowing hairs on the lower half of a giant bearded face. The top of this face including the eyes were obscured in the dark heights above, and though the face slowly bore down on me the upper half never came into view.

The mouth opened as the face descended, and a voice as loud as a thousand trumpets poured onto me like a torrent of raging water, scattering the remaining books and tearing them to pieces. As the voice increased in pitch and the mouth opened wider, it began to turn itself inside out and splayed open like bright pink bat wings, the color of which was so incredibly intense the piercing sound of the voice seemed to emanate from the color itself. As this pink skin pulled taught, I realized what was bearing down on me was a tremendous vagina, pulled open like the girls do with their fingers in the hard-core porno magazines. I had first seen this image as a curious young boy in a friend's father's skin magazine, and it had at the time disturbed me greatly, the picture staying in my mind's eye for weeks. Now that it was larger than life and screaming close, I was absolutely terrified.

It was one word this terrible voice of radiant color had been sounding, one word that had been crushing me under its weight, the word I'm sure I had been so frantically searching for among all those cobwebby books. It was an awesome word, terrible to behold, and it was a word that despite its absolute closeness, I could not understand.

I awoke with a start, the sound of the dream still ringing in my ears. The fire had burned down to glowing embers, and all was quiet around me save for the gentle sound of the bay rolling over the stones at the water's edge. I looked out over the starlit expanse of water in a sort of shock. Holy shit, man! What the fuck was that! A strong shiver ran the length of my body, and I realized suddenly I was very cold. I stood up and shook the cool sand off my clothes. What the fuck time is it? I thought. It was still dark, but the air had an early dawn feel. Maybe an hour before the birds start singing, I thought. I fumbled around in my pockets to find the second roach my buddies had left me, and when I had found it knelt back down before the fading heat of the fire pit and lit the thing on an ember.

What did that crazy dream mean? The thought of that giant screaming vagina gave me the willies. I shivered again and hit the roach hard, consuming it in three puffs. Dare I say it? Was I approached by God himself in this dream? If I was, it sure was an awful vision to have right before such a journey as I was about to undertake. I kicked some sand into the embers of the fire and turned for home. Bullshit! I don't know what that dream could've meant, but I'm not about to quit now. Not before I've even started. Besides, it was probably just demons whispering in my ear anyway.

Yeah, that's it, just whispering demons.

CHAPTER 4

The day of our departure found me awake at the break of dawn, bristling with an all-consuming excitement. I had hardly slept at all the night before, despite my valiant attempts to knock myself out with a sizable quantity of weed. Pete had said they would be by to pick me up early, and like most of my friends at the time their idea of early was hours later than mine, especially after all those predawn shifts working the first boat all summer. So, when they finally did roll up the driveway the morning had already passed well into double digits.

I could see right away the car was packed full of shit. The sporty lifting of the rear end the unloaded car had earlier displayed was gone. The car now rode low in the wheel wells with weight, and a mountain bike was strapped haphazardly over the trunk. Pete and Jen climbed out followed by Dylan who instantly flew into a fit of barking. Dylan was a young dog at the time, maybe a year old, and very excitable. He was by no means an aggressive pup, but the barking fits were at times a bit trying. He seemed to deal with most situations by barking at them. As the back-seat rider, I was to spend many hours beside him getting to know his loyal, albeit hyperactive personality.

As promised, I came out with a minimal amount of gear to add to the mix: my pack combined with another couple knapsacks stuffed with some odd bits of camping gear. I helped Pete unlash the bike from the back of the car and felt my heart sink when he opened the lid. The trunk was absolutely full. Every inch of the space was filled with something overlapping onto something else.

"Whoa, shit, dude," I exclaimed.

"Don't worry, man. Some of this shit I'm going to leave at my mom's place in Brooklyn. Like the bike maybe, and this shit here," He assured me, pointing generally at a mass of stuff. "

We'll be sleeping there tonight, so it'll only be cramped like this for a little while."

He punched a big dent into a large duffle bag and placed the knapsacks I had brought into the newly formed depression, slamming the trunk lid down to smooth out the lumps. My main pack would have to ride with me and the dog in the back seat for today, at least.

My mother was a little teary as I hugged my dad and her goodbye. I assured them I would be alright, bringing to mind the confidence I had that God would be watching over me. It was a long hug, my mother holding me a while longer than I wanted. They had seen me off once before already when I left for my short-lived college experience, but this was different, and we all knew it. There was no telling how this would all turn out, and it was often my mother's nature to expect the worst. But I was eager to hit this road I had been fantasizing about these past couple weeks and was really of a mindset to just snap off these home front relations clean. They waved goodbye as we backed out down the driveway and took a few pictures of the receding car. Goodbye mom, goodbye dad.

They say all roads begin right in front of your feet. In this case the road began on the cramped back seat floor pan of an old American car cluttered with empty coffee cups and soiled fast-food wrappers. It seemed so unreal; I almost couldn't believe this was actually happening. I watched the familiar landscape beside the roads of my childhood pass across the little triangle shaped side window of the back seat as we motored towards the ferry and felt the gentle tug of nostalgia in my guts. Away from me, demon! You will not hinder my passing today!

We caught the boat as it was being loaded and got a space towards the back. I had to get out and lean over the railing for this one last ferry ride across the channel in the warm sunshine. Pete joined me at the back of the boat as we watched the island gain in distance away from us. One of the deck hands on board, a fellow I had pulled many shifts with over the past summer, came up to us and asked me:

"Hey, man. So, is this it? Are you guys leaving now?"

"Yeah, man. It all starts here," I quietly replied.

He joined us in our rearward gaze, sharing in the moment. But for him it would be just one more of many rearward views on his daily back and forth crossing, briefly escaping the island's gravitational pull only to circle back again dozens of times a day. I knew that feeling well. I had been like a comet in an elliptical orbit, again and again returning to this place no matter how far I ran. But now, surely, I would have enough momentum to break free of this stifling gravity. This time I knew it would be different, it had to be different. For I had obscured my hasty escape in the smoke of the bridges I had burned in my passing. I wanted there to be nothing left on that island to be drawn back to. Nothing left to tempt me to return. Fuck that place, I thought as I watched the far shore recede behind us. I am never coming back.

The boat landed at the slip on the far shore with a thud, jolting all aboard with a quick forward jerk. When it was our turn to be let off the boat Pete mashed the gas pedal to the floor as we cleared the ramp, and the Oldsmobile's Rocket 350 engine roared under the effort of dragging the extra weight of all their shit up the hill before us until we crested the rise. Pete then set his foot to cruise and shifted down a little lower in his seat. The world was truly before us now.

Well, almost. There was just one last thing my companions needed to take care of before the trip got real. We had to stop off at the house of a coworker of theirs who had their last paychecks. It was on the way, so it shouldn't be a big deal, Pete assured us. The guy wasn't going to be home but had stashed the checks in an old coffee can on the back deck of the house he had been renting all summer. It would not take but a minute, and we would be on our way again.

We pulled up to a shabby looking one-story ranch house with an overgrown lawn and faded paint, parking in the washed out, pot holed dirt driveway. We all got out of the car to stretch. A little hiss of steam was coming out from the front grill, so Pete popped the hood to investigate while Jen went around to the back of the house to find the checks.

One of the first issues Pete had with the car when he pulled it out of the woods was a totally wasted radiator. If you poured water into the filler neck it would just run straight out the bottom onto the ground. He of course had been on a tight budget in the restoration of his old classic, so he scoured the town dump till he found a radiator from a junk car that mated up with the hose locations of the engine and held pressure well enough to work. Unfortunately, it was a bit too small for that big 350 engine of ours, having been extracted from some smaller car with a six-cylinder engine, so the Olds tended to overheat when pushed too hard. Flooring the car up that first hill under all the extra weight and then abruptly shutting off the engine had got the motor pretty well heat soaked, which caused the radiator cap to release some of the hot pressure built up inside.

I don't know what Pete was thinking when he reached for the radiator cap, and later when I asked him about it, he didn't have an answer for me. Suddenly a rusty green geyser of scalding hot anti-freeze blew out of the filler neck up his chest, and under his bearded chin, the force of the impact throwing him backwards and onto the ground with a terrible cry.

"Oh my god, Pete! Are you alright?" I exclaimed.

"Shit shit shit, God damn it! Fuck!" he hollered as he scrambled to get up off his back like an overturned crab.

Jen came running around the corner with the coffee can in her hand calling out "Peter, what's going on?" while Dylan was freaking out behind the windshield and throwing himself against the glass. I grabbed Pete under his arms and helped him to his feet. Immediately he ripped the T shirt from his chest and threw it off to the side where it let off wisps of steam as it lay there on the ground.

"What the fuck just happened?" screamed Jen, her eyes wide in alarm.

"The radiator! It exploded! I'm covered in hot antifreeze! Holy shit it burns!" and he broke into a run off around the side of the house.

We followed him close behind to one of those shitty outside showers attached to the side of the house. Pete attempted to turn the paint crusted faucet handles, and one of them came off in his hand.

"God damn it!" he cried in a desperate, high pitched exclaim.

Messing with the remaining faucet handle produced nothing, so he quickly abandoned the derelict shower and continued around the side of the house looking for a hose or a bird bath or something, anything with cold water.

"Here, here!" Jen hollered "There's a hose right here!"

Pete stripped off the rest of his clothes and started spraying the hose on his head and face, groaning loudly.

"Don't take your clothes off, Peter! You can't be naked out here!" she cried "Someone will see and call the cops!"

"God damn it, Jen I don't give a shit about that right now! My chest is on fucking fire!"

"Why did you mess with that radiator, Peter? I told you to fix that before we left! Why do you never listen to what I say?!" She berated. "Oh my God, Peter! You can't be out here naked in this person's lawn!"

"God damn it, God damn it, Jen! Go get me a fucking towel or something then!" he fired back, the hose blasting into his dreadlocks and water running in thick streams down his face.

She rushed off back around the house, while I just stood there with Pete. I didn't know what to do. He had the hose going and was standing in a muddy puddle at this point. Jen was off to get him dry clothes or whatever, so there really wasn't anything for me to do but stand there in shock. I had just started picking up his wet clothes when Jen came back around the house at a jog.

"Come on Peter." She pleaded "We should get out of here; the neighbors are watching us."

"Okay, okay! Fill up a jug or something with this water here." He commanded me, holding out the running hose in my general direction blindly. "We're going to need more water for the radiator, now that the anti-freeze is all over the fucking place."

I had no jug, of course, so I dashed around the house looking for a jug or something to fill with water. There was nothing. How could such a shitty rental house have such a clean yard? Fuck! I have got to find something; we have to get out of here before someone calls the cops on us! The coffee can! I can use that to collect the water for the radiator. Where's that coffee can with the checks inside?

I ran towards the car and saw it on the dashboard. I pulled the passenger door open and instantly released Dylan's fury. Barking like a maniac, he pushed me to one side and tore off towards Pete, catching the soft, wet spot on the ground where he had been blasting himself with the hose and promptly wiped out into a muddy pile of doggie disaster.

Holy shit, what a fucking disaster this was turning out to be! We've only been on the road for like half an hour and already shit has hit the fan. Fucking A man, what next? I came back with the coffee can and begin making trips from the hose back to the steaming hot radiator till I had it full to the top. I then quickly screwed on the cap and shut the hood.

By now Pete had his oversized corduroy pants back on, cinched tight with an old striped necktie as a belt, and was walking barefoot back to the car with Jen right behind him, leading Dylan by the collar. Into the car we all climbed again, hit the gas, and got the fuck out of there in a hurry. The road in that area wound through a wooded landscape spotted with small houses, but Pete took the corners with manic speed, attempting to put some distance between us and the recent radiator explosion.

We drove on like that for a short time in silence before Jen began berating Pete again. They argued back and forth with each other in the front seat, while I in the back seat attempted to ignore it, like a little kid whose parents were at it again. I plucked a piece of random paper off the floor, folded it in half, and rolled up a joint on my lap, blowing the first hit forward between my bickering companions.

"Chill out, you two." I pleaded and passed the doobie ahead to Jen.

That seemed to do the trick, and their bickering subsided. I stared blankly out the window as they passed the thing between them, processing the tense scene that had just kicked off our trip. What the hell had Pete been thinking? Wasn't "don't touch a hot radiator cap" like the first fucking thing you learned in kindergarten? Fucking A, Pete. Damn though, that must have hurt like crazy, and now Jen giving him shit about his dumb ass must have made the whole thing sting even more. We trucked on in relative silence for about an hour or so before we pulled over so Pete could put his sneakers on and finish dressing. Then Jen took over behind the wheel for the rest of the two-hour ride into Brooklyn, while Pete groaned and grimaced beside her.

It was dark by the time we crossed into New York City limits. I had been into the city several times in high school, for punk rock shows and weed runs, or whatever, but never had I spent the night. Brooklyn at this time was still pretty sketchy after dark. We would have to basically unload the car into his mom's apartment before we called it a night in hopes of discouraging the local lurking crack heads of the evening from knocking out a window of the car.

Finding parking close to the entrance of his mom's building was of course futile at that time of the evening, so we double parked out front and started moving bags and boxes of shit into the foyer. Pete's mom must have seen us from her apartment window above because she came down as we were unloading and gave her son a big hug. I could see him grimace from the painful burns on his chest, but he said nothing. He didn't want his mom to know about the radiator incident and had asked us not to mention it.

The building his mom lived in was one of those NYCHA projects and thankfully had an elevator, so we didn't have to schlep all that shit of theirs up multiple flights of stairs. Once we had everything of any value safely secured, Pete went back down to the car to find a good place to park around the block, leaving Jen, and me with his mother in her apartment. She had food cooking in the kitchen, so the apartment smelled great. Even more so, I'm sure, because we hadn't eaten anything since before we left that morning. Once Pete came back up, we all sat down to dinner together, and shared the food.

We sat for a little while there around the table once the meal was through and spoke about our intended trip. Pete's mom seemed a little indifferent about the whole thing. Maybe it was her way of coping with the thought of her son moving so far away. Besides, he had moved out of his mom's place and struck out on his own years ago already, so it wasn't going to impact her routine in any way. It was late by now, and his mom said she had to get up early for work, so we wrapped it up pretty quickly.

After his mom had gone to bed, Pete and I went out onto the little balcony that came standard with these apartments and smoked a bowl in the dark. New York City at night, late night, and still all lit up. There was no real view to be had from this balcony; we couldn't see the Manhattan skyline or anything. But the thousands of little lights in the adjacent apartment buildings and warehouses around us under a hazy orange sky devoid of stars made for a scene I had never witnessed before. Sleeping overnight in the city, it's not a big deal for most people, but it was a first for me. The first first of many firsts I would experience in the coming months.

CHAPTER 5

The next morning, we hit the road early, for real this time. We were headed up north to Ithaca, Jen's hometown, and it was bound to be a much longer ride than yesterday. We were out of Pete's mom's apartment and down onto the street somewhere between seven and eight to load up the car with what my companions decided they were going to take with them for their new life out west. It was a lot less stuff than what we originally left the island with, but even still the trunk seemed overstuffed. I was able to get my main pack to fit into the trunk now, but that was about it. I climbed into the back seat with the dog and made myself comfortable.

Pete naturally knew his way around Brooklyn pretty well, so he took us through a series of side streets and boulevards instead of taking the BQE out of the borough. Watching out the window I could say with complete confidence that I had no fucking idea where the hell we were. The views around me were all a jumble of nondescript red brick buildings covered in spray paint graffiti and elevated trains rumbling along tracks held up by gnarly iron beams covered in peeling green paint. And people, all sorts of people of every shape and size, crowding the sidewalks and striding out into traffic like they just didn't give a shit. Certainly, nothing like the sleepy roads that crisscrossed the island town I had just left behind.

At one point on our traverse through this foreign maze of concrete and steel, we rolled into a neighborhood where the most distinctively dressed men I had ever seen briskly moved about the busy streets around us en mass like they were on a mission of great importance. Most wore long beards, with curls of hair growing out from beside each ear, and all were identically dressed in a sort of black suit, with a black brimmed hat perched precariously on the top of their heads. Some wore a hat even more unique made of a brown fur and shaped like a stock pot, also riding high on their crowns. But they weren't alone in this city scene, their wives and children were out on the streets with them moving at the same deliberate pace and looking just as serious in their dark modest attire. I looked out the window wondering just who these people were. Then Jen beat me to the punch.

"Pete, who are these people?" she asked.

"They are Hasidic Jews. We're passing through Williamsburg now; this is their neighborhood," he replied.

"Who are these Hasidic Jews?" I asked, "And why are they all dressed up like that?"

"They are an ultra-orthodox religious sect of Judaism," He explained. "Great hats, right?"

We were stopped at a red light now, and a crowd of them were passing in front of the car from both directions. Man, what a crazy world this is, all these different people with different lives out minding their own different sorts of business. The only thing I could kind of compare the looks of these folks to were the Amish people I had seen on some family vacation a few years before. But unlike the Amish, these people drove cars, and smoked cigarettes, and lived here, in the city.

Just then a little boy with a little brimmed hat made eye contact with me through the window briefly before his mother yanked him along. The puzzled look on his little face I'm sure mirrored my own. Then the light turned green, and we were off again. Soon I noticed these interesting people with their interesting hats were gone, and Hispanic people now clustered the sidewalks. We had driven through their neighborhood and clear out the other side, passing through a whole other world in the process.

Before long we were mounting one of New York's free bridges into Manhattan. I could see the island city's impressive skyline moving through the faded framework of this heavy steel bridge as we cruised over. I was awestruck. New York's intensity was beginning to overwhelm me with a sensory overload. There was just so much to take in, so much to see and analyze. All these sights and sounds and smells I had been so voraciously consuming were now beginning to consume me. I had to close my eyes tightly for a moment and kind of reset myself using a method I first discovered as a child when I would find myself over stimulated by something. I would cup my hand over my eyes to blot out the light then apply gentle downward pressure just under my eyebrows, causing a sort of kaleidoscope of cascading colors to grow out from the center of my eyeballs in rippling waves for a few seconds before dissipating into blackness. I would then open my eyes again feeling a little less manic.

We were descending into the city now, and the buildings with their wooden pointed rooftop water towers rose quickly on either side of us.

The traffic down here in lower Manhattan was a bit more challenging than our earlier roll through Brooklyn, and at times our progress would be abruptly halted, prompting a cacophony of horn blasts to sound all around us. Pete piloted our old crusty vessel with skill through these troubled waters, bobbing and weaving with large yellow taxis and delivery trucks. Soon we were again on a comparatively open road keeping the East River on our right, headed north, and hammering down. I took this opportunity to suggest we twist one up in celebration of our acceleration, and they readily agreed. But by the time I had the thing in play there was nothing but brake lights ahead of us, so Jen had me clip it for later lest a neighboring car on this highway parking lot we were stuck on smell the smoke and alert the authorities.

"Fucking traffic," Pete exclaimed "We gotta get off this road and onto an uptown avenue before I lose my fucking mind!"

It took a while before an exit off this clogged artery of pot holed pavement presented itself, but once Pete had the real estate open in front of the bumper, we were off, bobbing and weaving again along a wide uptown avenue.

We were making much better time now, and before long came up on the George Washington Bridge and our final exit from New York City with its busy streets and its myriad of people. The bridge's pale blue towering pylons loomed large before us as we turned onto the structure. This bridge had a cleaner, sharper look to it then did the first, metal framed expanse we had passed over earlier and rose much higher over the river it crossed. I could see way up the Hudson River, with its rocky palisade like cliffs and smooth waters, until it bent out of view. We touched down in New Jersey and soon merged with what would be a reoccurring route for us over the next few weeks: Interstate 80 westbound. Once we had settled into the speed of the open highway, Pete suggested we re-spark the clipped joint from before so the monotony of suburban New Jersey might not drive us to tears. It was a good thing we did too because there really wasn't much to see until we got to the Delaware water gap.

As we approached that landmark cut in the Appalachian Mountains the scene quickly became greener, with mountainous outcrops of gray stone draped in moss and foliage. I had come to this place as a pre-teenager with my parents for a weekend campout a few years back and had fallen in love with it right away. Afterward I came back through the gap whenever I could. During my brief attendance at college, I had always gone out of my way to take this route on my back-and-forth travels if nothing else so I could pass through this gap. I would always pull off the last exit in New Jersey, park my ride, and walk out to the river's edge to engage with the local land and water. Dozens of times I had been here now, and I asked Pete to take that exit once more so I could share this place with my friends, and perhaps visit it for the last time for who knows how long. We pulled off into the little parking space provided for the local fly-fishing enthusiasts and took the dog for a walk, as it were.

We walked along a sort of unmarked path above the river. It must have once been an actual road because there were the remains of several little houses rotted into their foundations sporadically placed along the wide path's edge. Eventually the way just sort of quit at a steep drop near the water. Here we could go no further, so a bowl was packed, and we spent some time looking at the trees.

It was getting past noon now, we were getting a tad hungry, and there were still many miles to go before we reached Ithaca. So we made our way back to the car and had a little lunch from the trunk consisting of one of Pete's mom's reused to-go containers of last night's dinner passed around communally. We then hit the road once more.

We had to make some time now if we were going to have a couch to crash on for the night, so there could be no more pleasure stops till we got close, just breaks to let the dog piss and to top off the gas tank. We followed the same route I had always taken when I traveled to and from school, through the Pennsylvanian wilderness via I-380, and eventually back into New York State. Somewhere around Binghamton we broke left and took a more subtle route into Ithaca. We were in Jen's neck of the woods now, and she had us cruising the unknown back roads where the possibility of a police presence was significantly reduced. It had been dark for a few hours now, so you couldn't see anything out the windows beyond what the headlights illuminated, which was a great shame according to her as there were a few beautiful roadside sights we were missing on account of the darkness we found ourselves traveling through.

"Don't worry." she assured us "We'll be in town a couple days and will have time to see some of what Ithaca has to offer."

Pete had been there with her a few times before and had some sights of his own he was excited to share with me.

"There is this amazing junkyard in the hills outside of town," he described. "The place is huge, takes up an entire old farm, on both sides of the road. The deeper you go into the junkyard the older the stuff gets. It is awesome."

It was past midnight when we finally rolled into town. Jen had arranged for us to meet up with some of her old high school friends to stay with for the first night, and then to stay with her mother for the rest of our time there. Jen's friends turned out to be about a dozen kids at someone's parents' house. These parents were apparently away for the evening, so it had turned into a classic high schooler house party complete with a half keg of cheap beer and a ridiculously colored two-foot bong well before we arrived. We got into the spirit straight away. Jen introduced us to her friends, and we got to talking about the subject of road tripping around the keg before long.

"Oh, man I so want to do that," one of the guys was saying to me. "Just travel around the country, and follow the Dead, man."

"Jerry is dead, doofus," replied the other.

"Well, follow Phish then. They're not dead yet." And they roared with laughter, patting each other on the back.

"Where are you guys going to sleep when you stop at night?" a fashionable looking girl with an unnaturally colored spray tan asked me, pushing her way between the laughing dudes.

"We're going to camp, mostly, I guess. Try to find the state parks and stuff, ya know." I told her, awkwardly draining my solo cup of its lukewarm contents. "Can't really afford to be getting hotel rooms every night. Maybe sometimes though if we can't find any place better."

This girl seemed to find my response unsatisfactory in some way and sort of scrunched up her face.

"I went camping once," she admitted to me "So many bugs."

"Yeah, that's nature I guess," I replied. "Excuse me while I fill this cup."

I stepped to the keg and reached for the pumper tap for a refill of piss water, then wandered off to find the whereabouts of that two-foot bong working its way around the crowd. I found it just as Pete was clearing twenty-four inches of thick off-white smoke from its day-glow tube.

"You wanna pull?" the guy holding the slide asked me. "Plenty to go around."

"Yeah, man. Let me get a hit on that," I replied, and I sat down next to my friend on the sofa.

Pete had a good cough going so I handed him my beer, and he took it down, placing the empty red cup on the coffee table in front of us. The kid at the foot of the bong reloaded the slide and struck the lighter.

"Ready?" he asked me, looking up with a crooked grin.

"Go," I said and started pulling. I stopped just as the smoke load had been brought to the top of the tube, capped the bong with my hand, and exhaled. Once I had completely evacuated my lungs of air, I went back in for the kill. It had been about a year since I had pulled a bong rip of that size, and I expected it would hit me hard, but I was not prepared for the impact. I couldn't even clear half the tube before my cough reflex caused me to force the hit back into the bong, blowing a quantity of stinky bong water out of the slide and onto the carpet.

"Shit," I feebly muttered between full body coughs.

I reached for my beer in hopes of soothing the shredded esophagus I suddenly suffered from only to find the cup empty where Pete had placed it.

" Shit, shit." I wheezed dryly, attempting to get up. My head was swimming now, and my throat was on fire. Pete grabbed me by the arm and helped me to my feet.

"Come on, bro, let's get you a refill on that beer before you cough out your lungs." And he walked me back to the keg.

Ahh, sweet, sweet nectar of oblivion, I thought as I drained my plastic cup, my head tilted back, my blood swollen eyes staring into the kitchen light above me. What kind of cheap ass local swag was this here beer anyway? Damn, but it tastes like pure fucking gold right now. I refilled the cup once more and returned to the sofa to apologize to our host for the bong water party foul.

"Dude…" I said "Dude, sorry about the bong water. That hit totally shut me down."

"Nah, it's cool, man," he assured me. "Shit happens."

Shit happens indeed. I was fucking stoned to the bone.

CHAPTER 6

I woke up face down on the living room carpet. For a few confused moments I wondered just where the hell I was, but a torrent of snapshot memories quickly filed in the gaps, coming upon me with enough strength to force a foul-smelling groan out from my pasty mouth and into the shaggy floor I rested my face upon. I pushed myself up off the carpet and took account of my surroundings. I was alone on my knees in the living room of a strange house with a significant headache that actively increased in intensity as the seconds passed. Scanning the room, I zeroed in on the digital display of a VCR and acknowledged the time. 6:39AM. What the fuck? My internal clock was still set to those brutally early morning shifts and had forced me awake even in the grip of a wicked hangover I was now only just beginning to appreciate. I scanned the room again, looking for any other signs of life. Nothing except the stale leavings of a recently exhausted party; clusters of partially empty solo cups, over full ash trays, empty snack chip bags surrounded by oily crumbs. I brought my hand to my face, squeezed my brow, and groaned again. So thirsty, must piss. Must find toilet and drinking water.

I scrolled back through last night's scattered memories, looking for the placement of the bathroom, and found it right where I had left it. Relieved, I stumbled into the narrow room and momentarily hit the lights. The sudden illumination instantly proved too intense for my throbbing head to bear, so I cut the switch again before the incandescent light burned a hole in my brain and relied instead on the ambient morning glow bleeding in through the daintily curtained window to light my way. Pissing into the bowl below without swerving I discovered was incredibly difficult, so I rightfully concluded that I must still be drunk. Once I had succeeded in making a mess of the family's toilet bowl I stepped to the sink and gazed into the mirror at myself. What a sight I was. Blood shot, puffy eyes, parched lips, and the fabric patterned marks across one side of my face that could only be produced by my lying motionless on the carpet for hours. I must be the only one awake, I thought.

A smoky stale flavor of partially metabolized cheap beer and hours old bong rips consumed my senses of taste and smell and reminded me; oh yeah, water, that's right. I am really fucking thirsty, so I shuffled away to the kitchen to find that heavenly liquid and banish this foul taste from my mouth. When I came around the corner, I was surprised to find some random guy maybe ten years my senior sitting at the kitchen table stroking an enormously obese black and white cat on his lap with long, slow passes.

"Whoa! Hello!" I bumbled out, obviously startled.

"Good morning!" he announced loudly, stone faced and menacing "Can I pour you a drink?"

I noticed then he had one of those huge liter sized German steins on the table beside him a little less than half full with beer. The mug was one of clear glass, so I could see the horizontal foam lines of his progress through the consumption of his morning beverage.

"Uhh, no. Just water, I think. So thirsty."

"Come on! It'll take the edge off that hangover you got there."

"I don't know, man. I don't feel so good."

"Fuck that! Grow a dick and have a drink with me!" he barked and waved me in closer with his free hand.

I was pretty sure this guy was not partying with us the night before. I had no recollection of him whatsoever, but here he was wide awake and pulling liters off last night's keg during the breakfasting hours. Maybe he was someone's older brother or something, come to check up on the condition of their folks' un-chaperoned house. And here I was, the first drunk kid to regain consciousness. Continuing to refuse his offer to pour me a morning beer would most likely cause me some trouble in the short term. Okay, I'll roll with this, I thought. Maybe it will help my hangover.

"You have a cup?" I asked.

He released a sort of burp/exclamation hybrid, and grabbed a random solo cup from the counter, poured out its flat contents into the sink, and reached over to the keg pumper tap to fill it up. All this he managed to accomplish while still seated in a kitchen chair with a morbidly corpulent two-tone cat spilling over his lap.

"So, what's your story?" he demanded of me, handing the cup of warm keg beer across the table. "I don't recognize you. Who are you here with?"

"Jen. I'm on a road trip with her and her boyfriend, Pete."

He looked at me hard for a moment, and replied "Oh, Yeah. I remember that guy. Hippie ni**er, right?"

I hesitated for a moment, struck unexpectedly by the slur. I didn't often hear the word used much growing up despite being a white kid from a predominantly white town. It was a word representing a sentiment of violence I had been brought up to reject. For all its faults, my church with its widely diverse congregation gave me that at least. And now, here is some guy summoning up this violent sentiment, staring me down threateningly. Challenging me. Do I confront the slur against my friend and against my morals, or do I ignore it in the hopes of avoiding trouble. "What the fuck, man?" I swiftly decided.

"Hey, don't get all pissy. It was just a joke," he folded instantly. "They're still together?"

"I hope so," I replied, thoroughly disgusted now with this character. "They're my ride out of here."

He seemed to take great pleasure in this last statement and shook with enough laughter to finally dislodge the large cat from his lap. "You're alright, kid." he decided and rose from his chair, plucking his almost empty extra-large beer krug from the table by the rim. "You're alright."

The enormous cat now so recently evicted from its warm perch lumbered across the kitchen, parked itself by its empty food bowl, and began eyeing me distrustfully. This fat cat here would obviously not be so easily convinced of my "alrightness".

"Sparky cat, don't be such a bitch," he barked at the lump of cat at his feet. "Don't mind her. She just wants more food."

"Should someone feed her?" I asked.

"Jesus Christ, no!" he exclaimed as he left the room. "Don't you think that fucking cat is fat enough already."

Alone again and thoroughly unnerved by this guy's aggressive energy I upended the warm beer into my mouth and then went to the sink for the water I so desperately needed. It was cold and clear and tasted vaguely of chlorine. I was downing my second cup when the guy started to bang on a bedroom door.

"Time to get up, assholes!" the guy hollered.

He started banging on every hollow core door in the house, yelling obscenities and racially derogatory comments at the supposed occupants of each room. All my shit was still in the car and I had awoken with my shoes on, so I went for the back door, hoping to avoid another one-on-one encounter with an unstable racist redneck with a morning drunk on.

Dylan was thrilled to see me, having spent the night in the car, and welcomed me with peals of high-pitched barks. I let him out for a morning piss on the lawn, and he barely got a few feet from the car before he raised his leg at a bush. It was one of those really long dog piss sessions where their eyes kind of roll back in their heads and they almost smile. What a good dog to not piss on the car seats. I sat on the grass by the car, looking back up at the house. I could still hear the guy yelling inside, but there were other voices answering back now.

Dylan had just sat down beside me when Pete came out from around the back of the house with his shoes in one hand and a backpack in the other. Dylan, of course, instantly shot off like a bullet towards him. He dropped the shoes and backpack and knelt down, catching Dylan in his arms in a big hug and taking him to the ground, laughing. I got up and walked over to where they were wrestling.

"Who is that crazy ass redneck in there?" I asked.

"The kid with the big bong last night. This is his parents' house, and that loudmouth in there is his older brother," he explained. "He's pissed he wasn't invited to the kegger last night, but you can see why. He's a total fucking asshole."

Jen had joined us on the lawn by now, accompanied by the bong kid, who proceeded to apologize for the ruckus his older brother had created.

"I'm sorry about that, guys," he said. "He's such a fucking dick. It's a good thing there's still beer in the keg, otherwise he would be even worse."

The older brother inside started hollering again, and there was a loud crash from the kitchen.

"God damn it! My mom is gonna be so fucking pissed. You guys better get out of here before some other shit happens."

We were already leaning in that direction anyway, so we bid our goodbyes and hit the road once more, now in search of breakfast. Jen knew a little diner in town with cheap eats, so we went there and each had a big plate of scrambled eggs with bacon and home fries. The greasy food was absolutely glorious to my beer pickled insides, and I drank what must have been a quart of water to wash it down. Jen suggested we make our appearance at her mom's place next and get settled in, so that is just what we did.

Jen's mom lived in a trailer park surrounded by fields of cut grass. Hay, I guess it was. Scattered sporadically were giant rolls of the stuff that broke up the otherwise empty landscape. The trailer where we would be staying was all the way at the end of one of the little streets of the trailer park, where the neighboring fields just sort of merged with the lawns without so much as a wire fence. We went up to the porch and Jen knocked on the screen door, which I thought was odd at first figuring a mother daughter relationship could do without the niceties of knocking, but when her mother opened the door I began to understand why. She gave her daughter something of a half hug, saying she didn't know she was coming, and gave Pete and me a disapproving glance when Jen reminded her that we would be staying there a few nights and that they had talked about this already. It was painfully awkward standing there with Pete, even more so because we had only just finished burning down a huge spliff on the ride over from the diner.

"Come on, mom," she said embarrassingly "Remember when I called last week, you said it would be alright for us to stay a few nights with you?"

"Ok, ok. But Sam is not going to like it," she said abruptly as she turned back into the trailer.

Sam, it turned out was Jen's mom's sometimes boyfriend who occasionally would stay at the trailer when he was not out on the road driving an eighteen-wheeler around the east coast for weeks at a time. It was just our luck he was due back that night, and he of course was not expecting us to be there sharing their little love nest with him and his lady friend. It was after dark when he rolled up in his bobtail truck, revving the big diesel engine, and purposely blocking in the Oldsmobile. He stormed into the trailer, I guess assuming our car was the ride of some other guy who was with his woman. Finding us, a trio of shaggy kids in the living room, apparently wasn't much better.

"Who the hell are you?" he asked Pete and me generally.

"Calm down, Sam." Jen's mom called from the kitchen. " They are my daughter's friends, and they're all here for a couple days."

The man just harrumphed, dropped his duffle bag by the door, and went into the kitchen to get to the bottom of all this.

Pete and I looked over at Jen simultaneously. She just shrugged, turning up the volume on the TV with the remote to overcome the raised voices of the two lovers in the kitchen arguing about our presence. This was going to be an awkward couple of days, no doubt.

CHAPTER 7

I slept on the couch that night, though perhaps "sleep" would not be the best choice of words. The couch was one of those two-seater things with the high arm rests, so I couldn't really stretch out. Plus, it possessed an odd chemical smell that encouraged a headache. By early morning I had given up and rolled out my sleeping bag on the carpeted floor. My companions had the use of the trailer's single guest room, which was really more of a storage closet full of boxes and other junk, so they dealt with cramped quarters as well. Dylan slept in the car because Jen's mom would not let him in the house. He probably had the best sleeping arrangements out of all of us. And this trucker guy, Sam, he snored, and loudly too. At least it would only be a few days here, I told myself. I'd just have to tough it out.

Sunrise found me awake, and it being the first Sunday on the road I felt compelled to attempt this communion ritual I had talked myself into. Imagine how pissed Jesus would be if I bailed on this promise the very first Sunday out on the road. I had to give it a shot. So I slipped out of the trailer using the trucker's snore as a cloak of sound and retrieved my pack from the trunk of the car. Dylan started barking good mornings at me of course, so I had to let him out to join me. I walked out to one of those big round hay bales to get a closer look and found it was totally rotten. Why would a farmer go through the trouble of cutting and bailing this hay, only to let the bales rot in the field? Surely the farmer must have had reasons I was not aware of. I ran my hand over the damp dense straw and smelled the earthy musk it gave off. It smelled like good soil, healthy soil. I'll take my communion here, I thought.

I sat down cross legged on the moist earth and watched as Dylan sniffed around another round hay bale maybe twenty yards away. I tried to clear my mind of all the background noise that always chugged away in there and think about the sacrifice Jesus made, being brutally murdered by being nailed to a cross. He was an innocent man, as the story goes, and could have stopped his murder at any time by calling down a raging fury upon those who wished to kill him. He could have changed the game any way he saw fit and saved himself the agony of this terrible death. But he didn't. He chose to die so that I might live. Even though I was a wretched hopeless sinner who himself deserved to be hung upon that cross. Still, he chose to save me and countless others like me: a fucking heavy story to say the least even if you don't subscribe to a faith in the impossible.

With this thought washing my mind clean I took the bread, broke it, and remembered him. Then, with the dusty dry matzo cracker catching in my throat, I cracked open a little can of grape juice, gave thanks, and washed down the flavorless cracker with the sugary blood of Christ. Dylan had returned to me now and was looking at me in a puzzled way. I smiled at him, and he began to sniff around in earnest once again. I wrapped up my little ritual by singing a stanza of amazing grace alone in the field bathed in morning light. It felt good and right. This would work, I knew it. God would smile down on me and watch over me in my travels. I stuffed the crackers and the empty grape juice can back into my pack, then fished out my stash box. I was rolling up a number when I noticed Pete trekking across the field towards me. Excellent, I thought, we can share the morning doobie.

"Whattcha doin out here, bud?" he asked me.

"Praising Jesus, and smoking pot. Wanna join me?"

"I'll skip the Jesus part, but I will join you in that joint." And he sat down next to me.

Dylan came running back from an adjacent field and started licking my friend all over his face. We both started laughing. These were real moments we were having here; the kind of moments people never even notice themselves having. Folk will spend their whole lives chasing after these moments not ever realizing what it was they were looking for. We had it right here. The morning sun lifting the scent of the damp earth around us, laughing together about nothing, getting high, this was it. This is what passes people by when they're not paying attention.

We walked back to the trailer to get Jen. She wanted to go see her grandmother for what might be the last time, and while she was doing that, Pete and I were going to check out that monster junkyard he had described earlier. Everyone was up and awake in the trailer when we got back. Sam sat at the tiny kitchen table scowling at us, lording over his coffee and cigarettes. The air was thick with smoke and bad vibes. It was obvious we were not wanted, so we got our shit together and headed out of town for the day.

Jen's grandmother lived in an old farmhouse maybe fifteen miles outside of town. It was a classic old-time looking place with clapboard siding and a sagging front porch. The thigh high grass surrounding the house was at full late August growth: dry and brown and ready for threshing. With no one around to work the land, it seemed nature was reclaiming the lot on which her grandmother lived.

Jen led us around to the back of the house where we found her grandmother washing clothes with a washboard in a galvanized tub. Despite her advanced age, she seemed to have no trouble with this work for after we had all made her acquaintance, she refused our offers to help. Wiping her hands free of soap suds on her apron, she had us follow her into the addition at the back of the house, which turned out to be one large, sparsely furnished kitchen. The floorboards were those wide antique planks well worn with age, and in fact everything in the place looked like an antique. There was one of those old-timey black and white enameled coal ovens and a big galvanized sink. The open cabinets were stocked with dated-looking products and home canning jars full of pickled vegetables. Looking back, I wonder if this old lady even had electricity because I don't remember there being anything in the house that looked like it required power to operate.

Jen's grandmother was a lot friendlier than her mother and wanted to know all about our plans. She served us some homemade brown bread with butter made from a neighbor's cow, with water hand pumped from the well near the clothesline out back. It was absolutely the most delicious snack I had ever eaten. We all chatted for a while, and as the conversation turned towards family issues of no business to Pete and me we took our leave, telling Jen we would be back in the afternoon.

The junkyard was another twenty miles afield, down two-lane country roads past farms and forest. We came upon the place suddenly as we turned a corner. For about two hundred yards on both sides of the road, junk cars and trucks edged out of the underbrush. Set back behind the haphazard rows of derelict vehicles, a rickety old farmhouse could be seen poking its head above the fray. On the other side of the road was a big faded red barn also surrounded by ruined cars and trucks. We pulled off the pavement onto the rutted roadside, and I followed Pete into the yard. We came upon a low, long garage like shed cluttered with parts and junk which obviously served as a sort of office/shop for the place and found the owner inside with some of his brushy-bearded buddies covered in grease and drinking cheap beer.

"Can I help you fellas?" he asked us.

"Yeah," Pete replied. "Mind if we take a look around the yard?"

"What are you looking to find? I've got a lot of cars back there."

"Well, we're driving a 69 Cutlass. Don't need anything in particular, just want to check out all the old cars really," my friend told him.

"69 Cutlass, eh? Should be one back there somewhere. Remember that car, Bob?" he said to one of his greasy companions with a rotten-toothed smile.

"Yeah, we had some good times with that one," the other replied with a laugh.

The owner came in close to us as his crooked grin decayed into a stern scowl, all the more unnerving by being heavily weathered, smeared in grease, and partially obscured by his unkempt beard. "You kids can have a look around; I got no problem with that. Just don't let me catch you breaking any windows or there will be hell to pay."

Of course, we assured him, there would be no such nonsense with us, and with that we wandered off into the surrounding junk yard.

This place was amazing. All manner of vehicles piled and pushed together. Smashed cars, stripped cars, completely untouched classics covered in vines. And like Pete had earlier described, the farther you went back into the yard the older the stuff got. We were peeling away the rusty layers like an onion, heading back in time through the 50s into the 40s and into the 30s and beyond. I just could not believe what I was seeing. Large trees growing out from the engine compartment of a 1960s model Ford Fairlane. Three identical 1950s era Pontiacs with their matching translucent amber Indian head hood ornaments all in a row. A 1940s Dodge coupe with all its glass and chrome intact. It was incredible.

As we neared the woods line, the junk around us became hulking rusted farm equipment half sunk into the soil: disintegrating 1920s model T flatbed trucks and other amorphous, heavy iron debris impossible to identify. We climbed onto a piece of ruined farm implement that afforded us a higher vantage point from which to look back on the expanse of collected steel detritus. What a place! Pete had picked up an old license plate earlier and was now using it as tray to break up some weed on his lap.

"How much bud did we end up getting from the bong kid?" I asked him, vaguely remembering talking about going in on a large travel bag the night of the house party.

"One ounce," he informed me. "Don't you remember? Half of it's yours."

"Not really, man. I was fucking hammered." He lit the joint, and after taking two long puffs passed it to me. "This shit smells really good."

"Yeah, man. It's got a nice piney note. It's a real head high."

And indeed it was. We wandered on in silence for a time and eventually went our separate ways as we each zoned out on some aspect of this scrappy scene. We had been out there for a couple hours before I found that old Cutlass the owner had spoken of. It sat on its rims sunk into the soil up to the frame rails, with leaf litter continuing into the cab through its doorless sides and was boxed in between two old panel vans. I almost missed it because of the vans and the vines draped over the group like a leafy tarp. I clambered over the pile of cars and loose auto body parts surrounding it and dropped in through the passenger side. It was a 69 Cutlass alright. With the dashboard display divided into those three recessed circular gauges there was no question. I looked over into the back seat and found it full of well-preserved ring tab beer cans from the late 70s. Well, that explains the "good times" these old coots had back in the day with this ride, I thought. I have got to find Pete and show him this car.

I climbed out and made my way along the ridge of the front passenger fender. The hood and engine were gone, and I did not want to tumble into the open engine compartment, so I had to delicately untangle myself from the vines that encased this grouping of junk as I went. Once I was out, I spent the next twenty minutes trying to find my friend. I didn't want to call out his name because it felt somehow inappropriate to disturb the graveyard-like silence around me while I was so stoned, so I just continued wandering around until I found him behind the wheel of an old ruined army jeep.

"Check this thing out, man. This is awesome!" he exclaimed, pretending to drive the old wreck like a little kid.

"I found the Cutlass that guy was talking about. It's way back over there by those trees." I said, gesturing widely with my arm. "Though there's not much left of it."

I led him back to the spot where the carcass rested, and we climbed into the pile. He agreed that there wasn't really anything here we could use except the little thumb latch for the glove box, which our car was missing. I carried one of those pocket multi-tool knives everywhere I went so I was able to remove the latch from the wreck. Pete had grabbed some mini-light bulbs and some other little bits from other cars, and we thought that since we had seen most everything there was to see here and had been there for a few hours already we should probably get going. We returned to the garage and looked around for the owner but couldn't find him. We went around the back of the garage and wandered over across the street, but gave up after ten minutes or so of walking around the farmhouse where we assumed he lived. Oh well, we decided, can't wander around here all day looking for this guy. As much as we'd like to have continued grooving on all this old junk, Jen would be expecting us pretty soon.

We picked her up from her grandmother's and headed back into Ithaca town to see if we could find something to do for the evening. We didn't want to go back to her mom's trailer yet, not until it was time to crash out for the night, so we parked the car near the college and checked out the scene on the main street. There really wasn't much to do there, and since it was still technically summer the college kids had not yet returned, so the streets were all pretty dead. We got a bite to eat at some pizza joint and then went to see a movie at a tiny local theater. Jen had snuck a six pack into the place in a backpack so once the lights went out, we each had a couple beers to wash down the oily popcorn. The movie wasn't very good, but the beers helped make it interesting. Well, that and the fat bowl we smoked in the alley beside the theater right before we went in.

CHAPTER 8

That night, ol' trucker Sam came in drunk. I had been almost asleep on that uncomfortable couch when he crashed through the trailer's front door shoulder first, turned on all the lights, and began knocking around loudly in the kitchen. I pretended to be asleep because I just didn't want to have to deal with yet another drunken asshole, but that didn't stop him from being one without any help from me. He grumbled incoherently about "these God damn free loaders eating all the potato chips" and proceeded to crumple an empty cellophane bag incessantly in his search for the remaining crumbs. Don't blame me, I thought. I didn't eat your stupid chips. He also must have smoked a couple cigarettes back-to-back before he stumbled into Jen's mother's bedroom because he left behind a thick haze of menthol smoke in addition to leaving all the lights on. I decided to join Dylan in the back seat of the car for the night, which turned out to be a good idea because I was able to sleep undisturbed until well after sunrise for a change. Jen eventually woke me up when she came out to the car for something.

"Good morning," she said cheerily, her eyes squinting from the smoke of the cigarette dangling from her lip. "D'you sleep better out here?"

"Yeah, Sam came in all drunk last night making a bunch of noise and smoking like a chimney. I couldn't take it anymore. It was much better out here with Dylan."

"Yeah, we heard him too. We're gonna leave tomorrow. My mom is acting all weird, and Sam is being a dick, so just one more night here and then we're gone, ok?"

That was fine by me. I was eager to get back on the road and continue this trip. Having to deal with all the aggro assholes in this town was beginning to get old. I wanted to see the Rocky Mountains and the Pacific Ocean already. Enough with this place, man. Let's go.

We spent the day out hiking around a nearby state park. It was sunny and warm and unpopulated enough that we could let Dylan run free off the leash. Jen had put together a picnic lunch for us, so around noon we posted up on a big flat rock by a stream and had a nice little sit down.

It was hot in the mid-day sun, so after we had eaten and burned up a doobie Pete suggested we all go for a swim. I was automatically hesitant to strip off my shirt because of my deep-rooted self-image issues: you know, the fat kid boy boobs and all. But I forcefully pushed that hangup aside and peeled off my clothes like the rest of them. I still felt uncomfortable being outdoors in my underwear in the company of other people, one of whom was a real live female, but I knew this westward adventure was going to demand I step out of my comfort zone on a regular basis. So I just went with the flow and made sure I wasn't caught sitting in any position that might accentuate the adipose rolls clinging to my mid-section.

The stream wasn't very deep, but there were places where we could sit on the stony bottom up to our necks. The water felt great after our sweaty hike, and we lingered there for some time, long enough for Dylan to fall asleep on the bank. Later, when we were laying on that flat rock drying out in our underwear, I noticed how bad the burns from the radiator explosion were on Pete's chest. There were dozens of white blisters across his pecks, and one big water filled bubble over his heart.

"Holy shit, man. Your chest looks terrible," I remarked. "Does it still hurt?"

"Not so much anymore. I'm just trying to not pop these blisters," he replied as he gently poked the biggest one with a single finger.

Once we had thoroughly sunned ourselves dry, we continued our walk, eventually coming upon an impressive waterfall. We stopped here for a while again, taking in the beauty around us and finishing off the roach from our picnic lunch. This walk out here in the woods was the perfect reset from all the negative energy we had been picking up in town. Hopefully, we could keep some of these good vibes handy for our last night at Jen's mom's place, I thought.

It was late afternoon by the time we got back to the car. Jen's mom had mentioned that Sam and her would be off on a dinner date or something that evening. So we were planning on using the kitchen to make a proper dinner for ourselves, figuring this might be our last chance to use a kitchen stove for a while. We stopped off in town to grab some things from a supermarket, and while my companions were inside, I took Dylan for a walk around the edge of the parking lot. Dylan was watering a little tree when a cop car rolled by real slow. The mustachioed patrolman behind the wheel gave me a hard look as he passed and pulled around next to a row of shopping carts at the side of the building, parking there. Great, I thought. Now this negative shit is going to land on us too. I continued around the far edge of the pavement, letting Dylan lead us with his nose until I saw my friends emerge from the store each carrying shopping bags. I met them at the car.

"See that cop over there?" I asked Pete, nodding my head slightly in his direction. "He was just hawking me pretty hard. Better be careful pulling out of here."

"Great, that's just what we fuckin' need," he said as he placed the bags in the trunk.

We pulled out of the parking lot and onto the street like we weren't being watched. But we were of course. The cop pulled out right behind us and followed us at like a four-car distance. This had gone on for about five minutes when Pete abruptly pulled into another small shopping complex and parked the car. We watched as the cop continued slowly on, turning at the next light.

"Let's sit tight for a minute," Pete said, "We got a shit ton of weed in the trunk. Don't need any trouble."

We of course whole heartedly agreed. Getting popped with a big bag of weed would definitely put the brakes on our plans. I looked around this complex we had randomly pulled into and noticed a thrift store tucked in between a dry cleaner and a Chinese food place.

"Hey, let's check out that secondhand shop over there. That'll kill some time."

It wasn't much of a store, but it did have some stuff to pick through. I found an old faded black hoodie with a big hole in the sleeve for a couple bucks and a dated looking Walkman complete with headphones for a dollar. I hadn't brought a Walkman on this trip, figuring I should travel light. But now that I could get one for a dollar, I thought, why not. I always liked the insular solitude a Walkman could afford. And who knows, with the periodic arguments my companions often engaged in, the noise canceling effect of headphones might come in handy. Just need to get some batteries. I caught up with Pete as he rummaged through a box of loose cassette tapes.

"Anything good?" I asked him.

"Not really, just a lot of crap," he replied, as he ran his hands up to his wrists through the pile.

I took over when he lost interest and confirmed his report. Homemade copies of obsolete pop acts, top forty country hits, classical orchestral movements. Basic thrift store crap. Then towards the bottom I found one worth taking: a Judas Priest album without a case. That might work, I thought, and popped the tape into the Walkman, figuring I could get it for the cost of the Walkman.

The ride back to the trailer was gratefully uneventful. The cop that had followed us must have found something better to do because we never saw him again. We got back to the trailer as the sun was going down and found it deserted as promised, so we started on dinner straight away, lest old trucker Sam come back early and smoke us out. They had also gotten a twelve pack of hard cider, so we all got pretty lit up after the meal was through. Jen turned in before us, and Pete and I took the remaining ciders and Dylan with us out into the moonlit fields.

Soon we were running around in the dark with the dog and trying to climb on top of those rotten round hay bales. Most of the bales we tried to mount came apart in musty clumps, but I was able to get on top of one and stuck a couple empty bottles neck down into its top to claim its peak for our people. Eventually, once we had spent our drunken energy, we turned in as well, and I chose the back seat with the dog once again.

In the morning, we found that Jen's mom and Sam had not returned the night before, and we still had the trailer to ourselves. Jen found a message on the answering machine from her mother explaining they had spent the night in the sleeper cab of Sam's truck at some truck stop just off the highway, and they would be doing the same thing tonight. It was tempting to have the trailer all to ourselves again for another night, but in the end we chose to split like we had planned. So we hit the road, leaving a thank you note on the table and our dirty dishes in the sink.

We were about half an hour on the road when my companions started arguing about something that had happened at the gas station we had stopped off at on our way out of town. I guess Pete had been overly flirty with the girl at the register, and Jen had been right there next to him. Pete figured that since she had been right there to witness it then it proved he wasn't trying anything funny. But she wasn't buying it and took offense at his logic. They each were trying to get me to see it their way, but I really didn't want to take sides. These quarters were just so close, I thought it best to remain as neutral a party as possible. At least I've got this Walkman here, I thought as I fitted in the new batteries I had just gotten at the gas station.

I was halfway through the second side of the tape when I felt the car lurch and loose speed. I leaned forward to see what was going on and found Pete looking pensively at the speedometer, hoping some answer might be found there. But there were no gauges besides the fuel, speed, and temperature, and no idiot lights had come on. He was at a loss.

"What the hell is this?" he asked the car desperately.

The Cutlass just continued surging and loosing speed even more and was starting to make a popping sort of sound in the exhaust. He pulled the car off to the side of the highway and had a look under the hood. There was nothing out of place that he could discern besides those ubiquitous wisps of steam from the radiator, a reminder that, like some wild animal, the car might bite back.

"What do you think is the problem?" I asked him.

"I don't know, I don't know," he softly cried, shaking his mop of dreadies back and forth as if to swat away the flies of anxiety.

He started the car again and stood over the shuddering engine, holding onto the raised hood with both hands and looking rather limp.

"We need to find a repair shop or something, I think," he decided. "This doesn't sound good."

We climbed back into the car and attempted to reach highway speed again, but the popping noises only sounded all the more. The car seemed to have hardly enough power to realize thirty miles an hour. Then Pete lost his cool and started pleading with the car aloud, crying out for the malfunction to stop.

"No, please no! Don't do this to me! No, no, no!" he cried, grasping onto the wheel, white knuckled with both hands, and shaking his dreads even more.

An exit was coming up about half a mile ahead, and at times it seemed like we were not going to make it. Other cars were blowing by us like we were standing still. I could see my friend's tearing eyes in the rearview mirror in between the tossing of his dreads. Dylan was starting to whimper, picking up on his anxious panic, while Jen stared straight ahead, jaw clenched. I was feeling the panic now too. What would we do if the car were dying? What would we do if we found ourselves abandoned out here in western New York State with no means of transport? It would mean our trip, however short lived would be over. I would again have to return to the island, defeated. Powerless in the face of this latest development I found that like Dylan, I felt like whimpering too.

Maxing out now at maybe fifteen miles per hour we limped down the long exit ramp. As the trees along the ramp broke up, a big gas station sign on a single pole came into view.

"There!" cried Jen. "There's a service station, Pete, there!"

Popping and shuddering we pulled up to an open garage bay door. A clean-cut mechanic in a blue jump suit looked up from his work inside.

"Oh thank god!" she declared.

Pete popped the hood as he climbed out of the car and met the mechanic as he reached under the hood to release the safety latch.

"Oh please!" he cried. "You have to help us! Our car, it's dying! Please!"

"Ok ok, don't worry, sir," the mechanic calmly stated. "What seems to be the trouble?"

"She's shaking and making a popping sound! No power. Oh please, you have to help us!"

"Yes of course, sir. I think I know what the problem is. Have a seat over there while I look into this." He pointed over to a bench on a grassy patch under a tree.

While Pete had been having his own breakdown with the mechanic, I had been studying the picture this garage presented. The workspace was immaculately clean and orderly. There was no clutter, no rusty greasy junk pushed to the side like you so often see in a mechanic shop. There were neat rows of service manuals above well-lit work benches, a huge red multi-drawer toolbox trimmed in gleaming chrome, and large expensive-looking electronic diagnostic equipment draped in neatly coiled spools of colored test wire. This was a professional in every sense of the word. I pointed this out to my friend as we stepped over to the shady bench, and that seemed to help settle his nerves a bit.

We watched the mechanic slip on a pair of cream-colored exam gloves, grab a couple of small delicate screwdrivers, and tuck in under the hood. A minute or so later he emerged with some small component in his hand, which he held up in the daylight and studied with squinting eyes. We watched him then enter his garage and choose one of the thick service manuals from the shelf above his work bench. He paged through the book for a minute or so, took a note of something onto a piece of paper, and disappeared into the shop office.

"This looks good, man," I said, "We might be back on the road in no time."

"God, I hope so," he replied.

Ten minutes or so later, the mechanic again reemerged from his office and strode straight up to us.

"You need a new set of points," he said flatly, handing the small component to Pete for inspection. "You should also change the distributor cap and rotor as well. As you can see here," he continued, pointing to the component in Pete's hands "… these contact points are really quite pitted and burnt. I am surprised this car was running at all."

"So, the car is going to be ok?" Pete asked.

"Yes, of course," the mechanic replied "This is a common problem with these older cars fitted with breaker point ignition systems. It's an easy fix really. Unfortunately, I do not have the replacement parts in stock and would need to order them."

"How long would that take?" Pete asked.

"At least two days. None of my local suppliers stock parts for cars this old anymore, so I need to order them from a distributor out in Ohio. I can see you're just passing through this town; do you have a place to stay while we wait for the parts?"

After a moment of silence, Jen replied, "I have an aunt that lives nearby. Maybe she would let us crash there for a couple days. Can I use your phone?"

"Of course, ma'am. Right this way," and they stepped into the office.

Pete started laughing out loud in relief, and I joined him in his release. This felt like a real close call. If that mechanic shop hadn't been right there off that well-placed exit, we would have been fucked. And, to top it all off, the shop was run by a real professional who quickly got to the root of the problem and put our minds at ease. It was a stroke of good fortune to be sure, be it an intervention of divine nature as I was inclined to believe at the time or a particularly good roll of the cosmic dice which required no belief on my part at all to operate. Still, I wanted to think Jesus was looking out for us, so with a gaze to the heavens I thanked him there aloud on the spot.

CHAPTER 9

Jen was able to get through to her aunt without any difficulty, and she agreed to host us for however long was necessary. Jen, we came to find out, was not too thrilled at the thought of staying with this relative because of some family issue we knew nothing about. But given the circumstances it would be better than renting a hotel room or pitching a tent by the highway. She described this aunt of hers as a compulsive talker who would not let anyone get a word into any conversation and would suffer no silence in any exchange she found herself in. So we were prepared for this when she arrived, rolling up in her huge wood paneled station wagon.

She was friendly enough, almost too much in a saccharine superficial sort of way, and just as Jen described, she cut us off halfway through whatever question of hers we attempted to answer. I learned early in life you can learn a lot about a person if you just let them do the talking, so beyond my initial introduction I kept my mouth shut. It was not like she would have let me finish any sentence I started anyway.

This aunt lived maybe twenty-five miles away from the service station in one of those little cul-de-sac developments with identical looking, evenly spaced new houses and manicured lawns. She pulled into the clean, stain free driveway and up to a wide garage door, parking the car there. We were asked to remove our shoes at the front door, but she did allow Dylan inside with us, surprisingly. She directed us to make ourselves at home in the living room, which we found populated by large white couches and cream-colored deep pile rugs. Great, I thought. How the hell are we going to make it through this without leaving our dirt stains on this lady's furniture? She struck me as someone who would have a hard time handling stains on her shit. I looked over at Jen, and she just rolled her eyes. Pete leapt into one of the big white couches with abandon.

If the thought of dirtying her white sofa occurred to him, it certainly didn't cause him any pause. Dylan climbed right up there with him, and I was again surprised when she returned into the room with sodas and said nothing of the dog's presence on the couch.

She then picked up her monologue where she had left off, telling us about her husband and two sons and their many great achievements. Periodically she would present us with some question, but as always would pick up on some word of our response and run with it before we had completed a sentence.

This went on for over an hour until it was quite dark outside. I began to wonder where this husband and these sons were, as it was well into the evening hours and there had been no sign of them. Looking around the room, I could see nothing that spoke of a male presence in this house at all. No male shoes by the door, no glossy magazines dedicated to men's interests on the white coffee table, nothing at all that would be indicative of male teenagers residing in this clean room. I was totally zoned out on this thought, not paying any attention to her latest testament to her family's unprecedented success at whatever she was talking about now, when Pete nudged me in the ribs with his elbow.

"I think I should take Dylan out for a walk before it gets too late," he interrupted "Yo, why don't you come with me?"

Jen shot a hard look at Pete as if to say, don't you leave me here alone with her, but I don't think he even noticed. I followed him to the door and out onto the front lawn.

"Holy shit, man! That lady is hard to handle."

"Yeah man!" I replied "Have you noticed how she goes on about her husband and sons? Where are they? I don't see any evidence of them here at all."

"Yeah, she's divorced, and the sons live with their dad. He has sole custody."

"Wow. How 'bout that, the way she goes on about them you'd think, well I don't know. She's really in some deep denial, huh?"

"Yeah, I don't know the whole story, but something is not right with her."

"Ya think?!" I sarcastically replied, mentally adding up all I had yet seen of this character. "I hope that guy fixes the car soon."

"No shit, dude. Come on; let's find a place to smoke a bowl."

We were probably only gone for half an hour, and when we returned Jen's aunt announced that pizzas had been ordered. She asked if any of us wanted refills for our sodas and left the room before any of us could answer. She was not away for more than a second when Jen began directing a muffled rebuke at Pete through clenched teeth.

"Fucking asshole!" she hissed. "Don't leave me here alone with her again."

"Don't worry. You can take Dylan out for his next piss."

She responded by punching him in the arm with enough force to make him wince.

It was past ten at night by the time the pizzas were on the table, but Jen's aunt didn't seem to be running out of any steam just yet. She just continued her monologue over a single slice of pizza placed perfectly on a plate of fine china before her. Eleven o'clock passed without a break in her speech, and by midnight I could see that we were all visibly exhausted. I sat there staring blankly at that same piece of untouched congealed pizza between her animated hands, not listening at all to what she was saying, when I realized she had stopped speaking and was looking right at me.

"Huh, what?" I blurted out.

"I said, you look tired," she repeated "Are you ready for bed?"

"Yeah. Uh, yeah that sounds good," I mumbled.

"Ok, then. Let's get you all off to bed."

She led us upstairs to her kids' rooms, setting up my companions and Dylan in one room and me in another. She left me alone there without a word beyond goodnight, again catching me off guard. I was gearing myself up to have to listen to some rambling tale about the talents and achievements of the room's "real" occupant, but I was surprisingly spared this trial.

In sudden silence, I studied the foreign room I now found myself in. It had the initial appearance of a well-kept teenage male's living space, with sports posters tacked to the walls, a row of clean, unworn baseball caps on a shelf, and some other sparse furnishings one might find in a student's room. But something about the space felt off and cold. I opened the closet and found it empty. Pulled open a few drawers of the dresser and found them empty as well. No one lived in this room, I realized. It was beginning to feel like her estranged family might not even really exist. Well, at least I wouldn't need to feel weird about sleeping in someone else's bed, I thought, because it seemed no one ever slept here. I hit the lights and slid under a set of cold, clean sheets. I was indeed pretty spent from the evening's thrilling festivities and drifted off into unconsciousness with a quickness.

That night I was again visited by strange and troubling dreams. I was in a dark cave dimly lit by some unseen source. It seemed to me that I had been in this cave making my way further into its dark recesses for a very long time, but there was no memory of what had come before. I was struck by the warmth of this place as well, and I remember wondering why that was. Caves were supposed to be cold places, from my experience. Yet this place was almost hot. I began to feel a little panicked, and it seemed like the cave was contracting without changing shape. Was I getting bigger?

Before long I was on my hands and knees clawing my way along. I could see an opening ahead, and I knew somehow if I could make it to that opening, I would be ok. I picked up the pace attempting to reach this slit in the wall, but my back was up against the ceiling now, pressing down on me. I dragged my form against the rock, grasping for the opening. I was able to pull myself into the slit up to my waist when I either grew too big to fit the rest of the way through or the slit had contracted tightly around me. I was trapped.

I could see into the room now that I had so desperately attempted to enter and found it to be a vast empty space. I was aware of the walls of the room stretching out away from me, but I could not discern their likeness. It was all just a great inky blackness around me, or rather half of me, because I was now fused to the wall from the waist down and could no longer feel my legs at all. In fact, I was the wall and realized that I didn't have arms anymore either. I was just this endless wall in the darkness.

Around this time, I noticed a figure of a man appear from the darkness itself. The figure moved closer to me without walking. I was beginning to feel a terror slowly building inside me as this figure drew closer and its features became apparent. It was an incredibly old man. The skin of his face was like leather, and he was dressed in long overlapping rags. A long gray beard obscured the mouth, and the eyes were shut. The figure was right before me now; I had no choice but to exist there face to face with this vision because I was a frozen wall. The eyes then popped open to reveal deep empty sockets that emitted a kind of whistling wind, the only sound in this dark cavernous place.

The figure then came alive before me and grabbed onto its cloak of rags, ripping the garment off and presenting its naked body to me. It was a women's body: young, curvy, and voluptuous.

I strained to move away from this androgynous creature, or at least to avert my eyes, but remained as frozen as stone before it. The creature now reached into my mouth with both hands and began pulling it open and pouring itself inside like some clumpy rancid oil. I was gagging, I was dying.

I awoke face down in a cold sweat and reactively leapt out of the bed without thought. I stood there silent and still for a moment in shock, staring at that colorful row of unworn ball caps on the shelf before me, my heart pounding in my chest.

Whoa, that was a really heavy dream, I thought. I gave myself a shake and registered the need to piss. Ok, I thought, it was just a dream, just a dream. I could still taste that clumpy oily flavor in my mouth somehow. I needed to get a glass of water to wash out that memory.

I quietly opened the door and made my way to the stairs in the dark, descending lightly on the carpeted steps. In the kitchen I found a coffee mug by the coffee maker and used that to hydrate myself with multiple cups of tap water as quietly as I could. I could see from the digital display on the stove that it was a little after three in the morning, and I didn't want to wake anyone, so when my bladder reminded me that I still had some unfinished business, I thought it might be better to find a downstairs bathroom to use instead of the one by Jen's aunt's room. But I hadn't yet been acquainted with this downstairs bathroom, so I had to find it.

There was a little hall off the kitchen that possessed a few doors. One of these doors was sure to be the bathroom, I figured. The first one I tried had a washer dryer double stacked inside. Nope, that ain't it. The second one was the door to the garage, which I was startled to see was nearly full to the ceiling with piles of paper and plastic shopping bags from various department stores full with unopened merchandise of all sorts. Clothing, home decor, small electronics, kitchen equipment all new in their packages spilling out of over stuffed sacks. I paused here for a minute in awe looking at the cascading drifts of consumer commodities filling the space. Oh my god, I thought. This lady lives here alone, in denial about her family still living here with her, and hoards the results of her compulsive shopping in an otherwise clean and orderly house.

"Are you looking for something?"

I spun around automatically and found myself face to face with Jen's aunt in a pink night gown so sheer it was almost transparent.

"Uh…The bathroom. I'm looking for the bathroom," I bumbled out.

"Right behind you," she said flatly as she reached past me to shut the garage door, brushing my arm heavily with her breasts.

"Ok, thanks," I whispered, trying not to look at her nipples through the chiffon of her nightgown.

I backed into the bathroom and shut the door. Oh man that was fucking weird. She probably thinks I was snooping around her house or something. But her night gown, I could see right through that thing, her nipples, her bush, all of it. Who does that with strangers in their house? So fucking weird.

I finished my piss and hesitated to open the bathroom door again. I hope she's not out there waiting for me, I thought, as I amassed the courage to try my luck. Upon opening the door I found myself alone, so I took advantage of this unexpected windfall and sprinted back to the bedroom. Before I drifted off again, I wondered how my nighttime encounter with Jen's aunt would play out in the light of day. I guess I'll find out in the morning, I thought.

I was not the first to wake up once the sun was shining. I knew this because I could hear the aunt going on like she had the night before down in the kitchen. I hope she's talking to my friends down there and not just to herself, I thought. I heard the phone ring at one point, which got my hopes up that the car might be ready. I made my way down to the kitchen to take account of the day and found my friends together with the aunt around the kitchen table. Jen's aunt greeted me cheerily, as if our nocturnal encounter had never happened, and offered me a breakfast of some sugary, brightly colored cereal. I could see from the empty bowls unnaturally stained with brightly colored milk in front of my companions that this appeared to be the only option. I accepted this offer and sat down next to Pete.

"I heard the phone ring before, is the car ready?" I asked.

"No, that was some other call. I'll call the mechanic a little later to see if we can get an idea of when the Olds will be ready," Pete informed me.

"Man, I hope it's ready today."

"Yeah, you and me both."

It was a rainy gray day outside, and the weather colored our moods as such. Jen's aunt was not as talkative today and left us alone in the living room for some time. She had a big TV and a cable box with about a hundred channels of shit to choose from, so I joined my friends for a while as they surfed around from crappy show to crappy show.

Around mid-afternoon I decided to take advantage of a break in the rain to go for a little solitary stroll outdoors. I took leave of my companions, slipped on the black thrift store hoodie I had scored in Ithaca, and set out in search of some unpopulated woodland area to reset my thoughts.

I was able to find a place not far away that suited my needs well enough, despite the surrounding suburban-flavored development. The area must have once been farm fields, because I was able to discern its edges from the old wire farm fencing hidden in the brambles around the borders of the development. I found a space in between two identical tract houses where I could access the woods and dove right in. It was one of those patches of woods too small and close to houses to be used for anything like a public park or nature walk and too big to just bulldoze clear for expanded lawns. Plus, it had a little stream running through it that served to shunt the storm water runoff away from the streets. This stream had cut a moderate ravine, so it turned out to be a nice little place.

Birds were singing, the water was trickling, and the sun was finally popping out from behind the rain clouds. I lingered here for some time enjoying my solitude, eventually coming upon what must have been the old farm's dump. Trash from the 1920s to maybe the 1960s covered one side of the ravine bank like a rusty broken bottle-studded blanket and spilled into the stream below. Some of the larger chunks of metal debris lay in the stream bed itself, the water passing through the rusted holes of chrome trimmed retro household appliances and vintage auto body parts. I kicked around in the dump for a while looking for anything interesting, but it was hard to break through the surface of this amorphous mat of rusted shit. So I went back down to the stream bed to see if the water had found anything for me. Right away I spotted a tarnished brass belt buckle in among the stream bed pebbles. It had some nice patina to it and looked mad old. I checked my belt to see if the shitty nickel-plated buckle it came with was removable and found that it was, so there in the stream bed I swapped out the shitty one for the cool old brass clunker and counted myself blessed.

The clouds had again begun to cover up the sun, and before long the rain returned, prompting me to draw my hood around my head and wrap up my little walkabout. I found Jen on the front porch chain smoking cigarettes when I got back.

"What's up?" I asked her.

"My aunt is driving me crazy," she said with wide eyes. "We need to get the hell out of here."

"Any word on the car?"

"No, Pete hasn't called yet. He keeps saying he will, but whenever…" Just then the phone rang in the house. "That had better be the auto shop."

We entered the house and found Pete on the phone with the mechanic. It was good news, sort of.

"He says he just got the part in," he began as he hung up the phone, "but since it's the end of the day, he'll start on it first thing in the morning. Said the car should be ready by about ten tomorrow morning."

Jen sighed and said, "Ok, at least it will be ready tomorrow."

We all looked at each other in silence. Alright, so just one more night in this awkward, creepy house, I thought. Just one more night and we can hit the road again.

CHAPTER 10

Our final night under that roof passed without incident. No more disturbing dreams or inappropriate nocturnal nipple displays, just the silent oblivion of restful sleep. In the morning she treated us to a better more balanced breakfast of bacon and eggs instead of the day glow sugar cereal she had for us the day before. She had a pot of coffee on too, so the whole meal really hit the spot.

As breakfast was wrapping up, we found we had to ask her more than once to drive us to the mechanic shop because she kept stalling and changing the subject. I don't think she wanted us to leave on account of what was surely a crushing loneliness she suffered under. But we had no patience to entertain the thought of sticking around for even a second, our youth was burning away by the minute. It was time to go, whether the car was ready or not.

By mid-morning we were again in the parking lot of the mechanic shop beside the highway, despite the aunt's occasional "wrong turns" and her snail's pace when she was on the right track. We all thanked her for her hospitality, and she began to get all choked up. Pete backed out of that scene in a hurry, hightailing it to the garage office, leaving Jen and me to cut it off with the sniffling aunt. We were at a loss, each not knowing quite what to do in an increasingly awkward situation. After a moment or two in silence, we each gave her a half-hearted hug, grabbed our bags and walked away. We did not know what else to do. I of course didn't know it at the time, but that strange ownerless bed she had provided would be the last mattress I would sleep on for months.

The car was ready shortly after the aunt finally drove off, and I chipped in my third for the bill, breaking the first one of those travelers' checks I was flush with. We filled up the tank at the attached gas station and hit the road once again. Pete was thrilled to discover the car now exhibited more power than it had ever done before, and he laughed aloud when the tires chirped as he pulled out of the station.

"Holy shit, man! The Olds got some nut now! That guy hooked us up right!"

We shared his smile in silence, listening to the smooth acceleration radiating up through the floor pan. What a car, I thought, sinking into the back seat as we powered up the onramp and onto the highway.

We had maybe a hundred miles to go before we got to the western border of New York State, and it was still before noon. We should be well into the foreign land of Ohio by nightfall, I thought. I broke out the stash box and rolled up a fresh joint. What would the Midwest be like? I wondered. Was Ohio even in the Midwest? I smiled at my ignorance. Ohio was one of those places I had never paid much mind to, so the thought of eventually going there had never really come up. Perhaps it now loomed so large in my mind because it was going to be the first state we would pass through that I had never stepped foot into before. It's funny I would imagine a place like Ohio as such a faraway foreign land when it was just another neighbor of New York.

These thoughts now mingled with a completely fabricated imagining of what might lay ahead of us, obscured by a cloud of thick weed smoke. In my mind I could see great stands of mighty trees growing beside powerful, wide rivers moving in slow strength. I could see rolling green hills beneath an endless blue sky. I could see a people undefined, scattered throughout this landscape and moving around inside of it. God damn, this was some good weed.

Before long, Pete announced we were passing into Pennsylvania. That shook me from my introspective Ohioan fantasy and back to the present moment.

"Wait, what? I thought we were headed towards Ohio?" I asked, clearing my throat of a smoke-induced phlegm.

"Have a look at the map there, Smokey. There's a little finger of Pennsylvania we have to pass through first." And he passed the national road atlas back towards me.

I traced the highway with my finger and sure enough, a little piece of Pennsylvania jutted north toward Lake Erie. It seems that whoever oversaw the striking of the state lines back in the day had arranged for a little lakefront property for the keystone state. I raised my eyes from the map and sent them out the window. It all looked the same as ten minutes ago. What is in a state line, really? A change in local laws perhaps? The nature of the land paid no mind to these arbitrary borders, only another name and a different color license plate.

Who were these people that populated this little finger of land? Did they take some pride in this small stretch of lakeshore they possessed, sandwiched between two other states? Did they experience this land differently from their neighbors to the west and east? Did they consider themselves distinctly different from some eastern Ohioan, or some western New Yorker? I passed a quiet chuckle to myself, thinking of the futility of my ponderings. Who knows, who cares? Here we are passing through at upwards of seventy miles per hour with no intention of getting off the highway. If this place does have an identity, I am not going to be making its acquaintance today.

"Okay, now we're passing into Ohio," he proclaimed after our brief taste of Pennsylvania.

"Yo, I see on the map here we're running parallel to US Route 20," I pointed out. "Let's get off the highway and cruise some two-lane blacktop for a while, maybe find some lakefront parking and check out the water. I've never been to a lake as big as this Lake Erie."

"Ha, Route 20! Why not?" he replied and took the next available exit.

US Route 20 held a special place in all our hearts, being the main drag through the town of the upstate college we had all spent some time at. It had been our weekend escape route and was the main street where the pizza joint and all that sort of thing was. Looking on the map now, I realized that Route 20 was actually the main street for dozens of towns all across America. In fact, it ran from Boston clear across to the Oregon coast, cutting through a few major cities along the way. The road even cut through Yellowstone National Park, right by "Old Faithful". What an intriguing thought: you could be standing at the beginning or end of this road, depending on your perspective, and be facing an unbroken trail of pavement through a little bit of everything this land has to offer, clear over to the other side of the continent.

This section of Route 20 had a similar feel as some of the New York sections of the road I had traveled before, minus the cows and fields of central New York. Jen found on the map some little lakefront public park which turned out to be a shabby sort of dead end. Perfect for our kind of relaxing. We all climbed out of the car and waded through the weeds to get to the shore. It was rocky and absolutely covered with incredible amounts of wave-driven plastic trash. We stood there for a moment, taking in the juxtaposition of a placid expanse of shimmering water ending in a densely packed garbage pile at our feet. Jen was the first to break the silence.

"Oh, my God," she said softly. "What a mess."

Dylan was already at the water's edge sniffing around, so we followed him out onto the beach rubble. We found a grouping of larger rocks arranged in such a way that we could all have a seat not far from where we parked the car. Pete picked up a random plastic picnic plate from the detritus surrounding our circle and proceeded to roll up a spliff. We sat there silently passing the thing between us, listening to the shore birds talk amongst themselves and the water gently folding itself over the garbage-strewn rocks. Randomly, I began picking up all the blue colored bits and pieces of plastic within reach of my sitting rock and arranging them in a pattern on a large flat stone beside me. Jen soon followed suit, and then Pete as well.

Before long we had scoured this small section of shore for every piece of blue colored plastic we could find and had accumulated a sizable pile of blue hued bits on the rocks where we had started. We gazed upon this misshapen sculpture somberly. This was just a small stretch of shore we were playing on, like 20 yards, and look what we were able to collect. What kind of people are we to create such waste, to choke our shores with our discarded convenience? The obviousness of all this trash here really struck a chord in me. I felt a little pissed off at humanity in general, but more hopeless as the thought wore on. What could one do against the onslaught of millions of shitheads not giving a shit? From an early age I was taught to take care of your trash, to not just drop it on the ground. Most everyone I knew was similarly inclined. So who were these millions of litter bugs that could supply us with these hundreds of blue plastic fragments on this sixty-foot section of Lake Erie shore? I noticed that Jen was still at the task of collecting, but now on the hunt for green pieces. Shrugging off these sour thoughts, I joined her in this pursuit.

We were on that beach for quite a while; I'm not sure how long. At some point, it became apparent that the weather was changing, and not for the better. A bank of dark clouds had rolled in from the west and was beginning to blot out the sun with its ominous advancement.

"I think it's time to go," Jen suggested, her raised voice almost lost in a gust of cold wind.

We all climbed back into the car and headed out to the road. The windshield began collecting rain drops by the time we hit the pavement, and before we had clocked a mile the storm was upon us.

Sheets of heavy rain descended and drew close around the car like gray curtains. The wipers could barely keep up with the precipitous onslaught, and our view quickly became seriously obscured. Pete slowed the car down to a jog, his face close to the steering wheel, his eyes squinted in concentration. The wiper blades as it turned out were not up to the task at all and tended to smear the water rather than wipe it away. After a minute or so the driver's side wiper arm began lagging behind its mate on the passenger side, gaining in delay on each pass until a quiet sort of pop sounded, and the driver's side wiper arm fell limp against the base of the windshield.

"Fuck, what happened!" Pete exclaimed. "I can't see a God Damn thing!"

"Pull over, Peter, before you kill us!" Jen replied.

"Jesus, take it easy! I have this under control," he barked, leaning over towards the passenger side to get a clearer view of the road's shoulder. Heavy drips of water were now beginning to drop from where the windshield met the roof and onto Jen's knees.

"God Damn it, Peter! This car is such a piece of shit!"

"Shut up, shut up, shut up…" he grumbled through clenched teeth.

Pete steered the car onto the dirt shoulder a little faster perhaps then he should have and dropped the right front wheel into a big pothole hidden under a puddle. The car bottomed out with a loud thud and sent a fountain of muddy water into the air.

"Holy fucking shit! What the hell?" Jen yelled, her hands on the dashboard.

"Shut up!" he cried and stepped out into the rain.

Dylan, picking up on the energy displayed would not sit still and dove into the front seat as Pete shut the door, briefly landing on the horn.

"What?!" Pete yelled into the windshield; I suppose assuming Jen had sounded the horn for some reason.

The passenger side wiper was still flapping back and forth at full tilt. Pete grabbed the driver's side arm, and it momentarily jerked to life, pinching his finger before again going limp. I couldn't see very well out the windshield at this point, but I could sure hear Pete's cursing. Dylan, of course, began barking in every direction in response to Pete's animated frustration, adding to the chaotic nature of the moment. After a few minutes in the rain, he climbed back into the car soaking wet, his dreads dripping. We all sat there for a minute in silence watching the rainwater slide down the glass.

"I think the shaft is stripped," he declared in a low tone.

"What does that mean?" Jen asked.

"It means the wipers are fucked," I replied.

The obviousness of my response was enough to break the icy air, and we all began to laugh together. What else could we do? We were getting schooled on the trials of traveling and were going to have to learn to take this kind of shit in stride if we were ever going to make it out here on the road.

So there we sat, passing a roach around for fifteen minutes, listening to the radio and scanning the map for a campground we could aim for. Eventually the rain let up enough to drive without wipers, but it was still drizzly. We were going to have to find a place to stop for the night, before the sun went down, and deal with this wiper issue.

It was well into the afternoon at this point; we had only a few hours of daylight left, and the sky still looked as if it could release another shower at any moment. Jen found some county park where campsites were available. It was maybe twenty miles or so west of Cleveland. We were still well east of that city, so we left old route 20 behind and got back on the freeway headed west. Before long, an urban landscape began to materialize out of the misty gloom. Traffic up to this point had never been an issue, but wouldn't you know it, as soon as we crossed into the city limits traffic slowed to a crawl. About this time the rain came back into play. We were progressing slowly enough that some degree of visibility could still be had, plus the rain was nowhere near as intense as that first deluge that took out the wipers.

It took us about an hour to get through that city, but once we got through to the other side the clouds broke along with the traffic and allowed us a little open road sunset to drive off into.

The park Jen had found was a little south of the highway, out among small fields and suburban developments. It wasn't much to look at, but it was free. It was also totally unoccupied, so we had our pick of parking lot campsites. They were all basically the same. Each one had a little steel barbecue stand and your standard issue picnic bench next to a paved little square to park the car on. We took the one closest to a group of scraggly trees and brush and called the place home. I was the only one who had brought a tent, but since I was a single guy and they were a couple with a dog, I let them use the tent and took the back seat of the car for myself. This arrangement would work out nicely during our travels, as I always had a dry place all to myself to sleep, and it worked to my advantage right from the start because it rained that first night like all get out.

I lay there stretched out on the backseat, wrapped in my sleeping bag listening to the rain beat against the steel roof. The cloth headliner was long gone, leaving a skeleton of spring steel rods suspended below the sheet metal, so the impacts from the heavy rain fall resonated into the car as though I were inside of a drum. I wondered how my friends were faring out there in the tent, not that there was any other choice, really. That is unless we all just slept communally in the car, sitting upright in the seats. Even though it was storming out it was not cold outside, being late summer, so I did not give the issue too much thought. Before long, it would be morning, and we would be moving on again. This storm appeared to be heading east, while we were trekking west, so we were sure to clear this gray wet weather before long, I hoped.

I found that I couldn't help but replay these past few days over and over in my head as I lay there in the dark, at times laughing out loud and totally unable to fall asleep. This ever-present sense of excitement still permeated my being and kept the sandman standing outside in the rain. Jen had given me a few Percocet tablets she had left over from some dental procedure, and since the fire of mind apparently would not leave me, I decided to see if these pills might help knock me out. I washed them down with a mouthful of water, pulled out my road journal and then lit up a roach.

The thoughts continued for some time, unabated. I worked to pin them down by flashlight, chasing them as I drove my pencil across the paper. What might tomorrow bring, I pondered. What new experiences, new sights would I encounter as tomorrow's sun streaked across the sky? I had never felt such an awesome unfurling of potential future ahead, and the feeling consumed me. As the effects of the painkillers merged with the stone, I felt a sort of oneness with the present, with this random nondescript place I now found myself in, with the rain pounding the sheet metal roof above me, with the air, and the night. I felt completely in the Now like I had never felt before. Perhaps it was some cosmic force of the universe I had somehow tapped into that seemed to open my mind's eye so. Perhaps it was the very power of God himself touching my soul and lifting me up. Perhaps it was the three Percocet pills enhanced by the smoke of a roach. Whatever it was, it sure felt awesome to be alive.

CHAPTER 11

At some point during the night, the rain blew away on the wind, and we awoke to find the skies of dawn clear and blue. My companions had stayed relatively dry inside the tent, despite the steady deluge which had rode so roughshod over us all throughout the night. But their sleeping bags had become a little damp from condensation. So we lingered in that boring little campsite till mid-morning trying to dry out the tent and sleeping bags by draping them over the car.

Pete had made use of our idle time there by "fixing" the driver's side windshield wiper arm that had so hindered our progress in the rain the day before. He had taken two separate lengths of shoestring and tied each one to the loose wiper arm. Each length of string was then laid across the base of the windshield and into the car through the little triangle shaped quarter vent windows in the front doors. Operating the wipers would now be a two-person job, as the driver, and the passenger would each have to take turns pulling their end of shoestring to get the wiper arm to pass back and forth across the windshield. It was a ridiculous solution, no doubt, but it worked. The main drawback was that Pete now had no laces in his sneakers.

Our destination for the day was a state park called Indiana Dunes. It was right on the shore of Lake Michigan and had a bunch of hiking trails. We'd probably have to pay a fee to camp, but maybe because it was so late in the season we could get in there for free. It was worth a shot because there really wasn't much else around.

The interstate highway from Cleveland clear through to about where the park was located was all toll road. And since we were in no position to be blowing our money on tolls, we struck a course on a long, straight state route that would take us through a bunch of small local towns all across the heart of Ohio and

Indiana. Our old pal, US Route 20 was again to be our path, if at least for the morning.

There wasn't much to see out here, even on a side road like this, but it was better than the highway with its incessant billboards. We cruised at a good clip through farm fields and wooded patches. Past silos, and homesteads. Every twenty minutes or so we'd have to slow down, as the route would momentarily become some small town's main street. But often enough you could just blink and have just passed right on through the settlement, hammering down once again.

All morning we trekked on like this, burning down a few doobies along the way. At one point we missed a planned turn onto US route 6 without realizing it, being as blazed up as we were. Ten minutes on Jen noticed our mistake.

"We missed our turn, Pete. Turn around."

"Man, I hate going back. Is there some other road we can take instead?"

"Yeah, I guess," she said, studying the map. "There's a county road we can take at this next town that will take us west, and eventually back to Route 6."

That settled it, we bid adieu to Route 20 at the next town and headed off on one seriously back road. We hardly passed another car and often had to hang rights and lefts to stay on the road we wanted. Eventually we came up on the Maumee River and followed its southern bank for a while. Just past a little nondescript town we found a state park with riverfront access, and since the dog hadn't had a piss in a while, and frankly neither had we, we decided to stop in for a rest.

We found a little parking area there right down by the water, and it being about noon we figured we might as well make a picnic lunch out of it. Dylan had waded out into the river up to his chest, and Pete, after kicking off his loose shoes and rolling up his pant legs, waded in after him. I joined Jen at the trunk to see what we had to eat. Apples, a jar of peanut butter, a smooshed loaf of bread; that was about it.

"We're gonna need to hit up a grocery store or something," she remarked, as she carried our meager supplies over to a park bench.

We sat there munching on sliced apple and peanut butter sandwiches while Dylan munched on a bowl of kibbles. It was good enough. The scene was nice down there by the river. The birds were singing, and the sun was shining. After we had eaten, we spent another hour or so there walking the river's edge trails and puffing on roaches. At some point we lost the sun behind a growing bank of clouds, and by the time we got back to the car it was looking like rain again.

"Looks like we might get to try out the new wipers here soon," Pete said, as we pulled out of the park and back onto the road.

About fifteen minutes later the rain started in for real. Pete's shoestring wiper control worked well enough, but you had to be careful where the passenger side string was at when the passenger side wiper arm moved, or the movement of the one good arm would catch the string and pull it from your grip. Pete ended up not running the wiper motor at all after a while because the string kept getting caught on the passenger side arm. The novelty of the whole system wore off pretty quickly, and once the windshield seam started leaking onto Jen's knees again, we had to pull over so I could take over in the front seat.

I hadn't spent much time up there in the front seat so far, and found I rather enjoyed the copilot responsibilities of plotting our course on the road atlas and pulling the wiper string in time with the driver. Jen curled up in the back with Dylan, wrapping up in the colorful Mexican blanket that upholstered the shredded back seat, and together they passed out.

Pete and I drove on in silence for a while, the high from the last smoke degrading steadily, leaving us both bleary eyed and burnt. The road ahead of us was long and straight and seemed to go on forever with only farms and other rural monotony to attract our interest. I wanted to roll up another joint but couldn't let go of the shoestring as it was still raining steadily. After about an hour of this, we came up upon a sizable town near the border with Indiana. "The top of Ohio," the welcome sign claimed.

"Let's get some gas in this town here before we cross into Indiana," Pete announced. "I need to stretch my legs anyway."

We all agreed, and while he was pumping the gas, Jen, Dylan, and I took a walk around the edge of the station to let the dog take a leak. The sky hung low and dark over the farmlands around us, and puddles of gray water filled every low place, but the rain had let up a bit. Jen handed the dog back over to Pete once he had finished filling the tank and went into the station's convenience store to grab some foodstuffs for the trunk. I joined her to help carry the bags. She got a couple packs of cigarettes, a couple gallons of water, another loaf of bread, some more apples, and some junk food too. When we got back to the car, Pete took a look in the bags.

"What, no beer?" he asked.

"I'm not going back in," she replied, "If you want beer for tonight, you can get it."

"Come on, bud," he said to me "Let's get some beers."

So I returned to the store again, whatever. Pete grabbed a couple twelve packs and then proceeded to wander around the store, looking for impulse buys.

"What else should we get?" he asked me.

I just shrugged. I was still feeling pretty burnt and was content to just sort of silently follow him around the store. He ended up grabbing a couple packs of hot dogs for the campfire we expected to have that night, a deck of playing cards, and the ultimate impulse buy, a pouch of chewing tobacco.

"You chew tobacco?" I asked him.

"Nope," he replied with a smile.

When we got back to the car, it was Jen's turn to inspect the bag of its convenience store acquisitions.

"Chew?" she asked him, pulling the pouch from the shopping bag "What the hell are you going to do with this?"

"Chew it," he replied as he started the car.

"That's fucking nasty, Peter. Don't expect any kisses with this shit in your mouth."

He just laughed, popped in a thrash metal tape, and hit the gas. The rain had finally quit while we had been in and out of that little convenience store, but the pavement was still all wet, so we peeled out of the gas station with the engine roaring.

"Whoo hoo!" he hollered, followed instantly with peals of furious barking from Dylan.

"Jesus fucking Christ, Peter!" Jen exclaimed with a sly smile growing across her face, her hands braced on the dashboard. Her attraction to Pete's unpredictable nature seemed to be constantly at odds with her pragmatic demeanor. "Don't wreck the fuckin' car, you maniac!"

He replied by turning up the volume, until the speed metal guitar drowned out Dylan's latest fit of compulsive barking. I, in the back seat, again felt it necessary to roll up another fat spliff and began pulling big puffs off the misshapen burner as soon as I had rolled it. We had it down to a smoldering stump by the time we soared over the state line into Indiana.

The rain held off through the rest of the afternoon, which was good for our driving, and being that we were trying to make this lakefront park with enough daylight left over to see what the hell we were doing we were driving on now with some determination. There would be no more stopping till the dunes.

More than once we passed Amish horse drawn buggies, with their stoic passengers looking rather sharply at our speeding jalopy, leaving them in clouds of pre-emissions regulations dust. Seeing those Amish people working their lands and going about their business despite the secular sped up world around them reminded me of the orthodox Jewish people we had briefly seen as we passed through Brooklyn the week before. Their creeds and traditions were different, no doubt, but they were still a population apart from the general public, choosing a way of life steeped in traditions I didn't understand. I took them at face value, as it were, not giving much thought at the time to what it would really mean to be living under the weight of such traditions, and not realizing that I too was loaded with my own set of unbreakable, but at times bendable traditions of faith, compelled by guilt as I was with my Sunday matzo crackers and little cans of grape juice. They were my people in a way, though I'm sure both the Amish and the Hasidim would beg to differ.

I as of yet hadn't really grasped the full concept of religious faith and tradition, yet I lived with the consequences of it daily. My shackles of faith were all I had known thus far, having grown up immersed in the local evangelical Christian flavor. I talked like I loved God, like I loved Jesus, but what I hadn't realized yet was that I was really just terrified of their unpredictable, old-timey, Abrahamic wrath. I felt I needed to experience the guilt of my human desires completely to be absolved of them, so I carried that guilt around with me everywhere I went. It's a testament to the muted spiritual endurance I possessed that I could live under that weight and not be crushed by it. It also helped that I often devised brilliant methods of justifications I could use to do the things I loved and still be right from a "spiritually legal" standpoint, like listen to heavy metal, take this road trip, and smoke weed like a chimney. Lord knows the elders back in church would not approve of any of that noise, but that was really none of their fucking business. In the end it was just me, my sins, and my disapproving Jesus out here on the road.

Near where our little state route crossed I-69, we passed a big billboard advertising some small town's claim to fame as the place of interment of a fossilized mastodon skeleton. What a thought that was! A giant, hairy, elephant-like creature with its long curling tusks roaming these endless Amish corn fields. I imagined a bearded Amish man in his little black-brimmed hat steering a plow hitched to a giant mastodon! Jesus Christmas I was fucking stoned.

"I think we got about another sixty miles or so to go," Jen declared, pointing to some place on the road atlas and tapping the spot with her long thin finger.

"Good," Pete replied. "Cuz it'll be getting dark before we know it." And he gave the Olds a little more gas.

"Can I get a look at that map?" I asked, and she passed it back to me.

I spread the atlas out on my knees and traced our route thus far. We had really covered some ground since Ithaca. But we still had so much farther to go before we reached the Pacific Ocean. So much still lay ahead.

It was late afternoon when our route north finally appeared, and Jen made sure Pete didn't miss this one. The endless fields and silos began to change rapidly to suburbia again, and right about the time one could legitimately call it the evening, we passed through the gates of the Indiana Dunes state park. We came up on a guard shack splitting the way down the middle and found it unmanned. Once past the shack, the road widened considerably, and before long we rolled into a vast, nearly empty, windblown parking lot at the shore populated only by few lone cars. A large, two-story red brick building with cinder-blocked-up arched windows, shaped in fact like a single giant brick, dominated the shoreline, dwarfing the few small trees that stood randomly around it. The structure retained that stately, utilitarian beauty common in early century buildings despite its weatherworn façade. It remained there on the beach as a testament to the skill of its long-dead builders who probably never looked ahead to a time when such a vast fortress-like structure would be found obsolete and run down, its great halls nearly empty except for stacks of park service trash cans, one hundred thousand feral pigeons, and a scattered detritus of bird shit and beer bottle abandonment caking the floors.

We circled the lot once and came to rest near where the only other cars were parked.

"What a lonely scene," Jen remarked in a whisper meant for no one in particular.

We all climbed out and followed Dylan down to the water's edge. I stood there for a moment as my companions broke away and took it all in. I had never stood before a lake of this size; having grown up on the Atlantic Ocean, I found it difficult now to believe that this was in fact a freshwater lake before me, for the far shore could not be seen. Scanning the horizon, I could just make out the tops of pointy buildings due west and realized with a start that I must be looking at the upper floors of Chicago on the other side. I briefly imagined a submerged city at street level, canoeing around the ruined buildings, paddling into open twelfth-story windows.

The gentle waves lapping over my sneakers and soaking my socks dispelled this fantasy and I knelt in the wet sand and plunged my hands into the water just to see if it felt the same as the briny waters I had known all my life back home. The sand was markedly finer here than the coarse yellow material of New York's ocean shores, and the water itself did somehow feel different, but I could not place how exactly. Finally, I raised a dripping wet finger to my lips and searched for that sharp pang of salt in the water. I broke into a short laugh when I found I could taste none. A rising excitement tingled up the back of my neck as I stood up and stretched my arms wide towards the lake taking, deep breaths in through my nose and out my open mouth. What a delightfully foreign experience I was meeting with here. I of course had seen these great lakes on maps forever and had already met with Lake Erie's trash-strewn shore, but I was totally unprepared for the sheer size of Lake Michigan once presented in person.

Dylan ran up to me as I grooved on all this and dropped a handful of short happy barks, then circled around me a few times before tearing back off towards my companions. I followed with similar abandon.

"Wow!" I exclaimed, a tad winded from my short sprint on the sand. "Can you believe this is really a lake? You can't even see the other side! Look straight ahead, see those points sticking out of the water? That must be the tops of Chicago!"

"Ha, yeah. Cool," agreed Pete as he scanned the horizon, his hand to his forehead as if to shield the already departed afternoon light from his eyes.

Dylan, who had been running circles around our trio, suddenly shot down the beach towards a lone woman with a walking stick, still far off but walking towards us along the shoreline. Pete took off after him at a jog, and we followed his lead.

The lady greeted us with a raised hand and a smile as we approached her. She was older, maybe in her fifties. It's so hard to accurately judge an older person's decade when you're still just a kid yourself. She was dressed in layers of flowing dark fabrics and a long floral-patterned dress reminiscent of Victorian wallpaper, with a wild mop of curly salt and pepper hair that blew around in the breeze. She looked kind of like an old hippie, but darker somehow, gloomier, like a witch.

"Greetings travelers," she said as we approached, her palm still raised in greeting. "Heading west?"

"Yes," replied Pete, obviously surprised by her direct hit.

She turned her smoke gray eyes on me, and with a coy smile said, "I too once traveled west in my youth. Many things I've seen on the road, many lives I've lived." She then fixed her gaze on a zone above my head, her mouth slightly parted and inhaled sharply. "It's a long road," she continued, "and you all are still only at the threshold of your path. You too will see many things and live many lives. Walk with me back to the cars. It will be getting dark soon and we should not be caught out in the rains at night."

So we all walked slowly back up the beach, the wind at our backs. Occasionally she would stop and poke at something in the sand with her stick, and once stooped to pick something up. She had found a piece of cobalt colored beach glass polished by the waves like a gem. She held it out for me to see, sensing my interest no doubt. I noticed then that the backs of her hands were covered in faded greenish black tattoos of what looked like snakes that continued past her wrists and out of sight up her shirt sleeves and down her fingers under clunky ornate silver rings. It gave me the shivers, but not out of fear, rather excitement, anticipation. Jesus was there on my shoulder suggesting that what we had crossed paths with here was one of those Wiccan sorceresses the church fathers had warned me about, or worse yet, a demon. But my gut, always the bastion of reason, was telling me otherwise.

"It's wonderful how the earth can take our garbage and make something beautiful, given enough time," she remarked to me, taking the single rounded shard of glass and dropping it into a small bulging purple velvet sack that hung from her wide leather belt.

"I collect beach glass too," I told her, "though I've left it all behind."

"It's well that you did. Best to travel light when trekking west. You all still have many more possessions to purge, though, before your journey is complete; many more burdens to cast aside. Do not lament their loss once they have left you, the road will provide you with whatever you need."

We had reached the concrete boardwalk before the parking lot and paused there for a moment, Dylan too, having taken a seat next to Pete, was now positioned erect and stately like a statue dog. He had been on surprisingly good behavior the moment we approached this woman; he had not acted out or barked at her once, which was very unlike our hyper little buddy. This lady had some heavy energy for sure.

"Do you have a camera?" she asked us "I could take your picture here, so that when you are as old as I am you can remember this windswept moment with clarity."

"Yeah, sure," Pete replied.

"I'll get my camera from the car," I offered and trotted off to retrieve it. I grabbed a spliff I had rolled earlier too. We gotta smoke this lady out, I thought. It would be the right thing to do.

I returned with the little disposable camera my mom had gotten for me and handed it to the woman. We all sat in a row on the concrete wall that separated the beach from the pavement, with Dylan in Pete's arms, and smiled for posterity. When she handed the camera back to me I asked her if she would like to burn this joint I had with us.

She threw her head back in cackling laughter, and with a wave of her hand replied,"Oh, no. I'm far beyond that now. But thank you, truly." She then took my hand and said, "Blessed be with you on your journey to the western starlands."

I looked again into her smoky eyes and realized her pupils were dilated unnaturally wide. "Blessed be with you all," she declared with an overly dramatic flourish reminiscent of an actress exiting the stage, and abruptly strode off across the parking lot away from the few parked cars, barefoot, almost dancing in her movement.

"Huh, she's on foot I guess," Pete said, "I thought she had a car for some reason."

"She's probably too fucked to even drive," Jen snorted "Did you see her eyes? She's totally tripping or something. What was with all that crazy shit she was talking?"

"I don't know, she seemed nice to me."

"Oh, come on. You would like the weirdo stoner hippie chick. She's too old for you, Peter," she warned him.

"Hey, it's not like that!" he retorted.

"Oh yeah, what's it like then?"

"Easy guys, come on, the sun is going down, and I can see rain coming in out across the water," I pleaded "We should find a place to camp."

That settled the issue, and we all piled back in the car to see what we could find for campsites. There was a self-pay booth set up at the entrance to the campground, but we all pretended we didn't see it. It was almost dark anyway. The campground had lots of pull-off sites but was basically uninhabited. We picked a spot as far afield as we could find and cut the engine. There was still enough light to work with, so I helped Pete pitch the tent, while Jen rummaged in the trunk for their sleep gear and stuff. Once the tent was up, he asked me to help him find some firewood because he was going to have a hot dog supper tonight come hell or high water. I could already feel sprinkles on my nose, and the air had a heavy damp atmosphere of coming rain, but I obliged.

Finding suitable kindling in this well-used campground proved to be quite difficult. The trees were stripped bare of any deadwood within reach, and the underbrush was still green with late summer leaf. We eventually were able to amass enough material to make a go of it, having found a few charred lumps of wood in other fire pits, a mess of green twigs and some cardboard.

It was full on dark now and starting to drizzle. Jen had no interest in attempting a fire and had already retreated to the car with Dylan. I sat with my friend in the dirt and tried to help him realize his hot dog dinner dreams. The smoke of smoldering cardboard and damp, half rotten wood was a little overpowering, but Pete kept his face close to the sick little coals, trying to breathe life into his creation with minimal success. Soon the drizzle had turned into full-grown rain, and the heavy drops were crashing into his little pyre with sizzling impacts.

"Fuck this, man," I said. "I'm crying uncle."

"God damn it," he mumbled quietly, as I rose and retreated to join Jen and Dylan in the car.

"He's determined if nothing else," Jen said. I agreed, and we watched as he held a single limp wiener on a stick over the thick smoke. "He's going to eat that hot dog, even if it's raw, you wait." And shortly thereafter he did just that.

Finally, after wiping the smoky hot dog water off his lips, he rose and climbed into the tent. Jen and Dylan then left me to the car and joined him. It was early still, but dark and wet, so there was nothing else for me to do but ride it out and turn in as well. I sealed myself up in my sleeping bag and settled into the backseat.

My thoughts turned to the witchy hippie lady we had just crossed path with and her cryptic message. Her seemingly clairvoyant abilities to know who and what we were, and where we were going, were uncanny and mildly disturbing. Coming from my fundamentalist background, I couldn't help but assume the supernatural. It would be years before I understood that while she might have been under the influence of hallucinogens, all she really did was cold read us like any good fortune teller worth her beads would. But that night, as the rain beat on the car's roof and the smoke of my burning roach muddled my senses in the darkness, I concluded that she had not been a malevolent witch, or a demon, or even the actual human she actually was but an angel made flesh, placed before us by God himself to guide us on our path.

CHAPTER 12

We awoke to a clear sky, though everything was still damp from the rain. The firepit Pete had battled with so gallantly the night before was filled with a shallow pool of standing gray water, so I broke out a little hiking camp stove from my kit to afford us the privilege of having our breakfast hot. We toasted slices of bread and roasted Pete's remaining hot dogs, folding the dry bread around the wieners. We washed that championship breakfast down with a pot of weak coffee made by boiling the water and the grounds all in the same small saucepan, making the coffee a bit chewy. It was a rough sort of breakfast, but the best we could muster with what we had. Plus, since we had baked upon waking as was our custom, our appetite was sufficiently stimulated to tackle such fare.

Jen had found the camp toilets first thing, getting up before the rest of us, and had reported back that showers could be had there as well. They were both excited by that prospect, but I wasn't terribly interested, presently enjoying the road funk beginning to collect on my person. She had grabbed a couple trail maps from a kiosk near the showers as well, so by mid-morning we had packed a half assed picnic lunch and wandered off down the trails in search of all things good.

The day was quickly becoming hot and humid, charging the dense forest we walked through with an almost steamy atmosphere. Sometimes the trail took us through relatively open woodlands by sandy paths, and other times the trail became wooden plank causeways over swampy inland marshes full of singing birds and flying bugs. The biodiversity here was striking, and I began to notice unfamiliar birds by sight, but more often by their foreign calls. I guess I expected we'd be passing through the habitats of local animals I had never experienced before, but somehow I didn't think that'd be coming into play till we were farther on down the road.

We eventually came upon a tall, wooden, multiple-tier observation tower on the edge of a large swamp. There was really no other choice but to climb up and burn some more weed. At the top we found a few benches heavily carved with the graffiti of other climbers' names and tags, along with a long view of the surrounding swamplands below. Pete broke out a few choice nugs, and we got even higher still.

After ten minutes or so in the treetops, Dylan decided it was time to descend back to the earth and made his way down while we were busy wrapping up the session. He began barking for us to pick up the pace when he perceived that we were not moving as quickly as he liked and was very happy once we had reached ground level. High places tended to make him uneasy if he was not sufficiently distracted by something. Pete knelt down and gave him a reassuring hug, and I swear that dog smiled.

As we continued on, the path began to get sandier, and the trees began to space out around us. Before long, the way was leading us among big sandy hills which were in fact ancient sand dunes now studded with trees and brush. It was really getting hot now, and still very humid, so we were beginning to sweat pretty good as we climbed these hills. At one point, as the trail cut sideways across the biggest dune hill yet, Pete broke formation and began climbing straight up the sandy slope using all four of his limbs in the effort.

"Hey, what are you doing?" Jen asked him with some degree of exasperation. "The sign at the beginning said to stay on the marked trails!"

"Fuck the signs! Come on, let's all climb this hill before it gets away!"

"What the fuck is he talking about?" she asked me.

"Climbing this hill, apparently. Come on, I bet the view is awesome from the top."

This hill was pretty big and turned into all soft sand before long. We were all struggling in our prohibited ascent, our feet sinking in deep and losing traction with each step, our hands grasping at loose powder. The sun was full on now too and beating down on us, working to drive us back down the slope. Dylan crested the summit first and began barking encouragements until we finally joined him at the top. We were winded, sandy, and wet with sweat, but the view was incredible, spanning miles out over the lake. Far to the south, a yellowish haze shrouded an industrial landscape topped with the flame tipped smokestacks of refineries; to the north the cooling towers of a nuclear power plant could be made out among the hills along the shore. Due west was the Chicago skyline, now more visible due to our heightened vantage point. The heavy industry and urbanity that surrounded this place made it feel like an oasis of natural beauty, and I guess it really was.

Pete had his arms around Jen, attempting to get her to dance with him in the silence of that burning bald hilltop, and she obliged for a moment before she pushed him into the sand. Straddling him, her hands on his chest, she went in for a kiss. I looked over to Dylan awkwardly. Keep your lips off me was his reply.

For a moment I could remember the taste of the last kiss I had enjoyed and was brought back into the feelings I was stricken with when that girl dumped me just a short time ago. The swirling emotions were troubling and intense, and I wished I had my own girlfriend to roll around in the sand with, or at least that my companions would stop making out in front of me.

I was suddenly struck with an anger at God for allowing my first attempt at love to be shattered by reality, even though I had played the game according to his rules. It was those rules, in fact, that were the impetus of her leaving me, for I would not "go all the way" with her because of my convictions. I felt like I had blown my chance, the chance I had been so desperate for. I felt like a chump, a fool, and I felt it was ultimately God's fault.

That blasphemous thought was deflected before it really sunk in when Jen suddenly jumped up off Pete and declared, "It's too hot up here in the sun. Let's run down this hill to the beach and take a swim."

We took the slope in long flying strides, right at the very edge of control. Pete began to tumble head over heels, throwing a rooster tail of sand behind him. I myself lost control towards the bottom, landing on my side in the soft hot sand in a cloud of dry dust. Dylan shot straight for the water upon landing, and Pete was next, having shed his loose clothing all over the beach in his race to the water's edge. I plopped down into the sand and began fighting with my knotted sneaker laces.

I was pouring the sand out of my second shoe when Jen pranced past me and into the water after Pete in her panties and bra. She was up to her neck and in his arms before I realized that I had hawked her ass the whole way in. Waves of guilt and arousal washed over me in equal measure as I peeled off my T shirt, and a hefty portion of body image issues to boot,. Part of me wanted to stay there on the beach and remain clothed in their presence, but a stronger longing for belonging goaded me on till my pants lay unoccupied in the sand with the rest of the garments. At least the water would hide my pale, flabby shame.

The water felt so good after our trek through humid swamps and over dusty sand dunes in the blazing sun. Dylan had found a ratty old tennis ball on the shore somewhere and had engaged his humans in a game of toss and fetch which had him in and out of the water and yelping with joyous excitement at each volley. We laughed along with him, reveling in the moment. Before I knew it, I became the ball tosser, as my companions waded off together in buoyant embrace. I was on the fifth or sixth round of Dylan's game when I heard Jen moan in delight, despite their now significant distance from me. I was racked with conflicting emotions upon realizing what was happening between them underwater. I was embarrassed that I was there to witness their copulations, like I was intruding somehow, even though they obviously didn't give a shit. But more so, I was envious. I had had a similar opportunity not two months before during my brief stint as a boyfriend. She had pressed herself hard against me as we floated in the bay; we kissed and kissed and felt each other's bodies below the water line as if hidden from the sight of Jesus, but when it came time to take the next step, I instead asked her to marry me. I might as well have dropped a bucket of ice water on her. God damn, but I felt like such a schmuck.

After a while, they swam back into my territory noticeably glowing. Dylan had lost interest in the ball during this time and was now back on the beach rolling in the sand and on our clothes.

"Hey! Stop that!" Pete yelled. The dog jumped up and froze for a moment, his tongue and tail wagging in time before breaking into a full run down the beach. "Dylan, come back here!"

Off Pete went down the beach after him in his sopping wet underwear, leaving Jen and me bobbing in the water. I looked over to her, and she just smiled.

"You wanna burn one?" I asked her awkwardly. She just shook her head yes silently, gently smiling all the time.

At the foot of the big dune we had rolled down earlier, there was a small stand of scrubby trees and bushes that offered some degree of shade. So we gathered our loose clothes, shook the wet dog sand out from them, and made our way over to the spot.

I felt compelled to put my pants and shirt back on, despite still being dripping wet, because Christian shame is a mighty lord. Jen did not suffer from any such hangup and stretched out her full underwear-clad frame in the sand at the edge of the shade so the sun might burn the lake's moisture off her skin. This wasn't the first time I had seen her in her undergarments, but it was the first time I'd been alone with her like that. When we had all dipped in that woodland stream outside of Ithaca, I had felt awkward, of course, but Pete had been there too, which made it better somehow. Plus, her choice of panties that day had not been as revealing as the little lace number she had on today. She had her eyes closed as I rolled up a big spliff, and my desire to touch her with my eyes unnoticed was interfering with my work. Pete returned as I was lighting up the shoddily-built number.

"This is one ugly burner," he declared, as I passed the misshapen finger to him.

It was a thick one though, so it made the circle around our trio many times. Pete, after zoning out for a minute, handed the roach to me and lay down to nap in the shade. Jen moved out of the sun into the partial shade of the trees now too and sat cross legged beside me so we both faced the water.

"Light that thing up again," she asked me. I obediently obliged, and we consumed it down to nothing in silence. She then produced a cigarette from her little knapsack, lit it up, and leaned back on her elbows in the sand, stretching her pale thin body out once again. She looked beautiful there in the sparkling sunlight, the cigarette stuck to and dangling from her parted lips, her long straight hair drying to her shoulders. I tried not to think about it, remembering the church teachings about lusting after another man's wife and all. Even if they weren't actually married, it still felt wrong to entertain any sexual attraction to her if for nothing else than it would be a dick move on my part against my friends. Yea, but though the spirit may be willing, the flesh is most certainly weak.

"I am so glad we're actually putting some distance between us and New York," she finally said, snapping me out of my introspection. "I'm so fucking done with my family and all the bad shit back there."

"Yeah, I know what you mean. This trip is like a fresh start. We don't have to be known by our past mistakes and shit anymore cuz nobody knows us out here. We can be whatever we want!"

"Yeah. I like the sound of that," she replied, stubbing out the cigarette in the sand. Dylan had been lying next to Pete panting in the heat, his tongue waging and extra long somehow. "Come 'ere Dyl. D'you want some water, boy?" she asked. He jumped right up and came to us. There was no water dish with us she could use to give him a proper drink, so she just sort of poured the water from her bottle right into his mouth. At least half of it just went into the sand.

"Are you hungry?" she asked me as she attempted this inefficient water transfer. I nodded yes. "There's some apples in the bag here. Get me one too," she continued, gesturing towards her little knapsack. I again obliged, fishing out two choice examples. We spent the next half hour or so eating our apples together down to their cores and speculating on what the road might bring us next.

Eventually Pete woke up from his nap, and we put ourselves back together for our trek back to camp. We at first toyed with the thought of scaling that steep sandy slope so we could continue on the trail where we left it, but after looking up from the bottom, our necks craned skyward, we thought better of it and set off down the beach to find a place where a marked trail into the woods line might be picked up.

We walked the shore barefoot for almost an hour before we found what we were looking for, and it was then another hour in the mid-day heat on meandering trails before we made it back to camp tired, hungry, and terribly thirsty, having exhausted our meager supplies of water and apples. Jen wanted the camp shower even more then refreshments and left us to ourselves in camp right away. Pete and I, having nothing else to do, began drinking the lukewarm beers from the cooler and munching on nacho flavored tortilla chips. The first few beers went down hard because we were not accustomed to chugging warm cans, but with our thirst the way it was we found we were able to get past our initial aversion pretty quickly. We had a pretty good buzz going by the time Jen returned fresh and smelling of shampoo.

"There's no hot water there, the showers are cold," she declared flatly before climbing into the tent.

"Beggars can't be choosers, princess," Pete called out after her.

"Fuck off," she replied just as flatly as before from inside the tent.

"Man, I'm fucking hungry," he then said to me "Are there any of those hot dogs left?"

I rummaged through the cooler, searching blindly under the beers floating in melted ice water, and found a half pack of wieners, the naked hot dogs mingling with the water of the cooler in loose plastic. "Ah ha! Let's see if we can find some real wood for this fire tonight," he declared, as he rose and took the loosely wrapped and dripping package from my hand. "Four dogs… better than nothing," he stated, after briefly inspecting the hoard.

I dropped a few beers into the knapsack, Pete tucked a doobie behind his ear, and off we went with the dog in tow in search of combustibles.

We had to go far afield to find enough sticks to make a nice bundle, but it was just as well because burning weed in the campground during the daylight hours would probably not have been the best idea, even if there was hardly anyone around. We had no rope to wrap the bundle, so I used my belt, and I was pleasantly surprised to find that without the belt my pants now tended to slip down my hips as I walked. Life on the road was apparently slimming me down already.

We returned to camp about a half hour later minus the beers and the doobie and set to work getting a fire going. Since this batch of wood was more conducive to fire starting than the poor stock we had the night before, we had a merry little blaze going in no time. Jen emerged from the tent to join us just in time for weenie roasting. Pete had whittled her a green stick as well as one for himself, and together they held their processed meat tubes over the open flames while Dylan licked his chops. We all cut a section off our share of the weenie to drop in Dylan's bowl of dry kibbles; it was only fair. Again we wrapped our dogs in dry bread but broke out a can of cold baked beans which we passed around for dipping and scooping.

The setting sun found us reclining on blankets around our steel fire ring of meager coals, drinking the last of the now ambient-temperature beers. It was just after dark when we had our visitor. He emerged suddenly from the darkness, startling us all.

"Hello, travelers," he greeted as he stepped into the firelight. Dylan tensed instantly and began emitting a low steady growl. "My name's Jimmy, I'm camped a few spaces over. I spotted you when you all rolled in. Where you all coming from?"

"We coming out of New York headed west," Pete replied, his hand firmly latched to Dylan's collar. "How 'bout you?"

"Oh, I'm out of California, but I haven't been there in years now. Always on the move, ya know," he replied, squatting now by the fire. He was a thin white guy, maybe middle age, I guess. Dressed averagely, blue jeans, button-up flannel shirt tucked into his pants. He was clean shaven with a mustache and balding. Pretty normal at first glance, but something about the guy was off in an indescribable way. Something in his face, in his eyes. Dylan caught the scent, whatever it was, because his growling was beginning to intensify.

"You guys have enough to eat here? I have some burgers I can share if you all are still hungry." Dylan answered for us, breaking now into a full bark that would not be silenced. "Hey, I'm a nice guy, why's the dog gotta be barking at me."

"He barks at everybody." I replied, starting to feel a bit like barking myself.

"Nah, we're good on the burgers, man," Pete added. Dylan was losing his mind now, barking with all his might, leaning forward on all fours, held back only by Pete's steady grasp.

"Well, alright," the stranger said, rising from his squatting position. "I'm just a few spaces over if you change your minds. In the old Chevy van there, can't miss it." He waved generally towards the growing darkness. "Sleep tight, kids." And off he dissolved into the gloom, followed by Dylan's wild peals of barking.

"Whoa, what the fuck!" Pete exclaimed as he attempted to calm the dog down. "That guy was seriously sketchy."

Dylan was still growling but would occasionally break into a whimper that seemed to deflate his resolve. For a while, a sense of unease lay over our party. But soon enough the shadow the stranger had briefly cast on our evening was forgotten, and we finished off the beers and the firewood in quiet conversation, watching as the coals glowed in bewitching hues of red and orange.

Once the coals had burned down to ashes, we bid our goodnights, and climbed into our sleeping bags. As I lay there alone in the darkness, I found I couldn't get that stranger's firelit face out of my thoughts. The memory of that brief encounter was beginning to bring on a level of anxiety I had not felt yet on this trip, not even when cops were following us, or when that racist redneck crashed our hangovers in Ithaca. I tried to shake it off, but in the end his memory was there in the car with me as I drifted off to sleep. Then the dreams came.

I was in a gigantic derelict factory or warehouse or something that seemed to stretch on forever. This industrial space was populated by innumerable large and amorphous pieces of cold dead machinery embedded into the supporting structures all around me and draped in sheets of dusty cobwebs. As before, I was actively looking for something without knowing what exactly. I was peering into the dusty crevices of large iron gears and linkages, feeling the strong desire to reach into the dark spaces where my eyes could not go, but recoiling at the last moment in fear of unknown pains that might be inflicted once my hand was out of sight. This hall of abandoned, ancient machinery was silent except for my footfalls in the dust, and I found comfort in the solitude and quiet of this place despite the urgency I felt in my nameless searching.

At some point I found myself in a long room of peeling paint, the off-white color strips hanging down the tall walls like ribbons of flayed skin, the chips and bits of paint and other dusty debris thick on the floor like chunky dry snow. I felt I was getting close to what I was looking for, whatever it was, so I waded further into the loose debris. I was just noticing how tough the going was becoming when I became aware of a presence there not my own.

There was a man on a metal grate catwalk above me, speaking in gibberish. I could not tell if he was speaking to me or what, but his tirade appeared to be an angry one. He paced back and forth on his perch, his arms in animated motion, his legs unimpeded by the flakes of dry dusty paint that were now up to my waist where I was standing below him. Suddenly he became aware of me and pointed his tirade my direction. His anger and hate was like a blast of heat that pushed me back into the snowy paint chip pile. I could see his face clearly now, clear like crystal. It was the stranger that had invaded our campfire light.

I realized then I was dreaming, sort of, because I still felt I was in that decrepit hall of peeling paint and up to my waist in thick fluff. I had no control over the events unfolding here despite knowing it to be a construction of my mind, so I couldn't be described as "lucid," but I knew I was not awake. He was still screaming nonsense at me when I noticed he had something burning in his hand. I knew all at once what was about to happen and was already fighting against the material that thickened around me to get away from him when all the world turned to flame.

I was in a panic, surrounded and engulfed by fire. I could feel what felt like hard pinches all over me as if dozens of fingers were twisting my skin. "Is this what it feels like to be on fire?" I thought in a strange calm, separate from the panic which now consumed me. I was still flailing in burning paint chips when the man's roaring laughter began to change, began to take on an inhuman cadence that sounded like dog barking. Dylan!

I suddenly awoke to the sounds of the dog furiously barking again. I sat up and peered out the car window into the darkness to see what was happening. All looked quiet in the near-full moonlight; the tent of my companions was still there unmolested but shaking slightly from Dylan's frantic movement inside. I was about to lie back down when a flash of movement caught my eye in the brush just outside our campsite, a flash of white skin. It was that sketchy stranger, and he was naked! He was out there snooping around our camp in the dark bare-assed! You'd think I'd be spooked by this realization, but I found I was only suddenly angry: furious, in fact. Who does this fucker think he is? I thought. Probably a very bad man that we should avoid at all costs but I didn't care at that point. Fuck that guy, man he just set me on fire! I thought, mixing the emotions of my late dream with waking reality.

I rolled down the window and yelled out in a loud, low register "HEY!" Dylan was still barking so I couldn't hear if the guy was running through the brush or responding to my call in any way. I remained there with my head out the window for a few minutes as Dylan quieted down. I took his vocal de-escalation as a sign that the prowler had left, and eventually rolled the window back up and returned to my place of rest. It took a long while to pass back out after that episode. I had a strong adrenaline rush going between the intense dream and the subsequent realization that we had been snooped on by some free baller while we slept. At least we had Dylan as our sentinel, guarding our perimeter from undetected invasion. I'm going to give that dog the biggest hug in the morning, I thought.

CHAPTER 13

The next morning we held a huddle in the Olds to discuss what we should do next. While the stranger's night prowling had not really fazed me beyond indignant rage, it had shaken Jen considerably. She was still shaken, in fact, and wanted to leave straight away. Pete wanted to take his time, use the shower and the toilet before breaking camp, maybe even stay another night, just to show the creep we were not afraid of him. He didn't want to back down, didn't want to cut and run. I could see his point of view. I didn't like the idea of being run off by some weaselly fucker in nothing but his birthday suit either, but if Jen didn't feel safe, then what was the point in pushing it? I made my opinion known and reminded them all of our meager food supplies which would not really last another night anyway and that seemed to settle the matter. We would leave as soon as Pete had his cold shower, while Jen and I would pack up the car.

Pete really took his time, taking well over an hour to do his business. We had everything packed and ready pretty quickly and wound up waiting in the car for a while before he finally returned. I sat there in the front seat with Jen and Dylan while she chain smoked through her remaining pack of cigarettes. I offered to roll one up, but she refused stating again that she just wanted to leave. There was probably some terrible backstory to her extreme aversion to nighttime prowlers that I could only speculate on. I sure wasn't going to press her on it; lord knows we all need our privacy. I just hoped I could offer some degree of stability in the face of whatever was haunting her. We were a mini moving commune after all and should be looking out for each other, even if in practice this didn't always play out quite like it should.

On the way out of the campground Pete drove the Olds real slow past the site where the prowler's van was parked.

"No, Peter, please. Don't stop here," she asked meekly, sliding down in her seat.

"I'm not stopping; I just want to scowl at that fucker before we go. Where is he?" But there was no sign of him.

So that was it. We pulled out of the park and broke west once again, keen to leave that anxious bit of drama behind us. We chose US route 12 for our morning trek, hoping to spot a diner or some place for breakfast. We were pretty hungry, and there wasn't much left to snack on. Unfortunately, there wasn't much on the road for a while either, just rows of freight rail tracks and power lines rising from the swampy sides of the road. We stopped into a gas station to feed the car and raid the attached convenience store for sustenance, finding only the regular highly processed fare common to such rest stops. It would have to do for the time being, at least till we could find a proper supermarket or something.

Back on the road, the scene was rapidly changing from a low swampy brush-lined trace to a more urban landscape. Derelict urban to be exact. We were coming up alongside of the rust belt in all its corroded glory. We passed many large industrial facilities, mothballed and in various states of disrepair, with some being completely abandoned ruins. There were many roadside storefronts boarded up, and many empty lots where some once thriving business operation had been wiped away by the bulldozer. The area was starting to look pretty sketchy; perhaps that was the connection to last night's sketchy prowler. This whole area looked like sketchy prowler town. Pete kept it hammered down, and we met with no resistance.

The route was a wide three lane way that had obviously been built for a more prosperous time. We had it all to ourselves for the most part, sharing it only with a few semi-trucks hauling trailers of shrink-wrapped machinery on flatbeds, or overseas containers with bright foreign logos. This wide boulevard took us through the most derelict neighborhood I'd ever been in. The place was laid out in an orderly grid like a moderate city, but at least half of the row homes were gone, leaving empty overgrown lots full of trash scattered randomly block by block like a wide grimace missing half its teeth. Of the houses and business buildings still standing, half of those were burned out abandoned shells, most without so much as a piece of plywood to cover the gaping holes pane glass windows once filled. It was strangely peaceful here though, like a neglected cemetery. And people were still living here somehow just the same; their modest, well-kept little homes claiming space next to now unrestricted yard shrubs gone feral and knee-high grass.

Soon we came up alongside a vast oil tank city, rising over hundreds of sooty black railroad tanker cars in endless lines. Beyond were high-tension power line towers in multiple rows stretching away in every direction, here and there interspersed with heaps of black ashy dirt, gutted concrete buildings and piles of illegally dumped garbage. Far off in the distance, the billowing smokestacks of refineries and other heavy industry could be seen poking up behind the clustered rows of rail cars and large squat petroleum tanks; over all this a yellow haze hung like a ragged shroud. What a stinking shit hole this place was, and it showed no signs of letting up.

After quite a while of these unbroken views of a broken landscape, we were offered an entrance onto the I-90 toll road highway. We chose to pay the fare, just to get a move on out of this depressing scene, and with little fanfare or change in scenery we crossed over the Indiana state line into Illinois: more specifically, Chicago.

We were headed north now, directly towards downtown. It was mid-morning, and traffic on this weekday was beginning to thicken. I felt it was a good time to roll up another joint for what was looking to be some slow going ahead and broke out the stash box. I was a little alarmed to find our supply of nugs was beginning to look a bit light, but what could I expect, really? We had been burning like all get out the whole trip so far with no regard to moderation. No fat sack can hold up for long under that kind of attack. Well, no time to start rationing now, I thought, and rolled a comically large number despite our depleted resources. It was a scorched earth, human reaction to impending famine I guess; choosing to live in the moment, tomorrow be damned.

"I think I've found a good destination to aim for tonight," Jen stated as the spliff wound itself down. "Just across the Mississippi River over in Minnesota there is a nice big state park with campsites and trails along the river. It'll be a long drive though; we'll be driving all day if we wanna get there before sundown."

"That's ok," Pete replied. "It'll be good to put some serious distance down on the road today anyway. Fuck all this urban shit."

We agreed and decided we'd stay on the highway and attempt to make some high-speed distance. It'd be the farthest we'd yet traveled in a day, crossing two mid-size states completely. But judging from the map there wasn't much else out here for the likes of us.

This stretch of congested highway was all elevated above suburban Chicago, and since the land was so flat here near the lake we had quite the long view of Midwestern urbanity. This wide vantage consisted mostly of shitty billboards and power lines over low warehouse roofs. In fact, it seemed that the whole city was draped in a web of high-tension power lines propped up by hundreds of metal framework towers standing over the industrial landscape like erector set giants.

Soon the downtown skyline could be seen ahead, but this time not poking out of the lake. As we approached, I was struck by how small the tall-building-studded city center was compared to New York's Manhattan. Chicago was a major city no doubt, but it was so much flatter than New York, maybe because there was so much more space to spread out that building upwards was not as big a necessity here. I was just glad we were not going to be getting off the highway and into the city. I was really craving natural wonders, and the smoggy smell in the air was putting me off.

"This city fuckin' stinks!" I declared.

Jen replied by rolling up her window because that's about all one could do. "We're almost halfway through now," she added, after consulting the map again.

I reclined myself in the back seat, tired of these city freeway views and wishing to enjoy the heavy head high that last doobie had bequeathed upon me. I watched the gray scenery smear by my window for a time until my eyes became too heavy to operate and I slipped into unconsciousness.

I was roused from my nap by the car decelerating rapidly from highway speed. Pete was taking an exit into a rest area that from what I could see was the only structure of any size for miles across surrounding open crop lands. The Olds took the offramp like a plane landing on a runway, the big engine acting as a brake by loading up on our inertial forward motion, roaring steadily through the floorboards. We taxied into the automobile side of the facility and came to rest a little away from most of the parked cars and adjacent to some standard issue concrete picnic tables.

"God damn, I've got to piss!" Pete declared, as he hastily evacuated the driver's seat. Apparently, Dylan felt the same way because he shot for the nearest tree as soon as he got out of the car and proceeded to water it thoroughly.

After we all had our turn in the rest rooms, we shared a little snack and a stretch at the closest table and watched the traffic roll through. It was a busy little place here with lots of people coming and going, pissing and stretching. Pete and I thought it'd be a great idea to climb one of the little ornamental crab apple trees growing by our table. Jen stayed below and had a smoke.

"Hey, some of these little apples aren't half bad." Pete announced, after taking a bite from one of the larger examples he'd found high in the canopy. "Jen, go get a sack or something, we should take some of these for the road."

I tried one myself and found he was right. They were surprisingly sweet despite it being a little early in the season and these being more of the small, hard cider sort of apple. Jen returned with a knapsack and held it open so we could drop our picks inside from above.

Pete asked me to take the wheel for a while once we decided it was time to move on again. He had noticed my backseat snoozing via the rear-view mirror and had grown envious. I was happy to fill the driver's seat and jumped at the opportunity. It would be the first time I'd played the part of driver yet.

I cozied into the seat and summoned the Olds to life, reveling in the smooth rev of its big 350 cubic inch engine. Once we were back on the highway, Pete took a turn rolling one up, and we hot boxed the car as we sped along. There was no need to look out for turns or exits, as we were going to be on this same road all day. And there was no traffic to speak of, so I was free to completely zone out.

The land out here was all farms: crop lands specifically, dominated by corn and soybeans. There wasn't much to see, but it was still a hell of an improvement over the morning's desolate urban views. Jen informed me we'd be crossing the Illinois state line into Wisconsin soon, so I kept an eye out for a welcome sign lest I miss the only landmark of note for miles. It came and went with little fanfare.

I drove on for a few hours, sometimes listening to one of the few cassette tapes we had, sometimes in silence. Jen joined her lover in slumber at one point as well as the dog, and I found myself alone on the road with my thoughts. I played back the trip in my head so far, grooving on the finer points, and speculating on what adventures yet lay ahead of us.

Once the stone zone had worn itself out I became aware of a hunger for lunch. I spotted a truck stop just past Madison and made an executive decision. I was driving, right? So I'll choose when to pull off. My companions had no trouble with my choice once they awoke to find themselves as hungry as I was.

It was a big truck stop and busy too with the mid-day highway lunch crowd. The place was moderately populated with rough looking trucker dudes milling about the all-you-can-eat buffet and common areas. Their appearance ran the gamut from smoked leather skin-and-bones cowboys to the morbidly obese greasy loners who looked a little unsure of themselves now that they were out of their captain's chairs and on their feet walking around in public. We of course hit the buffet hard and loaded up on hot foods. It was the biggest meal we'd had in days and the most well rounded, including actual vegetables for a change. Jen had brought in a couple shopping sacks in a big empty purse-type bag and discretely filled up on food items that would transport well like hard fruits and breads. She also wrapped up some assorted meats in napkins for Dylan who we had left with the car.

On the way out Jen handed the purse of pilfered dinner rolls and such to me to carry out saying, "Take this to the car, and you and Pete take Dylan for a walk. Give him the meats in there too. I need to get some lady things." So Pete and I walked out through the front doors of the place with the big purse slung over my shoulder, all the while hawked by some manager-looking type in a white shirt and blue tie with a little plastic name tag over his front pocket who followed us out the front doors and stood in the entrance with his arms crossed, watching us cross the parking lot. Whatever, what's he going to do, kick us out? We were already obviously leaving.

Dylan was ecstatic over the assorted warm meats we brought him, and we enjoyed his enjoyment. Pete leashed him up once he'd licked his chops clean, and we took a stroll out towards the rows of giant semi-trucks to get a closer look at all that heavy machinery. The trucks were so much bigger up close and imposing all grouped together in tight rows, their chromed snouts breathing rippling waves of heat and diesel fumes. We were a few dozen rigs deep when a guy called down to us from the cab of a dirty blue truck.

"Hey, you guys holdin'?" he asked us. Pete handed the leash to me, grasped the chrome handle, and hoisted himself up onto the fuel tank step.

"Maybe," he replied. "What do you need?"

"Well, what do you got, man? I'm not picky."

"We got a little nugs, but that's our own supply. We're not looking to sell, really."

"Man, everything's for sale, or maybe trade, eh? How 'bout this CB radio here?" he asked, holding up the loose device, its power cords cut short. "A couple of joints for this?"

Pete looked at me, and I just shrugged. "Could be useful, man."

"Yeah, that's right. Shouldn't be out on the road without a CB radio. You can listen in on where the police are snoopin and call for help when you break down... Come 'on up in the cab, and let's make a deal. All of you, the dog too."

It was purely youthful indiscretion that allowed us to climb into a semi-truck cab with some mad sketchy stranger at a truck stop to make a half assed drug deal with no reservations at all, but we weren't afraid, indifferent as we were in our untouchable youth. I was stoked enough to be climbing into one of these big rigs to belay any alarms I should have been monitoring. Pete had to carry the dog up in his arms to get into the elevated cab of the commercial tractor. We found the cramped interior smelling strongly of armpits and ash trays and populated by empty soda cans and cigarette butts among other loose detritus.

"Let's see what 'cha got," the driver said eagerly. I broke out the little stash box that held enough loose weed to roll up like three or four doobies maybe. "That'll do," he decided "You got any papers to roll that up with? Yeah? Ok, roll it up into a few joints, and we'll call it a deal for the CB."

"Hold on," my companion said "Does this thing work? D'you got the antenna for this radio, or the thing to attach it to the dashboard?"

"Of course, it works, it was in use only yesterday," the man stated bluntly. "What you see there is what you get, my friend. It's a good deal, I'm tellin ya." The radio had "stolen" written all over it, missing the mounting bracket and with the power cord and the antenna wire both chopped off at about 4 inches. Some poor driver, maybe in that very same lot, maybe that very same day had returned to his rig to find that he'd been robbed.

"Alright, alright," Pete decided. "Roll a few up for the man. We can make it work." So I did and handed them over.

"You're gonna like this weed, it's real good shit," I told him, as he took the joints.

"Ha, I don't smoke this shit," he replied, as he slid them into an empty cigarette pack he picked off the floor. "Great doin' business with ya, boys. Safe travels out there," he offered, as we climbed down out of his truck.

"What's that guy gonna do with that weed if he don't smoke?" I asked Pete, as we walked back across the lot.

"Probably trade them for something else, something less hot. He'll have a better chance selling or trading a few doobies then he would a stolen CB radio. He just traded up."

It made sense to me, but suddenly I felt a little had.

"I hope this radio works," I said.

"I'm sure it will. We just need to find an antenna, then we can hook it up in the car. I like the idea of monitoring the radio traffic for information."

We found Jen waiting for us at the car.

"Where the fuck were you guys? I've been waiting here for like fifteen minutes with that asshole over there watching me!" She gestured behind her towards the front doors of the truck stop, where that white shirt manager was still standing cross armed. "I don't have keys to get into the car, Peter. What the fuck have you two been doing?"

"We got a CB radio from a trucker," I replied, once it became obvious that Pete was not going to take the explanation on this one. "We traded a few doobies for it."

"Jesus Christ, you two! What the hell are we going to use a CB radio for?" she asked in exasperation. "God damn it, unlock the car so we can get the hell out of here! Give me the keys, I'm driving!"

We rode on in silence for quite a while before Pete tried his hand at clearing the air with an apology. "Sorry, babe, we lost track of time."

"Yeah, whatever," she shot back. Silence again for a time.

"What'd you get from the store?" I asked, giving the air clearing a shot myself.

"Cigarettes, beer for you guys, more food stuff. I'm sick of peanut butter, dry bread, and apples, so I got some pre-made sandwiches and cold salads, and some ice for the cooler. Pete did you put that stuff in the cooler?" he replied that he had in fact done just that before we left, and that seemed to reset the mood back to neutral at least.

The landscape now was changing from the open farm fields of the morning to a more wooded, hilly area. Here and there, large outcroppings of mossy, blasted rock would occasionally present themselves through the brush on the sides of the highway. The route through here was really starting to look pretty and lush. It was mid-afternoon now, and I consulted the map to check our progress towards the river. We had made some good time today and better distance than any other stretch yet. Another couple hours and we should be crossing the Mississippi. The thought of that was enough to send the butterflies loose in my guts; I couldn't wait to see that mighty river of lore and legend.

Before long we began to pass signs heralding the river's approach, and when we came out onto a long flat bridge I excitedly asked Pete, who was now in possession of the map, if this was it; the mighty Mississippi.

"No, not yet," he replied. "This is the Black River, runs alongside of the Mississippi here. Then we cross a wide island and then the Mississippi. Just a few more minutes. Hold your horses, for fuck's sake." I was excited like a little kid, and I guess it showed. My companions were always so blasé in these scenarios while I always got all mushy, bubbling over with anticipation. It was just how I rolled. "Now, here it is."

And there it was indeed, wide and majestic. We were crossing it on a long highway bridge elevated far above its placid surface. The Minnesota side was rocky and tall and blanketed in trees. It was truly a gorgeous sight. When we landed on the far side, the highway veered right and began following the river north. I had some great views of the water and the islands from the passenger side as we continued towards our destination. Soon the highway moved away from the river and headed inland.

The next exit was ours, and we trekked to the state park by way of a few switchbacks and corn fields. It was a pay campground, or was supposed to be, but there was no one manning the front gate so we just rolled in and searched out the campsites. We found them far into the park, each site well insulated from its neighbors by thick foliage and sparsely populated by other campers, just like the last campground.

"This place is great," Pete exclaimed, as Jen shifted the car into park. "I think we might be able to stay a few days here, as long as we don't get chased off again by some bogus shit again."

"Yeah, fingers crossed," I added, and we all scrambled out of the car to check out the new digs. It was pretty standard, but clean. There even appeared to be some bit of wood on the trees that could be easily harvested for campfires.

"I wonder what the weather's gonna do?" I asked generally. "This's like the first day it hasn't rained since New York."

"I saw a weather forecast on a TV in the convenience store while I was waiting in line," Jen answered. "I think we're in the clear for as long as we're in this area, at least."

That was excellent news. It would be nice to dry out all our musty damp shit and not have to deal with more rain driving us into our personal hiding holes. We put the declining daylight to use and made ourselves at home. Pete and I went off in search of burning wood once we were settled and found enough to supply a blaze, returning with our bundles as dusk was well underway. By dark we were situated around our fire burning bright, passing joints and beers around and cheering our good fortune.

Jen wasn't really drinking like we were, she never did, but Pete and I were really starting to get lit up. The buzz was rolling in all the more because we never bothered with any sort of dinner before we started knocking the beers back, and I'm sure we were starting to get stupid. Jen took her leave and retired to the tent, leaving us to our revelry. After another few beers, Pete produced that pouch of chewing tobacco he had picked up on a whim back in Ohio.

"Ha, I forgot all about that," I said, as he pulled out a plug of tobacco and slipped it under his bottom lip.

"You wanna dip?" he asked me. I didn't really, but I was hammered and feeling belligerently curious.

"Yeah sure, why not." And he tossed the pouch over to me. I had never even seen chewing tobacco in person before, let alone deployed a plug into my mouth. I had no idea how much to take, or what to do with it once it was in there. So I winged it, grabbed a sizable pinch, and pushed it in, chewing on it like bubble gum. It was menthol flavored, so it was like woody toothpaste or something, and was a lot more intense than I was expecting. It activated my salivary glands instantly, and soon I had a mouth full of juicy minty tobacco mush sloshing around.

"Don't swallow any of it," Pete instructed, noticing my exaggerated chewing. Well, too late for that, as I had already inadvertently sent some of the strong juice down into my stomach. "Just kind of suck on it," he continued. I was clueless and had the shit running out of the corners of my mouth before long. After a few minutes I gave up, spitting the chewed wet lump into the fire.

"Yech, that shit is not for me," I declared and rinsed down the flavor with a long draught of beer.

Then the nicotine buzz hit me. I never smoked cigarettes, ever, so I had never experienced the nicotine rush that any regular tobacco user doesn't even feel anymore. Well, it hit me at a level off the chart. With the heavy beer buzz, the weed high, and the tobacco juice combined on an empty stomach I found my world was soon spinning, so much so that before long I began puking my guts out. I could hear Pete having a laugh about it as I dry heaved by a tree. I couldn't blame him; I'd have laughed too.

"Fucking shit, Pete..." I cried between involuntary heaves. "Get me some water."

And he did, hanging out with me till I had thoroughly purged myself of everything inside of me down to the bile.

"Go to sleep, man. You'll feel better in the morning," he suggested once I appeared to have stabilized. I agreed with his advice and climbed into the Olds to make an attempt.

I lay there in the darkness occasionally afflicted by waves of nausea and spins. Eventually my consciousness faded to dreamless black, and the world was no more.

CHAPTER 14

I awoke in a sickly sweat. The windows of the car had remained rolled up throughout the night and now the morning sun had turned my place of rest into a stinking, stuffy oven. I was also still zipped up tight in my sleeping bag, which of course only made it worse. It must have been the throbbing headache pounding away at my head which broke the bonds of sleep, for I found I was so delirious in mind when I opened my eyes that I was hesitant to embrace full consciousness. But once the heat-enhanced nausea began to wash over me, I was left with no other option.

I struggled to free myself from my zippered cocoon and was just able to pull the release handle on the passenger door before projectile vomiting the last dregs of stomach liquid I had left in me out into the dirt. I lay there half out of my sleeping bag, and half out of the car, retching into the dust involuntarily. What a miserable way to start the day. My companions came and helped me to my feet upon hearing my hoarse barks.

"Jesus Christ, man. You look like shit!" Pete informed me.

"I feel even worse."

"How much did you two idiots drink last night?" Jen asked us both generally. I just groaned and pleaded for water.

They each took an arm, pulled me from my rumpled wrappings and walked me over to the campsite's picnic bench. There they sat me down with a plastic gallon jug of water in the hope I could pull it together. I tried to keep it down, but I just kept on retching bile.

"Ok," Pete announced, "time to smoke some pot." And he began to put together a smokable number from our meager stash remains. A few puffs definitely settled my guts, and the dry heaves ceased. I still felt cramped and hollow on the inside and every manner of bad on the outside too, but at least I could keep some water in the hold.

"What time is it?" I asked, once the pressing need to puke had sufficiently subsided.

"It's about eleven, I think," Jen answered. "We were wondering if you'd ever rise from the grave. We were hoping to take a hike this morning. There's supposed to be some great views of the river from some rocky bluff here or something. We were gonna just go without you, but we were afraid you might be dead by the time we got back," she added sarcastically, with a chuckle from Pete. "Do you think you can pull yourself together for a walk?"

"Yeah, come on, man. Shake it off. A walk will do you good," suggested Pete. "Maybe you should have a beer too, a little hair o' the dog that kicked your ass last night, eh?"

The thought of a morning beer wasn't too appealing, but I remembered that hangover prescription that drunken racist jackass back in Ithaca pressed upon me did work pretty well last time. Ok, why not give it a shot. I couldn't feel much worse than I already did anyway, right?

The beer from the cooler was cold, crisp and remarkably delicious. After the twelve ounces I felt twelve times better, though still nowhere near a hundred percent. With my medicine imbibed I found I was able to pull my shit together, and before long we were out on the trail.

It was a bucolic scene out there in those Midwestern riverside woods. The birds were active and singing and the foliage thick and green. It was warm but not humidly oppressive like the dunes had been. Still, I kept a rolling sweat going as I walked, due to the frightfully intense hangover still there lurking behind those twelve ounces of beer and few hits of weed. I wasn't out of the woods yet, metaphorically at least. So I just sort of floated along, trying not to give the illness I carried any power of presence over me. Absent mind over matter, as it were. I kept up well enough, following my friend's lead, shuffling my sneakers through the leaf litter and grooving on the nature scene around me in my own little world. That single beer surprisingly had an effect on me. My stomach, empty these twenty some odd hours, was gently aflutter with liquid butterflies that tickled my insides whenever they drunkenly crashed into each other. I was beginning to feel a little "out of body," and the accompanying weed high only added to the feeling.

After an hour or so, out walking a generally upwardly inclined trail, we came upon a fantastic overlook. Man, what a view! We stood there together in silence taking it in. The elevation was such that you could see for miles out over the river into Wisconsin, probably could have seen further if the haze of late summer hadn't obscured the distant horizon. Far below a tugboat was pushing a barge down the river, tiny in the distance like a couple of bath toys bobbing away. I began to feel a little dizzy with vertigo and grabbed onto Pete's shoulder for support.

"Damn, man you're a fuckin' mess today."

"I'm sorry, Pete." I replied, "I think I need to sit down."

We all sat there in the grass for a few minutes while I got my head straight. We were still enjoying the view when it was suggested that we simply had to smoke some more weed because the view here was so great. We all agreed it was the right thing to do and rose to find a more secluded venue for our illegal ritual, since the main overlook where we were reclining was after all the main attraction at this park.

We ducked into the woods along the bluff's edge and found a little unmarked clandestine path in the brush that led away from the public areas. Soon the brush opened up onto another little rocky outcrop which also afforded quite the view but was definitely more secluded, being surrounded as it was by dense foliage. You could tell by the beer bottle caps, cigarette butts and other little bits of human trash embedded in the oft' trod dirt that this was the young adult smoking section where teenagers on family vacations escaped their parents briefly, and where road kids like us could find safe passage into intoxications.

We settled into a couple grassy nooks between the rocks and gathered what weed remnants we could muster for what was looking to be our last whole doobie. We combined the crumbs and shake from my stash box with Pete's last crusty nug and topped it off with a few skinned roaches. It was a nice big cone of a joint with faint oily spots soaking through where some clumps of resinous roach weed were pressed against the paper. It smoked unevenly and canoed hard whenever the cherry hit one of those oily lumps, but it gave clouds like a king and lasted more rotations than we cared to count on account of its gooey contents. We smoked it down to nothing in celebration of what we had achieved thus far. It was also sort of a closure event; having crossed the Mississippi, it seemed fitting to incinerate the last of our New York weed like some burnt offering to the spirits of the road. The absence of nugs ahead was definitely going to change our traveling dynamic. We'd been pretty much chronically stoned for our whole trip thus far.

I got to thinking about that, how we had managed to tear through a fat sack of good buds with reckless abandon in a little over seven days when it hit me; today was Monday. I had missed my Sunday communion ritual I had promised Jesus I would perform. I had been so lit up, and so disconnected from time, I had lost track of the days and blew through Sunday without even a thought to God's sacrifice.

Waves of guilt and fear began rolling over me in successive intensity; my heart started pounding along with my head, and nausea was creeping back. That must be it, I thought. God has laid this wicked hangover upon me as a punishment for forsaking my oath. I looked over to my companions, blissfully ignorant of the oppressive yoke of guilt now bearing down on my shoulders with increasing weight. Oh, if only I was like them, I briefly found myself wishing. If only I wasn't commanded to remember the Sabbath and keep it holy.

God damn thee, you ungrateful wretched sinner! I instantly shot back at myself, how dare you wish this cup would be passed away from you so you could live in ignorance! You can't keep one little ritual, one remembrance of his sacrifice for you?!

Worm! Feel the weight of that cross, you miserable dog! Feel the whip shred the flesh of your back to ribbons! Feel the spikes tear through the tendons of your wrists and feet! Feel the spear pierce your side! Feel the blinding thirst, the blazing Mediterranean sun draining your life away! Feel the brutal emptiness of watching your friends and brothers deny you, and mock you, of God himself turning away from you! He did this for you, you worthless piece of shit, how dare you!

My throbbing head was swimming in a murky torrent now, my guts doing flip flops. A thousand voices of pitiless judgment rang out in my ears in a deafening roar as curtains of shadow closed around my failing vision. The guilt of all heaven gave one last push upon my brow and I was down.

"Hey! Wake up, wake up!" Pete was sternly imploring while he shook me by the shoulders. I opened my eyes. His dready mop hovered over me as a dark silhouette against the bright blue mid-day sky. "Jesus fucking Christ, man! Are you ok?"

"No. I am a wretched sinner."

"What the fuck are you talking about? You just fell over, passed out! Are you alright?"

"I need to… I need to be alone," I stuttered as he helped me to sit up right. "I need to… take care of something."

"What? What do you mean, alone?" he asked as I struggled to get to my feet and swayed uneasily before them.

"I'm…I'll… I'll meet you back in camp. I need to…need to walk, alone for a while," I bumbled out as I stumbled off into the brush.

They called after me but made no attempt to stop me. I would have stopped for no mortal at that moment anyway. I drove forward through thick bushes and branches with no direction or destination, just the overwhelming urge to get away; away from explaining my convictions to my friends, away from the increasingly obvious ridiculousness of those convictions, away from myself, away from…dare I say it, God. I was terrified to accept how I truly felt.

Blindly I ran for I don't know how long, tearing through the brush indiscriminately before a tangle of vines took my feet out from under me. I landed in a heap of tears on the forest floor. There, prostrate on the ground, I prayed feverishly for forgiveness. Forgiveness for forgetting my oath of Sunday communion, forgiveness for being so intoxicated all the time that I forgot what day of the week it was, but most of all, forgiveness for entertaining the thought for even a moment that it sucked to be a Christian. Sucked so much that it felt like I was playing myself for a fool, holding myself up to pointless rituals and standards only because I felt I had to, or else I'd burn in hell. I lay there face down on the ground groaning and praying, at times grinding my forehead into the leaf litter in agony. Slowly the power of the guilt began to fade as I expended myself in penitence, and I eventually rolled over on my back, exhausted.

My mind was quiet then, and I felt empty. All there was in the world was here in my field of view, my range of hearing, in the atmosphere around me. Small birds sang and flitted from tree to tree above me and the afternoon sky shone radiantly through the green leafy canopy, sending dazzling gems of sunlight down around me. It was beautiful here, and for a moment I was truly alone with myself as I was, in the moment. Everything felt so right, so simple, so unmolested by anything. I closed my eyes and fell into a fitful sleep.

I dreamed then I was in church, the church where I had spent almost every Sunday morning since before I could remember, with all those familiar faces of the people who joined me every week. We were all singing a hymn like we did, each congregant taking the part of the harmony they could handle. I was singing too, of course, but I had no idea what the words were, despite the song being intimately familiar. I desperately wanted to sing correctly with the congregation, to be a true part of the harmony, but I was clueless as to what to sing. I looked to the hymn book in my hands, but the pages were all just jumbled letters and symbols. I looked to my fellow churchgoers around me to see if I could pick up on what was happening but found their faces strangely smooth and featureless. Up in the front, the preacher was raising his arms wide and opening an impossibly broad smile across his head. His face was wrong too, but instead of smooth it was sharp and angular, chiseled and cold. The volume of the singing was building, as his arms rose higher, until it was deafening. I looked at the people around me; their faces now looked like plastic masks with hollow eyes. Then came the fear.

This was all wrong. Who were all these strange beings around me blasting gibberish vocal music from their motionless mouths? These were not the people I knew. The urge to run took hold of me, but when I went to leave their presence I found they had circled around me, boxing me in, bearing down on me with their dark empty eyes. Their song now was just one repeating bark. Bark. Bark!

Dylan was straddling me, taking turns licking my face and barking. I looked in his eyes and saw life and love. God damn, I was happy to see him.

"Holy shit, there you are!" Pete cried as he burst in through the bush. "We've been looking everywhere for you; you've been gone for hours! Dude, what the fuck happened to your face?"

"Oh, Pete! I'm so happy to see you guys!"

"Dude, you're bleeding from your forehead! Did you pass out again and land on your face?" he asked a little frantically as he helped me to my feet.

"I love you guys!" I replied indifferently, throwing my arms around his shoulders.

"Ok, ok. Come on, man, let's get you back to camp. Jesus, you're a fucking maniac today!"

"Yeah, I'm feeling kind of insane. I think I…I think I need to eat something. I'm really fucking hungry," I suddenly realized. "What time is it?"

"It's like six in the evening, man. You've been gone for like five hours. What the hell have you been doing out here? You're all beat up and covered in dirt and shit."

"Sorry, man. I, uh… Wow, five hours, huh? Doesn't feel like it's been that long." I looked down at myself finally and caught sight of what he was seeing. I was dusty and dirty, my arms covered in red scratches, and my jeans were torn wide down by my calf. I reached to my forehead and felt the crust of dried blood. "Ok yeah, let's get out of here."

We walked about twenty minutes on another beautiful trail before coming out at the campsites. We found Jen waiting for us, pacing and smoking a cigarette.

"Oh my God, Peter, you found him!" she said "What'd you fall down that bluff or something? You look all torn up! Where have you been?"

"I'm sorry to stress you guys," I said, giving her a big hug. "I just had a freak out. I'm better now."

"Yeah? Well, come on then, let's clean you up."

She sat me down on the bench and wiped the dried blood off my face with a wet rag. Pete got a fire going, and we were dining on canned beans and bread before long. The food and water I was filling up on definitely evened me out, being the first bit of sustenance I'd had in over twenty-four hours at that point, and with a clearer head I began to reflect on my manic day and how I must have come across to my friends. They deserved to know what had torn me up so much, but I was too embarrassed to explain it, figuring they'd never understand. That they would think I was a fool for keeping these religious convictions. That maybe I would feel just as foolish once I laid my case out in the harsh light of reality.

I felt very alone but still very connected to them. Like the world around me was cut off by some invisible membrane. I could interact with everything on the outside, but I was still not a part of it. It seemed like everything in my life was a clash of contradictions like this. Who was I, really? I felt I had no idea. I looked at my friends in the firelight and felt love. These are good people; would they really be doomed to hell because they had not had their sins washed in the blood of Jesus? It just didn't seem fair, didn't seem right. What about all the people of the world, all the good and loving people who lived lives of secular righteousness or were of other faiths? They too, doomed to eternal damnation just because they hadn't been regulars at the same church I went to? It all felt wrong and left me altogether conflicted. I felt like I needed to face these doubts and explore them. If God was as real as I was taught to believe, as I wanted him to be, then there had to be observable, testable proof, right?

The possibility of there actually being no God was terrifying and sent shivers down my frame as I weighed the repercussions of that outcome. It was just too much for me to acknowledge after everything, so I attempted to shelve the matter for later consideration. I was feeling really fatigued mentally and physically and just wanted to call it quits for the day. I took leave of my friends and climbed into my backseat sleeping bag. I had tried to put my spiritual doubts aside before I made my bed but found them there with me just the same. I slid into sleep with the gut feeling that my faith was in vain.

I dreamed many dreams that night, most completely unrelated to anything of consequence in my waking life, but one dream stuck with me when my eyes opened the following morning.

I was alone out on a long, straight, two-lane road at night through a flat desert landscape dimly lit in hues of blue by a moonless sky; lit by starlight, I guess. It was dark, but I could see through the shadows. I remember the star-spotted celestial ceiling stretched out in every direction eternally, despite being framed by distant ranges of rolling hills and jagged mountains all painted black against the cosmos. All the flat land in between these raised edges was filled in with swirling scrubby brush and sandy stones. I had the feeling that to wander off the pavement into the bush here would lead me into total loss, into death. I felt no fear at this prospect, however, just that it was not the right time to step off the path into this ominous bush, that some other time might prove better somehow. I had been standing on the double yellow line of the road this whole time so far, one foot on each painted line. I looked ahead, far ahead, following the muted yellow lines away in the darkness. Would they ever meet? I had to find out.

I began walking at an inhuman pace, about the speed of a bicycle it seemed, and was covering a lot of ground quickly. Sometimes it felt as if I might lift off the ground and take flight, but there was always some weight keeping me terrestrial. I traveled like this for some time but of course came no nearer to where the parallel lines met because they never would; they couldn't.

I realized this suddenly and then found I was at a crossroads, where another two-lane road had cut across my path at a right angle. I stopped in the middle and swung around without moving like I was on a tabletop "lazy Susan," seeing all four corners one after the other. There was a rough-hewn wood post worn with time planted at each corner, all basically identical, marking the starting point of a slice of scrub desert landscape leading away for miles to a row of mountains back lit by a sparkling starry sky. Each one a quarter wedge of a giant earthen pie. Upon completing this rotational view, I realized that each wedge of landscape was identical to the next, and I had no idea from what direction I had come, or in which direction I should go.

This, instead of making me scared or panicked just made me very sad and hopeless. I felt like this was it, that this was all there was; just an eternally repeating spin. I looked down at my feet and saw I was standing on an old-timey wooden wagon wheel with heavy iron straps laid flat on the pavement, slowly rotating. I remember thinking the wheel looked cool, that I should roll it home, but which way to roll it? I looked up again; perched atop one of the four old posts was a very big mottled brown owl, big as a child.

I stepped off the wheel, instantly forgetting it, and walked up to the giant bird. It had deep wide eyes ringed in yellow circles; its brows topped with tufts of feathers angled away from the center of its face forming a V-shaped wedge on its forehead, the same shape as the land it stood in front of. I stood right before the bird now, completely unafraid and emotionless. Its size and the height of the post it perched on were such that I was at an even eye level with it. I looked deeply into those two inky yellow ringed pools and saw myself reflected back, or at least some approximation of myself. The face I saw in there was my own, but it was different. It was older. Much older perhaps, I couldn't tell.

Who sent you here? I silently asked the ominous bird. There was no response, only the silence of the dream.

Are you an angel sent from God? Are you a demon sent from Satan? Again, no response.

What are you? I implored, gazing deeply into those bottomless eyes.

We are dust.

CHAPTER 15

We spent another quiet day there in that riverside park, hiking around and viewing those long views over the river, and it was good. The weather was bright and cheery and, excepting the one church school group of loud kids dressed in loud colors we came upon at one of the majestic overlooks, we had the park mostly to ourselves.

Despite this perfectly acceptable presentation of a day, I still couldn't get totally past the issues which had so struck me down only hours before. More than once, I almost volunteered an explanation of the odd behavior I had expressed, playing out various scenarios in my head as to how I could go about these confessions to my friends. But in the end, I wussed out and kept my mouth shut, adding yet another layer of guilt on my soul for not having the balls to clear my conscious. I kept telling myself I was having a great day and that I didn't need to be feeling so guilty about all my spiritual baggage but, unfortunately, I wasn't buying it.

Finally, around that night's campfire I meekly broached the subject of religion with them, asking what their take on all of it was, though I already had an inkling they would be in the opposite camp as me.

"Fuck religion," Pete stated, with a determination I found myself mildly envious of. "Fuck all religions. Why do I need some asshole telling me how to think and live my life? We're all just animals, with animal needs and desires, completely natural desires. All these big, organized religions are just dreamed up stories to control the people and to keep their societies in line. It's just a way to keep the powerful in power and the weak in the gutter."

I didn't have a rebuttal. My guts were telling me the same thing, but my upbringing, my programming, was pushing back against that thought.

"I was raised in the church, Pete," I replied finally "I have convictions and beliefs I'm grappling with that don't jive with the world I find myself in. I don't know what to think anymore."

"I don't doubt it," he answered. "Look, I'm not going to sit here and tell you how to live, how to think. That's for you to figure out. If religion helps you sleep at night, then more power to ya. Just keep the Jesus shit to yourself. I'm not about to start joining any church any time soon."

"I know I know, believe me, I'm not into pushing these convictions on anybody else," I lied. I was in fact required by my church to do just that. "I love you guys. You all pulled me out of the depression I was locked in by offering this ride to me. I am so grateful to you for that."

"We love you too, man," he said, and Jen nodded her head in the firelight. "You'll find the answers to your questions, man, don't sweat it. Just live. Enjoy this life while you can. This is all we get."

That brief exchange was enough to settle the matter in my mind for the time being, and for the first time in days I felt the background anxiety throttle back towards a manageable level.

The next morning, we rose early and decided to hit the road again. The westward pull we all felt had overgrown this state park with its beautiful river overlooks, leafy woodland paths, and free Oldsmobile parking. The road atlas told of some epic country ahead, and we were getting anxious to get inside of those lands without delay.

We were only on the highway for maybe fifteen minutes when the right rear tire delaminated at over seventy miles per hour. It sounded like a bomb went off under my seat as the car lurched hard to the left. Luckily, there were no other cars around us on the highway when the tire blew apart because we were all over the road for a few seconds. We all collectively let out a multi-tuned scream, with peals of barking, as Pete struggled to steer the almost uncontrollable steel rocket safely to the side of the road.

"Mother fucker!" Pete cried as he forced the car onto the shoulder of the highway at speed, Dylan still hysterically barking with all his might.

"Stop, stop, stop!" cried Jen involuntarily, her hands planted on the dashboard bracing for some perceived impact.

And then we were stopped. We sat there frozen for a moment in silent shock. Even Dylan had stopped barking.

"Holy shit!" I muttered aloud. That was enough to convince Dylan he should pick up his furious barking where he left off, and that shook my companions into action. We all scrambled out of the car and gathered around the shredded remains of the right rear wheel. Most of the tire was gone, along with the hubcap, and the sheet metal around the wheel well was riddled with a thousand little dents and black rubber smears where shrapnel fragments of the disintegrating tire had torn past. In some places, the paint and rust had been blasted away to bare metal.

"Oh, shit! Look at the road behind us!" I declared, pointing back east. Like a trail of black rubber crumbs, fragments of our dry rotted snow tire lay all over the highway.

"We gotta spare, right?" I asked Pete quietly.

"Yeah... Yeah we do," he replied, still wide eyed. "Help me dig it out of the trunk."

The trunk was still packed tight with stuff, and we had to take out pretty much everything to get to the spare tire and the jack. I finally got a good look at what was back there and found it was just a lot of superfluous stuff that seemed unnecessary to me. But I could see Pete was getting frustrated digging through all his junk, so I didn't say anything. The plan was still to get an apartment in Seattle at the end of this trip, which was why all that household junk was back there.

The spare tire was a sorry example, to be sure. Bald down to the cords on one side and under-inflated. But it would be enough to get us to a gas station for air, we hoped. Together we repacked the trunk, leaving our shredded tire and jack for last, so we wouldn't have to go through this trunk digging chore again. Still, we were going to have to find another tire somewhere and soon because this spare tire didn't look like it had many more miles left in it, and if it quit before we had got a replacement we'd be screwed.

We took the next exit that exhibited signs of service station habitat and found one there straight away. There was an old automatic air machine in the back corner of the parking lot that took quarters to run, so we scrounged around the floor mats and fragmented carpet shreds till we had a handful of corroded green coins with which to feed the air machine. That poor old pump was on its last legs, shuddering and sputtering, and took over a dollar in coins to bring our soft tire to sufficient operating pressure.

Pete had gone into the attached convenience store while Jen and I struggled with the wheezing old tire inflator and asked the teenage clerk at the register where one might find used car tires at deeply discounted prices. The kid had no idea, but some other random guy there had overheard the question while pouring himself a cup of coffee. He stepped up and gave Pete a couple of junkyard options within a fifty-mile radius. So, after we had topped off the tank and grabbed a round of mid-western-sized syrupy fountain sodas, we plotted a course to the closest option we had been given.

The directions were straightforward, and after twenty miles or so on the interstate, we broke north into a moderately sized town. Near the edge of this municipality, out with the warehouses and small manufacturing facilities, we found the place as described. Though it wasn't really a junkyard so much as a scrap yard where people brought in truckloads of copper pipes, old car radiators, and aluminum pans to sell for cash. But there was a sizable pile of ruined cars stacked up in plain view at the far end of the dirt parking lot.

We parked the Olds in a dusty corner of the lot away from the large forklifts, flatbed trucks, and busy scrap yard workers pushing big hampers piled high with all manner of random metal fragments. Jen took Dylan in the opposite direction of all that industrial commotion towards the tall weeds while Pete and I made our way to the stack of crushed cars. They had all their roofs collapsed by the big forklift and were stacked now four cars high like cord wood but otherwise were unmolested. A late-70s-era, full-size, wood-paneled Buick station wagon sandwiched into the second tier caught my eye as still having one good tire in a position that appeared to make removal easy.

"There we go, man," I declared "That's a five-lug, 15-inch GM rim that should fit the Olds. Looks like it still got good tread on it too."

"Hmm, yeah," he replied, leaning in and inspecting the tire like a connoisseur of junkyard radials "I think you're right."

"Can I help you fellas?" We turned around to find an enormously fat guy in a tall mesh trucker hat with his greasy hands on the wide hips of his filthy mechanic's blue overalls. "If you've got scrap to sell you need to take it over to the scales."

"Nah, man… we're actually looking to buy a spare tire on a rim for our car."

"We don't sell used parts, buddy. This ain't a salvage yard."

"Aw, but mister, we're desperate. We had a blowout a while back, and our spare ain't gonna make it on the highway for long," Pete implored.

The guy twisted his face up to the side and sort of grunted disapprovingly. I didn't wait for him to finish with a worded response.

"Dude, this wheel right here," I said, pointing out the Buick's rear wheel, there at chest level with us. "This wheel would be a perfect fit for us and would be a snap to pull off. Look, we wouldn't need any machine to lift the car or anything, the wheel is right there." The guy's face began to un-scrunch a little in response. I continued. "We could pull off this wheel and be out of here in minutes, how much is the scrap price for a steel wheel with a tire still on it, anyway? Like, nothing right? Come on man, name your price."

He stood there for a moment, hands still on his ample hips, and looked us up and down. We were a dusty dirty duo to be sure, but we put on the "please mister" puppy-dog eyes as best we could.

"Alright, alright. Gimme ten bucks and it's yours. Just be fucking quick about pulling it off," he snapped with an air of frustrated disgust. Pete had a couple of crumpled fives produced almost instantly, and as soon as the money changed hands, I broke into a sprint back towards the car to fetch the tire iron. The lugs broke free easily, and as anticipated we had the wheel off and rolling across the dirt lot in about a minute.

"We should make sure it fits, Pete, just to be sure."

He agreed, and we set about jacking the car up there where it was parked. Jen and Dylan returned as we torqued down the lug nuts on what had turned out to be a perfectly fitting rim. There was no sign of the greasy fat guy as we repacked our bald spare tire back into the trunk, so like the crusty delinquents we were, we left our old, shredded tire and rim right there in the dust of the parking lot and gave the place our taillights.

Jen then laid out a course for us that shot directly west on a long straight US route parallel to I-90 through more corn than I had ever seen in my life. Pete hammered down and we flew along, the long stalks of ripening corn visually bent askew by our rapid passing. As we approached a moderately sized city we decided brake left and get back onto I-90 again, so we could keep up our speed, but the city's speed limits slowed us down before we could get to the highway, and the car began rapidly overheating. Pete thought it best to let the car rest a few minutes before we took off again, so we looked for a park or something where we could let Dylan have a good shot at clearing his bladder before our next long stint on the highway. There wasn't much, so we just pulled off in the parking lot of some random industrial complex and let the temperature needle sink back into an acceptable range. Jen took Dylan around the parking lot, but despite his intensive sniffing, he could not find a place he found suitable for peeing. After about ten minutes we all climbed back inside and rolled off again. As we came up on our turn, we passed a tall water tower perched on a large industrial building shaped and painted like a giant ear of corn.

"Well, that's kinda corny," Jen declared, frankly.

Back on I-90, we found the views still dominated by endless rows of monoculture corn presided over by frequent billboards of immense size imploring us to visit the local car dealership or eat at the local family friendly restaurant. We also began noticing recurring billboard themes, messages spread out over multiple façades: messages of faith and commerce and offers of "free ice water." Since there wasn't much to see once you got over the immenseness of these endless fields of corn, and since we no longer had the weed to blur the tediousness of midwestern driving the roadside commercials became our sole entertainment on our late morning fly by. Some were really quite a sight to see, with cutouts of waving cowboys, unnaturally colored dinosaurs, and gigantic apple pies

After about an hour of this journey through vast seas of maize, Dylan started crying the pee-pee whine with growing intensity. Pete began the slow deceleration process to prevent the car from overheating from a rapid stop, and we rolled off the highway into some random little burg. There we found signs suggesting we visit a park presided over by the figure of a green giant. How could we refuse?

There, towering over the trees, his giant green hands on his giant green hips, was the larger-than-life representative of frozen vegetables everywhere. Dylan was straight up crying at this point, desperate to piss, so we parked without delay and approached this effigy of the lord of prepackaged peas and carrots in supplicant reverence. Dylan laid his offering right there at the giant's feet in the form of a neat little pile of brown dog shit, to the monocle dropping gasps of the other pilgrims who had gathered there. Pete laughed aloud as Dylan finished his ritual with a long, raised leg piss against the dais the green statue stood upon and proceeded to strut about the grounds beaming with pleasure.

"God damn it, Peter! Why didn't you stop him?" Jen asked. "We have to pick up that shit now. We can't just leave it there."

"Why not?" he replied with a chuckle.

"Get a fucking plastic bag, now. You're picking that shit up!"

"Ok, ok," he said in feigned exasperation. "Where am I going to get a bag from?"

"Here, Pete," I offered, pulling a shopping bag from a nearby trash can and dumping out the ketchup-stained empty fast-food containers.

So the dog shit offering was removed despite Dylan's best intentions, though there was nothing to be done about the long stream of dark yellow dog urine running down the concrete and away from the giant green man, gleaming like liquid amber in the sun. We were getting some hard looks from the other frumpy families stopped there to view this American wonder made low by our dog's bodily functions, so we loaded up into the car once more and put that scene in our rear-view mirror in a hurry.

We crossed a little river outside of town; and beyond the highway opened up in a dead straight line away to the horizon. There was one single roach left now rattling around in the bottom of the little Mason jar, just big enough that we could all get one good lung full of smoke. I lit it and pulled my share, passing it forward to Jen. It was gone to ash by the time Pete had finished his pull. We all held in our portion of smoke as long as we could and blew our exhale in the direction of a compatriot in the spirit of wasting nothing. And that was it, the very last of the weed. Though, I'm sure if you searched the car well enough you could have found a few more moldy roaches under the seats.

There in my backseat world, enhanced by a moderate head change, I took in my surroundings as I found them. The torn and faded black upholstery of the car, the little yellow squeaky toy duck perched on top of the sun-split dashboard, blistered from years baking in the sun. A knot of wires and duct tape drooping out from under the center of the dash, and a wide variety of books, papers, maps, and other random items tucked and stuffed into the metal skeleton of what was once the roof's headliner. This was our home.

Through the bug-splattered windshield, I could see the great grassland expanse of middle Minnesota spread out to the horizon in every direction, the interstate ahead cutting through the endless rows of ripening corn in a laser straight path. And the sky; deepest impossible blue broken only by a few marshmallow clouds combed thin by upper atmosphere winds, with not an aircraft in sight. The entire world laid before me, framed by the windshield and bathed in the radiant light of the Now, we travelers following the eternal route of the sun. Speeding along in hopes of reaching that point on the horizon where the sun meets the land before that burning disc has the chance to. "Sioux Falls, sixty nine miles" read a lonely green and white sign blurred by our rapid passing. Overcome by numbing mid-morning fatigue, I closed my eyes and drifted away on those sky-high Great Plains clouds.

I awoke to the rumbling sounds of the car in rapid deceleration.

"Where are we?" I asked.

"South Dakota. Just crossed the state line, pulling into a rest stop for a minute," Pete replied.

I climbed out with the rest once we had parked and had a deep breath. The air was clean, yet thick with some unknown fragrance, and the hum of early autumn bugs rang from the tall grass all around us. I made my way to the rest stop toilets in a sort of a bleary semi-conscious haze. Something was different here. This earth had a foreign feel to it like nothing I had yet experienced. I was midway through a long piss when it hit me. I was west. I had made it. I was truly in another land now, the mythical land of the west. A smile broke across my face from ear to ear and I laughed aloud, my voice slightly echoing off the tiled rest room walls.

I was still glowing with that thought when I returned to the car, finding my friends there having a light lunch. I grabbed an apple and a stale dinner roll and joined them in the grass in front of the quietly hissing car.

"This is it, guys," I said after a few bites of my apple. "We're really in the west now. This world feels totally different here somehow, ya know?"

"Yeah, man. I can dig it," Pete agreed.

"There's a park ahead called the Badlands, it's got all these crazy land formations and stuff in it," Jen added. "I saw a brochure up at the bathrooms for it just now. Here, check it out." And she handed me the folded glossy paper.

"Whoa, man that is so fuckin' cool!" I exclaimed after just a cursory look at the pictures it contained.

"We should be able to make it there by dusk, and camp," Pete stated. "Unless some shit stops us. But one way or another, we're going to see that place."

"Well, come on. Let's go!" I said, rising to my feet.

Out on the road, the billboards took on a fevered pitch, with one theme occurring with increasing frequency. Wall Drug. "Where the heck is Wall Drug?" More like what the heck is Wall Drug. Being stoner kids, we couldn't get past the "drug" part without the fantasy of some crazy roadside store that sold wares on par with the fabled coffee houses of Amsterdam or something. But we of course knew that couldn't be it. "Free Ice Water" "Homemade Donuts," "5 cent Coffee," what could this place be? Some glorious diner, a diner with cowboys and dinosaurs and who knows what else? We decided we'd have to find out once we got there, wherever the heck there was.

In the meantime, we were hauling ass. The speed limit in this state was seventy-five miles per hour, which was the highest I'd ever seen or even dreamed of being legal. The speed limit being what it was, Pete felt it acceptable to push the car a good fifteen to twenty miles an hour past that so as to "go with the flow of traffic" and soon pushed the envelope further, giggling like a schoolgirl as the speedometer inched closer to one hundred, touched that line, and then stepped over it.

"Jesus Christ, Peter! Slow the fuck down!" Jen implored over the roar of the engine, obviously not feeling as giddy about our excessive rate of travel as he did.

"Ok, ok," he answered and let the car drop into a conservative eighty-something miles an hour. "Look at that sign!" he suddenly added, "a CORN palace? We have to check that out, it's probably made out of corn!"

"Why are you so excited about corn?" Jen sarcastically asked, still apparently displeased with the incredible speed our rickety old car had briefly achieved.

"Aw, come on. It'll be weird. We have to go see it. We'll probably never be back this way again." And he took that next exit with no further discussion.

We followed the signs through town towards this attraction and rolled up in front of the hall in a cloud of overheated anti-freeze steam. That changed Pete's mind about stopping and getting a good look at this temple of corn. Plus, the place looked locked up anyway. We circled the block to keep the air flowing through our overworked radiator, admiring the colorful onion-shaped turrets and the dioramic pictures of farming life fashioned out of thousands of ears of multi-hued corn plastered all over the sides of the building. After our one pass around the place, we headed back to the highway to resume our westward race, crossing the Missouri River just outside of town.

"Well, that was corny, eh?" he jabbed at her. She did not answer.

After another hour or so of incessant billboards and rolling prairie we came up on a roadside attraction that we had to check out for real; a "Show" consisting of dozens of old cars and junk.

Plus, the car needed gas, and we all needed to piss again. We had to pay to get in, but they let us take Dylan inside surprisingly.

The place was like an automotive oddity museum with more crazy stuff all over the walls than you could take in at once. Old enameled signs, old pictures, car parts, license plates, deer antlers, buffalo heads. It was intense. We worked our way through the indoor maze of the place and found our way to the back door. Outside was even more stuff. Old cars and tractors and trucks, crazy medieval-looking iron farm implements, sheds full of more bric-a-brac, train cars, a little schoolhouse. I was really digging this place, and Pete was too. But Jen was not as into it. She humored us for a while, but after about an hour of our boyish excitement over old rusty junk she had had enough.

"I'm hungry, Peter. Let's get out of here." We conceded without protest. We were hungry too.

Outside next to the place was a mid-size gas station serving not only automobiles, but semi-trucks and other highwaymen. Attached was a fried chicken place with a self-serve, all-you-can-eat option that we took full advantage of, stuffing ourselves to the point of nausea with greasy fried chicken and sides. It was getting to be late afternoon at this point, and we realized all at once it would be getting dark here sooner rather than later. If we wanted to reach the Badlands to camp, we would have to get moving and not let any other roadside weirdness distract us from our destination. We had about a hundred miles to go and a little over an hour before the sun went down.

Since we were heading due west at this point, the late afternoon sun was blazing in through the dirty windshield, fiercely obscuring the view of the road directly ahead. The sky slowly came alive in fiery color as we approached the Badlands, as dazzling as it was blinding. Soon the landscape began taking on an other-worldly air, lit up as it was by the setting autumn sun. Strange peaks and points of striated earth began to jut out of the ground around us. And then we were inside.

The Badlands. This place looked like something out of my dreams, lit as it was by the failing sun. In silence we motored through the park, making our way to the campgrounds, awestruck by the alien world around us. We came up on another self-pay kiosk and ignored it like the others. We were on a roll with the no-pay game and were not about to break that streak unless forced.

The sun had dipped below the pointed peaks by the time we found a place to park and pitch the tent. After the camp was set up, Pete and I took to looking for stuff to burn for a campfire. There was nothing there of consequence, just some green shrubby stuff that resisted our efforts to molest it valiantly. So once the darkness wrapped itself around us, we returned its embrace and gazed at the infinite stars in the inky blackness of space above. We lay out on the warm hood of the car, our backs propped up on the windshield, and took in the cosmos in all its immensity. The quiet was almost oppressive there in the moonless black, but the breathing of my companions next to me filled me with a sense of belonging like I had rarely felt before.

These moments were so charged with meaning, with purpose, that I almost felt lightheaded in their presence. I felt an emptiness inside of me that required no filling, a void of bliss, of contentment. I said a little silent prayer of thanks to God for this, and the blissful feeling sort of melted away in response. In the distance a coyote yelped, breaking the silence of the expansive night, and a collective chill ran down our frames. Even Dylan let out a whimper, faced with such wilds as he had never experienced. He jumped up on the car and joined us, sharing our laps in anxious repose.

Then someone nearby started coughing, followed by muffled laughter. After a brief return to prairie silence, the cough and laughter sounded again. Pete rose to investigate.

"I see a lighter striking inside that tent over there," he announced. "There's people smoking weed in that tent." He stood there for a moment longer, then began walking in the direction of the flickering tent.

"Pete! Where are you going?" Jen asked in a whisper as forcefully expressed as she could without breaking the reverent quiet of the world around us.

"I'm going to say Hi. I'll be right back."

After a few minutes, we could hear Pete coughing and laughing now in that neighboring tent.

"Aw fuck that!" I said. "Come on, let's join them."

In the tent, we were introduced to two girls in matching pajamas about our age. Their thick accents instantly placed them as hailing from Boston. They were on the return leg of a summer road trip around the west and were now headed east. They had good weed and a little five-inch-tall bong too, so we all got pretty lifted. Sitting together in a circle, cross-legged on the earth, we passed the piece around and let the conversation loose. We told them our plans of heading to Seattle, and they told us of some of the places they had seen. It was nice to have a good hang with people who were not spooky aggro freaks for a change. We hadn't really had a normal conversation with anyone outside of our trio since we left Ithaca.

They had been camped in the Badlands for a couple days and suggested we all try to catch the sunrise and then go for an early morning hike before the mid-day sun beat the earth with its heat. They also warned us that park rangers regularly checked the cars to make sure daily payments had been made. So we'd have to shell out some bills. Ok, it was looking like this place was well worth it.

Eventually we decided it was time to wrap it up. We all had one more round of the bong before retiring to our rooms. The night was still warm, so I left the windows of the car half down to let in the nocturnal grassland atmosphere. Far away I could still hear those coyotes crying, their calls entering the cab through the windows like wisps of smoke, and through my closed eyes I could still see all those glittering stars sweeping across all existence. At peace with it all, I drifted into nothingness.

CHAPTER 16

The excited anticipation of exploring these Badlands had me awake before dawn. Well, that and the brisk damp of the morning air wafting in through the open windows. Remembering we had all kicked around the idea of catching the sunrise over these otherworldly peaks, I quickly got my shit together and attempted to rouse my companions. They had all changed their minds at some point during the night and were now more interested in remaining within their warm cozy sleeping bags than joining me in the chilly pre-dawn hour. But Dylan was game and followed me into the bush.

It was misty in the early light, with the cars and tents of the campground covered in fine wet dew. The grasses were heavy with cold wet as well, dampening and weighing down my tattered and torn pant legs as I trudged toward the closest hill. The light was beginning to grow now, and it quickly became apparent that a dense fog hung low over the world here this morning, so much so that you could not even see the tops of the tallest peaks. Far from being the glorious, vibrantly colored break of day over this rocky moonscape we had hoped to witness, the sunrise instead turned out to be a slow turn of the dimmer switch, giving gradual definition to the low gray cloud bank enveloping us.

Still, it was a new morning in a strange foreign land, and it was beautiful even draped in drab mists. I attempted to climb a small hill to see if I could get above the fog while Dylan barked at me from below, hesitant as he was to follow me into the clouds. I could see nothing but billowing mists from my vista so I descended again, thinking perhaps I should give sleep another shot and wait for the fog to clear out. Dylan, on the other hand, was of no mind to return to bed and began spurring me on to play, somehow finding a nice thick stick somewhere that Pete and I had missed in our fruitless firewood search the evening before. The game was that age old canine sport of alternately trying to get me to take the stick from his bite but then not letting it go once I grabbed it. We went on like that for a few minutes, growling at each other and tugging on our end of the stick when one of the Boston girls started coughing in her tent. Dylan promptly abandoned his prize stick, and bolted towards them, barking all the while. That woke everyone up proper, and before long we were all standing around the Boston girls' little white gas camp stove boiling watery coffee.

"So much for the sunrise, eh?" Pete stated, looking away into the fog.

"Yeah, I don't know…" said one of the girls. "This is some wicked crazy shit! We've been here for a few days now and never saw any fog at all."

"Well, when it clears we should all go for a hike." I suggested. "I'm dying to check this place out."

They all agreed, and we hung around the camp there engaging ourselves with breakfasts and bong hits till the clouds began to lift. The girls informed us they were going to split after the hike, as they were on something of a schedule and had to be back in Boston in a couple of days. So we helped them pack up their tent and break camp. Then when the opaqueness of the mists dissipated sufficiently, we set out into the Badlands.

The landscape was striking. Fantastic land formations fashioned by the movements of water and wind over unfathomable spans of time had exposed striped lines of alternating muted colors that from a distance looked smooth as wet clay but upon closer inspection had an impasto gravelly texture, hard like concrete but loose on the surface in a way that made gaining a foot hold difficult. We all had to climb these crazy dream-like peaks; even Dylan followed us up onto some of the smaller ones. Pete and I, in true testosterone fueled fashion, had to keep finding the bigger, harder-to-summit peaks and quickly left the girls behind. And poor Dylan, afraid of heights as he was, still attempted to follow us wherever we went until he got himself onto a high ledge with no way down.

There in a panic he began to wail the most terrified dog cry I'd ever heard. Pete shimmied down from a ledge above him and took him up in his arms, held him tight and carefully made his way down to the girls waiting below. The poor pup was so shaken, still whimpering and trembling even after both Pete and Jen tried to comfort him. It had only been an hour or so since we had set out, but he was done with this place and would not go on. Jen chose to take him back to camp, and the Boston girls were ready to hit the road anyway, so Pete and I said our goodbyes and continued into the wilds on our own.

It was getting warmer now; the fog was completely gone, burned off by the growing intensity of a late summer sun. Down in these dry barren valleys, the brightness and heat began to become oppressive. Still we pushed on just to see what we could see. By mid-morning, we were getting baked in the sight of the naked sun. Pete stripped off his shirt and proceeded to continue the random climbing and descending that had characterized our explorations thus far. My shame would not let me follow suit, plus my flabby pale white torso would have surely turned blistering red if I exposed it to the unrelenting sun like my friend. As it was, I could feel the skin on my face begin to tighten from the dry dusty heat. A powerful thirst was also beginning to make itself known.

"Pete, did you bring any water?" I called out to him from a ten-yard distance.

"No. You?" he replied. I shook my head.

"We should probably head back; I'm feeling mighty thirsty."

With visible hesitation he agreed, and we began to make our way back the direction we had come. As we got into the bottom of one of the parched little valleys, I spotted something emerging from the rock-hard soil below, something that looked like an animal skull.

"Whoa, Pete! Check this out!" I scrambled in close for a better look.

Sure enough, it was a skull. Kinda like a big dog skull or something, upside down and partially encased in the hard dirt. In fact, it looked almost the same as the dirt, cracked and lumpy and gray. And with the way erosion had worked the peaks and pinnacles of this place into odd bone-shaped formations it's amazing I even spotted it.

"Holy shit, man! That's a fossil!" he declared as he caught up to me. Without a second thought I gave it a hard touch to see if it might come free, and the exposed portion crumbled in my hand.

"Mother fucker!" I cried in alarm. The fossil bone was softer and looser than the surrounding soil. It was an instant loss. "Shit, man. I broke it," I added, letting the fragments and dust fall through my fingers.

"Oh well," Pete said. "At least we got to see it once. We're probably the only two humans to have ever seen it, so that's gotta count for something, right?"

"Yeah… yeah, man you're probably right. That's a heavy thought."

"Come on, let's go. God help us if some park ranger finds us out here with fossil dust on our hands. That skull was probably like a million years old."

He was right; in my youthful indiscretion I had probably committed some grave act of archaeological desecration by even touching a fossil. Best to put some distance between us and that scene.

The heat out there was really hitting now, and as with most hikes it seemed the way out was longer than the way in. it was also getting hard to tell the hills and valleys apart, everything was starting to look the same.

"Are we going the right way?" I asked.

"Uh, yeah. See that hill?" he pointed, "I'm pretty sure we came from that way."

I was not as sure, but I followed him just the same. I didn't have a strong sense of direction back towards camp anyway. Finally, we came up on a taller hill that we could get on top of. The view that vantage point afforded settled the question; we were off course, but not by much. We were able to sight a line back towards the cars and tents and were back in camp a little after noon. We hit the water like fiends, taking down a gallon jug between the two of us. Jen and Dylan had been napping in the shade of the car and emerged while we were rooting around in the trunk.

"What time is it?" she asked blearily. "You guys were gone for a while."

"Yeah, it's a hot dusty world out there," Pete stated. "I have no idea what time it is, feels like noonish."

"We found a fossil skull!" I added excitedly.

"And… you broke it," he followed, punctuating his statement with a long draught of water.

"Nice one," Jen mocked.

We spent the remainder of the afternoon bumming around camp. The Boston girls had left Jen with one nice nug, and we broke it into as many tiny pinners as was possible. After all those nice thick doobies we had at our disposal through the beginning of the trip, those thin twiggy joints left us only with a mild head change and the taste of burnt paper in our dry mouths. But beggars can't be choosers, and we were grateful to have even that. Once they were gone, who knew when we might get more.

As dusk approached, Pete and I again went foraging for firewood, finding enough fragrant brush to have a small blaze to welcome in the darkness. We burned down the last of those pitiful pinners together before my companions turned in, leaving me alone there in my thoughts to rake the glowing coals.

I felt wonderfully blank, and open, despite the religious doubts and guilt ever present in my personality. Times like those, alone in the dark, alone in a faraway land, I felt almost free of the weight of my convictions. Convictions I never really chose to bear but rather were chosen for me. The rebellious side of me bristled at the thought of being forced to adhere blindly to biblical doctrine, especially when I gave the concept any unbiased thought. But the other half of me convulsed in the abject terror at the alternative: eternity in hell, whatever that meant. Be it the hell of popular culture, with the fire and the brimstone and the devil poking his fork up your ass for ever and ever, or just the cold darkness of being "separated from God," also a vague concept all the more frightening in its ambiguousness.

These threats worked to keep me in the direction of the faithful, against my will even. I knew the church fathers would not be approving of damn near anything I was doing out here on the road. I knew because they told me so when they all heard I was going on this trip, warning me earnestly that I risked my very soul by living on the edge of God's graces as I was. I had to convince them, convince myself really, that I would be ok, that I was going to spread the good news to the lost souls I encountered here on the road, that I would live as a Christian example to all these new-age Wiccan hippie Buddhists, and that would protect me from God's wrath. At least that's what I hoped.

Except in practice, I was doing no such thing; forgetting the Sunday communion, taking the lord's name in vain, lusting after my friend's wife, well, girlfriend. But most of all, not proselytizing the good word to the lost. God, I felt like a fool, like a worm, torn between two minds. How could I convince these "lost souls" that my way was the way, when I didn't even really believe it myself?

Bah! I shook these thoughts from my mind and dusted the ashes from my pants. I'll just take it like I always do, I thought, one day at a time. The coals were almost cold now, with only the faintest orange sparks occasionally lighting up. I kicked a little dust on the ashes to finish it off and trekked through the tall grass to that little hill I had mounted in the fog at dawn. The sky was crystal clear blackness now with ten thousand, nay, a hundred thousand tiny points of sparkling light. The cosmos spread out before me in all its glittering glory, its magnitude, yet conversely, its insignificance. Under the weight of the darkness, I lay down on my back and let the cosmos lie on top of me as, in my virginity I imagined a lover would. I let it have me.

Perhaps this is God, I thought. All this that I can see, this infinite space. If God is everything, then he is also me, right? That thought gave me a shudder. No, that can't be right. It's a sin to play God, to be God. We're supposed to need God with all our hearts. How can we need him if we are him? But then, why does God need us to need him? Why does he need our praise, our supplication, our devotion? And if so, why does he set up his religion at the exclusion of others, others who would have no chance of ever hearing the "good news?" Why would some of his humans get the "chance" at salvation, while others might live their whole lives without ever hearing his name and then be doomed to hell because of their ignorance?

It all felt wrong, fundamentally wrong, and deeply unsettling. I prayed to him there in the night. I prayed to him to give me guidance, to give me strength there upon that hill in the starlight. I prayed that I might find my faith confirmed in some way and, in desperation, gave it all to God, as it were, and nodded off there in the open.

I wasn't asleep for long. The cold awoke me with a start, and upon sitting up I heard the cry of the coyotes in the darkness, now much closer than they had been the night before. Not wanting to face a band of wild nocturnal hunters out on their turf, I hightailed it back to the car and called it quits properly, rolling up the windows all the way this time.

The next morning was a lot colder, so we all decided to break camp and check out nearby Rapid City and the surrounding areas instead of roaming the painted hills of the Badlands again. Plus, we hadn't paid the camp fee and didn't feel like risking another round of theft of services.

We were out on the road early and ran right into this much-anticipated Wall Drug place just outside of the Badlands. We could tell right away this was going to be a cheesy tourist trap sort of scene, but we rolled in just the same. Our initial observations were confirmed quickly, and we stuck out like sore thumbs as we wondered around the premises. We were looking pretty crusty by that point, not having showered or laundered our clothes in over a week; Pete and I especially since we had spent the better part of the day before trekking through the dusty Badlands. We goofed off a little bit, checked out what there was to check out, and had our "free ice water" and a bite to eat at the attached family restaurant.

Jen collected a handful of local brochures for us to peruse at the table while we finished our five cent coffees and our bacon and eggs. There were all sorts of campy low-budget attractions available to the family vacation crowd, but they all required some admission fee and would probably prohibit Dylan form entering. But there was one place available to us that we knew would line up with our lifestyle; the giant stone heads at Mount Rushmore, that place of vulgar American exceptionalism blasted out of the very living rock. It required no money to enter and was open to canines of all breeds. So we set a course for this professed national treasure and hit the road.

Mount Rushmore was one of those places I had heard about from before I could remember, like the Grand Canyon, or Niagara Falls. Now we were about to witness this monument in person with no knowledge of it beside the obvious: four dead presidents' heads carved into a mountain. We rolled into the large, surprisingly empty parking lot and instantly spotted two old-school VW camper buses parked in parallel, each facing a different direction so their side doors opened onto each other. Pete rolled by slow, and between the two we caught sight of dreadlocks and tie dye.

"Hippie kids!" he exclaimed "Awesome, let's go say hi!" And he parked a few spots away.

They had seen us too and knew right away we were travelers like them. So when we approached, they came out to meet us, the guy going so far as to embrace Pete just like that. They were a guy and a girl, each with their own bus as a home, who had only met a few weeks earlier and had come to the stone heads for the same reason we had; because they were there, and they had never seen them in person before.

We all did the introduction game; where we were coming from, where we were going. The guy's name was Brian, and he came out of Georgia. He had a mess of misshapen dreadlocks, a sparse, young man's beard, a pair of ratty old denim overalls over a tie dye t-shirt, and a pair of Birkenstock sandals. The girl, Zoe, was dressed similarly, with nappy Anglo dreads and hemp rope accouterments. She was from the Olympic Peninsula in Washington State and was on her way back there after some trip to Michigan. They were your archetypal Dead lot kids, complete with the VW buses. Zoe also had a little white dog called Moe whose curly coat had formed into little dreads as well. We all hit it off pretty well and together went to witness the granite likeness of presidents past.

The heads were indeed huge, towering above the rubble and conifer trees below. But I couldn't get past the feeling that the mountain face would probably look a lot better if it had been left as nature had made it. Apparently, I was not alone.

"It's kinda sad, really," Brian said quietly, after we had stood there before them for a minute or so. "This was, well, this is a sacred mountain to the Lakota people here, and we've gone and blasted the faces of old white guys into it. It's really kinda fucked up."

"I wonder what it used to look like," Jen added.

"Probably a whole lot better," I answered.

We all had a sad chuckle and turned to leave. Brian suggested we all park at this public golf course where he'd been working part-time all summer and hang around for a few days. The people in charge there didn't mind, as long as the vehicles were road legal. Then we could all pile into one of the VW buses and head into Rapid City for the evening and kick it on the street. That sounded like as good a plan as any and we took off in a little caravan down the mountain road, trekked to this liberally minded golf course, and lined up the vehicles under a big tree at the edge of the dirt lot.

We spent another couple hours there, just goofing off, kicking around a hackysack, and talking about traveling. As it turned out, there was apparently this whole subculture of kids traveling around the country like we were, moving from place to place, sometimes following bands or festivals, and sometimes just moving around from "kind" place to "kind" place where other travelers congregated. We didn't realize it when we started out, but we were in fact traveling road kids like them, and like countless others out there all over America, all over the world in fact. It felt awesome to be a part of something like that, part of an underground society of travelers. As the conversation continued, I began to realize I didn't really want to stop traveling once we got to Seattle, I wanted to keep going and see it all.

Later that evening, down in Rapid City, after hanging with the local hippie kids, smoking bowls in alleys, and sharing a couple bottles of cheap bum wine sweetened like candy, I asked Pete how he felt about our proposed destination and the ending of the trip that would entail.

"I don't know, man. I'm thinking I'm kinda over the Seattle idea now."

"I know, right?" I agreed. "This traveling thing is awesome, and there's people like us, lots of people doing it. I don't want to settle down now. I wanna see it all, man."

"Jen, what do you think?" Pete asked, turning to her.

"I'm game. Seattle's all rain anyway, right? Let's see where the road takes us."

So this is it, I thought. We're really going to do it. Honestly, I'd always wanted to do this, ever since I was a kid. I always liked the journey far more than the destination. Whenever I had gone on family vacations, or on weekend road trips during my brief stint in college, I was always a little bummed once we got to wherever we were going, and even more bummed once we returned home. I remember especially the trip I took with some friends over spring break, driving my half-dead station wagon as far south as our short time allowed. We ended up landing in Virginia Beach and had a blast, camping out every night. In my mind I never really came back from that road trip, dropping out of college shortly after we got back. Now, in a way, I was just continuing the same road trip, after a brief hold over in my hometown.

I was back on the road, seeing the world like I'd always wanted, and there was no telling where it would lead me. I felt drunk on the thrilling anticipation of what could come next. Well, that and the sweet bum wine.

CHAPTER 17

We all got up late the next day. Like noon kind of late. The sweet bum wine we had all been passing around the night before had given me a nice roaring high while we were chugging it but had now left me in the possession of a real skull splitter of a headache for my efforts. Even though we were all saddled with similar states of hangover, we got our shit together quick enough to roll into Rapid City again by early afternoon with a mind to just to get out and about and shake off the shakes. Even though our overnight parking arrangements there at the golf course were safe from harassment, they were also frightfully boring. None of us gave a shit about golf, and apart from knocking little balls around there really wasn't much else to do.

Rapid City on the other hand was sufficiently entertaining to distract us in our idleness. It had a crusty, rusty, anything-goes sort of feel to it with lots of back alleys into which to duck. Not that there was much to duck from; I don't remember seeing a cop once the whole time we were there. That day we ended up clustering up with a group of hippie hybrid skater kids and other youth loitering around the downtown area.

As evening approached, word started going around about a bonfire lit party up in the hills outside of town once the sun went down. It was a Saturday night after all. We went with the flow, naturally, and by dark were up on a wooded hill shared with a cluster of tall antenna arrays overlooking a section of the streetlight-lit town below.

Despite the roaring oak pallet-fueled fire and the orange municipal lights below, the sky still retained a deep darkness that caused the stars to pop in twinkling bursts. The drink of choice was again bum wine, sweet and rapidly intoxicating. The cheap wine was apparently a thing with the kids in this town; local cultural flavor, if you will. There were also some thin blunts going around in the firelight, and I hit those whenever one would pass. The combination of the sugary wine and the tobacco wrappings of the blunts got me lightheaded quickly. Since I wasn't a smoker, tobacco-wrapped blunts always hit me hard. And the elevation above my natural sea level habitat there in the Black Hills helped to get me higher still.

Somebody started drumming on a spackle bucket or something, and I found myself awkwardly stumble-dancing around the blazing pile of pallets with a few other random kids. It was very liberating, twirling around in a blur with abandon. I felt wild, filled with unholy glee, and the absolute unbridled feeling of not giving a shit about anything whatsoever.

The rest of the night is just random snapshots of memories, jumbled and out of order. I remember talking to some girls without awkwardness, and them not being repulsed by my advances. I remember throwing more pallets onto the fire with some other long-haired guy. And I remember Pete, much later, attempting to convince me that we had to go, that our ride was leaving.

I awoke the next morning in the backseat of the Olds, my sneakers still on, with my sleeping bag draped over me like a blanket. My first thought was dread, dread of what was sure to be another brutal hangover. But as I rose and looked out the windows at the two other VW buses, under the big shade tree, and the rest of that nondescript parking lot, I realized I felt ok, considering how lit up I knew I had been. I had that sugar crash headache thing going on, and was thirsty like a sonofabitch, but felt fairly straight apart from that. Ha, well I guess I'll go take a piss, I thought.

Standing in the tall weeds off from the lot, my yellow stream running strong, I realized I still had one of those pints bottles of bum wine in my jeans front pocket. Pulling it out I could see it still had a couple pulls left. Well, down the hatch, I laughed aloud as I slung the now empty flask deeper into the tall weeds. Dylan, out of nowhere tore past me to chase after it.

"Dylan!" cried Jen, "get back here!" I caught his attention, once he had found the empty bottle and was satisfied it was of no interest to him and led him back to the cars.

" Good morning!" I said cheerily.

"You're awful chipper today," she answered. "I figured you'd be sick as a dog."

"Yeah, I don't know…I feel ok."

"Hey, isn't today your birthday?"

"Oh, shit, yeah!" I then realized. "I totally forgot. Maybe that's why I feel ok; it's like a birthday present!" I added with a short laugh before a second, more grave realization came up beside me. Not only was it my birthday, but it was also a Sunday. Maybe God was cutting me some slack, I thought cautiously, allowing me a little birthday present despite my sins. I gotta duck out soon here and have my communion ritual before he changes his mind and slaps me with another killer hangover.

So I hightailed it off into the tall weeds to take care of my spiritual obligations without delay, slightly buzzing now from my breakfast of sugary wine. I kept it quick and simple, and it felt sufficient to stave off the ever-present guilt. Cleansed as I was by my little DIY ritual, I could now enjoy getting dirty all over again.

Apparently, the decision to hit the road again sooner rather than later had been made at some point during last night's revelry. I didn't remember agreeing to it but was fine with the idea. I was eager for whatever was coming next. Brian had some sort of unexplained business outside of town he had to take care of first, and Pete went with him. That left me with Jen and Zoe and the dogs. We all went into town again so Jen could do some laundry, and once she had a couple machines loaded at the local laundromat they set me up in a little park while they also took care of something, I didn't know what. Normally I'd be feeling a little put out, being the odd man out everywhere, but I guess that bum wine was still working its magic because I really didn't give a shit. I happily set up on a park bench in the warm sun to doodle and write in my road journal, chuckling to myself that I had actually been so occupied by this road trip that I had again lost track of the days, almost missing Sunday for a second time and not even realizing it was my twentieth birthday of all things. My teen years were now officially over, even if I still felt like a kid.

I was only alone there for fifteen minutes when the girls returned with some big shopping bags and big smiles.

"Happy birthday!" they sang in unison, producing a supermarket issue, unnaturally colored cake sheathed in a clear plastic bubble from one of the bags.

"Holy shit, thank you guys! I don't know what to say." I was almost choking up with touching surprise. "This is so nice."

They placed the cake on the bench, and we all had a round of hugs. It was nice to hug girls, to have them close, so close the patchouli scent in Zoe's dreads transferred into my patchy juvenile beard, filling my world with the essence of the fairer sex. That was just icing on the proverbial cake.

We then sat on the grass there in the sun and shared the sweet supermarket treat, eating it with our fingers for lack of utensils. They had also gotten a big gallon jug of Pisano wine and a few small paper coffee cups so we could have a few drinks without garnering the sort of attention chugging from a gallon jug in public would attract. The flavor of the artificial vanilla frosting clashed terribly with the wine, but it was the thought that counted to be sure. I felt loved, and it felt good.

We met up with Pete and Brian later that afternoon and bummed around downtown for a while looking for a scene to connect with. Pete was specifically looking for one of the kids from the party the night before who had drunkenly promised him one of those magnet base antennas he could use to hook up the CB radio we had gotten from that sketchy trucker so many miles back. But try as we might, we could not find him, or any kids out and about at all. So we gave up and headed back to the golf course parking lot to while away the evening. We kicked a hackysack around till it got too dark to see, then retired into Brian's van for a few hands of penny poker. I had no idea what I was doing, having never played poker before, and quickly lost all my pennies. I was more interested in watching them all play anyway and worked a growing wine buzz as the jug's level receded.

As the pennies changed hands talk was had about the road and how we would all travel it. Zoe was headed home to the Olympic Peninsula and suggested we all aim for that landmark. Brian was torn, wanting to follow Zoe, his feelings for her contrasting with his desire to return to his home in Georgia, in the completely opposite direction. We, of course, had always planned on heading west to Seattle, and the Olympic Peninsula was just across the sound, so it wouldn't be too far a leap for us in our original plans. Though we were all kinda lukewarm on the whole Seattle direction by that point, we didn't have any other place to aim for so, why not? Besides, the road was long, and who knows what might come before we reached that western city, before we even left the state we were in for that matter.

We decided to caravan west towards the coast and see what happened, planning to each go our own speed, as the VWs would never keep up with our rusty rocket, and then rendezvous again at the Wyoming state line. Brian asked me if I wanted to ride with him on that first stretch, and I readily agreed. With that we called it a night.

It took them all a while to get their acts together and get on the road the next day, but eventually once everyone had rubbed the crust from their eyes and were loaded up into their respective rides we headed out to the highway. The Olds, moving faster than Brian's VW was soon out of sight ahead of us, while Zoe followed behind, somewhere back there in the rear-view mirror. She was the last one to fill up at the station, which put her at least ten minutes behind us, so we three vehicles were spread out on the road that morning by miles.

I had never ridden in a VW bus before. It was a different riding experience up there in the front seat of a flat-nosed van, all on top of the road. Brian's bus was a late 1970s model and pretty clean. You could tell he had an abiding love for his bus, as I found most VW owners are wont to do, and had kept everything tidy and in its place. And not surprisingly, he had a Grateful Dead tape playing as we drove. When it got to the end of the tape he popped it out and handed the cassette to me.

"Pick another tape, bro. There's a couple cases of tapes here between the seats."

I picked up the biggest case and opened the heavily stickered lid. It was full of bootleg cassette copies of live Dead shows, labeled in handwritten letters, dozens of them. I reached down and flipped the lid on another case; same thing. Ok, I thought, I guess it'll be the Dead again then. I picked a random one with a mid-80s date written on it, and popped it in.

"Good choice, man," he said, smiling and slowly bobbing his head to an improvised jam session caught mid-way through. "I love the Dead."

Yeah, no shit, I thought. I'd never been too fond of the Dead, having come from a "Heavy Metal" sort of background, cutting my teeth on the genres of thrash metal, hardcore, and punk rock. But I certainly didn't outright dislike the music. It was just another flavor of rock and roll after all. But I did have a few less than stellar interactions with their fans. Back in high school, I had gone with the older metal head kids I had been hanging around with at the time to one of the last Dead shows before the lead singer died. We had no intention of actually getting into the show, and they all enthusiastically busted on the band the whole ride there. No, we were after the drugs to be acquired in the parking lot. Talk about not fitting in; metal head kids in black, clad in boots and chains lurking around, asking about acid. We got the cold shoulder from every tie-dyed hippie kid we approached. I remember feeling super pissed at the attitude we were getting at the time, but who could blame them. We surely looked like narcs or some other unsavory characters. We ended up leaving empty handed, cursing all hippiedom for the perceived slight against our advances.

And then a few years later, during my brief stint in college, I again had dealings with the hippie community, and again found them haughtily aloof and generally dismissive of my attempts to win favor. These experiences left a bad taste in my mouth I was now desperately trying to wash out. I knew that to categorize a whole group of people in a negative light just because I had unpleasant experiences with a representative minority of the group would be detrimental to me, especially out there on the road. It was important that I was open to new things, new viewpoints. I didn't have to groove like they did, but I did need to be on a level stage. The Dead weren't all that bad, really. That 80s-era bootleg had some pretty catchy hooks and rhythms to it, and I found my head bobbing along with Brian's before long.

The music was only playing for about fifteen minutes when I felt the van lurch and loose speed. Brian turned down the volume and listened attentively to what his van was saying. The word apparently was not good.

"Fuck, I think I'm losing the engine again," he said quietly. "You hear that knocking?" I heard nothing. "Fuck, man. Not again," he added desperately, as he pulled the van onto the shoulder of the highway. I accompanied him to the back of the van, where he popped open the rear engine door and knelt beside his shuddering air cooled motor, radiating with significant heat. "I'm going to have to turn back," he stated with cold determination.

What? Turn back? Then where did that leave me? I thought, beginning to feel the edge of desperation draw close. My ride was miles ahead of us, and there was no way to get in touch with them. I was about to protest his engine's prognosis and the whole turning back idea when Zoe rolled up behind us. There we go, I though in relief, she'll surely give me a ride to the first rendezvous. She's still going west, still going home. She joined us at the engine, kneeling beside him.

"She don't sound too good," she offered. What they hell they are hearing? I thought. These VWs all sounded like lawn mowers to me anyway, I could not detect any sounds coming from that motor that would be indicative of impending engine failure. "You turning back?" she asked him.

"Yeah, don't have a choice. I'm not dealing with another blown motor on the side of the road again."

She reached in beside the engine and shut it off, then pulled the dip stick and studied the oil sample it provided, rubbing a little between her fingers and smelling it. "Main bearings," she declared, and Brian groaned. "Well, no road trip for you just yet," she added. "Head back to Rapid City, and we'll pull the motor before it gets worse. I've got another set of main bearings and some gaskets. We can get the rest from the local auto parts house."

I felt my heart sink. She's not going west till she gets Brian's bus fixed? Fuck, I'm going to be stuck. All my gear is in the Olds, what will I do?

"I'll give you a ride to the state line," she said, turning to me, sensing my temporary panic perhaps. "But then you guys will be on your own again."

"Thanks," I replied, swallowing the lump of anxiety I had burped up. Of course, she wouldn't let me lose touch with my ride. See, these hippies are good people who care what happens to me, I thought, no need to freak out.

She then turned and embraced Brian. "Head back to Rapid City, I'll be there by dark." And they kissed.

Brian turned to me then, "Safe travels, broseph," he offered. "It's a long road. I'm sure we'll meet again." And he gave me a hug too.

So now I was behind the windshield of yet another flat-nosed van, looking down on the pavement flying away beneath us. Zoe's bus was an older model than Brian's by a decade or more and showed its age thoroughly. The upholstery was torn and faded, and the edges of the laminated windshield were milky with water contamination. But it ran a lot better and had much better acceleration. I hadn't noticed on Brian's bus, because I had nothing to compare it too, but Zoe's engine was quieter and smoother. The van handled better too and didn't feel as much like we were plowing through water at highway speeds.

"How did you know his engine was about to blow?" I asked her.

"Ha, yeah, it's an art," she replied with a laugh. "My dad's a VW mechanic, and I was raised on these things. I've had this whole bus here apart a few times already. My dad gave this bus to me on my sixteenth birthday, and I rebuilt everything with him."

"Wow," I exclaimed, wide eyed.

"Brian's bus looks really clean, but it's falling apart underneath. I don't think there's ever been any major work done on it in years. He's lucky he's even made it this far."

I was impressed; a girl who worked on her own vehicle. Talk about challenging my preconceived notions of hippies. I felt a little small next to her in that light. We rode on in silence for a time, while I chewed on these fresh revelations.

"You wanna see something cool?" she asked me randomly, breaking the silence. Of course I wanna see something cool.

She pulled off into a rest area and had me join her at the back of her faded red van. I noticed then that instead of the stock rear metal bumper she had a log of wood, like a fence post or something bolted in its place.

"That's so cool," I told her.

"Yeah, I sold the bumper to some other kid once when I needed some money. I like the log better anyhow."

'Ha, yeah," I agreed. "It's awesome."

"Ok, see this here?" she asked, pointing into the now open engine compartment. "Watch this."

She popped one of the clear reverse light housings out of the sheet metal, took one of the wires coming out of the back of the housing and attached it to something on the engine, maybe the ignition coil? It was hard to tell because she was so fast. The reverse light started flashing. Fuckin' A, she's made a timing light. She aimed the flashing strobe down at the crank shaft pulley, and with her other hand moved the little distributor insignificantly.

"See? Pretty cool, right?"

I was floored. That was probably the coolest thing I'd seen, ever. I was flooded with feelings of admiration and inadequacy in equal measure. She tightened down the jam nut on the distributor and shut the engine door.

"Ok, that's better. Let's roll."

We spent the rest of the ride taking turns talking about ourselves, where we came from, what we wanted out of life. I mentioned the spiritual conflictions I had been laboring under, and she briefly explained a few other ways of viewing spirituality. Eastern philosophies and Native American ways of looking at the world and our place in it. I was riveted. I had always been taught to view any other belief system with a mixture of distrust and disdain. That reflexive approach was still there, but I consciously pushed back against it more and more. I was beginning to feel pretty bummed she was not going to be caravanning with us anymore, and I told her as much.

"Aw, you'll be alright," she replied, shrugging it off. "I got to help Brian. He'd be lost without me," she added with a laugh. "You know, you guys should scrap the whole Seattle idea. You should travel around more before you settle down." I had to agree. "There's this place in Colorado, up in the hills outside of Boulder. The town is called Nederland, but we all just call it Ned. It's a really kind place, lots of travelers pass through there. You guys should go there and see what happens."

"Would you meet us there later maybe?"

"No, once I've got Brian squared away, I've got to get home. I've also got to lose Brian too somehow, let him down easy. He's a nice guy, but he's not really my type." My brain did a flip flop. Wait, she doesn't even like him? "Yeah, I don't know," she continued, maybe sensing my virginal confusion. "He's kinda, I don't know… lame."

Mind sufficiently blown. Blown like Brian's knocking engine. This chick was the coolest thing ever; independent, capable, kind. Man, I wanna be like her, I thought.

Then we were crossing the state line into Wyoming.

"Here we are," she said, "They should be at this rest stop up here." And there they were, Pete sitting cross legged on the hood.

The meeting was bittersweet. We explained what had happened, why we were so late getting to them, and what had happened to Brian and his bus. Pete was visibly bummed, having bonded with Brian at some point over the past few days, but shook it off as Zoe brought up Ned and Colorado.

"Just above the town," she explained, "there's a dirt road that leads into the piney woods. Follow it to the end. There's a sort of a rocky overlook there, cleared for parking in between the trees. The road kids stay there when they pass through, and the park rangers never hassle anybody unless they act like idiots. This time of year you'll probably meet some other travelers there too. Check it out, you won't be disappointed, I promise you." We then all had a round of hugs and watched her as she hooked around the center median and went back east into South Dakota.

"That was one cool chick," I told Pete on the side. "She built that bus she's driving, knows it inside and out. She made a fucking timing light out one of the reverse lights and adjusted the timing right there on the side of the road."

"Get the fuck out!"

"Yeah, man. What a woman."

So there we were, back to our core trio again, but now with a different view, a different direction. We decided to go west just a little further, just enough to hit the Devil's Tower before we broke south because the landmark was just too close to pass up. It was getting late in the day, after all the delays and hangups so we got back on the road and bee-lined it to that crazy tower straight away.

You could see it coming from a distance; a giant stone pillar, dark brown, almost black against the bright blue sky, its shank scored with deep vertical cuts, like some monster had clawed against its side in an attempt to mount it. The local Lakota had a similar explanation myth, attributing the ridged formations that ran up the sides to the claws of a giant bear that had tried to climb the tower in pursuit of a few wayward children who had scrambled up its sides in a panic. It was easy to see how a story like that could be born here; the place looked like something out of a myth. I couldn't wait to hike up to it, to touch it and see how real it was.

We rolled into the park with a few hours of daylight to spare. I made it known that I was going to climb up to the base right away, and if they wanted to join me. Jen said she wasn't feeling well and just wanted to nap, and Pete decided to stay with her and support her in that venture. So I set out on my own, determined to make this natural monument's acquaintance.

The trail towards the towering stone monolith led me first through a field populated by dozens if not hundreds of prairie dogs, chirping and scurrying from hole to hole, often poking their little heads out of their little hills to track my progress across their land. Then it was on to the tower itself. It grew larger and larger as I approached, until it dominated the landscape in front of me. The sun was nearing the horizon as the trail began climbing through the rubble at the base of the giant column. I came to a fork in the trail. It didn't matter which path I took because the trail was a loop around the base. I went right and quickly passed into the dark side of the formation. It was noticeably cooler on that side where the sun was refused late day access, but I had a good sweat going, having hustled thus far to get here before dark.

I approached the vertical wall of the tower as soon as the trail came close and laid my hands upon it, hoping to feel the spiritual power of the place, or something. I don't know, I was just going with my gut. I continued on my circumambulation once I had thoroughly explored that patch of rock surface and soon came out into the setting sun again. The light was dazzling after my passage through the shade, and I stood there for a few moments soaking in the warmth, my back against the rock face, feeling the accumulated heat radiate out of the rock and into my back. What a glorious place, no wonder the indigenous peoples here revere this part of the land.

I quietly meditated on nothing for a while, just listening to the songbirds and the breeze blow through the tall pines. When the sun finally dipped below the hills, I made my way back down, arriving in camp with the growing dark. I joined my friends around a little blaze they had made, and together we talked excitedly of the future, alternately passing around a big can of beans and a jug of wine in communal spirit. And it was alright.

CHAPTER 18

The next morning, I accompanied my companions back up to the tower along the same route I had taken the evening before. It was just as impressive the second time around. I took many detours temporarily off the trail to explore anything that sparked my interest, often accompanied by Dylan, but I always jogged back to meet up with my friends before they got too far ahead of me. It felt good to be out hiking and sweating in the sun, and I realized suddenly I was glad we had run out of weed and were not experiencing this place in a fog like we so often did. Not to say that if we did have doobies to burn I'd be turning them down or anything. But after weeks of chronic marijuana use in every situation we found ourselves in, to experience a day in a "normal" state turned out to be something of a head change all on its own. So later, when we were perched on a cluster of big boulders at the foot of the Devils Tower and Pete lamented on our lack of bud for the occasion I found for once I didn't agree with him.

We spent the afternoon cleaning house, pulling everything out of the car and laying it out around the campsite to get a good look at it all. Some of the duffle bags of their clothes and stuff had gotten wet from leaks through wheel well rust holes and dry-rotted trunk seals back when we were passing through the seemingly constant rain of the rust belt and had never dried out. That persistent dampness had in turn bloomed into spotty black mildews on anything cloth or paper. These musty things were now all spread out in the sun to dry fully for the first time in weeks.

It was a sizable pile of possessions, and now that it was all out in the open they started seriously looking at what was there and what was worth hauling down the road any further. Since an apartment in Seattle was no longer the goal, a lot of their junk no longer had purpose. I stayed out of that minefield and let them duke it out. Jen was of a mind to travel light when it came to Pete's stuff and kept pressuring him to leave behind this or that item she thought had little or no value. This of course annoyed Pete, so he would then demand she put aside more of her musty clothes and books to leave behind in passive aggressive retaliation. In most cases, they ended up denying each other and refusing to let go of any particular item in question.

By the end they had separated only a fraction of the stuff, which I dispatched to the park dumpster with haste lest they change their minds and pack it back into the trunk. It wasn't much of a load lightening, but it was something. I went through my shit too. I was already operating on a minimal amount of gear anyway, so I didn't have much to cull. But I did offload some surplus cold weather clothes I hadn't even worn yet.

While in the trunk, Pete also found our baldy spare tire had now gone totally flat; this meant we were again without "insurance" out there and would need to go on another junkyard mission. He also took the opportunity to engage in a little preventative maintenance and snooped around under the hood looking for anything out of place. Every fluid was low to some degree, but he had at least a quart of everything on hand. With every reservoir was topped off, he gave the engine a thumbs-up. Tomorrow we would start our southward journey into Colorado and beyond.

That night, long after they had turned in, I set off on my own into the darkness, just to get a better look at the stars. I had been trying to sleep for some time but could not stop my brain from running, tossing and turning for hours in a semi-conscious state. So I had abandoned the back seat of the Olds in hopes of calming my mind with the black of night.

I didn't have to wander far to catch the view. The sky here seemed so much bigger somehow, and the starlight sharper in the prairie silence. The mountainous tower's inky black silhouette could still be made out against the sky, mostly because of the stars it blocked but also because of some unperceived presence it put off, some black illumination, some aura unseen. Was it all in my head? I swore I could feel the energy of the place radiating through me in delicate waves. I stood there, alone in the starlight, my arms outstretched impossibly wide to the cosmos in the attempt to absorb this energy I was feeling.

Then an owl called, and close. Its booming hoot made my heart skip a beat. I smiled broadly once I realized what it was and tried to narrow in on its location when it called again. In a big solitary tree deep into the tall grass, totally denuded of foliage and set off a little from the camp's cottonwood grove was the place where the night raptor was perched. I made my way to it, slowly so as not to drive the bird from the tree. I knew it could see me; it was an animal specifically adapted for seeing shit in the dark after all. But I just hoped that if I approached easily it might not feel the need to wing away.

I was able to get pretty close, closer than I'd ever been to such a big bird. I could see its outline against the starry sky, much like the tower. It sort of reminded me of the tower in a way; erect and dark, lording over the landscape in the blackness. And it was big, startlingly big with twin tufts of feathers off its head that looked like pointed horns. I could not make out the features, but its outline was sharp and clear. Then something was wrong, I could feel the bird's gaze boring into me, right into my head, my soul even, and I was frozen in place as the stars began run down the surface of the sky in bolts of glowing light. The owl was close now, somehow right in front of me, standing before me as big as a man. I still could not make out its face in the darkness, but I knew it was familiar somehow. I peered in closer, closer, the face almost discernible. Then it was all clear in an instant, the face was my own. Instantly the creature unfurled its giant wings before me in a roaring gust of wind, and I awoke with a holler.

The dream had seemed so real, so viscerally real that I had a hard time being okay with the realization that what I had just experienced was all in my head. I climbed out of the car again, for real this time, and stepped out of the cottonwood grove towards where I had only just been standing in my mind. There was no solitary leafless tree, no giant shadowed owl, only starlit darkness low over the prairie, and the Devil's Tower looming dark in silent mystery.

We hit the road early the next morning, grabbing coffees and prepackaged sugary breakfast cakes from a local gas station near the park. With our sights set south, we hammered down backcountry roads through ranch and prairie unbroken for miles. I chewed on my latest dream as I sipped my watery coffee in the back seat and watched the rolling grasslands fly by.

Naturally, I wanted to know what it meant, if anything. Was it my subconscious trying to tell me something? Was it God? A demon? Something else; something more primal? These dreams probably didn't mean anything, I attempted to assure myself; just an overactive imagination and the chronic weed high starting to wear off. But a part of me was nervous there might be some sinister message behind the reoccurring themes, something demonic. For the dreams were always dark in their intensity. So much so that I didn't want to delve too deeply into what my subconscious was trying to tell me. My faith in the existence of God as I had been taught to know him may have been rapidly corroding, but my belief in Satan was as alive as ever, and I was still confident he had it out for me personally. The dreams were probably coming from him and his demon minions whispering confusions into my sleeping ears. I said a little silent prayer for guidance and protection, as much as by a force of habit as by the faith that Jehovah God was even around to hear it.

After an hour or so, near the junction of the I-25 interstate, we spotted a little corrugated metal fenced yard of wrecked cars and other random scrap. Since we once again were in the market for a spare tire, and the highway proper was before us we decided to check the place out, despite there being no sign out front indicating the place was any kind of a business, let alone a salvage yard.

We pulled in through the open steel gate, bumping in the rust-colored ruts of the dirt drive, and up to one of those work site trailers used as field offices for big construction jobs. The trailer was in rough shape; its aluminum skin torn in places, exposing stringy yellow insulation that hung like dirty ribbons from open wounds. The door swung open with a rattling slam as we approached, and an impossibly thin, leathery skinned dude popped his stubbly gray-haired face out at us.

"What kin I do ya for, fellas?" he crowed from his perch. "Y'all sellin, or buyin?"

"We're looking for a spare tire on a rim, sir," I replied. "We saw this place from the road and were hoping you might have one that'd fit our car."

"Well…ain't much left here, as you can see." We looked around at his suggestion and confirmed his statement. The place did have a rather picked-over appearance, with random vehicles in various states of disassembly in amongst drifts of junk and garbage and crisscrossed with deep ruts cut into the oily dirt from the likes of a big pay loader or backhoe. The place looked more like an illegal dump than anything else.

"Well, mind if we have a look around?" Pete asked the old guy.

"Have at it, fellas! Five bucks if you can find one."

That was a good price, to be sure, and we began searching the piles of debris in earnest, hoping to find a whole set if we could. But, like that crusty old coot said, there really wasn't much there to find. The wheels we did find either had garbage flat tires on them or were the wrong size rim. We ended up leaving our car up on the jack, the front wheel removed so we could try out each potential rim on the hub. But again and again our hopes were dashed against rusted, mis-matched steel. Finally, under a pile of ruined kitchen counter appliances and lumber scraps inside of the overturned wreck of a panel van I found a tire on a rim that looked like a five-lug GM. I rolled it over to the Olds, and it slid on the hub like an oiled glove.

"Got one, Pete!" I cried. "It's bald as fuck, but it holds air, and it fits." He jogged up with a grin that faded when he saw the old tire.

"Fuckin shit, man. This tire is shit," he said bluntly, running his palm across the curve of the sad tread worn tire. "But it'll have to do. Gotta have a spare." I set about remounting the regular wheel and loading our new spare into the trunk, while Pete went to settle up with the master of this yard. He returned with a smile and a magnet base CB antenna.

"Check it out; five bucks for this too!" he gleefully announced, swinging the three-foot-long steel wand around like a fencing sword.

"Jesus, watch it, Peter!" Jen replied, symbolically stepping back like he had swung it in her face.

"Gonna hook this up tonight!" he continued, giving no notice to Jen's passing displeasure.

We were just pulling out of that trash heap when a big, shiny new, extended-cab pick-up truck with a construction company name on the door hastily pulled up in front of us, blocking our path. A tall, clean shaven man, his lantern-jawed face slightly concave and topped with a huge cowboy hat, emerged from the truck, strode up to the driver's side of our car and squatted down to our eye level.

"What the hell do you think you're doing here?" the man asked us, with a stern quiet I found unsettling. "Dumping garbage?"

"No, man. We were looking for a spare tire for our car," Pete responded meekly. "The old guy in there said it'd be ok."

"What old guy?"

"In the trailer there. He sold us a wheel."

The construction cowboy erupted in mocking laughter. "Goddammit, you all just bought trash, boy! I hope you didn't pay much." We were silent. "That old guy in there is a goddamn squatter! This here is my land!" he barked into our window. "This's all his trash here I've been clearing out. I done told him he's gotta beat it, that I'd call the cops on him if he didn't clear out, but I see he's still hanging around."

He paused, looking at us hard before continuing in a low gravely register. "Now you, you all get the hell outta here you God-damned hippies! Before I call the cops on you too!" He then stood and abruptly walked back to his truck, peeling away in a cloud of dust and flying gravel. Didn't have to tell us twice; we followed his instructions and got the hell out of there in a hurry, happy a shower of stones and dirt was all we had to contend with.

We stayed on the interstate through most of Wyoming, only breaking off onto a smaller US route past Cheyenne. We took this lonely stretch of two-lane black top across the border into Colorado, another far away dreamland of a state I never imagined myself visiting. It was flat and featureless on first impression, but I knew the mountains were coming. The Rockies. I couldn't wait to see them, to be in them.

It was late in the afternoon by then, so we began looking for a place to camp. There were no sanctioned parks in the area we found ourselves in, but the country looked empty enough that it probably wouldn't matter where we camped. We turned off onto an unmarked dirt track and took it away into the scrub till we felt we were far enough from the road that a campfire would not attract the unwanted attention of the police, or worse.

We found a little hillock shaped vaguely like a crescent and positioned the car in such a way as to complete the ring and block any view of the flickering light of a fire at night. In the center, we dug a small pit with our heels and gathered some brush for burning. Jen and I then pitched the tent, while Pete started hooking up our shadily procured CB radio he'd been waiting to use. He had it active in no time, and the tinny sounds of faraway voices soon filled the camp. We waited till the sun went down before lighting the fire, so our smoke could not be seen from a distance, and set about occupying the fading light of the evening with our new toy, the CB radio.

We were close enough to the interstate that we could listen in on all sorts of trucker chatter. There were also quite a few Hispanic voices too; whole channels seemed to be populated exclusively by Spanish speakers. We just listened, switching channels occasionally whenever we got bored with any line of conversation we were eavesdropping in on. We quit the game once it was totally dark, afraid to run the car's battery down, and gathered around our little fire. It was chilly out there on the prairie, as a good breeze had come in with the night, but the little rise behind us was acting as a sort of wind break. It was very dark out there that night as well, there being no moon and no light pollution besides our fire, so the stars were impressively bright. Now I wished I had some weed to smoke, the novelty of being sober wearing off. I was not alone.

"Sure wish we had a doob to burn," Pete announced generally. We agreed in silence.

The next morning we aimed southwest, towards Denver. The flat emptiness of the prairie quickly gave way to green irrigated farmlands and then suburbia with its billboards and fast-food joints. Our path to Ned would take us through Boulder, so we skirted the outside edges of Denver, passing through a few satellite cities before landing in metro Boulder itself. There we broke for lunch, setting up in the parking lot of a big supermarket with a name foreign to my east coast experience. Jen and I went in to stock up on supplies while Pete played Frisbee fetch with Dylan on the outskirts of the parking lot. We filled the cart with the usual fare: non-perishables, bread and cans of beans, junk foods. We also got a carton of smokes, a couple cases of cheap beer, and a couple gallons of cheap red wine.

"Sweet!" I said as Jen handed me the two big gallons.

"If Zoe was right, and there ends up being other road kids in this place where we're going, some booze to share may go a long way in being accepted. And if they turn out to be a bunch of assholes, we can use the booze as distraction and leave," she stated.

"And if there's no one there, we'll get fuckin hammered on our own!" I added,

"Yes. Yes, we will." And she patted me on the head.

The mountains ahead loomed large now, like a vertical wall of jagged gray stone. The sight of them as we approached was intimidating, for they were absolutely massive from below. Soon we were climbing, and the road began to twist like a snake. Rocky outcrops rose on either side of the two-lane way, and civilization quickly dispersed. We had another twenty miles or so to go, according to the map, and it was all switchbacks and building elevation.

The country here was beautiful and much bigger than the east coast mountains I had known. This was another major crossing for me in my journey of discovery, for all of us really. As with crossing the Mississippi, entering these mountains was like entering another world, like stepping through a door from flat prairie into towering mountains of stone. I could almost feel a change in the air, a change in some fundamental understanding of life I had held. These unexplainable feelings washed over me, and I began to feel lightheaded, dizzy even. We were gaining elevation rapidly now, and it was having an effect. I laughed out loud.

"What's so funny?" Pete asked me.

"Everything, my friend. Everything."

The elevation gain was beginning to have an effect on the car too, heralded by a growing gasoline odor coming from a carburetor set to sea level. The rich, partially combusted hydrocarbon fumes wafted in through the open windows, adding to our lightheadedness. The climb was making the car run hot as well, so Pete turned the heat on full to stave off the eminent boil over. Just past a large reservoir the climb leveled out, and we rolled into Nederland town, elevation 8236 feet above my hometown. We pulled into a gas station in a cloud of anti-freeze steam and rich exhaust fumes, turning heads upon our hissing, stinking approach.

"Better let the ol' bird cool off here awhile," Pete stated, and we settled in for a rest. We set up at a little picnic bench over by the dumpster, which gave us a nice view of the local traffic. We saw several VW buses and other hippie type rides piloted by long haired bearded fellows roll by, which we took as a good sign.

I spotted a pay phone close to our bench, so I took leave of my companions and placed a collect call to my parents on a whim. I had not yet contacted them since we left, and there was a good chance I might not get another opportunity for a while. Plus, I loved them and wanted them to share in the excitement I was feeling, having traveled so far already and now so high up in the mountains.

My mom picked up, and the operator connected us once she had agreed to accept the long-distance charges. We had a good long talk, and it was good to hear her voice. I gave her the abbreviated, G-rated version of the trip thus far, and she seemed genuinely excited for me. My dad was still at work, so I didn't get a chance to rap with him but promised to call again soon, at a time when they would both be home. I loved my folks. I was at an in-between sort of age where I just wanted to get as far away from them as I could while simultaneously wanting to remain deeply connected. These conflicted feelings, so ubiquitous in my life, just mingled with the rest of my lingering teenage angst to form the background noise of my daily doings.

Once the car had had a chance to catch its breath, we loaded up again for the final push, in the hope we could find this mystical road-kid camp before the sun went down. We took the road out of town Zoe had described, climbing steadily again and soon came upon an unmarked dirt road on our right.

"This must be it," Pete decided, and he steered the car off the pavement onto the dusty gravel.

The road was bumpy like a washboard, so it was slow going. Too slow to outpace the haze of dust our passing kicked up, so we traveled in a cloud of our own making. This was a dry place, from what we could see in the late afternoon light. Scrubby pine and rock lit strangely by the fading sun. Our dust, lit up by the same afternoon light, billowed behind us like a big dirty, ethereal cotton ball, mingling with the trees and settling on the rocks.

We were on that road for over a mile I think, bumping along at a crawl and bathing the landscape in fine dust. The sun was just dipping behind the forested mountains in blazing orange as the road broke apart into a myriad of little trails and parking places in amongst the crusty fragrant pines, dead ending where the elevation dropped off steep enough to stop a road in its tracks. Off in a central location, a couple of cars and a big white and mustard yellow van-nosed RV were positioned in such a way as to make the most of what view could be afforded by the elevation drop. We parked on the outskirts of the encampment and garnered our courage.

"I see Dead stickers on that RV," Pete declared. "I think this is the place."

"Should we just walk up?" Jen asked, speaking to herself as much as to us.

"Fuck it," Pete replied, swinging the heavy car door open, the dry squeaking hinges sounding abrasively in the quiet. "Come on, let's see what happens."

We approached with equal parts excitement and trepidation, not knowing what to expect. Would these folks be annoyed at our arrival? Would they be hostile to us? Would they be aloof dicks who would not give us the time of day? As we drew closer, more of the camp around us came into view. A few tents were scattered around the area. Some colorful Mexican blankets were hung on some ropes between trees, and a giant fire pit backed up against a huge boulder full of ashes and melted beer cans lightly smoked in thin wisps.

The sun was down now, and the orange light of its setting had degraded into dusk. The RV, its tie dye curtained windows flickering in candlelight, was ahead now. There were indeed Dead stickers all over the back of the RV, and it had a California license plate. A dog barked from inside, and Dylan answered immediately, shattering the mountain silence. The curtains in one of the back windows drew back in response, revealing a gaunt, brown skinned face framed by the aluminum window frame and set with a wide toothy grin.

"Welcome fellow travelers!" the head in a box exclaimed. "Welcome brothers, welcome sister!" The door of the RV swung open, releasing a crew of smiling, crusty hippie road kids with arms wide in unconditional acceptance.

This was the place, and we had arrived.

CHAPTER 19

It was a good thing Jen had thought to pick up some booze before we made our climb into the mountains because it helped to break the ice with our new camp mates straight away. We all gathered around the blazing pyre our hosts hastily built up and began passing around one of those big jugs of wine, making our introductions and sharing our stories.

We, being the newcomers there, naturally went first. Pete and I took turns, sometimes talking over each other, enthusiastically describing the trek which had led us to this camp, and in turn fielding a few pointed questions from the apparent leader of this outfit as to our hopes and dreams, where we wanted to go, and what we really wanted out of life.

This guy's name was Zedekial, or just Zed for short, and perhaps titling him as the "leader" of the camp was something of a stretch given the random nature of this group of road kids gathered there. But he was the oldest by decades and presented himself as the captain of the van-nosed RV anchoring the camp to this place in the mountains. Zed was a rail-thin, middle-aged black man with a huge toothy grin and a mess of short, wiry, salt-and-pepper dreads that stood out in every direction off his head. Dressed androgynously in a sort of hap hazard, nondescript way, in clothes ostensibly straight from a used garments donation pile. He had the look of a guy who might approach you on a city street asking for spare change. But that was like a disguise, there was more to him than that. He had this aura about him, an other-worldly way of looking into you with his big brown rheumy eyes that seemed to lay your soul open before him, as if he knew your answers before he had even asked the questions.

Still, despite the unsettling feeling of personal exposure during our initial conversation, I was left with a deep admiration for the guy. His intensity felt benign to me at the time and somewhat thrilling to boot. My first thought was that he may have been an angel in the flesh, or that the spirit was working through him at least. The wine and the altitude only helped to solidify such erroneous thoughts in my head.

After Zed came his "deputies," for lack of a better word; three high school friends from Long Beach California he had picked up off the boardwalk. These three kids were our age and had been traveling with him for over a year already.

Tick came across to me as the alpha of this Long Beach trio; a tall, thin, second or third generation Latino kid with a pockmarked, acne-scarred mug and a fuck all attitude. He carried an unkempt mop of greasy, curly, jet-black hair on his head and dressed with a seemingly wanton contempt for current fashion in grimy blue jeans and some well-worn random sports team t-shirt. He spoke in a snarky sarcastic tone about such subjects as fucking and getting fucked up and had an abrasive nasally laugh that pierced the quiet of the mountains. You could tell what Tick really wanted out of life because he would unabashedly tell you. He wanted to fuck it.

Aiden, a bit shorter than his buddy, was a little more concerned with the fashion trends party kids of the day displayed. He wore the common uniform of the 1990s raver; huge-legged pants, flat skate sneakers, and colorful baggy t-shirts with prints that played on popular commercial product logos, changing them into words that suggested sex acts or drug use. Except that since he was a road kid his clothes were filthy instead of squeaky clean. He too, like many of the other white road kids I met out there on the road had grown his hair into poorly made dreads that hung limply in dirty blond lumps around his spottily bearded young face. He was nowhere near as abrasive as his friend but still came across to me as unpredictable and potentially dangerous.

The third of this trifecta was Barb. She didn't speak much that first night, but my impression was that she was an equal player in Tick and Aiden's adventures, not just some sort of tag-along girlfriend. She, like Aiden, dressed the part of the crusty raver, hiding her ample curves under the baggy uniform, but had managed to keep her long, straight, mousy brown hair dread free. She also liked the wine, taking two long pulls for everyone else's one, but never came across as drunk.

Then there was Judith. After Zed, she was the next oldest in camp. She knew Zed and his crew from other times in other places but had not traveled to this mountain camp with them. Rather, she had already been there up in the mountains, spending the summer in the forest when the RV had rolled up a few weeks before. She really had the look of rugged mountain lady. Dusty, heavy-duty dark brown dungarees with aggressive tread hiking boots, tan button up shirt tucked into her pants, wide brimmed weather worn hat capping a long graying blond braid, and a big ass Bowie knife in a rawhide and beaded sheath that hung low off her thick leather belt. Her tent was about fifty yards out of our camp, and her capable, mature, almost masculine demeanor was about fifty miles away from the likes of dirty kids like us.

And finally, there were the runaway girls from Wisconsin. Two girls younger than any of us that Zed's crew had picked up off the streets of Boulder one of the times they had come down out of the mountains to "restock."

The younger of the two, Sherri, could hardly have been over sixteen. She was a very small girl, maybe five feet tall, with short, curly black hair that looked like it was in the process of growing back from a shave. She was very quiet, often wrapped in a big colorful Mexican blanket that dragged in the dust behind her, and tended to avoid eye contact. My first impression was that she had good reason to be "running away" from wherever it was she was coming from. She had the look of an abused bird in recovery.

Her traveling companion was a more gregarious, outspoken, hippie-themed girl named Summer. Summer was a year or two older than Sherri, but they had come from the same town and went to the same high school. She had apparently decided to take off with Sherri as a sort of chaperone, to make sure she wasn't taken advantage of. Summer looked as though she had lost a bit of weight while living out on the road because her homemade flower print and paisley dress and blouse seemed two sizes too big on her frame. She also had a young puppy she called Critter that ran about completely undisciplined with Zed's anxious little dog, Akasha.

These folks formed the core of the camp on our first night, and we all stayed up late getting to know each other by the firelight until we had emptied all the wine and beer bottles. Pete and I were the last ones to turn in, too excited to sleep. The feeling of acceptance into this tribe of travelers was palpable, and it felt good.

Dawn revealed more of the camp than was initially discernible in the fading light of the previous evening. The camp area around where we were parked turned out to be a lot larger than I had first realized, with other cars and vans parked away from our central spot in amongst the dry pines. I wandered a little away from our zone to have a piss and promptly found a tree which had been used several times to that end already. I watered down the shitty bits of paper and attempted to kick some dirt on the spot, but there was too much material there already. It was kind of a bummer to see that stinking pile heaped up against a tree, swarmed in green flies and drying in the sun, but what did I expect? Kids and vagrants squatting in the woods is dirty business. Not everyone is a boy scout after all. In fact, there were bottles and bags and all sorts of windblown trash all over the place I quickly came to realize. So, in the spirit of obligatory stewardship I began picking them up, returning to camp with my arms full of empty bottles and plastic wrappers.

"Well done," declared Zed as I approached the smoldering fire pit. "These humans are a dirty lot. Its good of you to pick up after them."

"Yeah, it sucks," I replied. "There's a big shit pile over there too. I guess there's no trash cans or anything around here, huh?"

"Pack it in, pack it out. At least that's the idea. There's a couple trash bags behind the RV. Dump that shit in there," he instructed.

On the far side of the camper, I found six or seven overstuffed trash bags, their contents spilling out under the camper, their sides torn open by animals. Well, their heart was in the right place, I thought, adding my armload of trash to the pile, the bottles rolling down and away from the heap uncontrollably.

A few of the others had joined Zed around the fire pit by then, and we all made the collective decision that breakfast was in order. They had a big trash bag half full bagels, crushed donuts, and broken muffins they had scored from a dumpster behind a bakery down below in Ned the last time they had gone for supplies a couple days earlier, and we tore into it with abandon. Well, not all of us. Jen would have nothing to do with a trash bag full of days-old baked goods for reasons I'm sure you can fathom, and Judith seconded her motion. But the rest of the party didn't seem to give a shit, myself included. I kind of liked how the frosted toppings and sweet fillings from the crushed donuts transferred onto the salty, garlicky bagels. The mixing of the incongruous flavors made for a sort of sweet and sour experience I found quite satisfying in my morning hunger.

Once we all had our fill, we engaged in some hardcore goofing off. I spent the first full day there chatting with the other folk, scribbling in my road journal and lounging around on dusty blankets in the shade of the pines. Nobody had any weed, or if they did they were not sharing it. But that was fine. I was enjoying the idleness of this new scene and found that idleness, in and of itself, to be sufficiently occupying.

Around mid-afternoon, Zed suggested someone should volunteer to go hunt for some firewood, as our supply of combustibles was greatly diminished. Being eager to be useful, and having had my fill of dusty lounging, I jumped at the opportunity. Pete and Aiden joined me, and together we strode off into the bush to see what we could find.

The area was picked pretty clean, so we had to trek far afield before we started finding firewood of any worth. But still, it was nice to get out into the forest anyway. It was hot and dry, and the air smelled vaguely of pine tar everywhere. Our hands quickly became sticky with the sap of the dead branches we were collecting. No one thought to bring a rope to bind our bundles of sticks, so I again volunteered my belt to the cause as I had done a few weeks before. My pants were now so loose without the help of my belt that I had to keep one hand in my pocket just to keep them from sliding off my ass. Day by day I was becoming more lean, more seasoned, more feral out there on the road, and I found the progressive change exciting.

Pete and Aiden chatted continuously as we hunted, mostly about drugs and stories about drugs. I just listened, like I often did. Listened to my companions' wild stories of hallucinatory excursions into inappropriate situations, but also to the forest around me, the few birds chirping in the pines, the soft crunch our footfalls made when small sticks were broken in the mats of dry needles. I soon found myself lagging far behind the other two, finding the story of the forest around me more engaging.

When we returned, we found that another carload of travelers in an old, heavily rusted Jeep Wagoneer with Illinois plates had pulled up and were mingling with our camp. Three kids from Chicago, in three dirty ball caps pulled low over their brows; Jake, Ben, and Tom. They had also brought beer; a couple cases of cheap cans, warm and agitated from bouncing around in the back of their truck on the ride into the woods. We started knocking back the beers with glee, completely indifferent to the elevated temperature of the beverages, and stoked the flames of the fire high in the fading light of the evening with the sticks we had only just gathered.

Later, after more than half of the beers had been drunk and the waxing moon had risen high above the trees, two of the Chicago kids produced a couple of djembe drums from the back of their rusted truck and began hammering away in the firelight.

The third kid came out with a half full handle bottle of cheap whiskey which began making the rounds. I took a long pull when it found me, absorbing the harsh burning the strong liquor instilled in my throat.

The warm fuzzies in my gut really lifted off then, having had no food since the dumpster donuts earlier that morning. Aiden and Barb began dancing in a slow, creamy sort of way, their arms undulating in a fluid continuous motion. Pete joined them, moving in more of a hopping skank, and soon a few others of our group had joined in, myself included. I had never really thought of myself as much of a dancer, always self-conscious to the point of stiffness. But that night, loosened by the alcohol and the mountain night I found I had enough rhythm to keep pace with these crusty dirt ravers. This went on for a while, I guess. My sense of time had become so polluted by then that it could have been fifteen minutes, two hours, I could not tell. All I knew was that it felt good.

Eventually I had to stop, my head spinning with fatigue, so I propped myself up against a tree in exhaustion and watched as the few remaining kids still swayed to the now slower, rolling rhythm the drummers were still producing. I was about to succumb to my drunk and nod off there against the tree, when a set of headlights cut across the camp, the headlights of a white, snub-nosed VW bus. The drumming continued as tall bald man with a huge reddish beard and heavy framed eyeglasses, dressed in long white robes, approached our firelit drum and dance circle, a large German shepherd trotting along at his side.

"Holy shit! Egg Man!" someone called out. Zed and the man embraced once he entered the firelight, which Aiden and Barb soon joined as a group hug. "You cut off your dreads!" Zed exclaimed, as he pulled away from the hug, his hands grasping this Egg Man's shoulders.

The Egg Man threw his head back and laughed aloud. "Yes, yes I did," was his reply.

He sat down cross legged by the fire, his big dog beside him, and proceeded to produce a tin box full of joints from his flowing white robe. He pulled two out and lit them both at the same time, sending one in each direction. The stereo of the drums ceased momentarily as each drummer pulled a few hits before renewing the beats in intensity. Soon we were all dancing again, except Egg and Zed who sat close to each other on the ground, rapt in eager discussion. After a few reels around the fire, Zed caught my eye and waved me in towards them.

"I want you to meet someone," he said to me, his voice almost lost in the echoing percussive atmosphere. "This is the Egg Man."

"Hey, man," I said, reaching out to grasp his hand.

"It's a pleasure," he replied. His smile was warm and sincere. He then said something else that was lost in the din of the drums but waved me on with a grin when I replied to his query with a questioning head cock. With that I rejoined the flow of the delirious dancers, my comprehension slowly fading into oblivion.

Finally, when I could dance no more, I climbed into the car, spent and numb while the drumming continued unabated. I lay there for a while and wondered just how the hell those two kids could keep up their drumming for so long without a break, when it abruptly ceased. The sudden silence seemed even louder than the rhythmic beating still echoing in my head, and with that I passed out.

I slept late into the morning, finally awoken by hunger, thirst, and the need to piss. I stumbled away from the camp and let loose a long, yellow stream into the dust, the impacts of my intimate liquids sending mud splatters onto my bare feet. Back in camp, I found the Egg Man hunched over the smoldering fire pit, attempting to breathe new life into a small teepee of sticks he had built, his white robes dirty with ashes. He rose with a wide smile in a cloud of piney wood smoke as I approached.

"Good morning!" he said cheerily, his eyes unnaturally small behind the thick lenses of his glasses. I noticed then that the long white cloak he was wrapped in was actually a thick bathrobe delicately embroidered over the left breast with the name of a fancy five-star hotel. "Are you hungry?" he asked. "I'm going to scramble up a whole bunch of eggs here in a minute."

The words "scramble" and "eggs" were enough to cause my guts to emit an audible growl, which he must have heard because he let out a chuckle once the rumbling had said its peace.

He got the fire down to a good bed of coals and dropped a comically large, restaurant-sized frying pan down on the glowing embers, unwrapped a whole stick of butter into the pan, and began cracking eggs one at a time into the sizzling fat.

"Help me out here, man. Start cracking these eggs into this pan while I stir."

I obliged and soon had released about two dozen of them, which he worked to fold with a small plastic spatula, dwarfed even more by the huge pan he was working in. He finished it off with some salt, and that was it.

"I hope you guys got plates," he said into the sizzling eggs.

"I think we have some paper plates or something," I replied. "We have some sliced bread, that could work well enough."

"Great idea!" he agreed "What else you got to add to this breakfast feast?"

"Hold on, lemme see." And I jogged off to the car. Bread, hot sauce, beans. I brought what I thought might go with the eggs, returning with a couple plates and a wad of newspapers that would have to do for those who had nothing to eat off of.

By now, most of the camp was waking up, drawn from their tents by the aroma of frying eggs, and were gathering around the fire waiting for breakfast to be served. Egg Man opened the two cans of our beans and dumped them into the steaming egg mess. "Ok, everybody grab a plate or whatever," he announced and began dropping spatula fulls of the beans and eggs into whatever the kids came forward with. I had an aluminum mess kit with two pans in it, and I let the runaway girls use the extra one, which they both shared. I also let them use my spoon, so I ended up sort of drinking the food off the side of the pan for want of a utensil. God damn, but the food was good. You don't know just how hungry you are till you've got food in your mouth after a good long fast.

Once the pan had been licked clean, another two joints were released, and with full bellies we reclined around the fire in the shade and digested. This weed the Egg Man was so generously distributing was killer, better than anything I had been smoking on the trip so far, and it left me with a buzzing high so intense it felt like the earth was gently vibrating.

The rest of the day was spent in much the same fashion as the previous one, with baked idleness being the common cause for us all. I wound up talking with this Egg Man for a while and found him to be a most interesting fellow.

"Where are you from?" he asked me as we reclined. "Your slight accent sounds vaguely familiar."

"I'm from New York" I replied, surprised I even had a discernible accent, since we are not known to have accents where I'm from. "Far eastern New York, out on Long Island."

"Ha! I'm from Long Island too! Nassau County." Then I got a whiff of his latent accent, his defenses coming down.

We went on to describe our hometowns in varying degrees of detail. I always liked to describe where I came from because it was often so very different from what most everyone else had experienced growing up, coming from a tiny island accessible only by boat like I did. But he was familiar with the place, having been out that way once before. His town, on the other hand, was foreign to me; one of those up-island towns with old Indian names I'd known only by the assemblage of their Helvetica-font letters on the expressway exit signs. Long Island was one, well, long ass island. There were many places west of Riverhead I'd never been to; likewise for anyone from the west end of the island, many of them had never been east past the last exit on the expressway.

But he hadn't been back that way in a few years due to a falling out with his family.

"I'm Jewish," he explained. "I was born into an orthodox family, a very traditional family, and they demanded I be a certain way, to act a certain way. They had a path all laid out for me I was not to deviate from; business school, orthodox wife, big house in the suburbs, lots of kids. I dropped acid a bunch in college, opened up my eyes. I just couldn't follow their path any longer. I tried to explain it to them, but they would have none of it and cut me off. So I dropped out and hit the road, been on the road ever since."

I was rapt. I wondered if his family were like those ultra-orthodox people in their prominent hats I had seen in Brooklyn on the beginning of our trip. So I asked him.

"The Hasidim? No, no," he replied with a laugh. "Not that orthodox. What about you? Zed tells me you are a righteous man. That you walk with convictions, he said."

I felt a flush of embarrassment. How did Zed know I was religious? Maybe the spirit was with him after all. And how would Egg take my faith, being as Jesus was supposed to be the savior his people had been waiting for but denied, and crucified. I attempted to explain my faith in bumbling awkwardness, and he listened with polite interest. But in the end, I'm not sure if he really got it, maybe because I didn't really get it myself. Not that it much mattered I came to realize, because he didn't believe in God one way or the other.

"I'm an atheist," he confessed. "I don't really think there is any God out there pulling the strings. I think this life is all we get. Maybe, if we're lucky, there's some kind of reincarnation or something, since matter cannot be destroyed, only changed and reconstituted. But we'll probably just come back as dust, since that's all we really are anyway. Just dust in space."

"Nah, fuck that," Tick chimed in, having dropped into our conversation from behind. "We'll probably come back as a steaming pile of dog shit, Ha! Picture that, reborn from the asshole of some dirty old dog!"

The thought of being born again in such a way was admittedly funny, albeit a little disturbing from my perspective. I let out a nervous chuckle involuntarily. "Don't get all bent out of shape, there church boy," he shot at me once he caught whiff of my reaction, his acne-scarred face twisted in an unholy grin.

Just then another car arrived; a shiny new SUV with a cargo pod on the roof. This new car had Tennessee tags and two blond girls at the helm. Tick promptly abandoned our circle and beelined over to them, instantly forgetting his blasphemous game of shock with me. He started macking it to them right away, opening their door with theatrical bravado and welcoming them into our camp. He led them over to our group around the fire and began introducing some of us. They were good-looking girls, in a generic sort of way, both with long blond hair and dressed in clean, sporty attire. What struck me was the polar opposite attitudes they expressed. One was bubbly and outgoing, greeting us all with a big smile, and the other sullen and withdrawn, refusing eye contact, her complexion almost gray compared to that of her traveling companion.

They went about setting up their new, bold-colored, high-end tent adjacent to where they had parked their gleaming new 4X4, assisted by Tick, Aiden, and Pete. I hung back from that scene, not wanting to get caught up in an old-time cock sparring session, and took to scribbling some thoughts into my sketch book. I was still chewing on Egg's admission of atheism, a term for me wrapped up with all the darkest evil the devil could muster.

I had never met anyone who flew the flag of the godless, not that I knew of anyway. I had always expected someone like that to be a very bad person indeed. But this Egg Man, this gentle, selflessly giving goofball in a bathrobe was not at all what I envisioned when the church elders warned me about those lecherous minions of Satan, those hopelessly lost souls in league with the devil. How could this be? How could someone with such a good soul be in the employ of the evil one? This was going to call for some serious reflection, some serious prayer. And what better time and place than this? Tomorrow was Sunday, and I had all the time in the world, with shit to do out here in the woods but just sit around and think about it.

CHAPTER 20

It was cold that night, colder than it had yet been on the trip. It was the fall season after all, so what more could be expected. We had been enjoying an unseasonably warm climate all the way so far, but like all good things that couldn't last forever. Everyone had turned in early once the sun went down, including me, driven into our tents and cars by a stiff breeze bearing down on us from the north. I lay awake in the back seat of the Olds for a while unable to sleep, listening to the wind whistle through the pines, overcome by a distinct feeling of loneliness despite being surrounded by the communal camaraderie of the other folk in camp. But it wasn't a social loneliness; no, it was something deeper, something fundamental. My dreams were dark and cold all night, mirroring the atmosphere outside the car. I awoke frequently, nagged by some indescribable urging that seemed determined to disrupt my rest.

The last time sleep slipped from me I found the dawn was fast approaching, so I arose. It being another Sunday, I resigned myself for the ritual I had sworn to God to perform. I dressed, gathered my things, and slipped quietly out of camp, lightly treading the frosted ground in the stillness of the morning, my dirty black hoodie pulled tight around my head to keep out the chill.

Deep into the forest I went, wanting to put as much distance between my convictions and the camp as I felt I could safely do without getting hopelessly lost. I eventually found a lichen-encrusted boulder facing east towards a break in the trees a good way off from camp and felt it would do well enough. There I sat and welcomed the warmth of the rising sun. I performed my communion ritual, trying hard to really feel it, to really experience Christ's sacrifice. But it just felt empty to me. The feeling of emptiness rose in me as the sun rose till I was filled with angst and bathed in warm sunlight.

I prayed and I pleaded, but it did not help to alleviate the overwhelming feeling I had that I was out there alone, pleading and praying to no one but myself. Show me your face, God! I silently shouted to the heavens in impotent desperation, the morning sun sending daggers into my eyes. Show me so that I might know I'm not holding my life to these convictions in vain!

I took my time heading back to camp, hoping to compose myself, and chewed on these heretical musings like some giant ball of artificially flavored bubble gum as I walked. What if Egg Man is right? What if there really is no God, and all this guilt I carry around is unnecessary? What if there is only just the natural world by itself, for itself, indifferent to my prayers? What if I've been wasting my precious few years on this spinning rock fretting over appeasing a being that does not even exist? The thought made me mad, made me feel like a chump. But what if he was wrong? I shuddered to think of the consequences of that outcome; it'd mean a ticket to hell for sure for that gentle giant. Maybe even hell for me if I continued to doubt.

"Fuck!" I yelled aloud in desperation, kicking a stick lying in my path. The flying stick smacked loudly against a nearby pile of sun-dappled stones, instantly pissing off a large rattler snake that had been catching what it could of the morning sun. "Whoa, shit!" I exclaimed, lurching back from the rattling coil of death. The serpent watched me as I backed away, slowly tightening its coil as if winding up to strike. That was enough to clear away the clouds of doubt for the moment; fight or flight has a way of prioritizing matters of immediate importance. I hustled back to camp flushed with adrenaline, keeping a keen eye on where I put my feet.

I found Zed alone by the fire pit when I returned, his back to me, hunched over a boiling pot of tea.

"Blessings on this morning," he announced, his back still to me. "Join me for the bitter tea?"

I sat beside him cross legged in the dust without speaking. There over a small bed of coals, segregated from the rest of the large fire pit, a dented and smoke-stained aluminum tea pot steamed thin wisps of vapor in the chilly morning air. He had two chipped, mismatched coffee cups set up on a flat rock and a fat bundle of some gray leaves on an oval, tarnished silver plate tied up tight with string, the end of which was smoldering like a fat cigar.

He took the gray bundle in his hands and blew gently into the embers. A thick, fragrant smoke was released as the stump sizzled and popped, the vapors of which rose about his face, swirling around his little dreads and into the air around us. He coughed deeply a few times, then handed the bundle to me, motioning me to do the same. So I did, and the smoke rose around my face as well. It had a distinctive smell, somehow familiar, though I could not place from where. Letting the smoke wash over my face had a surprisingly soothing effect, and I felt the cold uneasiness that had haunted me all night rise with the smoke and dissipate into the trees.

"What is this stuff?" I asked him.

"Sage. The smoke has a cleansing effect," he quietly replied as he poured a very dark tea into the cups. "Here, let us sip the bitter tea and talk."

I took the old coffee mug and put it to my lips. The liquid was scalding hot, so I blew a few puffs of breath across its surface. The warm steam felt nice on my face after my chilly morning walk. I took a sip and found the flavor indeed incredibly bitter. I looked to Zed, and he looked back at me from over the rim of his steaming cup, his eyes peaceful and serene.

"So, tell me about your faith," he directly asked me as he sat in a lotus like position, his mug of tea in his lap, cradled between his ashy hands. "You follow the teachings of Jesus, yes?"

"Yes, I do," I replied. "Church of Christ, actually. How did you know?"

"Mmmm…" he hummed, taking a moment before he continued, without answering my question. "The denomination is not important. They are all basically the same once you cut away the ceremonies and traditions. Jesus was a good man, with some very good core ideas, ideas shared by many different faiths and traditions. All of the organized religions of man to some degree, actually. Though, over the centuries his followers have corrupted almost everything he ever said. So much time has now passed since his days that it's near impossible to know for sure what he really wanted of his followers, if anything beyond living right lives. And there are some who suspect that he may have never even existed at all, that he was just a character dreamt up by Hebrew dissidents and used to legitimize a political movement against the Roman occupation that grew far beyond its initial purpose, taking on a life of its own."

We sat there in silence for a few moments, my emotions swirling madly inside from rage to hopelessness to fear. Was I under attack, or was he throwing me a life ring? The signs of this internal struggle must have been apparent on my face for he continued.

"How do you feel about what I've just said?" he asked gently. "How do my statements make you feel, in your body?"

I groaned audibly. "Not too good, man. I feel kinda sick to my stomach."

"You are searching for the truth, and there is no nobler pursuit. But I feel your journey is far from over. There will be many hardships and many trials to face before you will know in your soul what you desire to know. I can sit here and tell you anything, any manner of bullshit, but in the end, they will only be my truths, not yours. You need to find those truths for yourself." He took another long sip of his tea, gazing into the steaming vessel once he had pulled it from his lips.

"You have goodness still in you that most no longer possess," he added, looking me now in the eyes. "Many have let their goodness waste away. Many have chosen to spend their goodness on cheap thrills, on dust."

"I feel very alone," I added involuntarily.

"You are alone. We are all alone in this life. That is why we crave each other's company. That is why we travel together."

I felt like running away into the forest just to get away from his piercing gaze, but I was frozen there, my cup of tea radiating heat into my hands almost unbearably.

"You have a positive energy that is very strong; your aura shimmers like amethyst. Even now you sparkle in the morning light." He sat there for a few moments staring intently, seemingly fixed on some point above my head. "You are welcome to travel with me, with us, for as long as you need to."

A shimmering aura? I had no idea what the hell he was talking about. "Uh, thanks," I replied, sipping the astringently bitter tea again. He continued looking intently into my eyes a few moments more and then emptied his tea in one gulp.

"You're welcome," he stated bluntly as he placed his cup on a stone by the fire. "Now, let me smudge you to close our communion," he added, reaching for the sage bundle.

He took the sage then and relit it on the coals of the fire, stoking the cherry gently with his breath as he had done before. Once a good cloud of smoke was emanating from the burning end, he took the bundle and sort of waved it slowly around me as he hummed quietly in a low register till I was wrapped in the strong smoke. He then took my hand and bid me to rise with him. "Blessings on you, brother," he whispered as he embraced me tightly. He then collected the smoldering sage, teapot and cups and took them into the RV, shutting the door behind him.

I sat there alone for a while, processing the experience and absorbing what warmth was still radiating from the fire pit. What the fuck was that all about, I thought. I didn't feel he had come at me from a malicious place, but still, he was challenging me and my faith at a very fundamental level. But wasn't I lately challenging myself in much the same way? My doubts by now were too strong to shelve for later consideration, too strong to simply to ignore, and Zed's little impromptu one-on-one ritual with me only shook my foundations even further. God, I just wanted to close my eyes and make the conflictions go away, so I in fact found myself engaging in just that. I sat there in my self-imposed darkness, trying valiantly to think of absolutely nothing. But I couldn't get the thought out of my head; I am no Christian. I am a fraud. An absolute, bold-faced lying fraud, wasting my youth in the pursuit of inanimate doctrine, too afraid to make my life mine, too full of doubts to give it to Jesus.

Judith then approached, joining me by the fire pit and shattering the silent spell of my introverted thought.

"Good morning, kid. How'd you fare through the chill of the night?"

"Oh, fine," I replied, opening my eyes again to the radiant morning. "It's pretty cozy in the back of our car."

"I much prefer a tent myself." I imagine you do, I thought. "I was going to go hunt for some mushrooms this morning, see if the frost left me anything. Would you like to join me?" she asked as she squatted down on her haunches beside me, the heavy leather sheath of her big knife thumping against the ground as she perched.

"Sure, that sounds good. Thank you."

"No problem, kid," she replied, rising with me.

I followed her out into the forest, the frost of the night now totally turned into dew. It was much warmer already, and the sun was beaming through the canopy, illuminating patches of damp pine needles all around us and producing amorphous blobs of blazing light all over the forest floor.

"It's beautiful out here, don't you think?" she asked me. I agreed, and we continued in silence a while longer. "I heard some of what Zed was saying to you this morning from my tent," she finally ventured. "He's a very spiritual man, you know. Something of a guide, really. But I differ from him on some points. He can be brash and reckless, but his heart comes from a good place, I believe. He's helped many kids on down their paths."

I made no reply but continued walking by her side. It was indeed beautiful out here in the forest, and I felt grateful to her for inviting me along. Occasionally she would stop and kick some needles, I assume looking for these elusive mushrooms, but she never bent down to collect anything. I had no idea what to look for, really. Mushrooms, I know, but I wasn't seeing anything obvious growing out of the ground.

"Not much out here, huh?"

"Oh, no, there's plenty to see out here, just not what we're looking for," she answered, stopping again for another kick in the needles. "Sometimes it's the search that's more important than the finding. Sometimes it's all about the seeing."

"I saw a rattler snake out here this morning when I went out at dawn, right over there on those rocks," I blurted out, suddenly recognizing the place from only an hour or so before.

"What? There's no rattlers up here at this elevation. And it's too late in the season for them anyway," she declared. "It's impossible."

"Well, I saw a big-ass snake there in the sun on those rocks just this morning. I kicked a stick and it smacked against them. The sound the snake made when the stick hit sure sounded like a rattle to me."

She looked at me hard. "I find that very hard to believe. I've been out in these woods all summer and I've never seen one. Maybe you only thought you saw one."

"I don't know, Judith. Looked like a fucking killer snake to me." She still did not appear convinced.

"What were you doing out here at dawn anyway?" she continued, turning her hard gaze away from me and continuing her slow trek between the evenly spaced trees.

"I was, uh…" I suddenly felt like I was caught redhanded doing something sneaky. "I was communing with God, or trying to anyway."

"Trying?" she asked, stopping again and turning back around to face me.

"Yeah, I try to do that every Sunday, to commune with God. But it felt empty this morning, like I was alone."

"You demand he show up, prove himself?"

"Yes, I did." And the fear began to rise.

"Well, maybe that snake was sent by the spirit of the one you seek." That sent a shiver down my frame so intense she must have noticed my contortion. She continued, "Many of the Native Americans believe the snake is a bad omen."

"What does it mean?" I asked a little desperately, instantly jumping to a demonic conclusion.

"That's not for me to say. Like Zed said, you have a long road ahead of you before you'll find the answers you seek. Keep searching and you will find what you are looking for."

We continued on in silence for a moment before she suddenly laughed aloud. "Look!" she said then, directing my attention to the treetops with her outstretched arm. "A hawk is passing overhead. Now that is a very good omen, so take heart, kid."

I followed the large, mottled raptor with my eyes till the canopy obscured its passing and continued looking blankly into the treetops long after it sailed beyond sight, my neck craned skyward. I wished I could fly away, wished I could soar like that hawk, high above my troubles.

Back at camp I found most of the residents awake and milling about, it being near noon by now. I spotted my companions over by their tent, and strode directly toward them. I caught Pete by surprise with a big hug.

"I love you guys," I exclaimed giddily.

He laughed. "You alright, man?" he asked, his wide smile cracking crookedly across his face. "You goin off on another freak-out in the woods all morning?"

"Nah. Well, yeah, I guess," I stumbled out goofily. "Nah, I'm fine."

"That Jesus shit is gonna be the death of you, bud."

"Don't you talk shit on my Jesus!" I shot back with a grin, feeling a little belligerent in my mental fatigue. He threw his arm around my shoulder, pulling me in tight. I could see Jen nearby shaking her head, a half-smile splitting her dour countenance as well. I really did love these guys. These were my people; they had my back and I had theirs. I'm not so alone, I thought. I am a part of a much larger community here that I am only just beginning to discover. I am part of something larger than myself, here on the road with these kids. The concept was fulfilling, empowering even. And for the first time all morning, all forever really, I felt like I could really grab this life by the balls free of guilt, free of second guesses. This was my life to wield; this was my birthright.

The rest of the day wound away like the ones before it, and as evening approached I found myself kicking it again with Egg Man and his big German shepherd. The conversation made its way seemingly on its own towards what I had been into all morning, so before I knew it I was telling him all about what both Zed and Judith had said to me. He stroked his long reddish-brown beard as I wove my little tale, often letting a side smile loose when matters of spirituality factored in. When I was done, he voiced his opinion.

"I love Zed, but he's no kinda spirit guide," he declared with a laugh. "Take anything he says with a grain of salt."

"What did he mean by seeing an aura around me?"

"Probably just an acid flash back," he laughed. "Nah, there's people who believe that we all have this colorful aura of light around our heads that most of us can't see. I'm a skeptic, I need proof, scientific proof before I will subscribe to something like that. I sure as hell have never seen an aura. But I can't disprove it either, so I'm willing to admit that I could be wrong. I've seen some crazy-ass shit while on acid," he added. "But my gut tells me that it's bullshit. All in your head." And he tapped his temple with a finger.

"What about Judith sayin' that the snake I saw was some kinda ominous vision?"

"It's true, we are pretty high up in elevation here for rattler snakes, and it is pretty late in the season at that, but I bet if you asked a real expert they'd concede that it is possible, however slim, that you did come up on a rattler snake."

That was a relief, partly anyway. It was not so easy for me to sweep away the perceived presence of the evil one so easily, even with a rational explanation at my disposal. I let out a long sigh.

"Come on, let's smoke a joint, that'll settle your mind," he suggested, leaning forward, looking at me from over the rims of his heavy eyeglasses. And he produced his little tin box again from under his dingy bathrobe. Once we had passed the thing back and forth between us enough times to achieve the desired effect, my curiosity got out in front of me, and I asked him the question that had been rolling around in my head since the night we met.

"Dude, what's with the bathrobe?"

"Ha! You like it?" he asked, popping the collar with his thumbs. "It's a good look, right?"

"Yeah, you looked like some wandering prophet when you came into the firelight the other night."

"Ha! Me, a prophet!" he laughed. "A regular Isaiah, eh? No, I got it down in Denver last week. I closed a big deal, made a nice chunk of change and treated myself to the best hotel in town, complete with a posh spa treatment. The robe was so comfortable I decided to keep it."

"A deal?" I asked. He held up the still smoking roach between his fingers with a grin. "Oh, yeah. I get it. A deal." And I received the roach from him one last time, pulling the last few puffs from its ember and exhaling the thick smoke into the mountain atmosphere around us.

CHAPTER 21

I awoke the next morning to someone pounding ferociously on the window of the car. I hollered out in alarm, sitting up involuntarily. There on the other side of the glass was a clean shaven, scowling face in a tan Smokey Bear hat, glaring in at me.

"Hey! You in there! Get your shoes on and get out of the car!" he yelled, turning away once he felt confident that I'd gotten the message.

I looked out the window towards the rest of the camp as I struggled to pull my sneakers on. The park ranger was marching off towards the RV with determined strides. Fuck, what's all this about, I worried. I was just getting out of the car when Zed emerged barefoot and shirtless from the camper, his hands up at chest level, palms out.

"What seems to be the trouble, officer?" he asked passively.

"We've been getting complaints down in Nederland; vagrants shoplifting all over town," he stated, hands on his hips. "I know it's your people."

"No, sir. It's not my people, I assure you. We're peaceful, law-abiding citizens here."

"My ass!" he snorted, making a head nod towards the cluster of shabby tents by our car. "Listen, you all have been up here for weeks already, longer than you should be. And I didn't start getting these complaints till you all showed up. That's right; I know when you all arrived. This is my beat; I know what's going on in this forest. I'm giving you two days to clear out, or I'm getting the state troopers up here, you got it?"

"Yes, sir. Of course, sir," Zed answered, his hands still up by his chest. "We certainly would not want to overstay our welcome here in your beautiful forest."

"See that you don't."

Zed then held out his hand. "I give you my word, sir; we'll be gone in two days." The ranger eyed Zed and his outstretched hand with hard suspicion for a moment before finally meeting Zed's hand with his own and shaking it firmly.

"I will hold you to this," the ranger declared, coming in closer to Zed and prolonging his grasp a few moments past the normal amount of time generally allotted for handshakes. Zed held his ground as they stared each other down. The ranger broke it off finally and strode back off to his truck.

I watched his white and green forest patrol vehicle crawl away down the gravely road with a few of the others in the camp who had emerged from their tents awoken by the commotion.

"Fuckin' six up pigs!" Tick cursed, spitting into the dust at his feet.

"No, no, that guy was alright," Zed corrected. "He gave us two days to leave; he didn't have to do that. He had good energy, despite how he rolled in here. He will keep his word, and I will keep mine."

So we began to make our preparations to break camp. Around the breakfasting fire we debated what our next destination should be and our means of attaining it. Or rather, they did, since they had been doing this traveling thing for a while already and had a handle on where to go next. I didn't much care where we were headed next, as long as it wasn't in the direction we'd come from, and my companions felt the same. A few southern locales were put on the table, but it was quickly decided upon to trek to a town called Quartzsite in Arizona. This town was something of a desert outpost that swelled in size in the winter months with hundreds of road travelers escaping the colder latitudes. There they would all converge, settling down in a sort of impromptu camp around the small cluster of cinder block buildings that made up the town. Some sort of a trading bazaar was also underway there during these winter months, dealing mainly in gems and minerals, though other flea market type stuff was on offer there as well. There could be opportunities to hustle up some money, they assured us.

But first, they would need to spend a few days down in Boulder to re-stock, and to pick up gas riders to help rustle up money for fuel. Since they were all pretty much broke, and the trip ahead was going to be a whole lot of miles, they were going to need all the help they could get keeping fuel in the tank. This they said they could accomplish by picking up riders who would either chip in cold hard cash if they had it or would work for their ride by begging for money at the truck stops, which in the road parlance of the day was called spainge'n, or by providing some other kind of service to help keep the ride rolling along. They figured, since the winter was approaching, there would be enough of a pool of road kids in town looking for a ride south they'd have their pick of the best. Sounded like sound logic to me. The only hitch was us. Would we really want to hang around Boulder for days, waiting to roll out? We were a self-contained, self-propelled entity not really set up to camp on city streets. So, we decided to push south on our own and rendezvous with them somewhere on down the road.

"Sedona," Zed decided. "We'll meet you in Sedona, Arizona. The place is super chill, super kind. You can camp out up in the national forest for as long as you need, but we really shouldn't be much more than a week."

"Sedona is beautiful," Judith added, "and a very powerful place. The mountains there are full of energy, positive energy."

She went on to describe the landscape of the region briefly, with its blood red rocks irregularly formed by the elements. It did sound striking, and with that we were sold.

"Now…" Zed declared. "Now we need to have a feast of thanksgiving. This place here has been kind to us, so we need to celebrate it. Tick, Barb, Aiden, I need you three to trek down into Ned and get the makings of a feast. Food, wine, you know what we need. Spare no expense," he added with a crooked smile.

"We're gonna need a ride," Aiden said. "I'm not hiking back up the mountain with a ton of shit on my back."

"The rich girls!" Tick exclaimed, jumping up from his squat. "Hold on, I'll get those little rich girls to give us a ride." And he strode over to their tent, popping his head inside. "All good!" he called back to us moments later, his thumb in the air.

"So, that settles that. Judith, Egg, what are you guys going to do? Will you travel with us?" Zed asked, turning his attention to them.

"No, I'm not ready to move yet," Judith answered. "I think I'll stay here a few weeks more; the cool weather here is feeling pretty good to me right now."

"Not me," Egg said, wrapped tightly in his dingy bathrobe. "It's too damn cold for me here already. I'm headed to San Diego. I need some ocean beach in my life. I'm gonna bounce out tomorrow morning."

"Good call, as long as you stay for the feast," Zed added.

"What about the two runaway girls?" Pete asked, prompting a hard look from Jen.

"We'll offer them a ride, but I'd really rather they make off on their own. They are both underage, and probably fugitives. Could be trouble for us if we got hassled by the cops."

"They'll be trouble for you too, Peter," Jen added, prompting him to roll his eyes.

I spent the rest of the morning kicking it with the Egg Man and watching the dogs roll around and play in the dirt. Dylan had really matured since we had begun this trip; and his overall demeanor was much more measured compared to Zed's kooky little dog, and especially to Summer's hyperactive, unsupervised, untrained puppy. The poor little guy was way too thin for a pup his age and craved attention to the point of desperation, which tended to annoy the other dogs. Summer didn't seem to be up to the task of caring for him, so he had sort of become communal property. The little pup really took a shine to Egg Man and his big dog who, though being more than twice his size, was perfectly gentle with him in play and limitless in patience.

"This little guy is so cute," Egg confided to me as he watched the little pup attempt to wrestle with his big stately dog. "That girl doesn't deserve such a sweet little puppy."

"I'm sure she loves him." I offered.

"I'm sure she does, or at least thinks she does," he conceded. "But look at him; he's hungry, he's dirty." He snapped his fingers and the pup instantly dropped what he was doing and came to him, abandoning his attempts to take down his oversized sparring partner.

"Yeah, that's true. Maybe she'll just give him to you."

"Maybe I'll just confiscate him for the greater good," he stated, gently stroking the young dog's head.

"You should ask her first."

"Of course, I'm going to ask her," he replied. "I'm just not going to let her say no."

Around noon, Judith approached Pete for a ride down into Ned to stop by the post office, and for a few supplies of her own from the supermarket there in town. He had been having some issue with Jen all morning, I wasn't sure about what, but I could feel the negative vibes radiating off them whenever I approached. Pete suggested I drive her down because he wasn't feeling up to it. So I agreed.

This was the first time we'd started the car since we got there, and it put up quite a fight. The cold and the elevation worked against the old vintage carburetor, throwing the air fuel mixture far to the rich side. But I eventually got her running, and down the mountain we cruised in a cloud of hydrocarbon fumes and dust.

"Got any music to listen to?" Judith asked me once we had pulled onto the pavement at the end of the long gravel road.

"Sure. Down on the floor there, there's a box of tapes."

"Aha!" She exclaimed, pulling out the old Judas Priest tape I had gotten from the thrift store so many miles ago. "I haven't heard this one in ages." She slid the cassette into the dashboard radio and started patting her hand to the beat on the outside of the door where she had rested her arm. I was really starting to dig this girl, or rather woman, since she was at least twenty years my senior.

On down the mountain we rolled, and before we had played through a second song we were rolling into the local supermarket parking lot. She said she wouldn't be long and that I could wait in the car if I wanted, but I had a mind to stroll through the store to get a little local flavor and maybe something to munch on.

The market was a small one, with a rustic western theme sparsely populated by mostly average looking white people, though I did spot a few hippie types. I still had a few bucks cash from the last traveler's check I broke, so I grabbed a few things impulsively to snack on. I was headed back to the front of the store when I came around the corner of an aisle and spotted Tick in the process of sliding a rack of shrink-wrapped pork ribs down his pants. I whipped around back the way I came before he saw me, so I wouldn't get caught up in any shit if he had been spotted by someone other than myself. Man, that was some bold shit, I thought, smiling to myself. That ranger was right; Zed's crew are shoplifting down in Ned. Guess that's what Zed meant by "spare no expense."

I made my way up to the registers in a hurry, just to get out of there before I bumped into Tick face to face, and got caught behind a few other shoppers in line at the one open register. Just ahead of me in line was a girl in a hoodie holding a single jar of red pasta sauce. Wait a minute, that's Barb, I realized as she half turned towards me, acknowledging me coyly with a wink. Oh shit, I thought, she's in here too. The person in front of her completed their business, and Barb moved forward to take their place. Instead of placing the jar of sauce she was carrying on the counter, she went to hand it to the cashier girl, and just as the girl was about to grab it I saw Barb sort of pull her pinky in on the bottom edge of the jar, which caused it to lurch out of the cashier's grasp, bounce off the counter, and hit the floor with a shattering splat, sending glass shards and red sauce everywhere within a yard of the register.

"Oh, shit! I'm sorry!" she exclaimed, as she quickly grabbed a handful of plastic bags off the counter and began to smear the mess in a bullshit attempt to clean it up.

"No, no, we'll get the mop. Don't use those bags, you're making it worse," the cashier girl was saying in a panic. All eyes were on this scene for a few moments, except for mine as I watched both Tick and Aiden calmly stroll out the front door of the place like they were invisible, their oversized pants and hoodies oddly lumpy. Man, I thought, I don't think I'd have the steady hand to pull off some shit like this.

"I'm sorry, I'm sorry," Barb kept saying as the girl left to get a mop, or somebody with a mop, or something. "I'll be right back," she said to the cashier in a bubbly, singsong way as she was stepping away. "I still need that sauce." And with that Barb retreated. I watched her as she made her way to the edge of an aisle then double back and stroll out the door herself. Their job was done.

"Excuse me, buddy," somebody behind me said. I turned around to see a pimply-faced teenager with a mop bucket. "Gotta clean up here, man." I stepped back to let him through.

"Over here," the exasperated cashier girl called to me from an adjacent checkout lane. "I'll take you over here. Will that be all, sir?" the checkout girl asked with a sigh once I had queued up.

"Uh, yeah," I replied absentmindedly. "Here, and one of these too," I added, grabbing a random Rocky Mountain themed postcard off a rack by the register and placing it next to my sugary snack cakes.

Judith was already at the car when I returned, sitting on the hood with a single shopping bag at her side.

"D'you see those guys in there?" I asked.

"What guys?"

"Tick, Barb, and Aiden. They were robbin' the place blind."

"Ha, no, didn't see 'em. Those three are like shoplifting ninjas." I just shook my head in awe and mild disbelief. Ninjas indeed!

The next stop after that sideshow was the post office. I had no idea where I was going in this little mountain town, so Judith had to direct, having been there once before. It took her a minute to find the place again, and we had to turn around once, realizing we had passed it, but we got there. While she was inside, I quickly scribbled a note on the postcard along with my parents' home address and joined her inside to buy a few stamps.

"Postcard to home?" she asked. I just smiled and shook my head yes.

Camp was quiet when we returned, with no one out and about except Jen, who was sitting alone by the cold fire pit, wrapped in a blanket.

"What's up?" I asked as I approached. She looked up at me with red puffy eyes. She had been crying.

"Nothing," she replied, returning her gaze to the ashes of the fire pit. I sat down on a log nearby.

"Where's Pete?"

"I don't know," she forced out, her response locked inside of a partially suppressed sob. We sat together in silence for a few minutes before she added, "I think Pete is fucking around with that little runaway girl."

"No! Really?" I spit out. "Why would he do that?"

"Why do you think?" she replied sharply, her eyes meeting mine like daggers. "He's always had the wandering eye; I know how he is."

I was at a loss for words, so I sat there and tried to picture where this would lead if it turned out to be true. Would this kill the trip for us? And for her, what would she do, go back to Ithaca and live in her mom's trailer with that smoking asshole trucker boyfriend of hers? Fuck! I hope she's just being paranoid or something, I thought. I liked our little group; I felt I could trust our little group. It would be a major buzz kill if Pete was actually doing what Jen was accusing him of.

"I'm sure he's not," I finally advanced. "He wouldn't do something like that."

"You'd tell me if he was, right?" she asked, her voice strained in desperation, her dagger eyes now blunted and soft. "Please, if you see him wronging me…"

"Yeah, of course," I blurted out, cutting her off. She continued looking into me, her soft eyes slowly hardening again.

"Ok," she said finally, her demeanor solidifying into an emotionless mask. She pushed herself up off her knees and stood. "Ok, ok…" she muttered, trailing off, looking blankly into the ashes of the fire pit. She then silently walked off towards Judith's tent.

I sat there alone for a time, chewing on this latest development. My traveling companions had always been hard on each other, at times putting me in awkward positions as the middleman between their arguments. It was uncomfortable, but I had grown used to it. I kind of felt like I was something of a balancing force for them, but maybe I was just deluding myself. What did I know of relationships? The only relationship I'd ever been in had barely lasted two weeks and ended in a fiery train wreck when my religious convictions crossed the tracks of our young sexual libido. How could I hope to understand what it took to maintain their codependency? I was succumbing to a suffocating despondency at the thought of it all when the Egg Man sat down on the ground beside me, a thick joint hanging from his lips.

"Here," he said to me, holding out the lit joint between his pinched fingers. "Smoke this, and it'll all be fine." I took his advice and started pulling. "Pete up to something shady?"

"Apparently so," I replied, exhaling my hit along with my response. "God, I hope not."

"Mmmm, time will tell. Hup, look here. We got company!" he declared. "Pinch that thing off, would ya. I don't like the looks of this character."

Over on the outskirts of camp, a sparklingly clean, two-tone VW bus had pulled up, and out popped a sparklingly clean, cookie-cutter hippie. He gave an exaggerated wave and began heading right for us.

"This guy's got narc all over him," Egg whispered to me, as he stood up to greet the newcomer. "Hello, sir. Can we help you with something?" he said aloud.

"Hi, guys," the stranger replied with a stiff familiarity. "I heard this is where the travelers are staying."

"Apparently so," answered the Egg. "You travelin' too?"

"Yeah, just passing through."

"Mmmm, yeah. Where ya headed?"

"South ways, chasin' the endless summer, ya know?"

"Well, you're welcome to park here for the night; you got as much right to this place as the rest of us."

"Oh, I have a place down in Ned to park for the night, I just thought I'd come up here and meet some fellow travelers."

"Right," Egg added sarcastically. "Well, you've met us."

"Say, d'you guys know where I could score some weed around here?" the guy asked, seemingly indifferent to Egg's sarcastic tone. I watched as Egg cracked a smile under his bushy mustache.

"Weed?" he responded. "Listen, friend. I think I know what's going on here, so let's cut to the chase. We're on the same team. You see, my partner here and I are undercover FBI agents, and we've been setting up these guys here for a big bust for months." I watched the guy's jaw drop as he stared blankly at Egg, who continued, "We've put in too much time and effort to have you come up here and blow our cover. I think it'd be best if you went back to your superiors and informed them that the Feds have the situation up here under control."

"What? No, you saying I'm a narc or something?" the guy exclaimed. "I'm not a cop!" We did not respond but stayed sternly silent. "You guys are just messin' with me, right?" Still, we remained silent. "Listen, I'll be back. I'll bring some beers and we all can get to know each other, ok? You'll see I'm no cop."

"Yeah, sure," Egg finally offered. "See ya 'round, buddy." And the guy walked back to his bus and drove away.

"That was fuckin' hilarious!" I told my friend.

"Ha! You like that? That guy is a total fuckin' narc. Good thing I'm bouncing out of here tomorrow; hopefully he won't be back till I'm gone."

"Yeah, us too," I agreed. Hopefully we'd all be gone by the time he came back. Narc or not, I did not like the energy I was getting off that guy. Call it a gut feeling, but that guy was not who he was attempting to be.

The remainder of the afternoon was spent around the fire pit, waiting on the supply party to return. Jen had gone off on a hike with Judith, I'm sure to confide in her over her relationship worries, but Zed, Summer, Sherri, and Pete had joined Egg and me there on the sitting logs and stones. I watched for any inappropriate signals from Pete or Sherri, for any signs that something was up between them. I saw nothing. In fact, Pete seemed to engage with Summer, Egg, and myself to the exclusion of Sherri, who sat silent, absentmindedly looking off into the forest while we tossed sticks for the dogs to wrestle over.

Egg began smooth-talking Summer, easing into his plan to take possession of her neglected puppy, and before long had leaned on her hard enough to convince her it would be the right thing to do; for her, and more importantly, for the puppy. It was sort of uncomfortable to witness, for me anyway. Nobody else seemed to mind, but it felt a little too heavy handed to me. Summer verbally acquiesced to his suggestions eventually, but I had a feeling she was only letting the dog go because she was made to feel like she was not up to the task of puppy rearing, which in all honesty she seemingly wasn't. Still, the whole thing felt dirty, but I kept my opinions to myself like I often did, for better or for worse.

The raiding party returned shortly thereafter with a startlingly large quantity of food, wine, and beer. Multiple racks of pork ribs with bottles of grilling sauces, stacks of big steaks, loaves of fancy rustic breads and rolls, all sorts of candy bars, and junk food. It was outrageous. And the booze, 4 big jugs of Pisano wine, two cases of beer, and a handle of vodka! How the hell these kids shoplifted all that loot was beyond me.

"Light the bonfire!" Zed cried, holding up one of the wine jugs by the finger ring. "Let us eat, drink, and be merry, for tomorrow we fly!"

Darkness fell fast, and soon the only light was the blazing orange glow of the fire. Multiple meats were searing over the flames, Egg man's doobies were working the crowd, and the wine was flowing liberally. I quickly lost track of time, as sobriety was strong-armed out the door, and soon found that I was totally wasted once again. I stumbled around, engaging in pointless conversations that amounted to nothing but felt epic and deep in the moment, to me anyway.

Eventually I succumbed to the overwhelming power of the wine and the weed and landed up against a crusty old pine tree a few yards out of the firelight. I sat there and watched the remaining revelers celebrate their collective dissipation in double vision, fighting to keep focus. I could see Tick making out with one of the rich girls, and her companion across from her, rather glumly chugging vodka straight from the bottle. I could see Aiden, his hands all over Barb, their faces pressed together over by the RV. I could see Jen, Judith, and Summer in a triad, wrapped in animated conversation by the fire. I could see Egg and Zed, also deeply engaged with each other in discussion. But where was Pete? And, more importantly, where was Sherri?

I began to get the spins, and my vision grew worse. I struggled to get to my feet, realizing that if I did not get to the car and my sleeping bag soon, I might never make it. I swerved and stumbled in the darkness towards the car, slamming into it with my body. Relieved, I turned back towards the party for one last look. My vision was damn near useless by this point, but movement over by the tents caught my eye. Someone was climbing out of the runaway girls' tent, shoes in hand. It was Pete.

CHAPTER 22

I slept in late, attempting to ignore my latest round of head splitting hangover. But even though I didn't emerge from the back of the Olds till late morning, I still turned out to be one of the first ones up. The only other one who had risen before me was Egg, who had already broke camp and left shortly before I had awoken. I found the spot where his bus had been parked noticeably empty. I had really enjoyed his company, and now that he was gone I found myself feeling the physical emptiness of his parking spot viscerally.

The morning was a brisk one, despite it being almost midday, and I shivered a little in my inadequate clothing there beside the car as I pissed my morning stream upon the tire. I pulled my dirty black hoodie over my head and approached the fire pit to take stock of the situation. It was a total mess. All the trash from last night's revelries lay strewn all over the camp, with a good deal of partially incinerated garbage still smoldering in the fire pit, stinking of burning plastic. The branches above the fire pit were also burned, as if the fire had grown to almost uncontrollable proportions at some point during the night. I sat by the pit and took it all in. Damn, what a fucking shit show this place was. I suddenly found myself totally over this camp. It felt spent, depleted, ruined even. It was time to move on down the road.

Someone began coughing in the RV as I sat there, a dry hacking cough that grew in frequency and intensity. Soon Zed came bursting from the door in a convulsive fit of coughing and grasped a near-by tree for support as he hacked away.

"You alright?" I called to him. He just waved, shook his head in the affirmative, and continued his hacking.

He eventually settled down enough to shake off whatever was ailing him and joined me by the pit.

"God damn garbage smoke!" he declared; his deep voice even gravellier than normal. "What a mess! Shit, look at these trees!" he added taking notice of the blacked limbs reaching a good fifteen feet above the fire pit.

"What happened last night?" I asked. "I got super drunk really fast and passed out I guess."

"It was a wild scene here," he answered, quickly followed by another brief round of full-body coughs. "One of those rich girls, the sad one, she almost burnt down the camp, the flames were so fucking high," he continued in between convulsive hacks. "She had been throwing all sorts of shit in the fire, something must have…" He paused for a moment to cough up a bloody lump of phlegm which he spit onto a rock near the pit. "Something she threw on the fire really took off and went out of control."

"Holy shit!" I uttered.

"Yeah, it was bad," he continued, shaking his head and clearing his throat. "Everyone was wasted and the smoke was thick, but that tower of flames sobered me up pretty quick. Luckily, I had a little fire extinguisher in the camper, and even luckier that it still worked. It was enough to bring the flames back down out of the trees".

"Holy shit!" I uttered again. I then realized the rich girl's shiny new SUV was absent, along with their tent. "They're gone." I said aloud.

"Yes, I cast them out last night," he said bluntly before hacking up another bloody clump of phlegm onto the rocks. "We're breaking camp today," he added after a few moments of heavy silence. "We'll leave in a few hours; as soon as we're ready. Your people will be heading south from here, right?" I nodded. "Good. We should only be a few days behind you. Now, help me rake this stinking shit out of the fire pit so we can make some attempt at breakfast."

Soon we had a nice clean blaze going. Jen joined us by the pit with some provisions from the trunk. A couple cans of beans were opened and poured into a pan over the fire, some sliced bread was placed upon a few rocks to face the flames, and Zed's beat-up old tea pot was positioned off to the side to boil.

With breakfast underway, I began rounding up the trash scattered all about the site. I performed this task alone, since everyone else was apparently still asleep. I gathered up a sizable quantity of garbage and dumped it onto the overflowing pile behind the camper. It was a disturbing amount of garbage, stinking and rotten. How Zed planned on getting all this trash down to a dumpster, I had no idea. A realization suddenly struck me then that laid bare the futility of my efforts. They would not bother hauling this trash out; they didn't even have enough bags to contain it all. And there was no way they would pack all this sloppy rotten garbage into the RV with them, no fucking way. That realization only soured my opinion of this camp even more. I walked over to the tent where Pete was still sleeping and attempted to rouse him.

"Pete! Wake up, man. Let's get our shit together and hit the road. This place is fucking beat." He grumbled and groaned in response, and I returned to the fire pit to see if I could help Jen speed breakfast along.

Judith and the runaway girls were already there at the pit, having only recently emerged from their tents. They were all just sitting around there looking blankly into the flames since there really wasn't much to do to speed along the cooking of beans in a pan. So I sat there with them, offering my support in their venture.

"Do you think you guys could give us a ride into Boulder?" Summer asked me once I had perched myself upon a log.

"Yeah, I guess," I replied, suddenly remembering what I saw the night before, and looking over to Jen. She did not meet my gaze, but I could see her jaw muscles clench.

"We don't want to ride with those assholes in the RV anymore," she added. "I don't trust those guys."

"Yeah, we can give you guys a ride out of here," Jen affirmed. "But no farther than Boulder."

"Thanks, that'd be great. Come on Sherri. Let's pack up the tent."

I sat there silently with Judith and Jen then as the fire gently crackled and popped. Should I tell her what I saw? What had I even seen, exactly? My blurry memory allowed me a single snapshot of Pete climbing out of the girl's tent. He was dressed, right? I thought to myself. Yeah, but he had no shoes on. Maybe he was just smoking up with her. Still, it was shady as shit, going off alone with her, into her tent. Surely he knew how Jen was feeling about the girl. Why would he risk her peace of mind if he was indeed innocent of anything shady? I was conflicted. I didn't want to throw him under the bus if all he was doing was just burning a little weed with the girl. But it looked bad, him emerging from her tent and all while everyone in camp was hammered. And I remembered how broken up Jen was at the thought of him cheating on her, and how she asked me to let her know if I saw anything fishy. Ugh, I need to ask him myself, I decided. If he did do something shitty maybe he would just work it out with Jen, and I'd be off the hook.

I stood up, dusted off my pants, and walked back up to the tent where my friend had been sleeping. I found him sitting cross legged on a rumpled mass of blankets and sleeping bags spilling out of the unzipped opening of the tent. I knelt beside him.

"How ya doin' there, bud?" I asked him. He groaned again like he had when I woke him up earlier, I could smell the sour booze breath in his utterance. "Were you in Sherri's tent last night?" I asked him directly. He looked up at me with a frown. "I was pretty shitfaced, almost didn't make it into the car. I thought I saw you coming out of her tent before I passed out."

"Give me a break, man. So what if I was?" he answered belligerently. I shrugged my shoulders in response. "Nothing happened, alright? You can tell my jealous wife over there that nothing fucking happened."

"I'm not going to tell her anything. You are," I stated, surprising myself in my assertiveness. "We're a team out here. If you're fucking around that might ruin the trip for all of us."

"I'm telling you, nothing happened," he said again, this time more passively in the face of my rebuke. "We were smoking a joint; she was feeling uncomfortable with all those people making out all over the place last night. She's had some bad experiences."

I sat there with him in silence for a time watching the girls pass plates of beans around the campfire. "Ok, this is all between you and Jen," I finally said. "I don't want to stir up this shit any more than it already is; I don't even really know what I saw anyway."

I stood up. "We're giving those two girls a ride into Boulder when we leave in a little bit." He looked up at me like a sad, hungover puppy.

"Ok, sounds good," he replied.

We were in the car and on our way down the mountain within the hour. We had our hugs and said our farewells to Zed and Judith, but left before Zed's three party deputies had awoken from their collective drunk so we could not extend the same pleasantries to them. Zed again described the area in the hills above Sedona where we should wait for them, going into deeper detail as to the exact area we should look to camp, and again assured us they'd only be a few days behind. We took a mental note and took our leave.

The ride down the mountain was a somber one without much talking. Jen was driving because Pete was too stricken with hangover to handle the task, and honestly, I wasn't that far behind him. She steered us down into Boulder and followed the directions Summer gave her to some park where they felt they could secure their own ride to warmer climes. We dropped them there on the city sidewalk along with their two small backpacks and said our farewells. No hugs were exchanged this time; the general distrust and malaise in the air was too strong.

The city was cold, gray, and bland where we left them, and the sky mirrored those colors. After these past few days in the green of the mountains, the change was striking. We hastened to put that atmosphere behind us, hitting the freeway south as soon as we had topped off the tank, looping around Denver proper and away like a slingshot.

And then, once again, there were three. The highway whined beneath the floorboards, sending that familiar low vibration up through the seats and into your core. Pete was unconscious in the back, curled up with Dylan, leaving Jen and me alone in the front seat. The impulse to inform her of what I had seen grew and subsided in intensity depending on how I looked at the matter. I felt I had an obligation to her, since she had expressly asked me to inform her if I saw anything off about Pete's behavior with Sherri. But I also felt an obligation to Pete not to unduly burden him with Jen's contempt if he in fact had not been up to anything shady with that girl. In the end, my indecision won out, and I kept my mouth shut.

We drove on for hours in relative silence, with Jen betraying none of her thoughts. It was slightly awkward there in the front seat with her, but I felt that none of her animosity was directed at me. By mid-day we crossed the state line into New Mexico and found ourselves in some little town just over the border, quenching the car's thirst for fuel and stretching our legs. We stopped into a fast-food burger joint for lunch. Jen picked at her soggy fries as Pete and I ravenously devoured the American fare, our hangovers now subdued.

"I want a shower tonight, Peter," she suddenly announced. "And I want to sleep in a bed."

Pete looked up from his half-eaten double cheeseburger. "Absolutely," he responded; his mouth full of food. "Let's get a hotel room tonight."

"Let's get one now," she shot back. "No more driving today. I want a shower now."

"Sure. Of course," he agreed as he returned to his burger with vigor. She stood up from the table then and walked out the door, abandoning her half-eaten meal. "Split the leftovers?" he asked me, reaching for the tray.

We found her out at the car, sitting on the hood with a cigarette hanging from her lip, the smoke curling around her head in thin wisps. "That hotel there," she said flatly, pointing to a long, single-story row of alternating windows and doors across the parking lot.

"You stay with the car," Pete told me. "I'll go get a room for us."

I sat there on the hood next to Jen, watching him trek across the parking lot. "Everything will be better once we've all had a shower," she said turning to me. "I promise."

The room was a single, so there was only one twin-size bed. Pete said there were no double bedrooms available, only singles were left. So that meant I had no bed of my own. I didn't mind sleeping on the floor though. It was carpeted and I had my sleeping bag. We grabbed a few things from the car and settled in.

The room was outfitted with your classic generic hotel furniture and had a distinct hotel room smell that seemed all the more potent for our having been living in the outdoors. It was odd to be inside again, in a room with a bed, walls and a ceiling. We'd been on the road for weeks now, and this was the first private room we'd had since Jen's kooky aunt's place. Dylan made himself at home right away, jumping up onto the bed and claiming his space right in the middle. I tossed my pack in the corner by the little table and chair that came standard with such a room and plopped myself into the hard straight backed seat.

Jen disappeared into the bathroom right away and was in there for over an hour. Pete and I passed the time surfing through the handful of local channels available on the mid-sized off-color television. Once she was through with the bathroom, Pete took his turn. He was only in there for a short time before

Jen got up off the bed and returned to the bathroom, joining him inside. The two of them then spent the next hour in there, settling their differences as it were. It was approaching the evening by the time they vacated the steamy little room.

"Your turn," Pete said to me, shirtless with a white hotel towel wrapped around his waist, his wet dreads limply collapsed upon his shoulders. "I'm going to go out and get a pizza or something and some beer. Take your time, I'll probably be awhile."

And with that, I found myself alone in that humid little white tiled room, accompanied only by my waist-up reflection. I stripped off my filthy clothes and inspected the strange naked body I found before me. The plump pale flesh I had left home with had noticeably deflated, strikingly so really, leaving me thinner than I could ever remember myself being. My youthful beard had overtaken my dirty face in fluffy clumps, and my hair had coalesced into a mop of short little four-inch dreads. I gazed into the mirror at this stranger before me and looked into his eyes, searching for something I might recognize. I was still there; it was still me. But I was different now in some fundamental way.

I stepped into the shower and let the hot water wash over me. The sensation was overwhelming; as if every nerve ending was being caressed in a warm wet embrace. The one bar of standard-issue hotel soap had already been put to work twice, but there was still enough of the pale white wafer left to lather myself up thoroughly. I opened my eyes briefly as the soapy foam was rinsed from my skin and watched as the dark gray scummy water swirled down the drain. It had been over a month since I had had a shower, in Jen's mother's trailer back in Ithaca, and it felt glorious.

I stepped out and dried myself with a couple of hand towels, since my companions had already used all the full-sized towels that had come with a room set up as a single. I slipped back into my dirty clothes and entered the cool dry of the mildly air-conditioned hotel room. Jen was in the bed with Dylan, wrapped in a blanket, watching TV.

"Feel better?" she asked me. I nodded yes." Me too," she finished with a smile. I could tell they had worked out their issues, and it lightened the atmosphere considerably.

Pete returned shortly thereafter with a pizza and a six-pack of tall cans. We made short work of the pizza, setting aside a few strips of crust to add to Dylan's kibbles, and then set about putting the beers away. Jen abstained from drink, so Pete and I soon found ourselves with a good buzz going. Well after dark, and soon after we had finished the last of the beers, Jen made it known she was ready to sleep. Pete and I were just winding up, so we chose to step out into the night to see if we could find a place that was still open within walking distance where we could pick up some more beer, leaving Dylan behind to snuggle with Jen.

We trekked a short distance to a gas station with an attached convenience store and got another six-pack of tallboy cans. Not wanting to disturb Jen by drinking in the room, we set off into the scrubby brush behind the gas station, away from the glare of the high-powered streetlights that bathed the landscape in the artificial orange glow of civilization. We found a dry wash studded with trash where the ruins of a cushion-less couch was abandoned. We dragged over a couple of old tires for footrests and made ourselves at home.

It was surprisingly quiet out there in the polluted scrub, with only the low constant hum of the nearby interstate, and we were far enough away from the streetlights to allow a few of the brighter stars to shine unimpeded. We lifted our drinks to our good fortune, our tall aluminum cans thumping together bluntly. We had come so far on this trip, engaged with such interesting characters, and been inside of such interesting landscapes. And now here we were in yet another foreign state; a desert state. The air had a warm, thin, dry feel to it and felt very open, very wide. It reminded me of the feeling I often experienced in some of my dreams, of being immersed in a sort of endless empty expanse that bled away in all directions. We sat there drinking our beers and describing the feeling to each other in turn.

We hung around there till maybe midnight or so, before hiking back to the hotel. We woke Dylan when we entered the room of course, prompting him to toss around a few loud barks, but they eased him back to his rest soon enough and we all settled down for sleep.

The room felt so small after being out under that endless sky, and quiet too, the highway sounds now muffled behind the walls. I lay on the floor, listening to the rhythmic breathing of my companions and staring into the impasto surface of the ceiling, studying the way the passing headlights caused the shadows to crawl across the textured surface. I had a pretty good buzz going after those last few tall cans and slipped into unconsciousness quickly, mesmerized as I was by the patterns of shadow altering the surface of the ceiling.

I dreamed then I was again out in that scrubby desert, under an endless starry sky. But it was much darker this time, for there were no offensive orange streetlights to soil the fabric of the night. I could just make out the silhouettes of buildings or structures of some sort off in the distance around me, as if I were in a landscape like the one I had just been walking through in waking life. But I had no concept of that in the dream, not knowing I was dreaming.

I began to make my way towards one of the closer structures, picking my way through the dry bushes. I could not tell whether it was a building or a large outcrop of rock, its inky black form constantly changing as I approached it. Sometimes it looked angled and man-made, only to become uneven and jagged as it changed positions in my advancement. As I drew close, it became apparent that it was a structure of some sort, made by human hands. It was an adobe dwelling, like the kind I had seen pictured in a little state sponsored welcome brochure I had grabbed from the burger joint earlier. There was a small opening low to the ground that served as an entrance into this dark, dried soil blister on the surface of the earth's skin. I felt compelled to enter, so I stooped down and shuffled inside on my knees.

It was impenetrably dark inside the earthen dome and surprisingly warm. I recognized a smell right away, a strong smell that filled my being. It was the smell of burning sage, like the kind Zed had smudged me with a few days earlier. I then became aware of the red-hot cherry of the burning smudge stick before me, slowly moving around in the air. This dull red glow began to grow and illuminate the space around me, and the being that wielded the stick emerged from the gloom. First the gnarled old hands, then the outline of the crouching form, and then its features fleshed out.

It was an ancient Native American man in traditional dress, his leathery skin creased deeply with age. He beckoned me to come closer, so I did, involuntarily. I knelt before him while he continued bathing me in the fragrant smoke, chanting a quiet string of unfamiliar sounds all the while.

His features were very clear now; I could see every thick stitch of his garments, every bead sewn into the hides. I could see his long braids of white and black hair running down over each of his shoulders and into his lap; I could see his dark rheumy eyes lazily following the trails of smoke the smudge stick was leaving in its passing. I felt an odd closeness to this image before me, as if he was an old friend, so I had no fear as he reached out and took my right hand in his.

He had given me something; he had placed something into my hand and closed it over with his own. I looked down at our two hands; his bony, leathery, dark-skinned hand over my young, soft pink one, and felt deeply ashamed suddenly. I looked up to him again to beg forgiveness for my skin, the skin of the invader, the colonizer, the enemy, and found his pupils were gone. His eyes now were milk white and opened wide. He was no longer chanting, but a humming sound remained, filling the air with vibration. Still I felt no fear, no apprehension at all. I gazed into his empty eyes, looking deeply. I saw nothing, an emptiness that rivaled space itself. The man then released my hand, and I looked to see what he had placed in it. It was a small, crudely formed owl pendant, made from wood, its eyes wide and blank like the old sage before me.

I am dreaming, I suddenly realized. I am asleep and dreaming. The little carved owl then disappeared from my hand in a puff of smoke. I looked up again to the old man and he was gone as well, only a thin atmosphere of smoke remained in the fading red glow of the smudge stick. Darkness then covered me again, and I was alone.

CHAPTER 23

The gentle yet incessant knocking of the hotel's housekeeper was what finally roused us from our slumber. The shades had been drawn tight, so the daylight had not been able to infiltrate our space with enough intensity to convince our sleeping minds that the day had broken and had in fact done so hours earlier. We hastily gathered our things and vacated the room once we realized we had slept over an hour past check-out time.

"I want pancakes!" Pete randomly announced as we climbed into the car. "Let's see if we can find a pancake house in this town."

We didn't have to look far. Just around the block from the hotel we spotted the telltale signs of such an establishment. Once seated in a large, high-backed booth, Pete got the biggest stack they offered, bathing the thick spongy cakes in amber syrup. Jen and I opted for more modest breakfasts but were still surprised at the amounts of food that came out on our plates. It was a lot of food to be responsible for, and we did our best to make it all disappear. We left that place with to-go containers full of what was left, feeding some of the eggs and sausage to Dylan mixed in with his kibbles.

Then we were on the road again, our bellies full and our lips sticky with artificial maple syrup. We traced the interstate for a short time before bearing right on US route 64 away into flat brown grasslands with dark hills looming low in the west. This stretch was desolate and striking in its starkness, its matted earth tones smeared by our rapid passing. The scrubby brown grasses of the flatlands gave way to stands of bristly dry pines and tan dusty rubble, rising on either side of the lonely two-lane road cutting through the canyon. We were in those rocky hills for a good while before coming out above a large lake where the land again became flat and wide around us.

We hadn't really said much to each other since we left the pancake place, awed into silence as we were by this new southwestern landscape as it played out across our windshield. Instead, the constant hum of that big V8 engine and the steady rumble and rhythmic thumping of the wheels passing over the highway's expansion joints filled the space where our conversations would have occupied. It would have been a good time to burn down a huge doobie, but alas, we had none to burn.

The flatlands again abruptly gave way to another stretch of piney rocky climbing, and with that we entered Carson National Forest. It was past noon at this point, and since we were now passing through National Park land, we thought there might be good camping spots where we might get to kick back a few days without hassles and see if we could meet this dry southwestern landscape face to face. We drove on a good distance into the forest and turned onto a random unmarked dirt road just to see where it went.

The road was heavily rutted, but not so bad we feared the car might get stuck. Pete steered the old tank on to the top of the ruts and attempted to ride them like rails, which worked for the most part with only occasional slips into the deep grooves. After maybe a mile or so in this way, the road leveled out and widened considerably. There we spotted a series of grassy patches that looked particularly inviting. It was there that we staked our claim.

We spent the rest of the day there enjoying the peaceful quiet the forest afforded us. It was obvious the site had been used frequently for camping by the well-constructed, well-seasoned fire pit and smooth flat tent areas. But as a nice change from our last woodland camp, there was no garbage of any kind around; it was completely clean. Not even bottle caps or cigarette butts. We set up the tent near the fire pit and set about collecting some wood for burning as evening approached. We didn't have to look far. Just a little way into the bushes outside of camp we found a nice little pile of seasoned, split firewood someone had stashed under a small camouflage tarp. We grabbed a few pieces for the night and returned with our spoils.

It was wonderfully dark out there in the forest once the sun had gone down, and not a little brisk. My companions huddled close together with their dog, wrapped in a blanket, the firelight setting their faces aglow. It was relieving to me to see them back on good terms with each other after their latest spat on the road down from Ned. Usually, whenever they would be engaged in a row, they would be quite vocal about it, arguing over each other and attempting to pull me into their side of whatever disagreement they were having. But this last time was different. The silence between them on the ride down from Colorado had been disconcerting and had me nervous our trip might have started coming apart under the strain of that silence. But they had apparently settled the matter back in the hotel bathroom and now seemed back to normal, occasionally bickering about some triviality as they always had but overall exhibiting every sign they were still in a committed relationship, albeit a sometimes dysfunctional one.

We stayed up a few hours past sundown before they took their leave of me and retired to their tent. I stayed up awhile longer, staring into the coals of the fading fire in silent thought and listening to the frequent hoots of a faraway owl. It had been quite a trip so far, and we had driven deeply into experiences beyond what I could have anticipated. I had stepped out onto this road with as open a mind as my hangups allowed, convinced I was ready for whatever was thrown at me. And it was these pre-installed hangups that were now becoming more and more apparent to me despite my efforts to ignore them. I was changing, my mindset was expanding, and it was fast becoming undeniable this journey we were on had already left its mark on me, despite me.

I now found myself often questioning beliefs I had always taken for granted, and frequently found them to be wanting. Again and again the faith I held so dear and which made up such a part of my personality, my very being even, failed to hold up to real scrutiny. Who was God, really? Some all-powerful force that demanded my unquestioning obedience, my unwavering devotion, my blind acceptance? Why? Why would he need that from me? Why would he have created me, instilled forbidden wants and desires in me that I was called upon to deny lest I forfeit my very soul to eternal damnation? Surely it was not God that sent these forbidden wants and desires; it was the Devil, right?

So why was there a Devil? Why would God, all powerful, allow some rebel angel the power to pervert his project? Why not crush the head of that snake under his foot from the start? Surely he had the power to do that. So why was the Devil allowed to exist in the first place? If God was omnipotent, then he must have known the Devil would arise and interfere with his grand project, perhaps even building the Devil and his evil works into his master plan.

But why? If he's this all-loving God, a God who sent his own son to die for our sins so that we might be saved, then why would he allow such evil to exist in the first place? If God is capable of preventing evil, then why would he allow it? Why would he need some grand sacrifice, his very own son even, to absolve us of the evil he allowed to exist in the first place?

Since childhood I was taught to know God as a just and loving entity, but the reality of the situation became increasingly at odds with that outlook. More and more, God was coming across as either impotently unable to control the balance of good and evil in our existence, or he was allowing it for some malevolent reason. Either scenario was viscerally unappealing and thoroughly disheartening. The foundations of my faith were slowly washing away like so much sand, leaving me with an ever-present sinking feeling that grew in intensity whenever I dared acknowledge it.

We spent the whole next day there in the forest, exploring the nearby trails and dirt roads and taking in all there was to see.

Nature, for the most part unmolested by humans as it was here, was becoming my solace and my peace. The gnawing doubts that often plagued me seemed somehow unimportant against the backdrop of the natural world, and the relief this afforded me was at times mildly intoxicating.

The next morning we loaded up and hit the road again, taking it slow through the forested valley. Soon we came up on the edge of that patch of parkland, crossing an obvious line into civilization.

Taos presented itself as a low dusty town of stuccoed cinder block buildings, rustic homesteads adorned with old wagon wheels, captive cactus, and stately willow trees, their long brushy boughs dangling over sun-baked, rust-free classic cars and trucks. It was an attractive-looking place, for the twenty minutes we saw of it anyway. US 64 took us right into the center of that adobe-colored town, where we took a sharp right onto State Route 68 and continued south into those signature scrub lands that characterize this part of the planet.

We drove on for a good long while before meeting up with the Rio Grande. There the road followed the river on our right, first through a virtual wilderness of scrubby hills before cutting through many little towns, ranches and homesteads as we continued south. The scene was a lot greener this close to the river, naturally, presenting as occasional groves of massive willow and cottonwood trees, and even a few cultivated fruit orchards.

Eventually Route 68 veered away from the verdant banks of the river into the flat scrub again and we soon crossed into the urbanized strip mall territory of a group of towns that had joined forces to create a minor city on the banks of the river. There we met up with US Route 84 and stopped for gas.

"Whoa, check out that old bus!" Pete exclaimed as we turned into the station. "Is that a taco bus?"

We climbed out of the car to investigate and found that indeed it was. The decades-old and long immobile school bus, crudely painted in the tri-colors of the Mexican flag, had been gutted of its children's seats and outfitted with a rudimentary kitchen, while a bank of windows on one side had been removed to create a serving window. Pete stepped right up to the counter with the determination of a man with the munchies.

"How much for tacos?" he asked the old woman inside, a goofy smile beaming across his face.

"Un dólar por cada uno," the woman responded in a monotone, with all the emotion of a stone statue.

"Holy shit!" Pete exclaimed, "only a dollar?" The woman nodded her head, indifferent to his culinary excitement. "How many do you all want?" he asked, turning to us. We just shrugged. "Ok, I'll take ten."

"Ok, diez tacos entonces," she stated flatly and turned to begin assembling the meat and bean filled hand food. I watched as she prepared the meal, adding some sizzling brown seasoned meat and a thick black bean paste, together with a dash of limp discolored lettuce and red onion chips into a steaming warm corn tortilla. She then rolled it up like a loose joint and dropped it into a small red and white checkered paper tray.

Once we had settled up with the old woman in the bus, we took our trays of tacos over to the motley assortment of dusty, mis-matched plastic chairs scattered around a couple rickety old tables pierced through with faded, beer logo-emblazoned umbrellas that served as the dining area for this establishment. On one of the tables a beat up, small plastic basket offered a few condiments to enhance the taco eating experience. These condiments consisted wholly of various brands of hot sauce, some labeled from their respective production facilities, some unlabeled and presented in re-used glass bottles.

"Ooh, hot sauce!" Pete exclaimed as we gathered around the table with the spicy condiment assortment. "Hmm, I wonder what's in this one," he added, holding up one of the unlabeled offerings, its discolored screw cap encrusted with dried sauce and dust.

"Oh my God, Peter. Don't use that, who knows what's in it!" Jen pleaded. "Look at it, it's filthy."

"What do you think, man?" he asked me, placing the questionable product before me for my closer inspection. "Is it edible?"

I took the bottle and had a look. The reddish sauce inside looked right, but the bottle was admittedly pretty gross. The original label had been roughly scraped off, leaving a sticky residue that had collected the saucy fingerprints of previous users. I removed the crusty cap and had a smell. A bouquet of vinegar and chilies with just a hint of industrial solvent responded to my inquiry. I dabbed a bit on my fingertip and went in for a taste.

"It's hot as fuck," I reported, the spicy sensation advancing across my palate with unnatural swiftness. "Try it."

He then ran the sauce through the same battery of tests I had and came to a similar conclusion. He applied the red-hued flavor enhancer liberally to a taco and began to macerate a bite of it in his mouth.

"You are crazy," Jen declared as he grimaced in mouth-burning pleasure. "You'll get the shits for sure."

Our thirst was significant once we had dispatched the heavily spiced meal, so we made our way over to the convenience store attached to the gas station to seek out soda. The cooler had all the name brands common to our experience north of the border, but also had rows of foreign bottles; Mexican sodas in tall glass bottles, their painted-on labels worn from multiple refilling. They were cheap too, so we grabbed a bunch, at least one of each of the brightly colored flavors available and took our booty out to the car.

We each knocked back a few of the artificially colored carbonated beverages before we even left the parking lot. I upended an orange soda, draining its contents down my gullet in the attempt to wash away the lingering burning still afflicting my tongue. The flavor of chemically enhanced oranges filled my being, my sense of smell more than taste, while my taste buds below registered only sugar; mouth puckering quantities of sugar. It was by far the most intense orange soda I had ever had. It might have been the black-market hot sauce still blistering my tongue that set the stage for that sensory shit show, because I was never able to repeat the experience with Mexican sodas again.

We topped off the tank of the car and rolled out of the parking lot. We made it only a few blocks before the car began pulling to the left.

"Fuck, we're losing another tire," Pete stated, once he had poked his head out the window at the next red light.

He steered the car, now with the front left wheel flat on the rim, into the nearest gas station, and we all piled out again.

"I'm going to change out this tire. Go inside and see if someone knows where a junkyard is so we can get a spare," he asked me.

I stepped into the gas station and up to the counter where a deeply tanned old lady with lots of gaudy plastic jewelry was seated reading a dog-eared old romance novel, an overfull smoldering ashtray at her side "Excuse me, ma'am, any junkyards nearby? We need a spare tire."

"Well, sure, hon," she responded with a smile, brandishing her yellow tobacco-stained teeth. "Just over by the airport, can't miss it." And she pulled out a local fold-out map from a rack on the counter. "Here, I'll show ya, hon." She delicately unfolded the map with her long bony fingers, the colorful plastic bangles on her wrists dully clunking together over her dusky liver-spotted flesh. "Right here."

"Thanks, ma'am," I cheerily responded, and she reached out and grabbed my hand above the wrist lightning quick.

"You may be lost now, but there is someone who can help you find the way," she stated, staring deeply into my eyes, her grasp tightening. "Jesus can guide you, Jesus can…" and she trailed off, her gaze intensifying in the momentary silence.

"You already know Jesus. I can see him in your eyes," she then stated in a low monotone voice. My heart was beginning to pound. "You know him, and you are turning away from him." I attempted to pull away, but she held firm, her grasp unnervingly strong for such feeble looking hands. "You mustn't turn from him, hon. Hell awaits the ones who forsake him. Eternal torment, everlasting pain." She continued her piercing gaze a moment longer before finally releasing me. "Safe travels, hon. Jesus be with you," she called after me as I made a break for the door.

"D'you find any junkyards nearby? Whoa, you alright?" Pete asked me, his demeanor rapidly changing once he saw the disturbed expression on my face. "You look like you seen a ghost."

"Yeah, nah... I'm fine," I bumbled out. "Weird lady in there, tripped me out. There's a junkyard over by the airport. Let's get the fuck outta here."

"Ok, ok. Help me pack this shit back in the trunk."

We found the junkyard as described, and I split off from my companions once the yard guy let us inside. I needed a few minutes alone. I wandered around the site in sort of a daze, aimlessly picking my way between the partially disassembled carcasses of ruined cars and trucks. I was supposed to be looking for a GM five-lug 15" wheel with good tread, but I couldn't concentrate. The creepy feeling the leathery old lady had just laid on me seemed only amplified by a churning in my stomach that was rapidly building in intensity. I sat down on a random sun-blistered automotive bench seat propped up against an engine block and laid my head in my hands.

Was that old woman a demon sent to torment me? Nonsense! She implored me to return to Jesus, how could she be of the legions of the dark one? But had I even left his good graces? I had my doubts, but had I really already forsaken him? My guts did a flip in my belly, and I belched a hot acid mouthful of partially digested, hot sauce-tainted taco. I groaned audibly and raised my head from my hands. Was she an angel then? Sent to keep me on the straight and narrow, to warn me of the hellish consequences of forsaking my savior, of breaking my oath? Again, my guts rolled in waves of increasingly intense cramps. Or was she just an eccentric old lady whose whole culturally defined personality was built solely upon American Christian televangelism and whose grip on reality was beginning to slip?

Cold sweats began to run down my forehead, and my legs began to tremble. Oh Jesus! Give me a sign! Am I living these convictions in vain? I cried silently to the hazy sky lowly hanging above the twisted piles of ruined motorized Americana. My stomach gave one powerful convulsion, and I projectile vomited a red and brown mass of watery mush into the oily sand at my feet.

I crouched there for a few moments, dry heaving my guts empty down to the small intestine. I am alone, I thought. I really am alone. There is no God; there is no devil. At least not how I was raised to believe, I can feel it in my bones. I stood up, my head still swimming, and grasped a hold of the door handle of a nearby panel van. My world tasted of artificial orange and toxic heat. My sinuses burned and my eyes watered to the point of blindness. I groaned again and spit, wiping the tears from my eyes.

As my eyes cleared, I realized what I was holding on to, noticing the hippie stickers on the windows of the van I was leaning on. Shaking off the effects of the continuing gradual loss of my faith and the more immediate loss of my lunch, I focused on the wreck I found before me.

I pulled the handle of the door I had been grasping, opening the sliding side hatch. Inside I found a disheveled wreck of items and trash; old clothes, cassette tapes, blankets. Hippie band stickers and taped up show fliers plastered the inside of the van. This was a road kid's ride, I realized. What happened to it to bring it to this junkyard death? I welcomed this sudden distraction from my troubles and climbed in to investigate.

Everything had a thick layer of dust on it, blown in from the surrounding sandy junkyard through the missing windshield. The dust caught in my dry, bile-burned throat as I dug around the remains of someone's prematurely ended road trip. It was pretty well picked over by whoever had abandoned this van to its fate, but I did find a crusty old pair of camouflaged cargo pocket pants that looked to be my size and a long-sleeve T-shirt tie-dyed in the color of flames with a silk-screened print of a pile of skulls on the front. I held the shirt up and had a good look. It was a fucking badass shirt but filthy, stained in transmission oil from being stuffed against the van's disassembled transmission case there in the back. I peeled off the dirty T-shirt I had been wearing for weeks already and slid into this new one. It fit like a glove. I stepped out of the ruined ride and dropped to my ankles the old shredded blue jeans I had left home with. The camo pants were smaller around the waist but fit snugly since I had lost so much weight on the road. I stood there in that wasteland of spent and discarded junk in my new outfit of previously discarded old clothes, my new skin, my head buzzing from a mildly ecstatic post-nausea high and felt somehow reborn. I can't wait around to see if Jesus will give me a sign, I realized. I need to go look for it. And if I don't find it in my searching, then fuck it. At least I tried.

I caught up with my traveling companions at the car as Pete was just tightening the lug nuts on a good replacement wheel he had found.

"Where'd you get the new clothes?" Jen asked me, eyeing me up and down.

"I found 'em in an old van back there" I responded as I threw my thumb back over my shoulder in the general direction from whence I came. "Good look, eh?" I asked, pretending to pop an invisible set of suspenders.

"They look fucking filthy, dude," Pete pointed out.

"I am fucking filthy," I chuckled. "I need a drink, I just puked my guts out back there; that hot sauce fucked me up, I think."

"Oh, shit! Really? he asked. "My guts have been rumbling. Wonder if I'm next."

"I told you not to eat that nasty sauce!" Jen exclaimed.

We blew out of Santa Fe on I25 south to Albuquerque, where we hooked up with I40 west and away into the desert afternoon. At one point on the highway, we came up behind a slow moving, rusty old two-tone Chevy van with Alaska plates, full of windows with little paisley curtains strung up to block the view inside. Even from a distance the ride had "road kids" written all over it, and when we came up alongside those suspicions were confirmed.

Behind the wheel, a shaggy dirty-blond-haired kid with a patchy juvenile beard smiled and waved as we passed them at speed. We waved back with smiles and thumbs up as well. We were of the same breed, the same subculture, traveling the roads of this land in search of kicks and enlightenment. It was an age-old pursuit countless travelers before us had engaged in and would continue to be a calling for a select few long after we all had settled down in our graves. We may all return to dust, but as long as there are feet to walk there will be a path to follow.

We pushed on at highway speeds all afternoon and into the sunset, by dusk coming upon the state line. Arizona; a land of endless desert and cactus, or at least that was the picture I had in my head of what it would look like. And since the darkness was now fast descending around us, the reality of this Arizonian landscape would have to wait till morning.

We grabbed a random exit to some dry little town a few miles in and tooled around the edges of the municipality looking for some dirt road or dry wash we could sneak our car down into and camp for the night. A good way out of town, we found such an arroyo dirt road and took it till it felt like we'd gone far enough.

It was dark out there in the scrubby brush, but since it was already so late and we intended on hitting the road again shortly after daybreak, we opted to skip the fire and just make camp.

I helped my friends set up the tent near the car, kicking the area clean of rocks and broken bottles. We then all sat on the hood of the car for an hour or so, checking out the stars and listening quietly to the far away howls of coyotes, as well as the not so far away sounds of small-arms fire. The place had a creepy atmosphere, a lonely desperate atmosphere, and we huddled close against it, Jen often shushing Dylan's low growls and whines. Eventually my companions and their dog retreated to the tent and I to the back seat of the car, where we waited out the desert darkness in fitful portions of troubled sleep.

CHAPTER 24

Dawn revealed a dry, desolate landscape. The shallow arroyo we found ourselves in was sheltered from long views by large crusty creosote bushes emerging from a hardscrabble ground littered with sun-bleached trash. We had our morning urinations into the dust and took off, passing the bullet-ridden, burnt-out remains of a large 1970s-model station wagon, buried up to the rocker panels in desert dirt.

We were back on the interstate in no time, pushing our olive drab tank up near eighty miles an hour down the wide straight-line pavement. We had the road to ourselves for the most part, sharing it only with a few long-haul semi-trucks looking to pass through this wasteland just as fast as their pre-set governors would allow. Pete switched on the CB radio to see what they all had to say, after fishing it out from under the front seat. He had never bothered to mount the radio to the dashboard, so it just sort of lived under the front seat with the floor trash, its cables climbing up the floorboards and under the dash like weedy bittersweet vines searching for the light.

We listened in to the trucker chatter for a time, switching channels whenever the conversations led into boring places, our attention span ridiculously short. The lingo they all used made understanding what they were talking about difficult, and even when we could figure it out, it offered no insights into our travels. We had hoped we could use it to stay ahead of speed traps and traffic problems, but it ended up just being a novel distraction we quickly grew bored of. I felt sorry for the poor trucker who had been robbed of this radio, whoever they were. He would surely have had better use of it then the likes of us. Oh well. Just slide the thing back under the seat and forget about it.

The interstate through this part of the country traced the remains of the fabled US Route 66. Sometimes riding right on top of it, absorbing its historical path. Sometimes veering away from long isolated runs of cracked two-lane blacktop, all but abandoned to the desert. Often along these forgotten stretches of pavement, the ruins of ancient service stations, diners, and hotels could be seen, cut off from the flow of traffic by the arrival of the interstate. These corpses of roadside commerce lay gutted and desiccated, occasionally accompanied by ruined vintage automobiles, themselves resigned to a similar fate. I would have loved to explore some of these places up close, but often there seemed to be no easy way of getting to them from the highway, short of just pulling over on the side of the interstate and hiking out across the desert scrub.

Slowly, the landscape began to change, the elevation gradually climbing, and the ubiquitous clumps of grass soon shared real estate with pinyon pine and juniper bushes. As we approached Flagstaff, larger trees came into play; ponderosa pines, tall and stately, rose on both sides of the highway, stubbornly remaining in place despite a mildly urban landscape building up around them. We quit Interstate 40 there, diving south onto Interstate 17 for a short time before grabbing the exit for State Route 89A towards Sedona.

Tall stands of pines now dominated the scene on both sides of the road as we pulled away from the metro area, its urban influence rapidly evaporating. The weather was cool, being by now well into fall, but we rolled along with the windows down anyway, enjoying the fragrant aroma of the piney forest we were passing through.

"It looks like we're going to be going down into a canyon here soon; Oak Creek Canyon," Jen announced after consulting our grime stained and wrinkled road atlas. "There's an overlook parking area right before the drop; let's stop and check it out."

The view from this overlook was impressive; a deep canyon of reddish rock studded with trees. The foliage of the deciduous examples in varying shades of autumn colors peppered in with the deep green cones of the coniferous stretching away from our vantage point by a mile or more.

"This is beautiful," she half-whispered in awe. We agreed in silent nods.

A steep switchback route awaited our decent to the canyon floor, or at least as close to the floor as the road would allow. The road clung to the side of the eastern slope, with rocky brushy walls on our left and at times steep drops down to the creek on the right. We continued on this road for miles at a nice slow pace, sometimes passing through tall stands of ponderosa pines, sometimes through groves of live oaks all the while taking care to not get run off the road by the huge tour buses we often passed.

Eventually, as we drew closer to Sedona, the rocks began to take on striking colors; bright shades of red and orange. Roadside resorts and recreation facilities began appearing along the road, then homes and small ranches. Then small desert themed shops began multiplying, tucked into the undergrowth.

And then we were in town. Low ochre-hued buildings lined the street, many offering upscale dining, southwest-themed art galleries, and expensive jewelry shops featuring turquoise and silver ubiquitously. The town had a sort of uncomfortable bougie feel to it at first glance. Coral-colored popped collared shirts and pastel-colored pleated shorts ready to golf. Big hair, salt and peppered in deep tan comfortable retirement. Small yappy dogs on short leashes with shorter tempers. It felt to us that if we stopped and started walking around we'd look pretty out of place in our grit and grime. Maybe even get hassled by the local cops. So we kept cruising around town, trying to find the road out into the mountains Zed had told us about. He had given us its name, an odd-sounding name we were sure we'd be able to remember, but now that we were on the ground in town none of us could remember what that name was, try as we might.

"You didn't write it down?" Jen asked, disapprovingly. "I asked you if you did, and you said yes."

"No, I did not; I never said I wrote it down."

"Yes, you did, Peter. I asked you and you said you had written it all down."

It went back and forth like this until Pete gave up and rolled into a gas station to ask for directions. He stopped the car short out front, giving us all an aggressive jolt and stormed inside, emerging moments later, his question answered.

"Schnebly Hill Road," he stated, starting the car and moving it over to the pumps.

"Oh, yeah. That was the name," I added cheerily, hoping to help deescalate their latest disagreement.

I joined Jen in the convenience store to gather some supplies for the days ahead, grabbing beers and the usual nonperishable foods we always stocked in the trunk while Pete filled up the tank. Once we were all set, we made our way out of town up to Schnebly Hill Road.

The road started out as a well-maintained, two-lane pavement but degraded rapidly as we climbed into the red-hued rocks and pale green scrub. Pavement ended shortly thereafter, with a warning sign ominously stating that rough roads were ahead for many miles to come and that you traveled at your own risk.

Up we climbed, the road steadily getting worse. The views were spectacular, colored with two tone peaks of red and pale yellow, beside melted looking buttes and mesas the hue of brick. It was slow going, so we had plenty of opportunities to catch the views from the windows of the car. There were other vehicles on the road up there with us, climbing and descending, but we had the only car. Only tour jeeps and all-terrain vehicles were up there with us, so we were very out of place in our old two-door two wheel drive coupe and definitely got some looks.

Around mid-afternoon, and maybe halfway up the Martian-colored canyon, the car overheated, blowing clouds of acrid steam out from under the hood. We had no choice but to stop. By chance, we came to rest near a prominent red rock outcrop. We all made for the feature and climbed aboard.

Sweeping views of the canyon below took our breath away. This place looked like magic, so it was no wonder Judith had talked about the land here with such a spiritual reverence. We sat there for maybe an hour soaking in the sun, our shoes off to the world. Pete eventually pulled his sneakers back on and climbed back down to the car to see how it was doing. He returned shortly.

"She's still hot as fuck," he reported. "I think we should camp here for the night."

"Hopefully, nobody fucks with us for camping so close to the road," added Jen. "There was a sign down where the pavement ended saying that camping was not allowed."

"Bah, we'll be fine," he dismissed. "We'll pick a spot off the road where no one can see us and won't pitch the tent till the sun is going down. Come on," he said to me. "Let's go scout out a spot."

The two of us scrambled down a few steps of the canyon below the rock outcrop and found a nice little nest hole like depression in the soil, surrounded by a couple of fragrant pinyon bushes.   "Perfect, this will do nicely," he declared and peed on one of the nearby bushes as if to mark his territory.

We heard voices as we climbed back up. Female voices. At the top we found a couple of pretty girls both about our age, a blond and a brunette enjoying the view we had recently quit.

"Hi! Great view, huh?" Pete proposed, deploying all the charm he could muster, while climbing up to join them.

"Hello to you too,"the blond haired girl responded. "Yeah, this is quite the view. You boys just passin' through?"

"Yup, we're on the road, traveling around the country." Pete stated. "Started out in New York. You?"

"Wow, New York! That's a long drive!" said the brown-haired girl.

"We're from Utah, traveling around the southwest, taking a semester off, ya know," added the blond. "New York is pretty far away; you all must have seen a lot of the country so far."

"Yeah, it's been a long, strange trip already," my companion chuckled.

"You all going to go through Utah?" the blond asked. "You think this view is amazing, you all need to check out Zion National Park, or the Canyonlands! Puts this place to shame."

"I don't know about Utah," Pete answered. "Ain't those crazy Mormon cops hard asses on travelers?"

"Yeah, I heard they can legally search your car just for having hippie stickers on the windows," I added.

"What? That's ridiculous!" the brunette laughed.

"I don't know, I'm afraid of those Mormons." Pete snickered. "Don't trust 'em."

"Do you even know any Mormons?" Brunette asked, her demeanor hardening.

"Uhh, well, no," Pete meekly answered. "I don't think so."

"Seems a bit presumptuous, don't you think?" brunette stated. "Two big boys like you afraid of some Sunday School Mormons." Pete had nothing. "You'd skip out on some of the best national parks in America just 'cuz you're afraid of a simple, modest people."

We stood there like mute idiots while she stared us down. "Come on, Sally," she finally said to her companion. "Let's hit the road before we scare these boys any further." And they climbed down off the rock.

"Smooth moves there, buddy," I chuckled as we watched their open-top Jeep continue on down the road toward town.

"Shut up," he replied, a bit put out.

We found Jen at the car, a cigarette dangling from her lips. "You two make some friends?" she asked sarcastically. "Those two girls left in a hurry."

Pete harrumphed. "Yeah, not so much," I added.

"Serves you right, Peter," she stated, pointing the two fingers that clutched her burning cigarette at him. He rolled his eyes.

"Alright, you two," I implored. "The sun's going down soon. I bet there'll be a great view of the sunset from that rock. Let's get our shit down to where the tent is going to go so we can relax and watch the sunset."

We pitched the tent snugly between those Pinyon bushes down the slope and tossed their bedding inside. There was a little half-assed fire pit nearby which had been used once or twice already, so we gathered a few of the dry branches lying around so we could have a little blaze once the sun was gone.

By sunset we were back on the flat overlook rock, waiting for the show to start. Shortly before the sun began its descent a couple young guys rolled up on mountain bikes, on their way back down from where we were going to be headed in the morning. They joined us on the flat rock for the sunset. The place where we broke down was apparently a pretty good spot; at least that's what the guys told us. They were locals, having grown up nearby, and said they knew the whole area.

"Like the back of my hand, man," one told us enthusiastically, presenting his left hand palm down and forcefully pointing to a space near the center with the other.

"This is a great place to watch the sun go down, especially if you're tripping balls," the other informed us. "You guys wanna burn a fatty?"

"Fuck yeah!" Pete exclaimed. And so, we did.

Their weed was super strong, and the joint was thick. I almost felt like I was tripping myself, mildly at least. The fiery glow of the setting sun set the canyon below us ablaze in impossible colors. It did not even look real, and I had to keep rubbing my eyes to make sure I was seeing it correctly. A few of the brightest stars began poking through the pink and orange curtain of the evening like pinholes torn into the fabric of the sky. I lay back against the rock, its surface still radiating the afternoon warmth, and let the colors wash over me. Soon it was dark, and the stars multiplied exponentially, their points studding the firmament like diamonds scattered across a sheet of glossy black velvet. It was kind of intense.

"Hey, we were going to light a little fire down below the rock for a while and stay the night here," Pete announced. "Do you think we'll get hassled by anybody?"

"Nah, you guys are good," one of the guys answered. "As long as you don't light some monster fire, and hoot and holler like a bunch of idiots, you'll be fine."

"Sweet. We got some beers, you all wanna join us for a bit before you ride back down?" Pete offered.

"Hell yeah, bro. That'd be sweet," he answered. And we all scrambled off the rock in the dark.

We all stayed up late, lounging around the little fire drinking beers and smoking joints. The kids told us about the forest at the top of the canyon, the area where we were headed. They assured us it was cool to camp up there for as long as we wanted, and that there were always people set up there in their camper trucks all summer. But now it was getting a little late in the season for that.

"It's gonna be colder up there then here," one of them continued. "You might even see some snow."

"Really? Snow, in Arizona?" I asked sarcastically.

"Sure, we get snow. What do you think, we're all just saguaro cactus and bleached cow skulls in the desert?"

"Ha, yeah. I guess I did," I admitted.

Eventually, the local kids took their leave, wished us well on our travels and rode off down the road, bombing the rocky path in the dark by partial moonlight alone. We called it quits shortly thereafter, Pete and I taking turns pissing on the embers of the fire to prevent any flare ups. I soon found myself alone in the back seat of the car, sealed up in my sleeping bag and thinking about whatever came to mind, riding the thought train from one subject to the next unable to sleep.

Before long, the subject of faith returned like it so often did, and I remembered that by daylight it would be another Sunday; it might be a Sunday already for all I knew, since I had no idea what time it was. I had been wrestling with my faith all trip and had come to some sort of decision the other day while I was puking my guts out in that junkyard. So, would I perform the ritual in the morning? Should I even bother? What did it matter if in fact there was no God? But if there was a God, a terrible vengeful God who smote any enemy the Israelites faced with fearful brutality, who sent his own son to die an excruciatingly painful and seemingly unnecessary death, who had the power to cast my soul in the eternal pits of hell for even doubting his existence, well, what then? Maybe I should cover my ass just to be safe, I reasoned.

I rose with the sun the next day and returned to the overlook alone to take care of my obligations. The air was brisk out in the open of this new day, with just a hint of frost in the darkest places of the landscape, faintly touching the earth like a whisper of the coming winter. I laughed at myself for my ignorance of the regional weather patterns, my breath hanging in the cold air of dawn in thin wisps of vapor. Frost in Arizona; a concept I had never thought to consider. This trip was so far challenging many of the concepts I held and presented a great many more I had in fact never even considered. This was not surprising, really. Wasn't that what I was after on this journey anyway, casting myself abroad as I was in youthful yearning, hungry for new experiences, and new points of view? Well, I was getting what I asked for. I was now reaping a harvest of deepening conflictions and doubts for my efforts. The sin of partaking of this feral fruit of road knowledge was rendering my heavenly passport void, I was now trespassing in the garden and it was only a matter of time before I was cast out for good.

I sat there cross legged on the overlook, my bag of crumbling matzo crackers in one hand and my five-ounce can of grape juice in the other, looking out on this world of stunning natural beauty below me and sighed. The nagging feeling that I was just hung up on unnecessary convictions was working to shake the supports my life had been erected upon, yet I still I felt compelled to observe this ritual. I had made an oath, and breaking my word felt like a legitimate sin.

So I again broke the bread and took the cup. I tried to feel the presence of God, tried to feel the sacrifice, the redemption. I prayed and praised and pulled my hair but all I felt was emptiness. I eventually completed the ritual by rote and packed up the remains.

I found Jen at the car, rummaging around in the trunk, the smoke from her cigarette hanging around her in the cold air.

"Good morning sunshine," she offered. "You look awful glum, you ok?"

"Yeah, I'm fine. Just thinking about shit," I replied, forcing my mouth into a smile.

"Aw, don't let shit get you down," she instructed as she came in for a hug. "Life is too short, ya know?" She gave me a nice tight hug. It felt good to be cared for, to be loved as I was. Better than anything else I could conceive.

We were back on that rough gravelly road by mid-morning, continuing our slow climb up to the ridge. The cool of the morning helped to keep the car's temperature within a safe operating range, and after a precarious and prolonged ride over roads not fit for the likes of a two-wheel-drive sedan with worn out overloaded suspension, we were able to crest the canyon rim with no further mechanical issues. It was approaching noon by then, so we stopped for a late breakfast and for one last look back at the rocky ochre landscape below.

Those kids who had smoked us out the night before had been kind enough to leave us with a fat roach, which we dispatched straight away. Just as we were climbing back into the car to continue our trek, Pete unexpectedly climbed up on the hood and let out a howl just as loud as he could, his voice descending into the valley below in muffled echoes. Dylan followed suit, not knowing what to make of his master's outburst, and continued howling in the car until Pete got down off the hood.

"What the fuck?" Jen asked in a sort of feigned exasperation.

"Just saying goodbye," he replied and steered the car back onto the path.

The road up here was worlds better than the rocky track we had followed up on the ascent. It was still just a dirt road but was remarkably smooth and rut free. We made much better time then and soon found we were deep into a forested wilderness.

A good many parking areas could be seen sporadically placed in among the pines on both sides of the road that must have served as the seasonal car camping spots the local mountain bikers had described. But there were no cars or RVs there now. We didn't see another vehicle for miles, parked or otherwise. We were about to just pick a spot to park, figuring we must be about where Zed had suggested we wait for him and his crew, when Jen spotted an orange VW Westphalia camper bus a ways off the road.

"Look, Pete," she announced, pointing over his grip on the steering wheel. "Road kids."

He slowed down to a crawl. There in front of the bus's open side doors a small fire pit smoked, and around the pit on some cut logs a group of hippie kids sat with a couple guitars, their white kid dreads hanging low over their shoulders.

"Excellent," he stated quietly. "Let's go say hi."

CHAPTER 25

Our new neighbors were a welcoming group, readily inviting us to settle in beside them and make ourselves at home. They were three kids out of Ohio, all about our age and dressed in the standard uniform of road kid hippies. They also had a friendly yellow mutt dog they called Sunshine and enough acoustic guitars and hand drums to start a band. And in a sense, they were a band since they all played together and had in fact been playing when we first rolled up.

Aaron, the owner of the van, had a collection of short dreads held out of his acne-scarred face by a dingy tie-dyed handkerchief, and was clad in a pair of equally dingy blue jean overalls covered in colorful paisley print patches. He played a twelve-string guitar and sang.

Amanda also had dreads, but a good six inches longer than her companion's, which were decorated with several large chunky beads and delicate rings of smaller seed beads of every color imaginable. She too was in old patched overalls and carpenter boots. She played guitar as well, a six-string, and sang as she strummed.

James rounded out their trio, his long golden brown hair dread free and loose to spill over his shoulders and frame his young bearded face. No overalls for him, just a checkered flannel and jeans. He played the hand drums, sang, and played the harmonica and flute. Together they could cut a good tune, as we would soon find out once the sun began to set.

But before that could happen, we all had to get to know each other a little bit first. This we did by sharing a communal meal around the campfire and exchanging the stories of our trips. They had set out from Ohio over a year earlier and had been pretty much everywhere in the lower forty eight states. They had kept fuel in the tank and food in their bellies by playing their music for handouts, as well as by hawking handicrafts they made at the various festivals and shows they followed. They must have been doing something right, since they did not feel as dirty and dangerous as Zed and his crew did despite operating on basically no money. They had a quiet peace about them that reminded me of the first traveler chick we had met back in South Dakota, Zoe. They came across as capable and trustworthy. We soon found our newly road hardened guard relaxed considerably in their presence.

We sat there in the firelight and listened to them play for hours, their music broadcasting out into the darkness of the night to mingle with the sleeping ponderosa pines.

It was cold the next morning, with a hard frost on everything. We shivered collectively around our meager morning fire while we waited for the breakfast and tea our hosts prepared for us.

"Thanks for the food," I said to Aaron between big spoonful bites of oats and raisins.

"Of course, brother," he replied. "Do unto others as you would have them do to you, ya know."

"Yeah, what goes around comes around," Amanda added. "Sharing the wealth is how we all get by out on the road."

"Well, we appreciate it," Jen stated while Pete nodded his head in agreement, his mouth too full of oats to speak. "Hopefully we can return the favor soon."

"Ah, don't sweat it," James replied. "The universe has a way of evening it all out. Someday we'll be hungry and someone will be kind to us."

"Still, we would like to cook a meal for you too, or something," Jen insisted. "But we might have to get some supplies."

"Why don't we take a ride back down to Sedona and hit up a grocery store or something?" Pete suggested. "We'll buy the next round."

"Ok, we'll see," Aaron answered. "It's a little late in the morning to start out on a trek into town now. Let's all take a hike in the forest today and see about making a run into town tomorrow first thing."

We set out walking around noon, following one of the many unmarked trails that crisscrossed the forest there. They had been going on daily hikes around the area since getting there about a week ago and had covered most of the ground surrounding their campsite already. Today we were going off in a direction they had not yet explored.

It was a dry, wild land without many permanent marks of humanity besides the trails and rough dirt roads we followed. The temperature had climbed considerably since dawn, and before long we had pulled off our sweatshirts and sweaters to take in the sun, unobstructed by any cloud cover whatsoever. We came upon a rocky outcrop rising slightly above the widely spaced trees and lay out there in the mid-afternoon sun for maybe an hour, drinking water and listening to James tool around on his flute. It was a relaxing way to spend the day, to be sure.

Pete and I got to talking to Aaron while he stacked a bunch of medium-sized rocks into a cairn, bringing up Zed and the crew we were there to rendezvous with.

"Maybe you all might like to caravan with us west. We're going to set up in a place called Quartzsite for a while and make some money working the gem show," he suggested.

"We'll see," Aaron responded absent-mindedly, his attention focused on the placement of the stones he was stacking. "We generally like to keep to our own schedule; haven't had much luck traveling in caravans."

By late afternoon we began to make our way back to camp. We had been out wandering around most of the day and were feeling the fatigue. My companions and I especially, since we had spent the better part of the past two months either driving in the car or lounging around some fire pit. These kids were in better shape than us, and it was obvious. I felt a little self-conscious of this fact, though to their credit, they never gave even a hint of judgment.

The ambient lighting of the forest was beginning to darken as evening approached, but we were still no closer to camp from what I could discern. Jen began to voice her concern about her desire to not have to spend the night in the open forest. But our guides assured us we were on the right path and would be in camp before dark. And sure enough, just as the path began to disappear into the surrounding darkness, our cars and tents materialized from out of the gloom. We were home.

We spent that next night much as we had spent the first, listening to the trio of travelers play their folk music by the flickering light of the fire. One of them had a long curved tobacco pipe he had packed with flaky tobacco and some other kind of dried herb, which was passed around many times and through a few refills. I did not get stoned off those mystery herbs, whatever they were, but I did get a head change of some kind. Though I suppose that could have just been the tobacco itself working its magic on my system, unaccustomed as it was to the effects of nicotine.

Aaron was up at dawn, followed by his partner, Amanda. Jen joined them shortly thereafter, and soon they were making their plans to trek back down the canyon road into Sedona for supplies, and to wash some clothes at a laundromat. The trio of minstrels would ride with my companions, while I would stay behind with the dogs and the VW bus to hold down camp, keeping an eye out for Zed and company should they happen to arrive.

"Got any dirty laundry?" Jen asked me. I did of course, but I was wearing most of it, having shed the clothes I had brought with me along the way as they became soiled. All I had to add to the load was a couple pairs of stiff stocks and underwear. It felt a little too risky to handover my only clothes and spend the day out there alone in my under drawers. I wished them success once they had all loaded into the car and watched as the Olds pulled away in a cloud of reddish dust. And then it was just the forest, the dogs and me.

I had at first been apprehensive at the suggestion I remain behind alone with the dogs and assume the responsibility of making sure they didn't run off or whatever. But I was assured by Aaron and company that Sunshine was a well-behaved hound, and would do no such thing. And I had gotten to know Dylan well enough by then to feel confident I could get him to respond to my requests should he feel the desire to run off. Plus, the two dogs seemed to get along so well together, never getting snappy with each other, that in the end I felt I could handle the mutts and accepted the job.

We played with sticks for a while, with the two of them often engaging in a tug of war between themselves over the latest stick I would toss into play. But soon they settled into their own choice of stick, and both set about chewing their chosen chunk of wood to pieces. I took the opportunity then to lean back against the front wheel of the van and zone out in the silence of the forest, a silence broken only by the chewing sounds the dogs were producing. The effect was slightly hypnotic to the point that I passed out for a time, drifting off into an empty space devoid of all color and substance.

I don't know how long I sat there in my self-induced trance, but I was eventually aroused by the sounds of a large vehicle rolling slowly down the gravelly dirt road towards me, its decrepit exhaust system woefully inadequate at muffling the noise of combustion from the eight cylinders of its large engine. I pushed myself up from my seated position, stiff from sitting still so long on the hard ground and caught sight of the approaching machine emitting that deep rhythmic rumble.

The RV! The van nosed, dirty white and mustard-striped camper! The ride we had been waiting days to see; they had made it! I dashed out towards the road, waving my arms and calling out. Zed was at the wheel, his wide toothy grin splitting his dark face as he saw me. I directed him into camp, and he pulled up opposite the VW bus, heralded by the barking of the dogs I had been left in charge of. Zed hopped out first, meeting me in an embrace as I approached.

"Aha! We have found you!" he declared as he pulled away from his hug, hands still on my shoulders. "But where is Pete? Where is Jen? Where is your cool old hooptie hot rod car? And whose orange bus is this?" he asked inquisitively. I briefly explained why he had found me alone deep in the forest accompanied only by two dogs and someone else's van. "Fantastic! The more the merrier!" he exclaimed. "I look forward to meeting our new campmates!"

The RV was beginning to unload its cargo as he spoke, the side door bursting open violently. Out tumbled Tick first, dressed exactly as I had last seen him, save for a large red wine stain down the front of his crappy sports team T-shirt. He crashed into the dirt like a drunken clown followed by peals of laughter from inside.

Then out came the crusties; three gutter punk kids in filthy threads, one with a gallon jug of wine three-quarters empty swinging from his finger by the handle. They, with the help of Aiden who had emerged right behind them, helped Tick to his feet. Then out stepped Barb, a second jug of wine in her grasp, followed by another kid, his large dirty gray hoodie pulled up over his head. Then a tall, short-haired, hippie-looking guy, his long stride landing him feet away from the door as he stepped out. And finally, like a ray of sunshine, the most beautiful girl I had yet seen on the trip, her long dirty-blond curls forming a mane thick and vibrant around her pale moon shaped face.

The steady silence the forest had been supplying was now totally banished. Everyone was drunk to varying degrees. Some, like Tick and the crusties, were straight up shitfaced. Even the dogs were now barking along with the sudden mayhem, egged on by Zed's out of control little pup Akasha, whose apparent idea of inter-dog play was to basically run full bore into Dylan or

Sunshine and attempt to knock them over. I couldn't help but laugh at the instant chaos that had just spilled out of the RV, like some dirty clown car disgorging its ridiculous contents into a library full of old church ladies.

"Holy shit, dude!" I exclaimed to Zed, who had stood by me as his riders had piled out," where did you find all these crazy kids?"

He threw his head back and let out a deep and hearty laugh, which almost instantly brought on one of his frightfully intense coughing fits. "Picked them all up in Denver," he replied a few moments later as he shook off the effects of his perennially irritated lungs, clearing his throat and spitting a thick bloody lump into the dirt. "Couldn't of made it here without 'em."

"You wanna pull?" Barb asked me as she sidled up with her gallon jug of cheap wine, a slight swerve to her step. I took the jug and pointed the bottom towards the treetops, taking a long draught.

"Ok, listen up!" Zed announced. "I need volunteers, we need firewood, we need to set up tents! Look alive, brothers and sisters, we need to make camp now so we can celebrate tonight!"

He received a lukewarm response among his troops, most having already been celebrating for hours apparently. But one jumped to attention right away. The kid in the dirty gray hoodie stepped forward and stood before Zed and me.

"At your service, sir," he stated flatly.

"Thank you, Dustin," Zed replied quietly, placing his long ashy hand on Dustin's shoulder. "Come on, everybody!" he then called out over Dustin's head. "We need volunteers!"

The tall, short-haired hippie stepped up, with the beautiful girl beside him. "We'll set up the tents," he offered. "Where do you think we should pitch them?"

Zed pointed out a spot off behind the RV, and off they went. "Why don't you and Dustin here go rustle up some firewood," he then suggested to us.

I looked to my new co-worker, and he winked with a sly smirk. "Shall we?" he asked, holding out his hand. I received a firm handshake and an honest eye lock as we formally introduced ourselves. He left me with a solid first impression. I was pleased to make his acquaintance.

He had a nondescript sort of look about him, this Dustin, dressed as he was in oversized clothes in muted colors. He wore his dirty-blond hair in an overgrown bowl cut that tended to spill over his brow and obscure his vision. He spoke softly as we went about our task of collecting firewood and allowed, or perhaps encouraged me to tell far more of my story then he did of himself. Before I knew it I had described my background to him in far more depth than I had yet to anyone else I had met on this trip, more even then to my traveling companions.

But it wasn't all a one-way street; he did offer a little of his backstory in return. He had come out of a suburb of Seattle, running away from home over two years ago to flee an abusive step dad and negligent mother. He usually traveled alone, only taking up Zed's offer for a ride because it was getting cold in Denver and he was running out of choices and time.

"And here we are in Arizona, and it's still fucking cold," he added in mock exasperation.

"It should be warm once we're down out of the mountains," I suggested. "We'll probably start heading to Quartzsite soon. I can't imagine we'll be here for long. There was frost on everything this morning."

He moaned sarcastically in response.

Back in camp, things were coming together, albeit haphazardly. A good blaze was going, supplied by all the wood we had dragged in, which filled the ring of rocks someone had expanded to twice the size it had been previously. The tents were up, their duct tape-patched rain flies lending unnaturally bright color to the forest backdrop and everyone was more or less settled in, drinking their wine and talking their shit with the raised voices of the inebriated.

I sat on a log by the fire with my new friend and studied these newly arrived characters. Characters whose hands I had shaken, shoulders I had hugged, and names I had exchanged with as we all went about setting up camp earlier.

The three gutter punk kids had come out of New York City's lower east side squat culture and were an abrasive lot. Especially their alpha, Fin Rot. He was the tallest of the three, over six feet tall easily. He carried a collapsed and overgrown Mohawk that had knotted up into clumps of greenish tinted dreads, a few of which hung over his pockmarked, pimply brow like a devil lock. He wore a well-worn and heavily studded leather jacket over a ratty old black hoodie held together with random patches emblazoned with the names of punk rock bands. Below the waist he wore a tight-fitting pair of red plaid pants, also held together with patches and zippers with a pair of old suspenders draped uselessly at his sides and a black leather flag hanging over his ass, displaying the tattered remains of some graphic cut from a punk T-shirt that had been crudely sewn on with dental floss. And he wore boots, of course. Ruined ox blood, ladder-laced Doc Martins that rose to his mid-calf, the toe of one held together with duct tape. He seemed to be perennially frowning, even when he smiled somehow. I was instantly drawn to this guy since he was so different from all the other hippie-type travelers I had yet met on the trip. He reminded me of some of the metal head and punk rocker kids I had hung out with in high school and my brief stint in college except that he came across as way more severe. "What the fuck you lookin at?" he barked at me the first time I worked up the nerve to introduce myself. "You," I replied bluntly, he laughed and accepted me.

His buddy was stocky and short, shorter than anyone else in camp. His hair was short too, probably shaved to the skin not that long ago. He kept this greasy fuzz under a faded NY Yankees ball cap pulled low over his brow. He wore a satiny olive-green flight jacket with a little NYHC in an X button pinned to the left shoulder zipper pocket that these type of jackets all have and dirty blue jeans with the cuffs rolled up to expose his yellow laced black Doc Martins, still somewhat shiny despite their life on the streets. He introduced himself as Mickey and was a lot friendlier than his companion, giving me a sincere yellow-toothed smile along with a firm, thick-fingered handshake free of charge.

The third punk they called Spun One. He was fall-down shitfaced when I met him that afternoon, so I don't know if the phrase "met him" would even really apply. He dressed less the part of the gutter punk then his companions did, clad in skate sneakers, big baggy pants, and an oversized grimy sweatshirt that had at one time been an expensive fashionable article but was now tattered and emblazoned with his name, Spun One, in fluorescent orange spray paint scrawled off center across his chest, which was applied while he was passed out drunk awhile back by his traveling companions so he would be easier to find in the gutter.

The other two newcomers who had set up the tents were a dating couple. The tall, short-haired hippie dude called himself Charles. He dressed in blue denim overalls and tie dye. On his feet were well-worn Birkenstock sandals over wool socks, and on his head was a floppy hand-knit cap that a lot of the dread head kids wore called a tam. Except that he had no dreads, so it just lay flat on his head like a deflated mushroom. He was from Tennessee and spoke with a drawl.

The beautiful girl he was with who had so struck me when I first saw her step out of the camper was called Alexandra. She wore brown corduroy overalls and a thick earth-toned cable knit sweater. She too had the Birkenstock, wool sock combo thing going on. She smiled a lot, her face was just set that way, and she just exuded positive energy. She reminded me instantly of some sort of archetypal earth goddess. Her hazel eyes glittered like magic when I was close enough to perceive them. Wow, I thought, that Charles is a lucky guy.

So with those cats, plus Dustin and Zed's crew, there were now ten heads milling around the camp when the Oldsmobile returned from town. They arrived just in time to witness Tick and Fin Rot's latest drunken wrestling match escalate into a dusty shouting debacle.

I ran up to the Olds, half drunk myself and pounded on the hood. "They're here, they're here!" I shouted over the scuffle behind me, the dogs barking wildly. Everyone in the car sat wide eyed, their mouths agape. "Zed picked up a bunch of riders in Denver," I explained without prompting. "Come on and park. They got all kinds of booze and shit. Let's celebrate!"

CHAPTER 26

It was a wild scene that night, from what I remember of it anyway. They had lifted gallons and gallons of cheap Pisano wine from some store on the way, and I must have drunk damn near a gallon of it alone. The Ohio kids, along with Jen and Alexandra, set about preparing a meal with the supplies my companions had brought back from Sedona, while Aaron, James, Aiden and Charles hammered away on drums and guitars. I bounced around from group to group, talking the small talk and getting drunker and drunker.

At some point the sun disappeared, for I realized it was suddenly pitch black away from the now raging campfire. I had held back from partaking in the food they all made because I wanted other folk to get a shot at it first and also because I was more interested in drinking at the time it was served. But now, with the spins coming on in unpredictable waves, I realized I was mighty hungry.

There wasn't much left in the pan; cold rice and beans with little chunks of spicy tofu or something in it. I ate what was left right out of the smoke blackened frying pan with my fingers, licking it clean in drunken ecstasy.

"Hungry much?" Fin Rot sarcastically asked me as he approached my dusty fireside squat.

"Fuckin' A serious!" I exclaimed, smiling wide, the saucy bits of rice stuck in my beard and my teeth.

He sat down beside me, followed by Mickey and Pete and one of those jugs of wine. We passed it around between us, calling out various cheers, skols and saluds.

"A jug of wine, a leg of lamb, and thou!" Fin hollered out, holding the jug high with one arm while wrapping the other around Mickey's neck in a mock headlock.

A few others joined us, and more wood was tossed on the fire with more hooting and hollering in the darkness added in for good measure. I could hardly see straight by this point but was having too good of a time to call it quits just yet.

My memory is sporadic from here, with my world drastically reduced to the light cast by the fire alone. There were fewer and fewer people around the fire with me as the night progressed, with the atmosphere growing quieter and more subdued as those souls disappeared. My final memories consist of blurred images of Fin Rot and Mickey dragging their companion Spun One away into the darkness by his arms, his drunkenly unconscious body limp and uncooperative. I felt I was probably not far behind Spun myself and voluntarily stumbled off to the sleeping bag awaiting me in the back seat of the car before the same fate befell me.

I had no idea what time of morning it was when I finally regained consciousness, or if it was even still morning at all for that matter. All I knew was that I was cold, hung over, and had to piss so bad my whole lower torso ached. Outside I found less than half of last night's company present, grouped around the fire pit, their backs to the chill of the day. Fin Rot, Mickey, Pete and Charles were silently passing around a jug of wine three quarters empty, a breakfast of champions apparently. I joined them, and Mickey passed the jug to me. I took a pull and noticed the orange VW bus was gone.

"Where's the Ohio kids?" I asked the group generally, wiping the wine from my immature fuzz of a mustache.

"They split first thing," Pete answered.

"Couldn't fuckin' hang!" Fin added. "God damned pretentious, holier than thou wanna-be hippies!" he swore, punctuating his declaration with a wine-colored dollop of foam, spit forcefully onto a rock by the fire where it sizzled audibly upon impact.

"Aw, they weren't that bad." Charles stated, standing up for them in their absence. "They were good people."

"Piss on you!" Fin shot back. "You hippies are all a bunch of fucking dirt snobs. Your shit smells as bad as mine, even if you douche your dirty asses down in patchouli."

"What the fuck, man?" Charles responded, startled by Fin's unprovoked attack. Fin stepped around the fire pit and right up to Charles, invading his personal space deliberately and stopping within inches of his nose, their gaze locking in a simmering stare. A few tense moments passed while we all stood frozen, waiting to see what would happen next. Fin then performed an exaggerated sniff of Charles causing him to flinch slightly.

"Yup, you smell as bad as me," he stated, a wry smile exposing his long yellowed teeth. Mickey began to chuckle, followed by Pete and myself. Charles then ventured to smile as well, taking the crude joke for what it was.

The situation sufficiently defused, Fin returned to his space next to his friend on the other side of the fire pit, and the jug started up its rounds again. Charles, not surprisingly, stepped away soon after, leaving the four of us.

"Fuck 'em if they can't take a joke," Fin announced to us all and finished the jug, which he then slung away into the forest as hard as he could, the sounds of it shattering against a rock returning shortly thereafter.

I stepped away then myself, the sudden need to defecate startlingly urgent. I grabbed a handful of napkins off the floor of the car and strode off into the forest, hoping I could make it out of sight before I shit myself. I cleared a dozen yards or so and deposited my liquefied waste in a shallow hole at the foot of a thick pine tree dug hastily with the heel of my sneaker, the stinking steam rising around me in the brisk air. I was just wrapping up my business when I heard brush snapping and breaking another dozen yards or so deeper into the forest. Something large was approaching. I quickly put myself together, not wanting to be caught out with my pants down by who knows what, and stood by my tree waiting to see what was forcing its way through the undergrowth.

Then I saw it, or rather part of it, for most of its form was still obscured by the bushes between my vantage point and its movement. It was huge, as big as a horse. In fact, I thought it was a horse briefly before I caught sight of its long dark brown head and the massive rack of antlers riding on top.

It was an elk, just like the pictures I'd seen in nature shows. But it was so much bigger in real life than I imagined it would be. I crouched down by my shitting tree and watched its progress. It was not into hanging around, probably due to the sounds and smells of our nearby camp, so I only had those few moments to observe it before it trekked away out of sight. But those few moments, wow, what an animal! I was in awe. Having grown up seeing the local white-tailed deer of the northeast ubiquitously present in every patch of woods and backyard garden bed, the sight of so large a creature emerging from the underbrush looked like something from a dream.

I remained there in my crouch for a while after the creature passed, hoping to catch a glimpse of another passing elk. But that was it; there were no others behind the big buck. I stayed for a while there anyway in silence, thinking about what I had just seen, until the cold finally roused me.

I shivered as I walked back to camp, my innards hollow and grumbling. I found more of the campers up and around upon my return. Alexandra and Jen had joined us, as had Zed, Aiden and Dustin. They were toasting slices of bread over the fire and passing around a giant #10 can of cold garbanzo beans, its lid mangled and torn for lack of an actual can opener.

"We need to move this party off the road," Zed declared as we ate. "Me and Dustin will scout out a spot further into the forest. You all pack up the tents and shit and get ready to move. We should be back in about an hour."

The gutter punks grumbled, not liking to take orders from anyone, and didn't lift a finger to help. But the rest of us did our part, hastily breaking everything down in our own half-assed way. They were back shortly and led our party deeper into the woods to an overgrown grassy clearing. The spot was very secluded, which is why they chose it. We set about building a fire pit, smaller this time, and collecting wood while the tents were put up. We then spent the afternoon goofing off. It was chilly, so by evening most everyone had quit the campfire and was crammed into the camper playing cards. I stayed out by the fire with Dustin and the punks. There was still wine left, amazingly, so we passed the time by passing the jug.

"Where is all this wine coming from?" I asked, surprised that there were so many gallon jugs of it around.

"Zed's kids," Dustin answered. "They shoplifted every place we stopped. They got all kinds of crazy shit in that RV they lifted from stores."

"Yeah, mostly dumb hippie shit," Fin added.

"Whatever, that shit in there is worth real money," Mickey responded in his thick New York accent.

"Don't do us no goddamn good out here in the middle of fucking nowhere. Fuck, I wish there was some cigarettes." And Fin took a long pull from the jug.

"At least we got the wine," Dustin reminded us. "For now."

We stayed up late into the night again, stoking the fire high for warmth more than anything. Most of the kids who had retreated to the camper as the evening approached stayed in there, where we could hear their occasional bursts of laughter and see the flickering light of their candles in the windows. I stepped in as well for a few minutes, but there was no room, plus I got the feeling I was intruding on something. So I stayed around the fire with the punks and Dustin. We were joined briefly by my traveling companions, Pete and Jen as they made their way to their tent for the night. The rest of them must have all slept on top of each other in the RV because no one else ever came out. We all called it quits after the last jug was empty.

It was very cold that night, but I slept well enough with my wine buzz on despite the drafts blown in through the dry rotted weatherstripping of the car doors. I had a nice sleeping bag I could pull up over my head, so I was warm. The kids sleeping in tents surely had it rough, though. I didn't remember seeing those gutter punks with much gear at all; even the tent they slept in was Zed's. I thought about offering the front seat to them, but there was not enough room for them all. It would never work. So I resigned them to their fate and pulled my bag up tight under my chin. Survival of the fittest, I guess.

I woke earlier than normal, I think. It was so hard to tell without clocks around. It felt earlier than normal anyway, so I stayed wrapped up in my bag and stared at the steel roof of the car, fuzzy with surface rust and frost from my breath. What are we doing here? I thought. It's cold and boring; why are we hanging around? I guess Zed has his reasons, I figured. I sat up and looked out the window, wiping away the frosty fog. The three gutter punks were around the early morning fire alone, wrapped in tattered blankets, their backs hunched in the cold. They seemed so out of place in the forest, completely out of their element. They all came up in urban environments, Mickey especially, being born and raised on the lower east side of Manhattan. But they were troopers. The streets gave them that much. They may have come to the forest woefully unprepared, but they were making do without much bitching.

I stayed in the car a long time, writing down my thoughts in the dog-eared, water-stained journal until the need to piss forced me out. It was a lot warmer outside now, and the sun was dazzlingly bright, offering its warmth freely in the clearing. Most everyone was up and about. Only Zed was absent. I found my way over to where Jen and Alexandra were sitting on a blanket, tying up strings of hemp twine into braided bracelets, and sat down beside them.

"How'd you all sleep last night?" I asked.

"It was cold in the tent," Jen responded. "But Pete and Dylan kept me warm, so we slept alright."

I looked over to Alexandra, and she glanced uncomfortably towards Zed's kids. "It was weird," she said. "but it was warm. I stayed close to Charles."

"Weird?" Jen asked.

"Yeah, Zed and Tick climbed up into the top bunk and cooked something up. Heroin I guess. I don't know what it was, but they shot each other up and then got really weird with us. I don't trust Zed. He kinda gives me the creeps." She glanced back over to Tick, who had joined the punks around the fire, and was laughing in his nasally abrasive way. "Don't tell anyone what I told you guys, ok?"

We agreed, but what was the use? Most everyone had been in the RV with them anyway, so it could hardly have been a secret. Zed stumbled out as we spoke, as if somehow hearing our conversation. He stood in at the door of the camper and surveyed his rag tag kingdom, his gaze coming to rest upon us. The girls looked away, but I met his gaze.

He looked bad, worse than usual. He always looked rough, but now he looked particularly gaunt, his eyes sunk deep into their sockets. He gave me a forced smile when he realized I was not going to look away. His smile was like the grin of a corpse; his thin gray lips pulled back taut, displaying long crooked teeth protruding from their receding gum line. Another one of his coughing fits broke our gaze, and he sat down on a milk crate and began to cough so violently he threw up. Barb came to his aid, bringing him water. I came to him too.

"You gonna be alright, man?" I asked him. He looked up to me, compassion in his watery eyes.

"You are a true man of God," he answered hoarsely. I felt instantly awkward, intensely so even, given the gradual loss of faith I had experienced so far on this trip. He seemed to read my thoughts for he continued. "You may be questioning your beliefs, as you should. But you will find what you seek, I promise you." I looked to Barb, who had kneeled beside him. She had tears in her eyes. I went to step away, and he grabbed me by the wrist.

"Seek ye first the kingdom of God," he quoted, again locking my gaze with his own, "and all of these things will be added unto you."

That fucked me up, quoting scripture and all. I pulled away from his grasp. "Yeah, I suppose so," I answered meekly. He began coughing violently again and I took my leave, making my way over to the fire pit where the punks were routinely stationed.

"That guy thinks he's a real fuckin' prophet or something, huh?" Mickey stated, having witnessed our exchange. I looked to them all, hoping to find my footing. "You religious?" he asked me.

"I was, but I don't know anymore," I answered.

"Too many rules in religion," he stated.

"There are no rules, anywhere. The Goddess prevails!" Fin added.

"Don't mind him. He fancies himself a Discordian."

"Fuck you!" Fin retorted, slugging his friend in the arm. "Chaos is everything. You'd be wise to recognize that," he preached, pointing his finger at the two of us. "Consult your penal gland! There you will find the answers you seek, not in some fucking bible!"

My curiosity was piqued. What was a Discordian, and who was this goddess of whom he spoke? But I was afraid to ask, fearing Fin Rot's general wrath and more so, fearing the wrath of the God I was spurning. Pete approached us then.

"We're going for another ride down into Sedona for supplies, you wanna come?" he asked me. I did, good God how I did.

I rode down with Pete, Charles, Jen and Alexandra, with Dylan riding on our laps. It was good to get out of camp for a while. The ride down was slow, since the road was so bad, but Pete had navigated it now three times before and had developed a method of bobbing and weaving around the ruts and holes.

We were down in the valley by noon. It was downright hot in town after the past few days in the chill of the higher elevations, and it felt great. I waited with Dylan over by a bench near a row of shopping carts while my companions walked the grocery store. An older hippie-looking guy, in his forties maybe, came up to me while I sat there with the dog and greeted me warmly.

"Peace be with you, traveler," he offered. "You just passin' through?" He was dressed similarly to me, in dirty camouflage pants and long-sleeve tie-dye shirt, except that instead of a mess of short wiry dreads like me he had a long ponytail of graying hair and a seemingly hand-carved wooden flute slung over his back with a braided hemp rope.

"Yeah, man," I answered. "We're just movin', been up in the hills up Schnebly Road for days. Came down for some groceries."

"Gotta be getting cold up there," he figured. "Ain't you gonna follow the sun?"

"Man, I hope so. I'm ready to get on down the road."

He sat down beside me and produced a one-hitter dugout. "Burn one?" he asked. How could I say no?

We sat there and shared a moment, pulling hits in the public of a supermarket parking lot, yet somehow invisible to society. He had such good energy, clean energy. I hadn't realized how cold and dark it had become around me till our chance encounter. I told him as such, and he smiled.

"I could tell you were troubled in spirit," he said. "Follow your heart; it will show you the way." I looked down at the one-hitter dugout he was holding and noticed that it was intricately carved.

"Did you make that?" I asked.

"Yup. You like it? Carving wood brings me peace. Well, many things bring me peace, really, but sculpture is one of my favorites." He paused for a moment. "You know what, here. I think you should have this." And he produced something from his pocket, placing it in my hands. It was a little wooden pendant, carved into the shape of an owl. I looked up to him dumbfounded, half expecting him to be gone in a puff of smoke like the old Indian sage who had given me a similar wooden owl in a dream not a week earlier. But he was still there, smiling calmly.

"Thank you so much, dude. You have no idea how much this means to me."

"Peace be with you, traveler," he answered as he rose from his seat. "And stay true to yourself."

My companions returned less than a minute after he had strolled out of sight. I thought about telling them what I had just experienced but decided to keep it to myself. I felt spiritually recharged somehow, but the feral road kid attitude I had recently developed wanted to just keep that energy to myself. So I hid the pendant under my shirt in response.

It was near dark by the time we got back, so we set about making a communal dinner right away. All the pots and pans were crusty with previous meals, but we cooked with them anyway. We brought a couple cases of beer too, which were decimated quickly, mostly disposed of by the gutter punk trio. As they got drunker, Fin began to get agitated about some ritual he insisted he needed to perform.

"I need to have a hot dog tomorrow," he kept saying, while his buddy Mickey kept telling him to shut up. "No, mother fucker, I need to have a hot dog tomorrow."

"You are fucking ridiculous," Spun said, one of the first and only statements I think heard him utter the whole time I knew him.

"Fuck all of you!" Fin shouted, standing up from his squat by the fire. "Fuck this, I'm going into town."

"For a fucking hot dog?" Mickey sarcastically asked.

"Yes, for a fucking hot dog."

"Dude, town is like ten miles away, and it's pitch black, and we're way off the road. You'll get lost and freeze to death in the forest," Pete stated. "We were just down in town. Why didn't you ask us to pick up hot dogs?"

"I don't care how far away it is. I need to have a hot dog tomorrow." And he strode off to his tent.

"What the fuck is all that about?" Pete asked, voicing the question we all were thinking.

"He's a Discordian," Mickey explained. "He feels he needs to have a hot dog on Fridays."

"That's fucking stupid," Pete said, again voicing what was most likely a common sentiment among us.

"Don't tell him that," he replied with a laugh. "He's liable to start throwing punches."

Fin noisily rummaged around in the tent, cursing and grunting. Finally emerging with a single mid-size, book bag backpack covered in magic marker graffiti, apparently his only worldly possessions, and headed off into the darkness without so much as a goodbye.

"Fin Rot! Get back here you fucking idiot!" Mickey called after him.

"Fuck you!" came the response from the darkness of the forest.

"God damn it!" Mickey muttered quietly as he rose from his seat and went in after him.

We all stood silently, listening to the two argue in the woods, a little in awe of Fin's complete disregard for everything except his need for a hot dog on a Friday morning to complete some ritual he felt he had to perform.

I laughed to myself; it seemed so ridiculous. Here is this crusty punk rocker whose whole identity is built on crassly denying any and all rules, and yet he feels he must perform some ritual dictated to him by some farcical religion. Even if it was just eating a hot dog, it seemed the epitome if incongruity, of hypocrisy even. But then I thought of my own ritual, the Sunday morning communion I had promised myself I would perform. How different is that, really? I too had felt that I had to perform it, that I had no choice and got all worked up when I missed it. What made his need to have a hot dog on a Friday morning any different than my need to have a bite of matzo crackers and a sip of grape juice on a Sunday morning? Who's to say his religion, this Discordianism whatever that was, wasn't the true religion? Maybe I should start looking for a hot dog myself, I chuckled.

The two returned after about fifteen minutes of woodland arguing. Fin stood there sullenly silent before the fire, a frown creasing his blotchy, stubbly face. I wanted to ask him about his faith, to know what drove him to need a hot dog on a certain day, but there was no way in hell I was going to ask him anything now, not after that show.

As we all stood there around the fire sipping our beers in awkward silence, a big black tarantula strolled up to the fire pit, climbed up on one of the rocks and raised its four front legs towards the fire, while standing on the other four rears.

"Holy fucking shit!" Pete exclaimed. "Look at that big ass spider!"

The sight of such a huge arachnid in our immediate vicinity instantly separated those with a spider phobia from those who didn't. Half of our party lurched away reflexively with exclamations and expletives, retreating from the sight of a hand-sized hairy spider, while the rest of us leaned in for a closer look. I was amazed, having never seen one outside of a glass terrarium, and knelt down to investigate.

"Careful man, that fucker is gonna jump up and bite your face!" Mickey warned.

"Nah, he's cool," I insisted. "Look, he's just trying to get warm."

"I'm gonna smash that fucker!" Fin stated and raised his ruined boot.

"No! Leave it alone!" someone shouted. He put his boot back down.

The big spider stood there facing the flames, apparently warming itself for at least ten minutes, sometimes down on all eight legs and sometime standing on the four back ones. It was wild. The thing seemed completely indifferent to our presence and stuck around so long that we began to ignore it, to take it for granted even. Then, as suddenly as it had appeared, it climbed down off the rock and continued on its way, quickly disappearing as it walked out of the firelight.

CHAPTER 27

The muffled sounds of commotion outside the car slowly roused me from slumber. I opened my eyes, finding the interior draped in a grayish light, dim and gloomy. I wiped the fog off the window to see what was going on but still couldn't see. Holy shit! Could it be? I popped open the passenger door, still half in my sleeping bag, and got caught in a shower of cold white fluff.

Snow! And lots of it. It looked like nearly a foot of it had fallen on us over night. Everyone was agitated, on the verge of panic even. Zed was barking orders to break camp, kids were struggling to break down snow-covered tents; it was chaotic. I shut the door and set about getting my pants and shoes on. Pete pulled the door back open as I was pulling on my last shoe.

"We're bailing outta here, hitting the road now!" he said, wide eyed, his clothes caked with snow. "The RV won't start, has a dead battery. Jesus Christ, I hope the Olds will start, or we're totally fucked!" He climbed into the driver's seat, pumped the accelerator pedal a few times and turned the key. The engine turned over slower than it should have but started and stayed running. "Yes!" he hissed through clenched teeth. "Come on, man," he said to me "We need to clear a path to get out of here."

Where to even start? I thought, surveying the buried camp. Everything was under a thick blanket of snow. I scanned the scene, looking for direction. Charles and Alexandra were breaking down their tent, Dustin and Mickey were attempting to do the same with theirs, while Fin Rot and Spun sullenly looked on, their meager packs slung over their shoulders. I trekked over to the RV, the snow almost up to my knees, where I found Zed brushing the snow off the hood with a broom.

"Good morning, soldier!" he greeted. "Hell of a way to wake up, huh?" I shook my head yes and he tossed me the broom. "Sweep off your hot rod. We need your battery." I followed my orders and pushed the drifts of snow from the surface of the Olds. He joined me once I had the hood clear. "Pop the hood," he commanded. Pete joined us and opened the hood to expose our humming vibrating engine, idling high in the cold. Zed went after our battery with a wrench and pulled it out while the motor was still running. He then walked it back to the RV, dropped it in the battery slot and hooked up the terminals. "You can have it back once I get our ship started," he stated.

It took a good deal of cranking but the RV eventually roared to life, its rich exhaust filling the camp with hydrocarbon fumes. Zed then pulled out our battery while his engine was running and handed it back to me. "Thanks," he said and dropped his own old swollen and corroded battery back in its place.

By now everything was pretty much broken down and packed up. All the cook gear had been left out by the fire overnight, as well as the trash we had accumulated, so it all had to be dug out and packed up in milk crates and worn-out cardboard boxes. I'm sure we left stuff behind in the rush, especially the trash since it was all buried in the snow. Zed then rallied the troops.

"Ok, everybody," he announced. "We're headed to the highway. The snow is deep, so once we get moving we can't stop. Pete, you guys follow me, but not too close. Hopefully Schnebly Road has been plowed by the time we get to it. Ok, let's roll out."

Charles and Alexandra, their packs on their backs, approached us as Zed's riders filed into his camper. "Can we ride with you?" she asked. "We really don't want to be cooped up with those kids in the RV anymore."

"Of course," Pete answered. "Climb in."

The big camper lurched forwards into the drift, quickly coming to a stop. It then backed up and charged forward again now with greater speed, pushing away from the dry patch of dirt it had been parked on and blazing a trail through the virgin snow. Pete did the same and followed the tracks the big truck left in its wake. The RV was gaining speed as it progressed, plowing through the drifts, the evergreen branches heavy with snow showering them and us with powder and broken pine boughs as we pushed through.

How he knew what direction to drive I have no idea. The fallen snow cover had made the whole landscape uniform. We had made it into that clearing down paths unfit for vehicular travel in the first place, and now that the world was blanketed in white fluff it was impossible to tell where the path even was. But the RV pushed ahead, blindly, because to stop would mean instant traction loss. We would both be hopelessly stuck in the snow in the middle of nowhere. Stopping to make sure we stayed on the path was not an option.

We pressed ahead for a tense few minutes, and it was looking like we might never find the road when suddenly we were on it. It had not been plowed, not recently anyway, but there were the tracks of 4X4 trucks to follow now. And soon we came up on some sort of horse ranch complex or something off the road, surrounded by a large clearing. There we found the way plowed and clear. Together we collectively breathed a sigh of relief. Within minutes of hitting plowed road, we came out of the forest and face to face with the Highway, thundering with big-rig trucks tearing by in clouds of icy dust. We followed the RV up the on-ramp of Interstate 17 south and slowly matched the speed of the traffic.

The highway was clear and dry, with only short piles of snow running along its sides where the plows had earlier passed so we could travel as fast as the big camper would go. Before long we were dropping in elevation and the snows disappeared altogether. We weren't sure how far Zed was planning on going today; there hadn't been any discussion of that in the hustle to break camp, so we figured we'd just follow them and pull off when and where they pulled off, then talk out the plan once we had all stopped. We didn't have to wait long. About forty-five minutes down the road we came up on a rest area and followed them down the exit ramp.

We all piled out into the sunshine of the lower elevations and reveled in the temperate dry climate. Zed came up to our group as we stretched.

"Ok, guys. We're headed to Phoenix, maybe stay there a few days. We need to stock up; food, booze and gas most importantly. That's going to be a lot easier in a city. You guys still want to be caravanning with us?"

We all looked to each other and nodded in agreement. "Yeah, sure," Pete answered for us. "We're down."

"Excellent," he said and glanced over to his riders. "We're going to hang around here for an hour or so, see if we can't spainge up some cash for gas." I noticed then that Tick, Aiden and Barb had split up and begun approaching people, engaging in conversation. "Relax; wash up in the rest rooms. We'll hit the road again in about an hour."

We took his advice, using the rest area facilities for what they were worth and drying out our snow-dampened clothes in the full unobstructed sunshine. By this point, I had tossed out most of the clothes I had brought from home and was still wearing the oily fire-colored tie-dye shirt and camo pants I had found in that wrecked van back in New Mexico. I was feeling grimy and looking even worse according to the reflection the restroom mirror was giving me. I peeled off the shirt and found my form even thinner than it was on my last attempt at bathing. I had also developed a nasty raspberry-colored rash across my chest centered over my right nipple. The transmission oil in my shirt was irritating my skin, but I had no other shirt to swap out. So I filled the sink with hot water, plugging the drain with a lump of brown paper towel and did my best to wash the shirt with the hand soap provided by the State of Arizona, or whoever stocked those rest area bathrooms I found myself in.

The water quickly acquired a dull oily sheen, so I flushed it out and started over, only to have it quickly film over once more. I ended up playing this game a dozen times before the shirt stopped souring the water instantly. I rang it out and set to work washing my upper torso with the paper hand towels and soap. It felt pretty good, but I made a total mess of the sink I was working at, leaving a black oily ring in the sink and gray water all over the floor.

"Jesus fucking Christ, you taking a bath in here?" Fin Rot remarked as he joined me in the roadside rest room. I just laughed and headed back to the car, shirtless to the world, my four-inch dreads shooting out all over the place and my water-spotted pants stiff and slightly glossy with filth riding low on my hips.

"You're a real sight," Jen laughed as I approached the car. "You want a towel or something?"

"Nah, my shirt will dry out soon enough in this sun."

I hung around with my troop as they rummaged around in the trunk. Alexandra and Charles had struck some sort of deal with my companions for a long-term ride wherever we were going, so they were making room in the trunk for their packs by revisiting the possessions they had been carrying all this time: the apartment in Seattle now all but forgotten. They had a nice little pile of cast-offs set aside, a serious amount really. The two seemed to have come to terms with our current situation and were not as insistent on keeping all the superfluous stuff they had brought anymore. The trunk was now half-empty without our new riders' packs. We'd come a long way from my parents' driveway.

After an hour or so had passed, we began looking to Zed's crew for the signal to roll out, but they were all still goofing off, having given up on asking for handouts from the motorists who had stopped to piss. Zed was nowhere to be seen.

"What the hell are we waiting for?" Charles asked us all generally. "Look at those guys, they're just fucking around." And indeed they were. Tick was again engaged in some sort of mock wrestling match with Fin Rot in the grass beside the parking space, the two of them hollering and carrying on and drawing the attention of the motoring public. "Those idiots are gonna get the cops called on us."

"Hold on, here's Zed," I stated as he flung the door of the camper open, slamming it against the side.

"Yo, what the hell!" he admonished his crew. "Get in the van, now!"

They all slowly piled in, Tick and Fin laughing and pushing each other around. Zed waved to us from the driver's seat, signaling our departure, so we all loaded up as well and followed them back out onto the highway.

"Those kids are fucking nuts," Charles said to us all as we drafted the camper's wide ass. "Especially those gutter punks. Holy shit, what a crew of aggro crazies." We could hardly disagree. "Brother man, thanks for letting us ride with you; I don't think I could have taken much more of that one punker's negative energy," he confessed to Pete, grasping his shoulder from behind. "Jesus, that crowd. Whoa buddy, I would not want to be in that ride if it got pulled over."

"Yeah, it'd be trouble for sure," Pete replied with a laugh.

"Man, I'd be fucked. I really need to keep low key," he added cryptically.

"What do you mean?" Jen asked, turning to him from the front seat. "Are you in some kind of trouble?"

Alexandra looked to him with concern furrowing her brow. He met her gaze briefly, before directing it out the window into the blur of the passing landscape. "I'm in the Army, or at least I'm supposed to be," he confided. "I'm AWOL for about five months now." He then put his hand to his face, squeezing the bridge of his nose with his fingers. "I'm probably gonna go to jail over this."

We didn't have much to say, certainly nothing in the way of advice. Alexandra, sitting between us in the back seat put her arms around him. "We'll figure something out. Don't worry," she said softly.

"Just don't get pulled over," he laughed to our driver awkwardly. "Shit, I don't even have any ID."

The RV had changed lanes at some point, moving over to the left, and someone was waiving out the passenger side window, signaling for us to pull up alongside.   It was Tick, hanging halfway out the window, his greasy pockmarked mug grinning ear to ear. "Hey, we're going to stop for gas at the next exit!" he yelled over the roar of the highway. We gave him the thumbs up. "Hold on, stay right there!" he added and ducked back into the cab, emerging seconds later, pale pimply ass first, his hands grabbing each cheek so his grimy asshole was pulled taught.

"Oh my god!" Jen exclaimed, covering her mouth in disgust.

"How's that for low key, eh, bud?" I ribbed Charles. He just shook his head.

We followed them to the next available fueling station and pulled up to a pump as well. I volunteered to cover this tankful and went into my pack to grab another one of my traveler's checks. We had lived frugally so far, our spending focused mainly on gas for the car, but when I dug out my pouch of checks from my pack, I was a little alarmed to notice they were more than half gone. I was still rich by the standards my fellow travelers lived by, but I couldn't help but feel a little uneasy at the thought of running out of money out on the road. I guess I'll cross that bridge when I get to it, I figured, and went into the station to break that representation of a hundred-dollar bill. Zed was already at the register, counting out a wad of crumpled small bills.

"Ok, I've got eighteen bucks," he said to the cashier. "Open up the pump for eighteen, regular gas."

"Hold on, Zed," I told him, bellying up to the counter beside him and addressing the cashier. "Here, use this travelers check to fill that green car at pump four, and then use the rest for this guy's RV."

"Thank you, brother," Zed said to me, putting his hand on my shoulder.

"No sweat, man. What goes around comes around, right?"

"Do unto others as you would have them do unto you," he quoted in a quiet monotone.

There was some money left over, so I let them spend most of it on crappy snacks, cigarettes and beer for the ride, taking the rest for my pocket. I was everybody's favorite guy for a hot minute.

Back on the highway, we all got to talking, as is to be expected among people on long car rides. Charles let us in on a little more of his backstory, and what brought him to our back seat. He had joined the Army after dropping out of college and quickly realized he had made a mistake. The rigidity, the uniformity, the life of a soldier was not for him. He stuck it out for a while, then when he went out on scheduled leave, he never went back.

"I had been home partying with my old friends from high school," he explained. "We all dosed on acid one night, tripped my face off. Somebodies older uncle was there with all us kids, I can't remember his name. He had fought in Vietnam and it had really fucked him up. He heard I was in the Army and unloaded on me, asking me to imagine looking your enemy in the eye putting a bullet through their head, told me about seeing his buddies killed right next to him and innocent little kids blown apart by American bombs. Brought me to tears. The next morning, once I had come down, I just knew I couldn't go back. What if I had to kill someone in battle? What if I had to face the same shit this guy had? I couldn't do it." We all nodded in agreement. Killing people was definitely not something any of us were keen on doing. "I just sort of drifted for a couple weeks, hitchhiked out of state, got a ride with some kids heading west, and landed in Denver. That's where I met Alexandra," he added, taking her hand and smiling. "We hung around the scene there till it started getting cold at night, then met Zed one day and here we are."

"How about you?" Jen asked Alexandra.

"Oh, I'm from Boulder. I've done a little bit of traveling since high school, but this is the farthest I've been from home. I mostly just hung around Colorado, enjoying nature, kickin' it with my sisters and brothers, just enjoying life," she explained in her soft, melodic voice. "I was in Denver this last time only a few days when I met Charles. He has such good energy; I was drawn to him right away." Jen nodded understandingly.

We all gave them a brief account of our stories and what had brought us together to head out on the road. Neither of them had ever been to the east coast and were very interested in our New York experiences, especially Pete's New York City stories. The Big Apple to them was the stuff of movie legends. He made no attempts to dispel this notion, purposely choosing his wildest city tales and embellishing the details as much as Jen, who was already well versed in his stories, would in good conscience allow. It was nice riding with them; they were just lost kids like us, looking for the way, for meaning. They were not as pragmatically jaded as some of the other road kids we had met, and not as spiritually dirty, which was refreshing.

We were nearing civilization again. The wide rolling hills covered in grassy tufts and scrub brush were gradually giving way to civilization. We followed the leader into the satellite suburbs and finally into metro Phoenix proper. The city was not particularly tall but was dense and sprawling from what we could see from the highway. The camper took an exit, and we followed them in.

Down the streets and boulevards we rolled, cruising at a moderate pace. The air was strikingly warm considering the weather we started the day off in, so we had all the windows down, reveling in the warm breeze swirling around our heads. We had no idea where we were going, but it didn't much matter since we had nowhere to go. Zed must have known the city well enough because he pushed on without hesitation, rolling through stop signs dangerously, eventually leading us to a busy strip of stores and restaurants where pedestrian traffic was substantial.

He looped around the block and pulled up along the curb facing the back side of the strip of buildings. We pulled in behind him. "I guess we're here," Pete announced as he shifted the car into park.

We all gathered on the sidewalk by the RV, waiting to see what was up. The punks were visibly drunk, as were Zed's kids. Most still had a beer in their hand as they congregated on the sidewalk. Zed stepped out last and addressed the group.

"Ok everybody. We'll probably be here for a few days. That strip we just rode down is like the main drag of this town. Feel free to spread out and spainge if you'd like; you'll probably make a good coin. We'll all meet back here around midnight. There's a better place to park for the night a few blocks away. I've got something I need to take care of on my own, so I'll see you all later. Have fun, everybody."

The punks took off right away with Zed's kids, leaving our carload and Dustin. "What's up, guys?" he asked us as he stepped up. "This is a pretty fun town, ever been here before?" We all shook our heads no, none of us had. "Follow me then; I'll give you a tour."

We walked the strip for about an hour as the sun slowly set, checking out the scene as it was. As night overtook the light, we decided to split up. Pete, Jen, Charles and Alexandra wanted to sit down at some restaurant. Dustin said he didn't do restaurants and would rather try to score some forties and drink in an alley. That sounded more my speed as well, so we struck out in search of a convenience store that would sell us big bottles of beer without checking our IDs. We didn't have to look far.

The first place we went took my money without question. I had gone in alone because I looked a little older than he did, and it would be less conspicuous than the two of us in there at once. I grabbed four forty-ounce malt liquors in bright green bottles, made my purchase and stepped out the door like I had every right in the world.

"Aw, fuck yeah, dude!" he exclaimed as I met him around the side of the building. "Come on; let's find a quiet alley someplace."

We walked maybe two blocks away from the strip and ducked in alongside some low cinder block building facing a four-foot-high retaining wall. There we found a few milk crates and a mess of empty beer cans and bottles scattered about. We each pulled up a crate, twisted the tops off a couple of those big bottles of cheap beer and got down to business.

The beer tasted delicious. Enhanced by the risks associated with its procurement and its side-alley consumption no doubt. The first two went down fast for the both of us, for we had a job to do, goals to meet. But once we had our second ones open and a good buzz rolling we took our time, using our drinks more as hand props in our conversations. Again he had me opening up and baring my soul; he had a knack for that somehow. But he reciprocated in equal measure, matching the depth I would set. I, of course, unloaded the issues of faith which had so troubled me this whole trip and asked him what his take on God was.

"I wasn't raised in a religion, like you were," he admitted, "so, I can't totally relate. I get the concepts and all but never had much use for God. Frankly if he does exist, I don't think he's got much use for me. I mean, where was he when my mom would leave me alone as a kid for days with no food in the house while she went off on another bender? Where was he when her asshole boyfriend beat the shit out of me cuz I wouldn't suck his cock? Man, he was fucking absent. I've taken care of myself now for as long as I remember and never got no help from no one, either human or superhuman." He took a long pull from his forty and continued. "You know, this life is completely fucking absurd if you really think about it. It's all one big cosmic joke, and we're the punch line. Think of the vastness of space and time. Its limitless! And here we are with a few dozen years if we're lucky, kicking around this one tiny speck of a planet thinking we're the shit. Man, we ain't shit, and anyone who stops running the race for half a fucking minute and actually thinks about it can't deny it." I certainly couldn't. "We're totally insignificant against the background of the cosmos, and yet we can contemplate infinity. And by the time we've figured out what the fuck we're supposed to do with ourselves, it's like too late, we're dead. If God does exist, he's fucking with us. So, fuck him!"

He took another pull from his bottle, and I did the same from mine. "Ya know, if there is any meaning to life it's this right here." And he made a motion to the space around us, the dark and trash strewn alley. "The point is to have a good time and live well, wherever you are, whatever you are doing. To enjoy this comically short amount of time we get to live as best we can. We only get one pass through this life, and I'll be damned if I'm going to waste one fucking minute of it trying to please the unpleasable. To life!" And he raised his big bottle in the air. I met his bottle with my own, our vessels clanking loudly in the darkness.

"I think you're on to something, Dustin," I admitted, once I too had taken a long draught.

"You're God damned right I am." He laughed with an exaggerated wink. "You know, there's some good books you should try to read by this French guy from…"

"Hey-oh, what's going on down here?" We both wheeled around towards the voice above us. A girl, a crusty punk girl, her traveling pack strapped tight onto her back, her patchwork hood drawn close, framing her smudged face heavily tanned from spending most if not all the daylight hours out in the open. She had tall lace up boots caked in dirt, a beat up plaid pleated skirt like the ones worn by schoolgirls over top of a pair of pants that looked to be made almost entirely out of random patches of black leather and fabric. "You boys got any beer for me?" she asked, hopping down from the retaining wall we had been sitting below. I handed her my half-finished forty automatically. "Gee, thanks handsome," she said coyly before drinking about half of what was left and handing it back to me. "How 'bout you?" she asked Dustin, wiping her mouth with the sleeve of her hoodie.

"What's in it for me?" he asked with a smirk.

"I'll tell you my name," she offered. He handed her his beer. "I'm Amerika, with a K," she stated, fulfilling her end of the bargain, "but you can call me Ami. You boys just get into town? Don't recall seeing you on the street."

"Yeah, rolled in a few hours ago," Dustin explained. "Headed west."

"West eh?" she asked, dropping her pack, pulling up another milk crate, and taking a seat. "You all in a car or something, huh?"

"Yeah," I replied. "How'd you know?"

"You ain't got no packs," she stated bluntly, pointing out the obvious. "Ya know, I'm looking for a ride outta here soon. Got any room for a rider?"

"Yeah, actually," Dustin said, "I'm riding in an RV now; half hippies, half gutter punks." The girl raised her thick eyebrows in interest. "The guy in charge of the ride is a little controlling, acts like some kinda guru dad, but you know, a ride is a ride."

"Sounds promising," she said, stroking her chin theatrically. "What about you, you riding in this RV too?" she asked, turning her attention to me.

"Nah, I'm in a car with some other kids," I explained. "We're caravanning west."

"Alright. I'm intrigued," she decided, handing the forty back to Dustin and standing again. "Why don't you boys introduce me to your friends."

It was past midnight now, and the streets were a lot quieter in these early hours. The orange glow of high-pressure sodium lights lent a dreamy, unnatural feel to the city. We talked as we walked, Dustin and I each trying to keep the girl's attention and win her favor without being dicks to each other. It seemed we were succeeding for the most part, since she was being less guarded about who she was and flirting back at us with equal measure. She was obviously working her angle, securing a ride out of town, and we knew that. But it was still fun to flirt.

We had her pretty excited about the ride on offer as we turned the corner to the block where the vehicles were parked, and we were excited about having her climb aboard too. The more she volunteered about herself the more we liked her. Pete and the three others in my ride were standing by the open trunk of the Olds with Zed as we approached. We were a few yards away when the door of the RV burst open violently, with Tick and Fin Rot locked in battle, real battle. No play wrestling this time, they were both bleeding and yelling and throwing fists. Right behind them piled out Aiden, Mickey and Spun One. As soon as they got out in the open they started swinging at each other, landing punches and kicks, with Mickey attempting to pull back his friend as Aiden attempting to pull back his. Zed and my crew dropped whatever it was they were doing and rushed to the action. Our new punker girlfriend, Ami, stopped dead in her tracks.

"What the fuck's all this?" she asked, wide eyed. We didn't know for sure why, but it was obvious what was happening; a fight.

The two, evenly matched as they were, kept at it despite their friends' attempts at breaking it up. Other random people were being drawn to the commotion now as well; the noise of a fight always draws a crowd. Zed tried to step in, and Fin took a swing at him, grazing his cheek. That gave Tick an opening and he came at Fin with all his might, tackling him and driving him into the rear quarter panel of a parked minivan, caving in the sheet metal and shattering the big side window with the spikes on his leather jacket.

The random people who had gathered were hollering now to stop fighting, and someone yelled that they were calling the police. Fin pushed back against Tick, driving him back against another parked car and setting off its burglar alarm. I turned to my late drinking companions and found Dustin alone. Amerika the gutter punk chick was jogging away. She had seen enough and apparently had no further interest in catching a ride from the likes of us.

"Mother fucker," Dustin muttered as he watched her tightly turn a corner at the end of the block and disappear. Then we heard the police sirens.

Zed had climbed aboard the RV after his attempts at stopping the fight had failed and had collected the three gutter punk's packs and tossed them onto the sidewalk without a word. He then started the engine.

"Fuck, that's my ride!" Dustin exclaimed and ran towards the camper. I followed close behind, arriving just as the two fighters had stopped throwing punches, their rage sufficiently spent. Mickey and Spun already had their packs on. I went to grab Fin's from a bush where it had landed and brought it to him.

"What happened?" I asked him as I handed him his pack.

His face was lumpy and bloodied, and fury still raged in his eyes. He snatched the pack from my hands. "Fuck all you assholes!" he barked and strode after his companions.

"Come on, get in the fucking car!" Jen hollered at me from behind. I turned and ran back to the car. Dylan was barking and climbing all over us, the car alarm was still wailing, and now the police sirens were drawing closer, so close that I could see the red and blue flashes of light from the cop cars reflecting off the third story windows a few blocks over. The RV pulled away, and we followed them down the block and around the corner, passing a speeding police cruiser about four blocks from the scene.

"Jesus, fucking Christ!" Jen exclaimed. "Peter, the light is red!" The big camper plowed ahead, blowing through red lights without even slowing down. Pete did his best to keep up, blowing those same red lights in turn. "Oh my God, oh my God!" she cried.

The RV blew one last light ahead of the I-10 on-ramp, cutting off a panel delivery van, causing it to dive off the street and into some bushes to avoid getting creamed by the big camper. We watched the action mouths agape, frozen in apprehension, as Pete followed Zed up the on-ramp and onto the highway. It was a good thing it was so late at night or we would have definitely crashed into somebody on those streets.

Traveling the highway was better; there being minimal traffic, we were able to travel at speed in relative safety. Zed had his huge camper going incredibly fast, up over eighty miles an hour at times. The Olds had no problem keeping up, having been built with those kinds of speeds in mind, but the RV weaved all over the road at such a rate of travel. It must have been terrifying to be inside of that thing.

After about a half hour Zed began to slow to a more moderate speed and eventually took a random exit off the highway. We followed him down to the service road along a dark, desolate stretch, the only lights being the few high-powered lamps that lit the interstate. Zed took a sudden dive off the pavement onto a dirt road, and we followed him into a cloud of dust lit by our headlights alone.

He led us down this route for maybe ten minutes, tracing the track of a set of high-tension power lines away into the desert before abruptly stopping. We cut our headlights and were instantly draped in the complete darkness of a moonless night. We all climbed out of the car, our bodies stiff from the stressful escape we had just executed. Zed approached us alone.

"You all ok?" he asked us, his face obscured by the darkness. "I'm sorry about all that crazy driving."

"We're ok," Pete answered, taking a deep breath. "What the fuck happened back there?"

"Those idiots were all playing poker for cigarettes and drinking whiskey. Tick says that Fin was cheating. Fin said that Tick was cheating. You fill in the blanks." We all let out a chorus of understanding grunts and hums. "We're staying here tonight. We're out of Maricopa County and way off the road. I don't think we'll have any trouble out here tonight. Get some rest. We're close to Quartzsite. We'll hit the road once everybody is up and should get there by midday." With that he returned to his ride.

I helped my friends pitch their tents beside the car and bid them good night before climbing into the back seat. It was warm out there in the desert, too warm for my thick sleeping bag, so I attempted for a while to lay on top of it. But I still could not sleep, the adrenaline rush of our flight from Phoenix still coursing through my veins. I climbed onto the hood of the car, propping my back against the windshield, and basked in the light of the stars, so piercingly bright out here miles from light pollution. Gazing into the endless fabric of space had a calming effect, and I slowly drifted off into a fitful sleep devoid of dreams.

CHAPTER 28

I hardly slept. Lying on the hood of a car with the windshield as a pillow does not make for the most comfortable sleeping arrangements. So I was up before dawn, watching as the landscape around me slowly emerged from the starlight. It was pretty bleak there in the dim dawn. Far off in the distance, many miles away, a row of dark jagged peaks rose from the horizon like broken shards of earthenware vessels. And closer, sporadically placed all across the floor of the desert, were several tall saguaros standing like silent creatures, their arms raised in salute.

I slid off the hood and trekked off to take a leak. Not far from where we parked, I found the ground covered in shell casings of all calibers, the brass surfaces of the little cylinders catching the rays of dawn like metallic dew. Ahead I could discern a wide ravine and stepped towards it, the metal shells clinking under my feet. Down in the dry wash of the ravine, a number of ruined cars and large household appliances were tumbled on top of one another, riddled with bullet holes. It was eerily reminiscent of a mass grave and gave me a shudder to imagine it. But I pissed over the side onto the Swiss cheese-skinned corpse of a washing machine anyway.

I found Zed up and coughing his lungs out upon my return. He had the hood open on the RV and had been working on something before his lungs decided otherwise. He was spitting out the bloody bits as I approached.

"Oh, man dude. Are you alright?" I asked him.

"Yeah, yeah," he replied hoarsely, clearing his throat and waving his hand near the side of his head like he was swatting away flies. "You know anything about cars and trucks?"

"A little," I replied. "What's up?"

"I had like no brakes last night," he admitted. "I tried to stop for that first red light, but almost nothing happened." I raised my eyebrows in a sign of alarm. "After that I just kept going no matter what the traffic lights were doing."

"Holy shit!" I exclaimed. "I was wondering what the hell was going on."

"They work ok at slow speeds, but there's no stopping this tank once it's really moving. Must have fucked something up underneath when we were plowing snow in the woods yesterday. Pretty sure I ran over some logs and rocks," he reasoned with a chuckle. "The transmission has been slipping too. Do you think Pete might have a couple quarts of tranny fluid I could grab?"

"Yeah, probably," I replied, looking in under the hood with him. "What are you gonna do about the brakes?"

"Drive slow, I guess."

Tick and Aiden had emerged from the camper as we were talking and had together walked off a few paces where they stood taking turns with a pair of binoculars, checking out something off in the distance. They returned and conferred with Zed quietly for a few moments before setting off across the desert scrub. I caught a glimpse of Tick's face as he turned to go. Black eye, split lip, dried blood on his shirt. He looked like shit but appeared unfazed by his physical damage. I wondered what they could be doing, what they had been looking at, but I didn't ask.

My companions were waking up now, and I joined them at the trunk where they rummaged around for breakfast. I asked them all how they had slept. Their answers were the same; poorly. The ground was hard as a rock, and they had all been as agitated by our panicked flight from Phoenix as I had been. I think the only one who got any real sleep out of all of us was Dylan the dog.

We hung around there for maybe another hour, packing up the tents and checking out the vehicles. Pete did have a couple spare quarts of transmission fluid to offer Zed and took the opportunity to check all the fluids on the Olds as well.

Tick and Aiden returned carrying a large, flat, rectangular metallic object wrapped in a stained and tattered blanket and slid it in the door of the RV. I caught Tick's eye as he fed the object in to his partner and he smiled wide, exposing a freshly missing tooth before climbing aboard himself and shutting the door. We were underway not long after, following our leader's dust back out towards the freeway.

We were on Interstate 10 west for maybe an hour, traveling a lot slower than before on account of the RV's lack of adequate brakes. We were in some real deal desert now. It was flat, dry and hot, even for late fall. The warm air whipped through the open windows of the car, blowing the girls' hair around and filling the space with a dull roar of sound. There wasn't much to see out the windows, the terrain long and flat and populated with short thirsty bushes and tall thin cactus. I soon became mesmerized by the monotony of it to such an extent that I fell asleep.

I awoke to the telltale sounds of off-ramp deceleration and opened my eyes on Quartzsite, Arizona. At first glance I was unsure if it was the "city" described to me. The bustling market bazaar of gems and minerals instead looked like a half-abandoned desert outpost, its few low cinder block buildings in the minority among a variety of mobile home trailers, vans, campers and pop-up tents of all shapes and sizes. We tooled down the main thoroughfare past the few businesses housed in permanent buildings and pulled up in front of a sort of grocery/general store.

Our whole party entered the store at once, overwhelming the watchful eye of its cowboy themed proprietor and his one employee at the register. Jen and Alexandra got baskets and began to shop properly, while Tick, his face a bruised beat-up mess, set about creating a moving distraction around the store as a cover for Aiden, Barb and Zed to swipe whatever they could get down their oversized pants.

Pete, Charles, Dustin and I were only so much filler; milling around, picking up items and putting them back down. The poor shopkeeper couldn't keep up and didn't know who to watch. Tick finally pulled the "break a jar at the back of the store" trick, which worked to summon the register girl away from the front to investigate. The shoplifters then walked right out the front door, hopped in the RV, and pulled out of the parking lot. The cowboy shopkeep continued to follow us around trying to catch us in the act of theft, but the graft was over. I don't think he even realized three of our party had left the building.

Our remaining group gathered at the front of the store while the girls unloaded their baskets on the counter. I could see the smoldering fury in the shopkeeper's eyes as he surveyed our derelict troop of dirty kids, his arms crossed and his wide-brimmed Stetson hat pulled down low on his brow. He knew he had been robbed, but he couldn't prove it. He stood in the window, shooting daggers from his eyes as we left the parking lot, some of us in the Olds and some on foot. We met up with the camper crew in an adjacent parking lot and blew out of town, south on US 95.

We followed them down the two-lane black top for maybe ten miles before hanging a left down a dirt road away into the desert. It was slow going, as the road surface had formed washboard-like bumps that rattled our molars if we pushed the car above fifteen miles an hour, and the dust the big vehicle in front of us kicked up was choking. The scenery out there was delightfully foreign. Being off the highway and inside of this desert landscape made it much easier to appreciate the world around us. Traveling at the speed of a bicycle helped too. The dark, jagged hills that had been off in the distance all morning were now drawing closer and coming into sharp relief against the clear blue sky. And the tall saguaros, poking up from the scrubby brush all around us, had multiplied exponentially from their numbers near last night's camp.

Deeper and deeper into the wilderness we drove, maybe another ten miles before the way broke apart into many little ways and parking spots with little stone piles for fire pits. We were right up at the base of those broken peaks now, with one of the largest right before us. The RV made a hard turn, following the contours of the gravelly path, and pulled into a central campsite on the shore of a wide dry wash, presided over by a palo verde tree of substantial size. This was it; we were home.

Everyone piled out into the dry desert light. Zed stepped up to our group, his arms outstretched. "Here we are!" he declared. "Crystal Hill. This here is a very kind spot for travelers. We won't get hassled out here; we can make as much noise as we want." And he let out a howl with enough force to bring on a coughing fit, his guttural hacks echoing off the surrounding stony hills. "Find a spot for your tents," he continued once his fit had passed. "We're going to climb the hill in a little bit, see if we can't find us some crystals!"

I helped my traveling companions set up their tents and surveyed the scene around our new camp. We were not the only ones around. A good distance off I could see a big box of an RV the size of a semi-trailer parked by a small grove of palo verde trees, while closer to our group a brown station wagon with a matching brown canvass tent was set up. The owners of these vehicles were nowhere to be seen.

Our group was loud and colorful and shattered the stark silence of the surrounding desert the moment we arrived. Tick had finally changed his shirt from the grimy, blood-stained one he had been wearing from the moment I met him into a fluorescent orange number with the name of a construction firm on the back in big black letters that made him glow in unholy radiance in the full desert sun. And Alexandra, stripped down to cut-off corduroy shorts and an insanely colored tie-dye t-shirt, was equally as blinding. In fact, it seemed everyone had apparently chosen their loudest colors for our introduction to

Crystal Hill's wilderness. Even I, clad as I was in my dirty flame-colored tie-dye shirt.

Within the hour we were all climbing the hill as an obnoxiously bright group, stumbling and scrambling on the loose rocks, and broadcasting our cacophonous noise in every direction around us. Quickly we broke apart into smaller groups according to each hiker's level of fitness and determination. Being a nonsmoker, and generally of the determined mindset whenever faced with a hill to climb, I found myself in the leading pack with Dustin, Charles and Pete. We were the first to mount the summit.

The view from the rocky peak was breathtakingly long and clear. I don't know how many miles into the distance we could see, maybe twenty or more, but even at that hardly a sign of human construction could be discerned. Only a few rows of high-tension power lines and meandering unpaved roads and paths that might just as well have been desiccated arroyos cut through the desert floor. We four lads of the road stood in silence for a time, taking it all in.

"This is awesome," Pete muttered quietly, followed by a few murmurs of agreement among us.

Others of our group soon joined us in waves, and the noise of our humanity quickly polluted the serenity we had invaded. Zed and Barb were the last ones up. I could see Zed was struggling, breathing hard in hoarse raspy breaths and leaning on Barb for support, but no one else seemed to notice. Once he caught his breath enough to address us, he directed our attention to a slope a dozen yards down.

"Over there is some of the best chances we got for finding crystals and it's out of the line of sight of camp, so no one will see us digging," he explained. "No one is supposed to be using a shovel on this mountain, so keep your eyes open. It's a big fine if they catch us." He cleared his throat and spit. "And snakes, keep an eye out for snakes too. If you get bit out here, you're fucked." We all instantly began looking around on the ground for snakes compulsively, much to his amusement. "Don't worry everybody," he assured us with a grin. "They are more afraid of you then you are of them. Besides, it will be well worth the risk if we find a big crystal or two. A guy pulled a big beautiful two-pounder out of here a few years back and made a lot of money!" We all then began searching the ground for both crystals and snakes alike. "Come on; let's hike down to the mine."

The mine was a rocky dirt patch where the soil had obviously been disturbed before. Zed pointed out a few other areas nearby that looked similar, which prompted a few of our group to break off towards those areas. I started kicking around the soil with my foot right where I was and uncovered what looked like a tiny shard of clear glass right away. "Holy shit! I think I found one!" I announced. Zed and a few others came to investigate my claim.

"Yup, it's a crystal. Good eye, bud," Zed told me, rolling the small chunk of stone around the palm of his hand with his finger. "Ain't worth much, though. See here where it's broken? the tip needs to be perfect for it to work properly, for it to be worth anything." He handed it back to me. "You got the right idea, though. Keep your eyes peeled. You have your spirit in the right place; you might just find a powerful one."

We all spent less than an hour there, kicking the dirt with our feet. No one had brought a shovel, and no other crystals were unearthed, so most of our party quickly lost interest and began making their way back to camp. I ended up walking down with Zed, keeping my eyes to the ground for crystalline minerals and deadly reptiles both.

"You have good energy. I'm grateful you're in our caravan with us," he said quietly as we picked our way down among the rocks. "Life corrupts many people, yet your aura still glimmers with a purity I don't often see. I hope you will continue to travel with us, wherever the road takes us." I didn't have much of a response besides a stock "gee, thanks." He continued, "I know you are very conflicted in your convictions; I can understand where you are coming from. I was raised a Baptist; my father was a traveling preacher and dragged us all over the place preaching his good news. But I have transcended my roots and found a deeper spirituality that goes beyond any one faith. I can show you this deeper understanding, if you will but follow me." I felt goose bumps ripple up my frame, recognizing his bastardized quoting of Christ. "Ha! Gotcha!" he laughed, sensing my discomfort. "But seriously, travel with us and you'll find the deeper meaning you are searching for."

I stopped and turned to him. "You're an intense dude, man." I said to him point blank. "I don't quite know what to make of you."

"I'm just a man, a homeless traveler like you," he answered softly, squinting in the desert sun. "I have a book you might find interesting. Remind me once we're back in camp."

A new face awaited us down below; an older man in dusty old clothes, his graying hair and beard long and greasy. He had already made the acquaintance of a few of our troop, they all having arrived before Zed and I did, and now he made ours.

"Hi, I'm Timothy," he stated clearly, a smile visible behind his long overgrown mustache. "I'm your neighbor." And he gestured over to the old brown station wagon and tent combo a few yards away by throwing his thumb over his shoulder before reaching in for a handshake with Zed. "How long y'all planning on stickin' around?"

"Oh, a couple weeks maybe," Zed answered. "We'll see, wanna try to hit the gem show."

"Yup, me too. Been rock hounding my way around the southwest all year waiting for the tents to go up. You guys lookin' to trade before the show?"

"Yeah, we might be able to work something out. Come and sup with us tonight, pleasure before business."

That night we all got rip roaring wasted on wine. Zed and his kids had somehow lifted a few gallon jugs of the stuff from that little grocery store back in town, along with a few steaks and some other food. Plus, with the items Jen and Alexandra had actually purchased legitimately, we had quite a feast. Our new neighbor offered a couple larger logs for the fire, which was a big help, since the few bushy trees around the banks of the wash were pretty well picked clean of dead wood. Even with that, our fire was forced to remain meager and useful only as a source of light in the deep darkness of the desert night. The food was cooked on a couple white gas stoves to free up the flames for the purpose of ambiance alone.

A couple drums were brought out from the RV once we had all eaten, and we began dancing to the rolling rhythm. Even our neighbor, old gray Timothy, joined in, albeit hesitantly after being pulled to his feet by Alexandra and Barb. The wine can work wonders, not the least of which was our perception of the quality of the drumming. Often the two drummers, whoever they were at any given moment, would lose time with each other, throwing the repetitive thumping out of balance. But the dancers just absorbed the occasional disharmony, locking on to one or the other's line of beats until the two merged in synchronicity once again. And after all, we weren't out there in the middle of nowhere for a professional percussion performance. Our companions wove enough of a steady thundering beat to put us all into a sufficiently otherworldly trance, moving and shifting around the firelight as we were, like dirty ragged moths chaotically spinning around a lone light bulb in the darkness.

Again, I stayed up till the end, only making my way to my rest as the dawn approached. Timothy had succumbed to the wine hard and lay prostrate in the dirt beside the fire. Dustin too bedded down in the open, but of his own volition. The rest had retired to their respective places in the tents and the RV. I kept myself conscious just long enough to greet the sun as it cut above the horizon, then laid myself down as well in the back seat and allowed sweet lady wine to cover me over with the curtains of sleep.

The day was half over when I finally pulled myself from my wrappings, and still I found myself alone in camp. Timothy must have dragged himself back to his tent at some point in the morning, the full force of the sun surely driving him into the relative shade of his canvas shelter. Dustin too was no longer to be seen, also probably forced to retreat from the morning light, for even in late fall the heat of the day could be intense out there.

I took a quick look around camp. We hadn't even been there yet twenty-four hours and already our footprint was apparent. A few empty wine jugs, some broken, lay around the perimeter of our settlement, and the plastic wrappings of last night's dinner were scattered around the fire pit, flattened and dirty from the trampling of our dancing feet. God damn, but we humans are a dirty lot.

I looked then to Crystal Hill, quietly looming over us. It was Sunday again, the Lord's day. I sighed at the thought of it. Every mile I traveled seemed to take me farther and farther from the faith I had always known. The pointlessness of the ritual I still felt compelled to perform seemed more real to me than anything, but I gathered myself up for that obligation nonetheless. I tossed the unleavened crackers and a can of grape juice into a knapsack along with my beat up old mini-bible with a mind to climb to the top of that dry hill and face the pointlessness of it all head on. Zed met me as I walked out of camp.

"Good morning!" he crowed. "Or rather, good afternoon I suppose. You climbing the hill?" I shook my head yes. "Hold on a sec, I have something that may help you on your spiritual quest." And he jogged a few steps back to the RV. I followed at a walk, the listlessness of my mood preventing me from unnecessary exertion. "Here, have a look at this," he continued, meeting me as I approached the door and handing me a big paperback book. "If religion all is a farce, then this might just be the one true faith."

I looked at the cover. A widely grinning face with a pipe clenched in his teeth stared back at me with the friendly urgency of a mid-century salesman. "You might find some heavy truths in there, so prepare yourself," he added with a crooked grin. I made a quick pass through the pages, flipping them off my thumb. It looked like a zine I might have picked up at some coffee house or record store, only denser. The pages were packed with text of all fonts and sizes and interspersed with all manner of illustrations. I was attracted to it instantly.

"Thanks, man. I think I'm going to read this on the mountain top."

"That sounds like an excellent idea," Zed agreed. "Now go and be enlightened."

I was at the peak of that little mountain a short time later, my brow wet with sweat. I cozied into a little crevice and looked out across the plain, casting my eyes wide. The view was just as striking the second time around, the cloudless sky impossibly blue against the yellows, tans and browns of the land below.

I opened my knapsack and laid the contents out before me. On one side I had my bible, the cover so beaten I had reupholstered it in duct tape, on the other I had this strange-looking book I had just been given. I sighed and picked up my bible, opening it to a random page, and dropped my finger on a random verse in the hope some sign would be given. "Then Samson went and caught three hundred foxes; and he took torches, turned the foxes tail to tail, and put a torch between each pair of tails."

Jesus Christ, that's fucking brutal. And no help whatsoever. Let's try another one. I flipped through the pages again and placed my finger on another random passage. "Now, the day of the LORD is coming, cruel, and full of wrath and fierce anger… Their little ones will be dashed to pieces before their eyes. Their houses will be looted, and their wives will be raped."

Equally unpleasant and thoroughly unhelpful. Ok, one more time, Lord give me a sign, I spoke aloud on the mountain top. Give me an explanation to confront my doubts and settle my conflictions! Please, what is the answer I have been searching for? And I flipped through the pages once more. "However, the

Most High does not dwell in temples made with hands." Ok then, that's more like it. Let's get this ritual done.

I said a little silent prayer and attempted to clear my mind, which I found terribly difficult. I pushed ahead, ignoring the white noise in my head and broke the bread, taking a little and placing the stale flavorless bit into my mouth. This is the body of Jesus, broken for me. I then took the grape juice and cracked open the can, the sound echoing briefly off the surrounding rocks. I then took a sip of the syrupy liquid and thought of the blood that Jesus spilled for me, personally while the flies of doubt buzzed heavily in my ears.

The story seemed more and more impersonal, impossible even, every time I thought of it now. I sighed again. What's the point? I felt nothing, not even the ever-present guilt for a change. I looked again out across the desert and realized I did feel something. It was awe. Awe of the natural beauty spread out before me.

Fuck it, I said to myself, and chugged down the last of the juice. I then reached for the second book, the strange book, and flipped to a random page towards the back. "Quit waiting for someone to explain everything to you, there is no explanation!"

Bang! Like a smack in the face. I laid the book back down and attempted to chew on that for a second. I found my guts, my intuition agreeing with that statement despite the instant mortal fear it conversely conjured. Could the answer really be that easy? I picked up the book again. "The answer always was that you already had the answer."

My stomach did a somersault. Whatever this odd book of bold headlines and strange doctored pictures was it was hitting me right where it counted. I then dove in head long, starting from the first page, and ate heartily of its fruits.

I spent the rest of the afternoon on that rocky mountain top pouring over those blasphemous pages, until by the fading light of evening I reached the last page. "You are good enough," it told me. "You are clean enough, you are right enough, if, and only if you get right with "Bob" tonight."

CHAPTER 29

I found camp in a subdued mood upon my return. A small blaze of twigs and cactus bones gently crackled in the center of a circle of young travelers, their faces illuminated in the flickering light of flame. I joined the communion, setting my frame down between Dustin and Barb.

"Where have you been all day?" Pete asked me over the fire.

"Up on the hill," I replied. "Slacking off."

"Find any-big ass crystals?" Tick asked abruptly. I shook my head no. "We're going to have a go at it with a shovel tomorrow. Do you guys have a shovel?" he asked our detachment. We did not. "More crystals for us," he sneered, brandishing his missing-tooth grin again.

"God damn, but your face is busted," his buddy Aiden interjected. They laughed together. Barb then passed me a jug of wine.

"Go easy on 'er," she suggested. "That's the last one till we can get back to town." The jug was already half gone. Just as well; I was looking forward to getting some sober sleep for a change.

We lingered around the fire till the jug was empty. Zed and his kids ducked out first, followed shortly thereafter by the two couples, leaving only Dustin and myself.

"Hey, you still thirsty?" he whispered to me in the darkness. I could just see his mischievous grin in the failing light of the fire.

"You holdin' out on everybody?" I chuckled. He then pulled a pint hip flask of whiskey from his pants pocket. "Where'd you get that?"

"Zed's kids ain't the only ones around here with light fingers," he snickered. I thought back to the cowboy's general store. There was a small selection of liquors behind the register, seemingly out of the reach of thieves. Light fingers indeed; he must have snatched it while the cashier and the cowboy were hawking the rest of us. He twisted off the cap with a snap, took a pull, grimaced, and held it out to me.

"Thanks, dude," I said and took a pull myself. The whiskey was rough, especially after the sweet wine I had been drinking, and it burned my throat. But I held my composure and counted my blessings. "You're a real gentleman, my friend."

"Likewise," he responded as I handed the flask back to him. "Glad to be with you tonight."

We took our turns there together, passing the little bottle back and forth until it was finally gone. We stayed up a while longer, enjoying each other's company beside the glowing embers and the glow of the whiskey in our guts, until the chill of the desert night encouraged us to retreat to our blankets.

I dreamed that night that I was out on a road, some long straight road cutting through a desert not unlike the one I was sleeping in. My way was lit by starlight alone, yet the double yellow lines still glowed faintly as they stretched away indefinitely. I had the feeling I was walking with someone; a friend, all my friends really, coalesced into a single entity. We were experiencing this road together, hiking it in a state of heightened excitement like I so often did on those long, intense acid trips with my friends back home.

But whenever I would turn to share a knowing smile with this conglomerate person, there would be no one there. I was alone. I kept looking for my friend, kept calling to him/her in excitement, and kept finding myself alone out there on the road, my only companions being the dark, strangely shaped shrubs lining the way.

I felt awfully lonely the next day and mildly anti-social despite being surrounded by my fellow travelers in camp. So I did what I always do when I'm feeling spiritually constipated; I walk alone. I set out across the open desert, bee-lining towards one of the far-off high-tension power line towers seemingly miles away, knowing I couldn't get lost as long as I kept a few faraway landmarks in order. Apart from the single bottle of water I grabbed on my way out, I carried nothing but the clothes on my back.

There was no sign of a human touch out there at all; no garbage, no tire tracks. Only the faraway rows of the power line towers and a couple com trails streaking across the cloudless blue sky. And the silence, that's what struck me most of all. It was absolutely quiet out there. Only the sound of my foot falls on the gravelly ground. I hiked on for a long time, the tall steel-framed tower slowly growing in size as I approached.

As the morning progressed, the temperature began to climb. Soon I had a good sweat going and decided to peel off my shirt, since there was no one around to witness my pale, flabby mid-section. I had by this point already lost a significant amount of weight living like I was on the road, but I still felt terribly self-conscious about my body. I might not have been the fat kid I was in high school any longer, but I still felt like I was on the inside. The sun was dazzlingly bright, and I could feel its rays colliding with my bare white skin, so unaccustomed to daylight. Perhaps the sun will harden me up a bit, I thought.

I pressed on, following one random thought to the next and allowing the present to be, well, present. Soon, I found myself again in an internal debate on faith and its role in my life. That funny book I had just read on the mountain top really struck a chord with me like nothing else had before. The book portrayed itself as a holy joke, I thought, but at the same time was deadly serious and touched on thoughts and feelings I had been chewing on for months.

Could this "joke" religion really deliver on what it offered, a life free from the fetters and bonds of pointless bullshit? I mean, if there was no God, if all religion was just a sham, a method of societal control, then who's to say that this "Bob" could not be a vehicle to inner and outer peace? I surprised myself with the candidness of my inner heretical line of reasoning. For the first time, the hardwired aversion reflex to doubts of faith was weakening to the point that I could honestly debate the tenets of

Christianity with myself without being overcome with fearful guilt.

I was nearing the crucifix-like metal frame tower when the urge to shit came up from behind suddenly, interrupting my exercise in deep theological reasoning. Being in the middle of nowhere made the finding of a suitable place to deposit my waste laughably easy. I just stopped, dropped my drawers, and snapped a sticky one off right there in the dirt. It felt empowering in a way, being free to shit where I pleased, and I laughed aloud at the thought of it.

But then I remembered I had brought no ass wipe. That sobered up my nature-boy pooping glee in a hurry. Now what? I asked myself desperately. There were no leaves that I could use, certainly no paper of any kind. Only dry flaky cactus bones and rocks. I was faced with a serious choice. Do I continue on un-wiped and resign myself to everything that entails, or do I sacrifice my last pair of underwear to the vanity of personal cleanliness? I squatted there over my little pile mulling over the consequences of my choices as a few flies miraculously found me with uncanny speed and began buzzing around my bare ass. Fuck it, I said to myself, deciding then I'd much rather go free ball then to attract flies in camp.

So now I was naked in the desert, wiping my ass with my underwear and finding the event still strangely empowering. I rose, straightening my back, my business done, the entire organ of my skin now exposed to the power of the mid-day desert sun. I flung my arms wide and hollered aloud like an animal; a feral, dirty animal.

I was close to the tower now and anxious to complete my goal of reaching its shadow, so I pulled on my dirty old pants and blown out sneakers and continued on. A dull humming noise soon began filling my head. I hardly noticed it at first, taking the desert silence for granted. But as I drew nearer to the looming steel skeleton, the humming intensified. The sound seemed to be entering into my very being, dull and consistent. My ears registered the low rumbling vibration as well as my very flesh. It was the power lines themselves, radiating energy stronger than anything I had ever experienced up close.

The hum of all those moving electrons in the thick cables cascaded down the steel frame of the tower in unseen rippling vibrations that amplified the sound like a giant bell. I stood below this humming steel giant and gazed up into its towering heights. I felt as if I could almost see the air vibrating around the individual cables. A thought crossed my mind, a memory of hearing about how people who lived near these heavy power lines often came down with cancer. Could these vibrations radiating into me be doing the same? I didn't wait to find out and abruptly turned back.

Far in the distance I could see Crystal Hill, or what I was pretty sure was Crystal Hill. I set off towards that landmark, trusting my dead reckoning to guide me back to camp. I quickly lost track of the foot prints I had previously left behind, and since everything around me all looked exactly the same, I was left with nothing but the innate sense of direction that comes standard with humans to varying degrees. Apparently this was enough, for I was able to find my way back without much difficulty.

I found Jen, Alexandra and Charles alone in camp upon my return. The rest of our party, including our neighbor, was up on the hill illegally digging for crystals. I was famished and thirsty, my water bottle having run dry long before I even got to the power lines. I helped myself to an apple and a jar of peanut butter and reveled in the simple pleasures this vagabond life offered me.

We spent another relatively quiet night around a small fire, there being no booze or weed, or anything else to intoxicate us. We all spoke quietly among ourselves about varying subjects, from fantasies of finding big money crystals, to life on the beaches of southern California, to what we were going to do with our day tomorrow.

We needed more supplies; more food and more importantly, more wine. So Zed's kids were planning how to get away with hitting that same grocery store again, since it was the only one in town. They were going to need a ride, and naturally that responsibility fell on my party because we had a car with functioning brakes. Pete volunteered to shuttle the three of them into civilization while the rest of us stayed behind to try our hand at mineral digging. The miners had been basically unsuccessful that day, coming away with only a handful of tiny clear shards. Zed encouraged us all to keep at it, and to have faith in karma to reward us with crystals of monetary value. Karma! I couldn't help but snicker at his statement. With all the bold-faced theft and shady dealings he and his crew engaged in, it was a wonder the cosmos hadn't stepped in and snuffed out their luck already. All the more evidence of there being no higher power dictating the fates of mortals, it seemed.

I then shifted my attention to our neighbor, old gray Timothy, who had also been sitting beside our fire quietly carving a short chunk of broom stick. He had fashioned it down into a series of geometric shapes connected by a thin remnant of the original stick. He caught me checking out his work.

"You whittle?" he asked me. I had tried my hand at wood carving years ago in the Boy Scouts, but I figured that probably didn't really count, so I answered no. "It's a way to pass the time," he said, holding the carved piece of wood up to the light.

"That's pretty cool," I freely admitted. "I met a guy in Sedona that carved too. He gave me this." And I pulled out the little wooden owl pendant I had been wearing under my shirt and handed it to him.

"This is a nice piece of work here," he stated, intently studying the object. "Better'n anything I coulda' done." He handed it back to me, and I tucked it back under my shirt. "Why do you hide it, man? That's a beautiful piece of art that guy gave you." I didn't really have an answer. I agreed it was beautiful, and its provenance was personally special, considering how the owl often haunted my dreams, but I didn't have a good answer as to why I had been wearing it hidden. Perhaps it symbolized something I was uncomfortable with, something I didn't yet understand.

The next morning, the raiding party rolled out on their mission fairly early. After a meager breakfast, I joined the group of rockhound hopefuls and climbed the hill once more. All the remaining campers including the dogs went this time, leaving no one behind in camp. Timothy joined us as well, and we all took turns with the two shovels we had, Timothy's and a little folding army surplus shovel they found in the RV.

We spent half the day up there in the blazing sun and came out with nothing but tiny broken shards. Thoroughly discouraged, we trekked back down to await the return of the grocery store bandits and the wine they would bring. We didn't have to wait long. The advancing cloud of dust gave away their approach.

They rolled in triumphantly, with Tick sitting on the edge of the passenger side door, hooting and swinging a half-empty forty of malt liquor. Piled on the roof were a couple old oak pallets and a bunch of lumber scraps tied down precariously with a few lengths of old coaxial cable. They pulled up alongside the camp in a cloud of dry dust and all piled out. I, along with a few others, went and met them at the trunk. Again, they had somehow managed to swipe all sorts of stuff. Gallons of wine, forties of beer, all sorts of food stuffs. They even had a couple cartons of cigarettes. How the hell they consistently pulled off that level of heavy-duty shoplifting was beyond me.

So, you can imagine what happened next. We all ate like gluttons, drank like winos, and danced to the thundering beats of the djembe drums deep into the night around a blazing pyre of used building materials and shipping pallets. It was how we lived; it was the point of everything we did. We were misguided youth, adrift in a world we were either rejecting, or which had rejected us. We were a family of sorts, an impromptu tribe of feral children. Looking out for each other and sharing in the spoils of our efforts.

At some point I bumped into Barb between rounds of drunken dancing. She was off to the side watching the movement of the dancers and nursing a jug of wine to her head.

"Hey, can I get a pull on that?" I asked as I approached. She freely handed it over with a smile. "Thanks!"

"No prob," she answered and slapped me on the shoulder. She had sparkly eyes in the firelight, her eyelids low and relaxed. "You havin' fun?" she asked. I shook my head yes, and she grabbed me and pulled me into a hug. She had an ample figure hidden under her baggy road kid raver clothes. Her hug was tight enough that I could discern her curves against my body. She pulled back, grabbed my head in her hands and planted a wet wine kiss in the middle of my forehead. "You're a good kid," she laughed giddily. "Come dance with me!" And she pulled me back into the firelight.

I reeled around with her for a while before going off on my own. I was drunk, and I was a little intimidated by her. Plus, I wasn't sure if she was really Aiden's girlfriend or not. Sometimes they seemed to be a couple and sometimes not. I didn't want to get myself into trouble.

I bumped into her again later in the night. The drumming had ceased, and some of our party had already thrown in the towel. She was beside the fire with Aiden, the two of them drunkenly leaning against each other. I sat down cross legged nearby.

I was about to attempt to start up a line of conversation when the door to the RV flung open, and Zed came stumbling out in another full-blown uncontrollable coughing fit.

"Are you ok, Zed?" Barb called to him pleadingly. He just waved his hand dismissively, his breath too preoccupied to form a worded response. She groaned helplessly and sunk into Aiden's lap.

"He'll be ok," he assured her, stroking her hair.

"No, he won't!" she sobbed and broke down in a drunken whimper.

Aiden looked up and caught my eye. "He has cancer," he stated, answering my silent question. "Lung cancer. It's terminal. He's dying."

"Oh, shit!" I muttered, my utterance almost buried under Barb's whimpering cry and Zed's guttural hacking. I didn't have anything else to say. What could you say? I grabbed the bottle beside them and took a long swig. Jesus Christ, fucking cancer! I guess that explains a few things, I thought to myself.

Zed was regaining his composure, catching his breath, and spitting phlegm. I rose and brought the jug to him. "Have a pull?" I asked, holding the jug out.

"Thank you," he whispered and he chugged for a good ten seconds, draining a large portion into his throat. "Thank you," he repeated once he'd had his fill and wiped the wine from his mouth with his sleeve. He grabbed my shoulder then, squeezing hard. "Good night, my friend," he stated and re-entered his mobile home.

The specter of death is a sobering thing. I felt I could not continue in the revelry that night, and honestly the party was pretty well over by that point anyway. I made my way to my rest, and there in the dark of the Olds's back seat mulled over that inevitable end awaiting us all.

The feelings brought on by that thought surprised me. When I used to ponder my end, it would always be in the light of my Christian salvation, usually focused on the alternative to keeping the commandments. Hell, specifically. But if you take heaven and hell out of the equation, remove the prospect of an afterlife completely, than death is suddenly less terrifying, benign even. I found this realization pretty empowering, more empowering even then shitting out in the open desert. But seriously, if there is nothing after we die, if we just cease to exist, then all there really is for us is this right now, this very moment.

That thought added a degree of urgency I felt excited to fulfill and underlined a lot of what I had recently read in that strange farcical religious book. "Quit your job and slack off!" Well, I had already accomplished the first part, and now the rest was just coming naturally.

Everybody slept in late the next day, nursing their respective hangovers. And even once we were all up, we still did nothing of consequence. The past two attempts at digging crystals had yielded nothing but sweat and dirt, so we weren't very enthusiastic to have another go at it in the full sun. I had acquired a substantial sunburn from hiking around in the desert with no shirt on and was not too keen on making it any worse. So I just lounged around the camp with the rest of them in the partial shade of the palo verde trees or the shadow cast by the bulk of the camper reading my strange book, writing in my road journal, or chatting with my camp mates.

Alexandra spent the day weaving strands of hemp string into intricate lengths of knotted, beaded necklaces and bracelets, teaching Jen the art in the process. Intrigued, I joined them and made an attempt at it myself. The first few series of knots I tied looked like hammered shit, but I got into the groove soon enough, so that by the end I had a passable repeating knot necklace that I could hang my carved owl from. The two objects complemented each other nicely.

We all spent a quiet evening around the fire that night, saving what was left of our booze for the next night, which would be Halloween. Zed and company felt they had used up all the luck they had working that one grocery store and didn't want to risk hitting it again. So instead of getting shitfaced for a second night in a row, we kept it low key, opting to chat and pass around a pipe of tobacco that someone produced.

Zed's kids, as well as the rest of us, were feeling mighty discouraged over the prospects of finding crystals of any monetary value up on that rocky hill, mainly because we were a bunch of impatient kids who had grown bored with digging in the sun. Zed kept trying to keep our interest in the work, touting stories of huge crystals the size of your head, but he was fighting an uphill battle. He eventually caved and agreed to his crew's suggestion that we travel to San Diego and kick it on the beach through the worst of the winter. After weeks in the growing cold, and now the dry of the desert, the idea of slacking off on the shores of the Pacific sounded pretty inviting. We were all on board with the plan within minutes; we decided to stick around for another couple days there in the desert, then shoot west to the coast.

The next day, Pete, Jen and I, along with Charles and Alexandra, trekked into town to run some laundry and for supplies. The girls needed some things Zed's bandits were not grabbing, and we all had a hankering for some professionally prepared food instead of the canned beans, potato chips, and bun-less hot dogs we had been living on.

We found a diner in town that fit the bill and feasted on heavy, grease-laden trucker fare. Once we had our fill, we leaned back into our seats and digested over coffees and conversations. The topic quickly turned to our proposed westward push. None of our group had yet been to the west coast, nor seen the Pacific, so naturally we were all keen on the idea, but Jen struggled with some degree of trepidation.

"I don't trust Zed," she confided in us. "There's something off about him."

"Well, he is a thief," Charles pointed out.

"Yeah, but it's more than that," she answered. "He's manipulative. Look how he has his little family wrapped around his finger. They do whatever he asks them."

"Nah, I don't see that," Pete interjected dismissively. "They're all doing their own thing, just like us. If anything, they're just using Zed for his ride."

"I have to agree with Jen," Alexandra added. "He's kinda given me the creeps since that night in Sedona. But I don't feel in danger around him, I guess."

"He has lung cancer," I stated, as if that was supposed to explain why they felt creeped out by him. "Terminal lung cancer; he's dying. Ever notice how he coughs?"

That did seem to settle the matter though, and our conversation veered away from his perceived creepiness once everyone had expressed their surprise and dismay at the thought of his impending death. The thought of dying, especially from a prolonged and debilitating disease like lung cancer, was something our little group of youthful free spirits was not prepared to embrace, even if it was inflicted on someone they felt uncomfortable about.

We settled the bill soon after, splitting up the cost between us evenly, and stepped back out into the mid-morning daylight. There was still the matter of the personal supplies the girls needed, so we headed over to the grocery store, hoping the proprietor would not recognize us and take us as the thieves who had robbed him twice now. I chose to hang back; someone needed to stay with Dylan anyway, since dogs were not allowed in the store. Alone again, I strolled along the main drag, checking out the scene.

The roadside was reminiscent of a series of big yard sales widely spaced apart by empty dirt parking lots and small businesses. I stopped into a few of the faded pop-up tents and perused the dusty tables looking for anything that might temporarily occupy my interest. It was slim pickings. Sun-stained plastics, obsolete electronics, used car parts, and strange inappropriate articles of clothing. I kept moving, letting Dylan lead the way.

Eventually we came to a sort of indoor/outdoor book bazaar presided over by a leathery-skinned old dude who I was sure was buck naked until he turned to greet me, his only customer, and I found he had on the tiniest brown leather thong, the same color as his skin, which served to carry his cock and balls alone. I stepped back in automatic alarm, my societal programming not prepared to process the reality of a virtually nude shopkeeper.

"Welcome!" he greeted warmly. "If you got any questions, just give me a holler." And he abruptly left me to myself, surely accustomed to reading the level of discomfort he instilled in his potential customers. I mean, you don't just go and start a nudist bookstore without the expectation that your bare ass might scare off some of the dollars. But it obviously wasn't all about the profits with him. Indeed, it was surely a pure individualistic passion that powered his days, and the bookstore was probably just a vehicle to maintain the life he chose for himself. I felt an admiration for the man, a little envy even, but I still was not too keen on interacting with him and his cod piece again, so I ducked out and headed back to meet up with my crew.

I met them as they exited the store, each carrying two bags of goods. I grabbed a bag each from the girls, handing Dylan's leash off to Jen, and described what I had just come across.

"There's like a nearly naked dude selling books down the road there," I told them, nodding my head in that direction and eliciting a round of raised eyebrows. "Tanned like dark leather, in nothing but a thong. I doubt the guy has worn clothes in over a decade."

"Damn!" Pete exclaimed as we walked to the car. "That's crazy."

"Yeah, he seemed like an ok guy, he was…" And I trailed off, my attention being drawn to a face I thought I recognized; a girl's face, young and troubled.

About fifteen feet from us a small girl, dressed in ill-fitting men's clothes too big for her petite frame, stood staring at us, her wrist grasped by a larger, gray-haired man old enough to be her grandfather. He was leaning in towards her, hissing a whisper into her ear, his brow furrowed, his dry lips pulled back exposing his long-yellowed teeth.

It was Sherri, the little run-away girl from the Nederland camp! She yanked herself free from the old man's grasp and sprinted into Pete's arms, catching him completely by surprise.

"Oh my God!" she cried. "You found me!" And she turned back to the man who had remained where she left him, still as stone, his fists clenched in fury and fear. "This is my boyfriend!" she yelled at him. "And he's going to kick your ass!"

Pete's jaw dropped like a sack of rocks. I looked to Jen; she too was dumbfounded.

The old man took a step towards us. "I wouldn't do that if I were you," Charles stated flatly, accurately reading the situation he suddenly found himself a part of. The man paused, rage burning in his eyes. He spit on the ground in front of us, turned on his heel and stormed off in the opposite direction. We watched him as he climbed into a beat-up old camper and spun gravel out of the parking lot.

"Oh God, thank you Peter!" Sherri cried and wrapped her arms around him.

Pete, still with his mouth agape, looked to his real girlfriend then. There was fire in her eyes, wrathful furious fire. Sherri hadn't run to her for rescue, and she hadn't run to me either. She had run to Pete. Pete was her savior. Pete was her knight in shining armor. Pete was her "boyfriend."

CHAPTER 30

The ride back to camp was painfully awkward and disturbingly emotional. Sherri, who had in the Ned camp been as quiet as a mouse, was now unloading her soul on us in one long unbroken sentence.

The guy she just escaped had been her captor for weeks. He had picked her and Summer up near where we had dropped them off in Boulder with the promise to take them south. Within days the man became possessive, verbally abusive, and sexually suggestive to them both. When Summer protested his inappropriate advances on them, he pushed her out of his ride and left her on the side of the road in the middle of nowhere with no gear or jacket or anything.

Then Sherri was trapped and alone. The man slowly broke her down and twisted her perception of her situation until he had her under his command. He had apparently felt confident enough in his power over her to allow her to leave his camper with him, and that's when she saw us. It was the first time she had been outside his ride in weeks. Uncanny luck for her; perhaps there was a God guiding the fates after all.

She sat in the back seat, shaking and laughing manically in between breaths and fragments of sentences, while Alexandra stroked her hair and tried to calm her down.

I sat in the front seat between my companions and could see Jen's fists clenching. It was obvious we had most likely just saved this girl's life, but it also reflected badly on Pete, casting into doubt his story about what had happened between the two of them back in Colorado. Jen's confliction was obvious to me and probably to Pete too, for he just kept his mouth shut and his eyes on the road during all of this. "We should get the police involved," Jen finally said through clenched teeth.

"No No NO, please don't call the cops!" Sherri pleaded. "I don't want to talk to the cops! Just get me as far away from that fucking asshole as possible!"

And so we did, taking her back to our desert wilderness camp. Zed welcomed her with open arms and tears, as did Barb. Tick and Aiden were more pragmatic but welcomed her back just the same. She unloaded her story on Zed and Barb with the same intensity she had to us, while we stood by.

Tick eventually walked up to Pete and me and asked, "Ok, where's the booze? I'm about ready to hunt that fucking dirty old man down and slit his fucking throat! I need to take the edge off." We led him to the trunk, where he grabbed one of the forties we had bought, popped the top and started drinking. Sherri saw him and abruptly broke off her account.

"Hey, Tick!" she called. "Gimmie one of those." He grabbed another from the trunk and brought it to her. "Thank you," she replied, surprisingly coyly. Whatever had happened to her, locked up with some manipulative old dude, had altered her personality strikingly. Which was not surprising, I guess, who knows what manner of trauma she had endured at the hands of that dirty old man. We all just sort of went along with it, not knowing how else to handle the situation. We were just a bunch of kids with our own sort of dirty old man leading us anyway. Zed may not have been holding us against our will, but he was manipulative in his own way. She was still shaken by her experience and would no doubt struggle with the memory of it for life, but if she wanted a beer now, then I guess she could have a beer.

That broke the ice for all of us, and we began slinging jugs of wine and forties of malt liquor around like we were shooing away the bad energy she had just escaped. "Sisters!" she called as she drank. "Can I borrow some clothes? I can still smell that asshole on these dirty old clothes of his." The girls hopped to it and had her out of the ill-fitting outfit we found her in and looking more herself in no time.

Night fell, a fire was lit, and the djembe drums were produced again. Our pace was quickened this time, for a certain dark anxiety lurked among us all. Sherri attached herself to Alexandra for the most part as she got drunker and drunker, until she jumped up and began dancing with the few who were reeling around the flames. She made a few passes before aiming for Pete and throwing herself at him. He caught her reluctantly, grimacing as he held her limp form. Alexandra rushed to collect her, having been filled in briefly by Jen on the troubles Pete had created back in the Ned camp weeks before, but Sherri was not ready to be collected.

She broke from her grasp and began to reel around the fire once more, wildly drunk, her eyes going two different directions like a creature possessed. It was frightfully unnerving to witness but was beyond me in my youthful ignorance to do anything about. The girl surely should have been engaged in professional counseling after her ordeal, and probably earlier ordeals as well instead of getting shitfaced wasted with the likes of us deep in the desert, but there we all were, hammered and strange. It was Halloween night after all, so the darkness of the evening was fitting.

A short time later, she lunged at Pete again in front of Jen, this time passing out cold in his arms as she landed. Alexandra and Jen both helped to collect her from his awkward embrace this time and carried her off to a tent to lay her down.

The night got steadily hedonistic after that. The drummers, now Aiden and Charles, picked up the tempo to a feverish pitch, while Pete and Jen argued loudly off to the side of camp. I joined in the drunken dance with Barb, Tick, Alexandra, and even Dustin, who had never danced to the drums previously. I caught sight of Zed as we reeled around and saw him swaying in place to the beat, his eyes closed, a smoldering stick of sage in his hand.

I ducked out at some point to take another drink from an abandoned jug I spotted in the shadows, and when I came back

Zed was alone on a drum, beating a thick steady current of sound, better than anything I had heard out of any of the other drummers yet. Tick was locked in a swaying embrace with Barb, their mouths equally locked in sloppy osculation, while Alexandra swayed with Charles. Then they all split into single spinning atoms again for a moment, before Barb and Alexandra came together in a passionate embrace.

Zed slowed the tempo down and the movements of the bodies in the firelight became more fluid, more creamy. Pete and Jen were gone, probably off to their tent, and Dustin was gone off somewhere too. I sat back against a rock alone with my jug, my sight gently fading in and out of double vision and watched as the remaining dancers quit the ring of fire, its flames burned low, and entered one by one into the largest tent we had set up.

Zed's drumming was very slow now and quieter. Quiet enough that I could hear the giggles and moans of the revelers in the tent. Even in virginity I could fathom what they were up to in there and felt equal parts unnervingly disturbed and fiercely aroused, my Christian hangups around sex of any sort still tightly binding my perceptions despite the now rapidly eroding foundations my faith had been built upon. It was too much for me to picture, and I began to get the spins. I stumbled my way to the car and forced myself to sleep before the spins wound beyond my control.

I was hung like shit in the morning and reached for the partial jug of wine I had taken to bed with me straight away. A degree of shamelessness had emerged in my personality out on the road, and I no longer had any qualms with drinking upon waking, especially if it worked to dispel a hangover. I was not alone. I found Dustin and Pete by the ashy spent fire pit sharing an almost empty jug of their own. I sat beside them.

"How you fellas doin' this morning?" I asked them. They both moaned in stereo, returning my gaze with puffy, bloodshot eyes. I held out my jug towards them. "Cheers, brothers. To health." Dustin, who currently held their jug, returned the favor, and our big gallon-sized glass bottles clanked loudly, the new sun glistening off their surfaces, their paper labels stained bloody red with wine.

It was a shabby scene in camp, and an air of desperate pointlessness hung low over us all like a fog. Zed's coughing was an almost constant background soundtrack; what words he did speak were short and snappy, and to his deputies alone. Sherri was back to the way I first knew her; quiet and wrapped in a colorful Mexican blanket that dragged in the dust behind her. She spent the day whispering with Alexandra near the tent she had slept in and didn't really interact with the rest of us. Jen was nowhere to be seen, riding out the day in her own tent, no doubt.

Later, I found Charles and Pete sitting together in the shade, looking rather glum. I joined them, hoping to awaken some cheer. Easier said than done.

"Jen is so fucking pissed right now," Pete explained. "At me, and Zed, at herself, at everyone. Jesus, if we weren't way out in the middle of fucking nowhere, I think she'd have split for a bus home by now."

"We need to get out of here," Charles added. "I did some things last night, things I'm not proud of," he said, staring off into the distance. "I can't even look at Alexandra this morning."

I had nothing. The darkness of the cloud that hung over those two was thicker than anything I could swat away with whatever feel-good vibes I could gather. Shit, I felt a little strung out myself. So I left them to it. I found Dustin in the shade of one of the palo verde bushes, his pack emptied, the contents spread out on the dirt.

"Hey, bud," he offered brightly. "Big bummer in camp this morning, huh?" I agreed. How couldn't I? "Zed's fixing to split tomorrow, has he told you guys? No? Well, yeah, they're headed to O.B." I looked at him puzzlingly. "Ocean Beach," he explained. "It's a seaside neighborhood in San Diego, really cool place. He's already told his kids to start cleaning out the RV to lighten the load and make room for riders. We're heading down to Yuma first, see if we can't find some kids with cash." I felt a pang of hurt. Did Zed not want us to caravan with them any longer? "You guys coming, right?" he asked indifferently.

"I don't know," I answered. "Maybe Zed doesn't want us traveling with him anymore."

"Bullshit, man. Of course, he does. He needs people to prop him up, it's how he survives." I figured he was right, but I needed to hear it from Zed himself. So I went to the RV and knocked on the door.

"Come in, come in, brother," Zed told me after I poked my head inside. "Tick, Aiden, start emptying out the cargo hold and see what we can leave behind." They begrudgingly obeyed, leaving me alone in the cramped camper with our crusty old scout master.

"Have a seat, my friend," he told me, gesturing to the little pop-up table that came standard with mobile homes. "What's on your mind?"

I recounted to him what Dustin had told me and asked if he still wanted us to caravan. "Oh, yes, of course!" he assured me. "We need you guys; I need you guys. I'd like it very much if you stayed with us. You could even ride with us if your crew has had it with this life on the road," he added invitingly. "We'll do well in O.B. for the winter. It's a kind place; plenty of places to park overnight without getting hassled, lots of other travelers like us, lots of good times. Even Egg Man will be there," he added with a wink. "You two hit it off very well up in Ned. He told me he really took a shine to you. And who knows where we'll go once spring is upon us, the road is wide open! Northern California, the Redwoods, Mt Shasta? You heard of Mt. Shasta?" he asked me. I hadn't. "It's a powerful mountain, a magic mountain. It lies on a ley line like Stonehenge, in a vortex of earth's energies, and is one of the main energy centers of the planet, in fact. There are crystal caves there where you can contact the spirits of the earth and have visions of the future. We'll burn sage, ring the hand bell, get in touch with that vital earth energy. But you need to have your heart in the right place. Not everyone can connect with these powers. You, I think, have the right spirit to witness that power. You have a power yourself, like I've never seen in anyone who has not been training their mind for years. You have a raw power, a true power. Your chakras are already nearly in line. I can help you fine tune them. I can help you find what you seek!"

He was really spinning his web, and I was freely wrapping myself up in it. I wanted to follow this guy, I wanted to experience what he had to offer. I wanted to be able to live on the road forever, free from society, free from obligations. I wanted to ring hand bells inside of a magic fucking mountain, God damn it, man that shit sounded awesome! "Find out if Pete and his woman still want to follow me… uh, us," he corrected himself. "If they want to split you should wish them well and ride with me."

I stepped out into the blindingly bright noonday sun, my soul alight with excitement. I loved feeling accepted, I loved feeling I was a part of something larger than myself, and I loved feeling needed, just as I was.

When my eyes adjusted, I found Zed's kids and Dustin pouring out bags and boxes of all sorts of shit into the dirt. CDs, books, rumpled clumps of brand new t-shirts and tapestries with the store's tags still on them, small sculptures made from stone and wood and bronze thumping into the dust, and all manner of small expensive looking trinkets. The spoils of countless shoplifting excursions to hippie new-age stores all across the southwest and beyond. The pile was impressive. I began to root around in the detritus, helping sort like items according to their instruction. Dustin, Pete and Charles joined me, and we marveled at the merchandise they had amassed. It was loot in every sense of the word. Shady, stolen loot.

"What the hell is this?" Pete asked anyone within earshot, holding up a large bronze device or sculpture, decorated heavily in all manner of filigree and vaguely reminiscent of a king's scepter.

"That's a dorje," Barb answered. "It's something the Buddhist monks use."

I found another dorje that had been wrapped in a rainbow flag, but this one was even larger than the one Pete picked up and had an additional two ends protruding from its center like a cross. It was heavy, maybe 5 solid pounds, slightly tarnished, and looked incredibly old, like something from a museum. Then I saw the price tag; thirty five hundred dollars! Holy shit, these kids were fucking bandits!

We helped them sort and repack what they were going to keep for a few hours as we passed around the last jug of wine. They had boxes and boxes of incenses and fragrant oils, dozens of books, some of them beautifully bound collector's editions, hundreds of CDs and tapes still sealed in cellophane, more band t-shirts than I could count, hundreds of sunglasses of all shapes and sizes, all sorts of near-eastern jewelry items, sculptures and tapestries. Beautifully wrought items made from bronze, wood and stone. Japanese and Chinese looking sculptures, Tibetan religious items, Native American and Mesoamerican looking items. It was nuts. They had tens of thousands of dollars worth of stolen merchandise stuffed into that broke-down old camper.

I was in frightful awe of their abilities as thieves, and an equally fearful revelation dawned on me as I helped them load the boxes into the cargo hold; if I stuck with Zed and his kids, I would need to be ready to commit the same sort of acts. I would need to be able to pull my own weight once my money ran out. That thought took the wind out of my sails a bit. My faith in the religion of my youth was rapidly corroding away to nothing, but I still possessed a morality at odds with such gross levels of graft. It would be hard to justify such wanton theft with myself, even if I was godless. I would have to find other ways to hold my own on the road, other ways in which I could remain in some personal moral standing with myself while still being a productive member of the gang. There had to be a way. Then a small green figurine caught my eye. Almost unconsciously I snatched it quick before anyone else saw it, stuffed it into my pocket and spirited it away from the group.

Back at the Olds, I pulled the object from my pocket for a closer look. It was beautiful. Or rather, she was beautiful. A small, Chinese woman in traditional dress crouched on one knee. In one hand she held a delicate lotus flower, and the other was raised to her face, partially open. The figure was expertly carved from a single piece of lime green stone striated with fine blackish swirls. The stone was light weight, and if it were not for the black lines embedded in the stone I would have thought it was carved from some sort of artificial substance. I instantly fell in love with this little prize, this beautiful little girl. I had just stolen her without a second thought and was surprised at how easy it was. I guess I could swipe shit if the need arose, I told myself. Finders keepers.

That night was a quiet one. There was no more booze and no more desire to party. Pete and Jen kept to themselves, holed up in their tent with Dylan. Every once in a while I could hear one or the other's voice raised in protest or argument and I feared for their relationship. I loved the both of them and had naturally grown close to them over the course of this trip, but things were changing, for better or worse I was not yet sure. I resolved to myself to continue on this road even if they decided to quit it. I would feel them out in the morning and see where they were at. If they were done, then I would climb aboard Zed's ride, come what may.

Jen herself woke me in the morning, climbing into the front seat and shutting the heavy door behind her. "Hey, wake up!" she said softly.

"Good morning," I replied, rising to a sitting position.

"Listen, we have to talk. Pete and I have been hashing some things out, as I'm sure you know." I shook my head yes. "I'm pretty sure he did something with that poor runaway girl back in

Ned, but he swears to me he didn't. I know I need to get over it, but I can't shake the feeling that he's lying to me." I sat silent, not wanting to do anything that might be read into as me knowing anything, which in a sense I really didn't. "And that poor girl, abused by that old man, I really think we should get the cops involved or something, get that guy arrested, but Sherri does not want to talk to the cops because she's an underage runaway and doesn't want to get sent home to a situation even worse than being held captive by that old man, apparently. So, I need to breathe, I need to let sleeping dogs lie."

I didn't know what to say, so I kept my mouth shut, lest I make matters worse by the insertion of my foot into my gaping maw. We sat there in silence for a few minutes, watching the rest of the campers breaking down the tents. "Anyway, Alexandra and Charles are riding with us to San Diego. We're not following Zed to Yuma. We need to get away from those guys for a while, regroup on our own. Zed has a strange influence over everybody here, and I don't like it. If we all meet up again on the beach, that's fine, but I'm not following him out into the middle of nowhere again."

I sat quietly, taking her statements in. I was relieved her and Pete were apparently working their differences out again, and that we would continue traveling together. I was even a little relieved we were not following Zed anymore. I was deeply intrigued by him and the things he had to say, but in my gut, I knew she was right. I knew something was shady about that guy, you know, besides the obvious. "But first, we have to fix the tire again. We have a flat." I noticed then the car was sitting unevenly. "Pete says the spare is flat too, so Timothy is going to give us a ride into town to get it fixed. We'll need you to stay with the car, ok?" I shook my head yes. "Not too talkative this morning, eh?" she chuckled. "Don't worry, we'll all be ok once those crazy kids split. Then we can get our shit together and roll out on our own. Come on, let's get some breakfast." And she climbed back out of the car.

A group of us gathered at the fire pit, where an attempt at some sort of breakfast was underway. I grabbed a couple little pouches of instant oatmeal artificially flavored to resemble the taste of brown sugar and maple syrup, which I mixed with ambient temperature water in a coffee cup. It got the job done. I bumped into Dustin, who was engaged in a similar venture.

"Good morning, my friend!" he greeted me as he came in for a hug. "Looks like we're fixin' to roll out here soon. You guys coming down to Yuma with us, or what?" I answered no, and his face darkened. "Oh, no, really? Man, that's a bummer. I really, uh, like you. Like, uh, hanging around with you." And he averted his eyes briefly, his youthful cheeks noticeably blushing. "I was hoping to spend more time together."

"Don't worry, bud," I assured him. "We'll all meet up down in O.B. soon enough." He didn't seem convinced.

"Ah man, San Diego is like a lifetime away," he sighed. "Who knows what will happen on the road before then. I might never see you again." Now it was my turn to be unconvinced.

"Of course we'll meet again, dude, don't sweat it." And I slapped him on the shoulder. He responded by giving me another hug, tighter then before, close enough and long enough that I could feel him begin to tremble. I had experienced many an embrace with other guys, but this was different. He felt something for me, something I did not understand and could not fully reciprocate. I blushed myself then at the realization, feeling both honored to receive his affection and sad that I could not return it. He finally pulled away, his face contorted in emotion.

"Ok, you're right. We'll meet again soon," he said softly and then, lightning quick, kissed me on the cheek. I stood there in dumb shock as he hastily retreated into the RV.

"I think he's in love with you," sneered Tick from behind, obviously witnessing the exchange. I didn't know what to say. I liked Dustin a lot, more than anyone I had yet met on the road, but not like Tick was crassly suggesting. Though I was surprised to realize I was not automatically repulsed by the idea. I found his brief tenderness very endearing and felt a distinct sadness now that we would not be traveling together. I realized then I felt that familiar tickle in my guts, like when then ground gives way under you, like when you're struck with a crush. I put my hand to my cheek, touching the place where his lips had landed. What is this feeling, I asked myself. "Don't get all bent out of shape, dude," Tick barked, sensing my ponderings perhaps. "Whatever floats your boat is fine by me. None of my business what you all do with your dicks."

I felt instantly ashamed, and momentarily was taken with a keen desire to run. But I stood and stayed with the feeling. I did like Dustin, and felt that to deny it would be a sort of betrayal to the openness he had shown me in our time together. I did not feel aroused by him, per-say. The thought of his naked body did not bring up a boner. But I did feel love. Real, honest love. My shame gave way to anger briefly. Fucking Tick, always got to be a jerk about everything. I looked to him then, my emotions all over my face, and he chuckled in response. He saw he had gotten a rise out of me, and delighted in it. There was no getting ahead with him, he lived for this sort of shit. So I ignored his attempts at riling me further and walked off back to the Olds, now jacked up off the ground, its right rear wheel removed. Pete and old Timothy were standing there, looking at the dusty deflated tire laying prostrate in the dirt.

"Thanks for helping us out with a ride for our tire, man," I told him.

"It's no problem, kids," he dismissed. "It's the right thing to do. Plus, I need to get your crazy party energy away from me before I lose all my chances at redemption." He chuckled. "Jesus don't take kindly to all the drinkin' and dancin' like I was doin' the other night." I felt my guts do a flip. "I mean, you all can live however you want, but I've sworn an oath. I'm supposed to hold myself to a few things." Pete and I stood silently by. "But it was fun getting' lit up, though. Shoot, it'd been years since I got that drunk." He laughed. "Look, fellas, I'm not one to judge," he explained. "I was raised up a Mormon, not some watered-down LDS, but a real Mormon out on a compound in the desert. That sets you up to see the world a certain way. I didn't have a lot of contact with the outside world growing up, but I still figured out how to get myself in all sorts of trouble. By the time I was sixteen the old elders had cast me out, excommunicated me. I've been driftin' ever since. I still feel the pull to live my life a certain way, to be a man of righteousness as best I can, and helpin' you kids out of a jam is just the sort of thing I should do."

Aiden approached just as Timothy was completing his confession. "Hey, Tim. Would you be interested in buying a couple solar panels?" he asked. "We need to lighten the load; we'll let 'em go cheap."

"Thanks, but no, son," he answered. "All's I got is this old station wagon here. Can't rightly set up solar panels on that. Try asking Jake, down the way." And he gestured off towards the huge camper truck that had been parked the entire time we had been there, but whose occupant we had never seen.

"Is anybody even in that big camper?" I asked.

"Sure, Jake's in there," Timothy assured us. "He just don't like people so much, especially hard party kids like you guys." He laughed. "Go knock on his door; he might be interested in your wares."

Aiden thanked him and went back to his RV, briefly chatted with Tick, then climbed aboard their vehicle together with his partner in crime. Moments later they emerged carrying a large, rectangular metallic object, the same object I had watched the two load in the side door a while back outside of Phoenix. It was solar panels they had spotted off in the distance that morning, solar panels mounted to some piece of off the grid machinery out in the desert. Now they had these hot, high-tech pieces of equipment they needed to offload. I chuckled to myself at the brazenness of those two as I watched them carry the panels away towards the only other vehicle in the area. They came back a few minutes later empty-handed, with satisfied looks on their grimy, suntanned faces. The big old camper roared to life minutes later and slowly pulled away, leaving a fine cloud of dust in its wake. That truck had sat there innocuously the whole time, with never a peep out of its inhabitant, and now, after the briefest encounter with our crew, it breaks camp and leaves. I wondered who that Jake was who lived in that big camper. I wondered what his story was, why he would have nothing to do with us. But I would never know what his deal was. I would never even know what he looked like.

And that was about it. Camp was all broken down by now, our flat tire and our ruined spare were both loaded into the back of Timothy's wagon, and Zed had finished starting his ride with our battery like he had done once before in the snows of Sedona, his being dead again from days of accessory use in the desert. We said our goodbyes to the RV kids and to Zed, with mutual assurances that we'd all meet again soon on the beach. Sherri and Alexandra stood off to the side in an embrace, a series of handshakes and hugs were offered between us all, and Dustin once more gave me his farewell with a long tight hug. "I look forward to seeing you again, my friend," he told me, his hands grasping my shoulders with a tight squeeze, his eyes moist with emotion. And off they went, rumbling away in their own cloud of dust.

"Alright," Timothy announced. "Once the dust clears, we'll head out too. I can't fit everybody in the car, so somebody's gotta stay behind."

"I'll stay," I volunteered, remembering Jen's earlier instructions. "You guys shouldn't be too long, right?"

"We'll be a couple hours at least," he answered.

"I'll stay and keep you company," Alexandra offered with a smile. I thanked her, and soon we were alone, watching the dust clouds of our companions trail away into the desert.

It was an odd feeling, being out there alone after days of being surrounded by a bunch of loud and boisterous people, so I was glad to have the company of Alexandra. We set ourselves up in the shade of a palo verde bush on a couple of blankets and fired up the small talk.

"Thanks for staying out here with me," I told her. "I really appreciate it."

"Of course!" she responded. "Gosh, it's lonely out here though. I can't wait to hit the road again. I'm so excited to see the Pacific Ocean. Have you ever seen it?" I hadn't and told her as much. "I've done a bit of traveling, but I never had a chance to actually see the Pacific."

"Have you seen the Atlantic?" I asked.

"Ha! No, I haven't seen that ocean either," she confided. "Growing up in Colorado, you don't get to see much more than a pool or a lake." We shared a laugh.

We continued like that for an hour at least, sharing our stories and our love of traveling. She was so beautiful, and her voice so melodic, it didn't matter much what she was saying to me half the time, I just loved being at the center of her attention. I was a little unsure of how I felt about her participation in whatever they all had done in the tent together the other night, but since I didn't know all the details I could hardly come to a conclusion.

Besides, what business of mine was it anyway? I tried to keep an open mind about my experiences out on the road, tried to approach everything from a neutral perspective, but the strings of my faith, however denied, still held me in a net of preconceived notions about what was right and proper. I could push and pull against that net, and lord knows I did, but there was only just so far it would let me lean before I came up against something that stopped me, something I couldn't be "cool" with. Sexuality was one of those things. I wanted to know what sex was, I wanted it so bad it hurt my balls to think of it, but it had to be right, had to be with the right person. And since it was a reciprocal act, I couldn't do it alone.

"I like you; you know?" she said bluntly at one point. "I feel I can trust you, like no one I've met in a long time. Even more than Charles in a way." I felt lightheaded; butterflies were flip-flopping around in my guts like fish out of water. "I don't think Charles loves me anymore. He's been very cold with me since… since that night we all were in the tent together." What should I say? Was this my "in"?

"I just don't know how to feel." She continued. "I thought he was into our play that night, but I guess he wasn't." My imagination was running beyond my control. Play? What did she mean by that? She reached out and touched my leg, which sent a bolt of shivers cascading up my body. "I'm sorry," she said. "Are you bothered by this sort of thing?" Bothered? Jesus Christ, I didn't know what to think.

"Look," I said, catching notice of an approaching cloud of dust in the distance. "I think they are coming back."

She smiled knowingly and turned to see what I was seeing. "Good, I'm over this desert camp. You're a good guy, you know? I really do like you." My heart melted in place.

We stood up to greet the return of our companions, but when the car kicking up the dust rounded the corner it was instantly obvious that it wasn't them. The approaching vehicle was a little beige hatchback wagon, the windshield so shattered that all you could see of it was the white spider web pattern of its ruined surface emanating from one central point near the driver's side. As it drew closer, a reddish brownish stain could be discerned accompanying the shattered surface, trailing off the hood and over the passenger side fender. It looked like mud, thin mud. Then a realization struck. It was dried blood.

The car pulled right up to the fire pit, right into it in fact, knocking the few stones over and driving them forward like a bulldozer. When the car finally came to a stop, both the driver's door and the passenger door swung open simultaneously and out stepped two biker dudes in dirty blue denim and worn black leather, their long hair and beards greasy and unwashed. Each had a denim vest on over a leather jacket covered in well-worn patches, and as one turned to reach back into the car, I read what the wide patch across the back of one of their jackets said; Hells Angels.

The two guys strode up to us, one with a half-empty handle of whiskey, and stood silently for a moment, sizing us up no doubt.

"Howdy," one of the bikers said. "My name's Roy, this here is my brother Paul. How are you kids doin' today?" Both had deep-set eyes ringed in dark circles and looked like they hadn't slept in days.

"We're doin' alright, man," I replied, matching his piercing stare.

"Your car here don't look so good," the other one said, and indeed it didn't, with only three wheels on the ground, the fourth noticeably absent, its hub suspended in the air. "You two seem to be stranded, huh?"

"Our friends are in town with the tire, getting it fixed," Alexandra stated. "They'll be back soon."

"Well, then we haven't much time, do we?" Roy flatly stated.

The two stood there before us silently for what felt like an eternity. What did this biker mean by that? What did these guys have in mind to do with such a limited time? Why was there a body-sized imprint across the windshield of their blood-smeared car?

"Haw haw!" he started laughing gutturally, followed equally by his partner. "The look on your faces, God damn, that never gets old!"

"Relax you two," Paul ordered us. "We're just passing through, have a drink with us." And the two dropped into crossed legged stances in the dirt across from us.

Paul, who had been holding the bottle unscrewed the cap and flicked it away into the bush with a snap of his finger. "Won't be needing this anymore," he chuckled and took a long swig. Then he passed it to his partner, Roy, who took an equally long swig. Roy then held out the bottle to me. "Bottoms up, boy!" he ordered. I obeyed and took a pull. "Drink that shit like a man,

God damn it, you wanna look like a pansy waste in front of your girlfriend here?" I took another pull, drinking until my gag reflex forced me to begin coughing. The bikers loved that and guffawed heavily at my expense. "Ok, little lady, your turn." Alexandra took a pull, a long even pull, wiped her mouth, and handed the bottle back to Roy without even clearing her throat.

"That's what I'm talking about!" Paul declared. "See, boy. That's how you drink the whiskey." I was too nervous to feel even remotely offended.

The bottle made one more pass around before it was fully drained by Roy. "Aw, fuck," he groaned. "Now what are we going to do?"

"You hippies have any weed?" Paul asked. I didn't, in fact hadn't smoked in days, not since Sedona. The bikers were obviously unstable, probably strung out on crank or something, and were now on a whiskey drunk to boot. I wished I had some weed to smoke them up with. It'd probably level them out a bit, I reasoned. Then Alexandra came to the rescue.

"I have a joint," she offered, her soft voice in sharp contrast to their gruff cadence. "Hold on, I'll see if I can find it." She went to the trunk, pulled out her bag, and brought it over to our circle. "Here we go." And she pulled out a little decorated brass box, popped the lid and produced a single fat joint. Thank Christ, I thought. She lit it, took a couple big puffs, and passed it to Roy.

"Thanks, beautiful," he croaked and took a few puffs himself before passing it to his partner, who also took a few puffs in silence. Paul then passed it to me.

The weed was good. Really good, I could taste it right away. I wondered how long she had been holding on to that doobie. I exhaled a thick cloud of yellowish smoke into the dry desert air. The atmosphere had changed; the aggressive energy the bikers carried in with them had dissipated with the smoke.

"God damn!" Roy exclaimed. "This is some good shit." And he closed his eyes and took a few deep breaths. "Man, this is hitting the spot."

The joint went around a few more times till we had burned it down to nothing. Paul started to chuckle for no reason as his partner looked on with a smirk. "Jesus Christ I am high as fuck!" He laughed, and that broke the ice for all of us. We all started laughing.

"Ok, ok," Roy finally said, rubbing his face with his big grime-stained hand. "So, you kids are like traveling around the country I guess, right?" We shook our heads yes. "Man, that is the life. No one to tell you what to do, or where to go. Just the wide-open road," he preached. "How long y'all been on the road?" We each gave a heavily abbreviated version of our traveling stories while the two sat patiently and listened, their deep-set, bloodshot eyes almost gone behind their drooping eyelids. "Sounds like a good time," he decided once we had told our tales. "Me and Paul here have been everywhere, all over the U.S. down into Mexico, up into Canada. Haven't been home in years. Don't even have a home to go back to, really. We have brothers wherever we go, so home is where you plant your ass."

"It can get rough, though," Paul added. "I haven't slept in a real bed in months. Just couches, floors, out in the dirt. Shit, last month I was up in Idaho, freezing my ass off. Had to wrap up in an old carpet like a burrito to keep from freezing to death one night."

"But it's worth it," Roy answered. "I wouldn't trade it for the world."

"Alright, Roy," Paul said, after a brief silence. "We still have a job to do. Get your stoned ass up." And the two rose to their feet. "Thanks for the head change, kids." He held out his hand. I rose and shook it, giving the firmest handshake I could muster. "You know, you should really be more careful out here in the desert," he quietly stated, as he held fast to my hand "You got a beautiful girlfriend here, and we're so far away from civilization that nobody'd ever hear your screams." I felt the bottom fall out of my stomach. He held my hand a few moments longer, our eyes locked as he stared into my soul. He had dark, empty eyes; eyes of a shark.

"Can we have your lighter?" Roy asked. "We're supposed to burn this car down, and neither of us even has a match." Alexandra held out her lighter. "Thanks again, beautiful."

The two of them then climbed back into the little hatchback, backed up off the fire pit rocks, and drove off the road and into the dry wash at the base of Crystal Hill. I looked to see what the license plate read, thinking it might be good to try and remember something like that, but the car had no plates, Only bloody fingerprints on the back hatch door and smears on the bumper. I shuddered to fathom what we had just witnessed and how close we came to trouble the likes of which I could only imagine.

"Those were evil men," Alexandra said softly as we watched the dust of their passing fade out of sight.

Ten minutes later, our people returned. We filled them in on our brush with the angels of death as Pete mounted the wheel and stowed the spare in the trunk. They brushed it off, figuring we were exaggerating or something, but Timothy took our story to heart.

"If I see them pass this way, I'll try to steer clear of them," he said.

We thanked him heartily for his help and rolled out. It was well into the afternoon, but there was no way in hell we were staying one more night out in the desert. We all agreed we would try to push on into the night as far as we could, maybe all the way to the ocean shore if our stamina held out. We all had our reasons to put the past few weeks in our rear-view mirror. We all had our needs to push west and wash away our collective sins in the ocean waves.

I turned to look back one last time as we finally merged with the pavement, and far off in the distance from whence we came, across miles of open desert, a single, thin pillar of black smoke rose into the cloudless blue sky.

CHAPTER 31

It took about half an hour to clear the state line into California. Once we crossed the Colorado River, the landscape instantly changed from dry, open desert to green, irrigated fields. Greenery like we hadn't seen in weeks sprang up on all sides, the most striking of which were the tall palm trees, sharing the horizon with brightly colored suburban signage and tall streetlight poles. We picked the first exit advertising offerings of fuel and food.

We stopped at the first gas station we found, splitting the cost among us, and then rolled through a drive-through fast-food hamburger place.

"Make sure my burger has no onions, Pete," Charles asked from the back seat. "I'm allergic."

Pete placed the order, and we were soon rolling once again, skirting the highway west on a parallel street. Before you could blink, we had left the town and were out in open green fields, artificially irrigated against the ravaging desiccation of the desert looming just out of view over the horizon. We hung a hard left onto S.H. 78 south. Twenty miles or more we drove through fabricated farmlands before crossing an unmarked canal. The desert waited there on the other side; a native power banished to the periphery.

Pete hammered down now that civilization was again behind us, and the miles flew by at over seventy miles an hour. The land through here was of a different flavor of desert compared to the world of Quartzsite. The soil was brighter, the yellows and reds more vivid, and there were no more saguaro cactus sporadically stationed about. The land was more undulating as well, so that we often experienced the butterfly feeling in our guts as the speeding car crested the little rises in the road. At some point we cut through a sea of rolling sand dunes, soft and gleaming in the afternoon sun. Out on the dunes, quads, dune buggies, and other stripped down 4X4 vehicles could be seen tearing across the sand and shooting rooster tails of the beige dust behind them like the minions of some post-apocalyptic war lord.

"Oh, man! Check that shit out!" Pete exclaimed as he let off the gas in response to the sight, his excitement reminiscent of a boy with a basket of matchbox cars. "I'd love to be out on one of those quads!"

Then once again we crossed another border, leaving the organically shaped track of the desert for the geometric grid-like layout of irrigated farm fields, as humanity once again wrested control of the land from its rightful owner. We tore south on that wide-open road for another twenty-some-odd miles before coming up on Interstate 8.

West we pushed, towards the sinking sun, soon leaving the flat green fields behind us. Again we were in a dry, treeless desert, this time the color of beach sand. The land was bumpy, cut with washouts, and virtually devoid of any greenery whatsoever. It was striking how much of a difference industrial irrigation made to the landscape, how unnatural it was. If you were to turn off the tap to those grids of green fields, they would surely revert within weeks to the dry inert world we now flew through. I wondered how long it would take before those little strip-mall cities we blew through turned into dry, gutted wastelands unfit for modern human life.

The land slowly rose around us as we sped west, with hills of rocky rubble protruding from the desert floor in huge bursting blisters. On both sides of the highway these piles of pale stones were tumbled in great heaps, as if giant dump trucks had dropped their loads indiscriminately all over the place. We were climbing now, the elevation building, and it was slowing down our speed. The car was now loaded up with two extra people and their gear, and it made a noticeable difference.

The road leveled out for a while once we got past the fields of rubble piles, and opened into a scrubby landscape, populated by small bristly bushes. Evening was closing in upon us, and there wasn't much daylight left. We passed a sign announcing that we had another seventy miles or so still to go before we reached San Diego. That it would be well after dark by that point would make our entry into the city problematic, since we had no idea where to go besides a spot pointed out to us on the map. At the same time, the car was threatening to overheat due to the steady elevation gains we were climbing. We talked the issue over and decided we would find a place to camp between where we were and the city limits. The Arizona desert was far enough behind us now that we felt comfortable with stopping.

Jen studied our smudged, road-worn atlas, looking for clues as to where the best prospects of finding a clandestine sleepover site near the highway might be. She found a little town near the summit of the pass through the Cuyamaca Mountain range, just off the highway. It was well within the Cleveland National Forest area, so we figured that would give us the best chance of getting away with squat camping in the bush somewhere off the main roads. If we went much past that we'd start descending into civilization, where pitching tents next to our parked car might be frowned upon. But we still had a mess of miles ahead of us till we reached our new goal, and all through the mountains judging by the way the route snaked across the page of the atlas.

So on we pushed, often getting slowed down by the steady climb, as cars and trucks of more nimble natures blew past us in the passing lane. The evening had progressed to the point where headlights were required when Charles began moaning quietly in the back seat.

"Ugh, I think there were onions in that burger, or onion juice or something. My guts are cramping terribly," he complained.

"Are you going to be ok?" Jen asked him.

"I don't know. I think I'm going to throw up." He looked pale and clammy.

"Pull over, Peter!" Jen demanded. "Quick, before he loses it in the back seat.

No sooner had Pete pulled off on the shoulder than Charles lunged for the door, climbing over Alexandra and the front seat in his overwhelming need to get out. He stood leaning against a signpost doubled over, vomiting out the contents of his stomach at the pavement's edge. The car too, the ram air effect of airflow across the overworked radiator suddenly ceasing was now engaging in its own version of vomiting from the filler neck. Thick clouds of steam billowed out from the front grill, accompanied by loud hissing and gurgling with boiling, watered-down coolant spilling onto the ground under the car. "Looks like we're sitting tight for a little while," Pete stated.

We all climbed out and sat on the rocks on the side of the highway as Pete opened the hood, releasing a mushroom cloud of steam lit ominously by the headlights of the passing cars. There was enough of a shoulder where we stopped that our ride was well off the road, so there was minimal danger of getting creamed by a speeding vehicle. But it was still a little unnerving to be so close to traffic moving at highway speeds, especially for Dylan. The sounds of the tires humming on the road surface seemed to irritate him greatly, causing him to fly into fits of barking whenever a particularly loud set of wheels roared past.

Charles was able to regain his composure long before the Olds did, so we ended up being stuck there for nearly an hour before the car had chilled out enough to be ready for another go at the climb. It was totally dark out by the time we were back on the road. Nothing could be seen of the landscape we were passing through, which was too bad, since by then we were well into the National Forest.

We were nearing our destination, according to the map, when we rolled up on a line of cars stopped in the middle of the highway, their glowing red brake lights out of place in an otherwise dark expanse. It was a check point, a border patrol check point. We were close enough to Mexico for there to be the need, apparently. The lines of cars and trucks moved smoothly through the pinch as the uniformed agents waved them along, but as we approached in our beat up old hot rod an officer stepped forward and indicated we stop. He stepped to the driver's side window and had a quick look at us with a pass of his flashlight, which prompted a long low growl from Dylan.

"Good evening," the officer stated. "You kids carrying any drugs?"

"No, sir," a few of us replied simultaneously, which for once was true.

"Ok, how about any fruits or vegetables, any guns? Any illegal immigrants in the trunk? Any bombs, landmines or missiles?'

"Missiles?" Pete responded with a laugh. "No sir, no we ain't got no missiles."

The interrogating agent smirked. "Ok, move along." And he stepped back and waved us forward.

"Missiles?" Pete repeated as we pulled away. "Why the fuck would he ask if we were carrying fucking missiles?"

"To see how you would respond to such a ridiculous question," Charles answered. "You laughed it off because it was ridiculous. That shows him you are not nervous about something. Nervous people are usually nervous for a reason."

"They teach you that in the army?" Jen asked him.

"No, my uncle was a state trooper," he replied. "He gave me some tips on how to act if I ever got pulled over with weed in my pocket."

"Well, that was nice of him," Alexandra said.

Soon after we came up on our exit. We hung a right on the main drag and made a pass through town headed east. In less than a minute, we had left the town and were out in the dark countryside. At an intersection we spotted a dirt road leading off into the scrub. Pete took the turn, and we bumped along into the darkness, the way illuminated by our running lights alone so as not to draw undue attention to our presence. The dirt path was a service road for a stretch of power lines and was deserted enough for our needs. We picked a spot as secluded as was available and set up a little camp there between the humming highway and the backcountry road.

After we had the tents up, we decided to risk a little fire, just to give us something to congregate around. The piney dry boughs we burned produced a wonderfully fragrant smoke almost like some kind of incense. It was nice to be up in the mountains again with minimal ambient light pollution. The night sky was clear, allowing the stars to twinkle in the firmament, and the sweet smoke was somehow cleansing after the drunken revelry we had been enjoying the past few weeks.

I slept well that night, the low background noise of the nearby highway almost mimicking the sounds of the ocean washing down the shore. I drifted off wondering what the Pacific would be like, what it would smell like. I had been to the Atlantic shore countless times and could conjure up the feel of its presence effortlessly. Would the Pacific be similar? I could also remember how different the shores of Lake Michigan had been to any other body of water I had ever met; would the Pacific present itself like that as well? Eager anticipation shared my sleeping bag that night, and my dreams reflected this energy.

I stood upon the Atlantic shore of my memories, wrapped in the blanket of the night. Before me, the surf pounded in the starlit darkness. I could feel the pounding in my chest with each crash of a wave; I could feel the exhilaration rise with each successive swell. I was alone on that wide sandy beach, alone as I often was in my dreams, and it felt right to be alone there with the stars as my only companions. I felt as one with those stars, with the waves, with everything. I felt as if the very atoms of my being were the same as everything else around me, so the boundaries between my being and the world around me dissolved. I was no longer a body standing on the beach, listening to the crash of the surf, no longer the eyes gazing up into the night sky. I was the beach; I was the surf. I was the very night itself. I was the cosmos, infinite and eternal.

We arose with the sun, greeting the first light of day in mutual excitement, for today we would all meet the Pacific for the first time. Pete steered back onto the highway, and soon we were making our descent down the mountainside and into an increasingly suburban world. The highway leveled and straightened out as it weaved its way through a world of low buildings, low enough to be towered over by telephone poles and palm trees. As the morning grew, a haze became apparent, a haze that hung over all the surrounding metropolitan area. And then I caught a whiff of something blown in through the open windows, something intimately familiar; the briny aroma of the ocean.

The highway was wide now, four lanes in each direction, and the traffic was thickening. But we kept up a reasonable speed, it being still early in the morning. Both sides of the highway were dense with low structures of urbanity. We were well within the city now, and the brackish smell of the ocean was growing stronger.

We passed under the Interstate 5 exchange and were on the last stretch. The highway began to shed lanes until it was down to two. We passed a sign announcing the impending ending of the freeway and the low buildings gave way to canals and wetlands as we slowed down to accept the rumble strips cutting across our path. Finally, we came to the end to the highway and stopped at a red traffic light. Ahead, clusters of tall palm trees and green parks awaited. The light turned green, and we rolled into Ocean Beach, San Diego.

We found our way directly to the shore by way of a large, almost empty parking lot peppered with vans and capped-bed pickup trucks that to our eyes stuck out obviously as the rides of other travelers. Some with California tags and some from out of state, but all a little stained somehow from the life on the road. Pete aimed straight for the ocean, passing them all hurriedly, and pulled the car into a parking spot where the pavement met the sand. We all piled out into the sunshine and took our final steps west. Once on the sand Pete Dylan and I lost our patience and broke into a jog.

"Fuck this," Pete exclaimed as he approached the water's edge, kicking off his sneakers and struggling to pull his shirt off over his wide mop of dreads. "I'm jumping in." And he waded into the surf in his pants, diving into a small wave as the water reached his waist.

I peeled off my shirt, kicked off my shoes and followed suit, wading in deep wearing nothing but my filthy cargo pants. I made my way out past my waist before dunking my head in under the surface as well, baptizing myself in those western waters of my dreams now realized.

The ocean felt incredible after all those dry, dusty days in the desert, and I hollered aloud in ecstasy as I emerged from under the salty waves. This was it; the far western shore. I had made it. I bobbed with the swells for a while, an uncontrollable smile distorting my face. It was a Sunday, and I felt grateful, but I knew not to whom. I was confident now that God as I had known him did not in fact exist, and in all probability did not exist in any form whatsoever. But I still felt a feeling of gratitude, a sense of appreciation, and I yearned to give thanks to some great orchestrator for my current placement on the planet. But to whom, to what? I looked up to the sun as I floated, its light glittering in the water droplets riding on my eyelashes, and laughed aloud. I was adrift now, cut loose from my heavy convictions and on my own, completely alone. I swam over to my friend as he frolicked in the swells and embraced him heartily.

"Thank you, my friend," I told him. "Thank you for inviting me to join you guys on this trip."

"Of course, man," he replied with a wide grin. "This is fucking awesome, huh?" How could I disagree? "Guys! Hey, guys!" he shouted at the shore. "Come on in, the water's great!"

Our companions on the beach just smiled and waved. "I guess it's just you and me," I said.

"Fuck 'em, their loss," he dismissed, and dunked his head under again.

Eventually we quit the water and climbed up onto a rock jetty separating the two beaches, there attempting to dry our pants in the sun. Our companions had already climbed over the jetty and down onto the other beach, where a multitude of dogs ran and frolicked while their respective owners stood by. Dylan was tear-assing around the beach, chasing and rolling around with other random pups and kicking sand like a child in a sand box.

"Look at my boy go!" Pete laughed. "God damn, this place is awesome." And indeed it was. The first impression this beach was laying on us was great. The air was warm but not hot. The parking lot told tales of other travelers we would surely meet. There was even a section of beach devoted solely to dogs.

To the far right, past this dog beach, ran another long straight jetty jutting far out into the surf. On the far side of this barrier rose more of this beach city. To the left, a long wide beach of white sand stretched away maybe half a mile towards what looked to be a small hill or rise sheathed in one- and two-story buildings presided over by a few randomly placed palm trees. Also, down where that hill seemed to rise from the beach, a long pier shot out into the sea, much farther than the stone jetty to the right. Instantly I needed to walk out to the end of that pier.

"Yo, you see that long dock down there?" I asked him, pointing towards the structure. "Dude, we should walk down there and check it out."

"Shit, I'm down. Let's go," he replied, pulling his shirt back on.

Once we had all our acts together and got Dylan on a leash, we trekked down the beach in the soft sand towards the far side. We made our way towards a bustle of activity following a wall of stones marking the dividing line between the shore and the city. The rock wall quickly gave way to a poured concrete wall leading us towards a right-angle bend where the city streets came right up to the edge of the sand. Looking up one of the streets, you could see the strip was lined with restaurants and shops and clustered with all sorts of sun-dappled people out and about. There at that intersection of multiple paths I spotted a familiar looking van in an adjacent parking lot.

"Yo, Pete, check out that van over there," I said, directing his attention that way. "I think that's that van we saw on the highway in New Mexico a few weeks ago, the one with the Alaska plates."

"Oh yeah," he replied, squinting in the sun. "Let's go say hi."

The two of us broke off from our group to have a closer look, while the rest of our party took a walk up the strip. My initial observations proved to be true; it was the same rust-stricken, baby blue and white two-tone Chevy passenger van we had passed on the highway, and there beside the open side door stood the dirty blond-haired kid who had waved and smiled at us those few weeks ago.

"Hey, brother man!" I called out as we approached. "Remember us? We passed you all on the highway back in New Mexico a few weeks ago; we had the olive drab fast-back car with the New York plates."

"Oh, shit, yeah man!" the kid replied, reaching out for the customary road-kid hug. "Dude, you guys just getting to town?" We replied in the affirmative. "This town is pretty kind, you'll see. But you still need to keep your guard up. There's a bunch of tweekers on the beach here that don't give a shit about much," he explained. "Some of these smiling faces will try to rob you blind once your back is turned." We listened soberly. "And the cops. Six up can be real hard asses." And as if the police were waiting for their cue, a black and white cruiser rolled up on us, angling in and blocking the front of the van. "Ah, fuck me," the kid muttered under his breath.

"Good morning, gentlemen," the cop proclaimed sternly as he climbed out of his car, his partner joining him. "You two, don't recognize your faces. You just getting to my beach?" he asked

Pete and me. "Let's see some ID," he demanded before we could answer.

Luckily, we both had our wallets, albeit a little damp from our late dips in the ocean, and we were both clean as far as our permanent records were concerned. We stood there with the Alaskan kid while the cops ran our licenses in their car. I noticed while we waited that both crests of the front fenders were heavily dinged and scraped. In some places the paint was worn down to the primer. How many victims thrown over the front fenders getting cuffed did it take to cause that kind of wear? Jesus, these cops are no joke I thought.

"Ok, you kids are ok to go," the cop said as he handed our IDs back. "But if you plan on staying in town, you need to get California issued IDs. If I run your IDs again in a few weeks, and they are still New York documents, we're going to have problems. And don't think I won't remember you two, I never forget a face. Ain't that right, Jacob?" he asked our Alaskan acquaintance.

"Yes, sir," Jacob answered meekly. We watched as they climbed back into their cruiser and wheeled out of the parking lot. "Fucking cops. See what I mean?" How could we not. "Anyway, you guys got a place to park for the night? This lot is way too hot to hang around for long," he asked. We did not. "Fiesta Island, that's the place. The cops keep tabs on your vehicle though. Can't stay there more than two nights at a time, but there are other safe spots around too. Is your car legal?" It was. "Good. If your tags are expired, they will snatch your shit in a hurry."

"Damn, thanks for the head up, man," Pete stated.

"Yeah, of course, bro," he dismissed. "We'll be on Fiesta tonight. Come to our fire."

With that invitation filed away for future use, we bid our see you laters and continued to the pier.

The pier was long, especially so when looking at it stretch away before us into the ocean. We walked briskly west, passing other folk out strolling and a great many locals fishing, set up with aluminum lawn chairs and umbrellas in little day camps. The smell of fish guts drying in the sun mixed with the natural aroma of the sea itself brought to mind memories of my childhood, exploring the fisherman's wharves in Montauk with my dad out beside another ocean far to the east. I kept smiling to myself in mild disbelief that I was now in the presence of the Pacific, something I never thought I would see.

It took us a while to get out to the end, even at the quickened pace we walked. Looking west into the ocean didn't afford much perspective really, just the sea and the sky. But looking back towards shore was a sight. We were far enough out that most of the city shoreline could be seen. It was big, being a major city after all, but it was short. A small cluster of tall downtown buildings could be made out a mile or more inland against the horizon.

Once we had taken in the view, we headed back towards land, meeting the rest of our crew near the halfway point.

"Did you guys get hassled by the cops too?" I asked them after we had filled them in about meeting the kid from the Alaskan van. "They ran our IDs; told us we'd need to change them to California IDs in a few weeks if we want to stay for a while."

Charles's face went white. "Jesus, thank God I was not with you guys."

"Holy shit, yeah. You would have been fucked, huh?" Pete stated.

"I would have been arrested on the spot if they figured out who I was."

"But you don't even have an ID, right?" Jen asked. "You could have just gave 'em some fake name."

"Even without an ID they would have probably snatched me till they could figure out who I was. I'm living on borrowed time."

"Well, we'll do whatever we can to deflect them if it comes to it, and you can make a run for it," I assured him.

"Ha, yeah, then they'll just gun me down," he laughed. "Nah, I'm gonna have to face the music sooner or later. I'm resigned to that. But in the meantime, I'm going to enjoy myself. No use worrying about the future, cuz all we have is the present, right here, right now." And he grabbed Alexandra and Jen and pulled them into a hug. "Come on, we saw a taco place on the strip that smelled awesome. Lunch on me."

The tacos were rolled up in thin little sticks and were deep fried, I think. They were amazing and cheap too. We ate a whole mess of them, then walked off the full stomachs up and down the Newport strip till evening approached. We then stopped into a local supermarket, got a few beers and some food stuffs and headed back to dog beach to get the car. As we drew near to its place in the parking lot, we saw that another police cruiser was parked behind it, blocking it in, while a cop was at the driver's side of our car looking at the registration sticker and writing something down.

"Better hang back a minute," Pete cautioned. "The car is legal; they'll probably leave once they've confirmed it with their station or whatever." And sure enough, after a few minutes they rolled off. "Damn, six up is no joke here though." He added as they exited the parking lot.

We climbed aboard and rolled out. Luckily, Fiesta Island was an actual named place on the map, not just road-kid slang, so we had no trouble plotting a course to its location. The island was a strangely shaped lump of sand in Mission Bay connected to the mainland by a thin spit of land bridge. The landscape looked to me like one big dredge spoil dump, colonized by grasses and a few small bushes alone. The road followed the switch back shoreline exactly, never tracking inland at all. On the water side we would occasionally pass a parked car, van, or RV, some of which had little campfires going. The scene looked pretty good for the likes of us. As we rounded a corner, we spotted the

Alaskan's van parked alone, a little blaze burning away in a cut-in-half fifty-five-gallon drum beside the van. We pulled up opposite and joined their camp.

"Welcome to Fester Island!" one of the kids told us as we climbed out. "Don't mind the smell, it's just sewage."

CHAPTER 32

We all kicked it around their little fire of scrap lumber and nursed our warming beers as the fading light of evening was replaced by the orange background glow of urban municipal lighting. The few seats available to us on the beach consisted solely of a couple empty spackle buckets and an old flat tire on a steel rim blistered and flaking with salty rust. Those accommodations were claimed by the others quickly, so I just parked my ass on the hard sticky sand of the shore for lack of a better option. Jen produced a pack of hot dogs for us all to share and fried them up in the Alaska kid's smoke-stained frying pan.

We got to talking over our meager meal and shared our road stories with each other. Only one of the kids we supped with was actually from Alaska. The other two were from Oregon and New Jersey, respectively. Jacob, the shaggy blond kid Pete and I had spoken with over in the hot lot earlier, was from Fairbanks, and this was his rusty old van. He had set out with a group of other kids from his city over a year ago, looking for adventure. Over the months on the road, he lost the kids he had left with and picked up new riders along the way, including a girlfriend.

The girl, the one kid from Oregon, had been riding with him for about six months. She was a small grimy sprite with thick nappy dreads, speckled with heavy colorful glass beads, which she wore tied up on the top of her head so the individual dreads splayed out like the leaves of some wild plant.

The other kid was a hitchhiker out of suburban New Jersey, on the road for about as long as we had been. They had picked him up at a truck stop in Arizona the week before. He was a nondescript looking fellow, bearing no outward allegiance to any particular scene, which was unusual among the road kids I met out there. Most were of the dead-head raver skater type to varying degrees and wore a standard sort of uniform that placed them in those camps. But some, like this Jersey rider, could not be pegged so easily.

This uniform of course, had its drawbacks and advantages. Looking like a dirty road kid set you apart from the general populace and put a target on your back that law enforcement could aim for. But having a generally accepted uniform to follow did lead to sense of belonging and helped to keep the community of travelers coherent, like a tribe, so it could work to your advantage to don the garb of the road kid. It certainly expedited acceptance when groups of travelers met in the field. But it wasn't absolutely necessary, as this Jersey hitchhiker and the others like him I met plainly showed. Real travelers wore an aura of the road around them that shone like a beacon and could be discerned from a distance if you knew what to look for. Even if they weren't dressed in the standard crusty hippie raver uniform they still stuck out like sore thumbs in a crowd of regularly showered and laundered normals.

Eventually it was time to turn in. My companions took the tents into the low scrubby dunes, while I stayed with the car. Our campmates all bedded down in their van, pulling the little paisley print curtains across the large windows the vehicle emerged from the factory with. Jacob informed us shortly before we all quit the fire that they would be rolling out in the morning to start their journey north towards Oregon and the scene his girlfriend had originally come from. They had been harried by the cops one time too many and were itching to get rural again. He invited us to caravan but admitted in the same breath that we'd probably do better to stick around OB for a while, since it would be cold and wet for another couple months up north where they were headed.

I was abruptly awoken the next morning by the hard rapping of a heavy aluminum flashlight butt on the window beside my head. My eyes popped open to lock with those of a square jawed cop peering in at me in the dim light of dawn.

"Wake up, kid!" he sternly demanded. "Time to move on."

He stood there a moment longer, glaring hard before turning and joining his partner in their black and white cruiser. I sat upright in the car and watched the officers slowly drive away. I realized then that the Alaskan's van was gone. They must have broken camp well before dawn, for I had not even heard the engine turn over. Well, they missed out on one last run-in with OB patrol, I thought, lucky them. The cops in this town were really proving to be hard asses, and I began to worry we'd soon find ourselves as harried as our late friends.

My companions emerged from the misty morning dunes shortly thereafter. They hadn't even seen the cops, but Dylan's growls had awoken them. The pup must have heard them stopping near the car and automatically went into alarm mode. Luckily, he did not fly into one of his barking fits. That might have prompted the cop to take a peek into the dunes. The sign posted on the route in clearly stated: "No camping, no tents." The "no camping" part apparently didn't apply to vans and cars, but I did notice there was not a single tent on the shore. If the cop had made a big deal out of my companions tenting it in the dunes, they would surely have found out Charles's fugitive status and probably locked us all up.

With that potential shit show avoided, we loaded up and headed back down to the beach to see what the day had in store for us. We were just climbing out of the car in the parking lot beside dog beach when we heard a familiar voice call our names from afar.

"Halloo! Pete!" cried the voice. "Over here!" We turned our attention towards the raised path separating dog beach from the parking lot, and there on that high stone way walked a man in white cut-off jean shorts and white v-neck t-shirt struggling to slow the advance of two large dogs by their leash; a man with a wide grin and large, thick eyeglasses. "You made it! Welcome, my friends, welcome to OB!"

"Holy shit, it's Egg Man!" Pete exclaimed. And we trotted across the parking lot to meet him. He caught Pete in a cheerful embrace, laughing heartily.

"Welcome, brothers, sisters. You all just rolling into town?" He had shaved off his large beard since last we saw him, and it changed his appearance dramatically. His large heavy glasses now looked even more oversized on his stubbly head. "Where's Zed, and the kids?" Pete and I began to excitedly fill him in with disjointed segments of our story since last we met, all out of sequence to the actual timeline of events. "Whoa, whoa! First things first," he laughed. "Come with me to the end of the jetty. My boys need to run in the sand and we need to smoke a few bowls."

The raised path led in a straight line out towards the ocean, ending finally in a jumble of large, jagged boulders. We clambered down onto the dog beach side and tucked into the sand. Egg released his dogs, who took off running, followed by Dylan once Jen could get him unlatched from pulling so hard on the leash. "Ha! Look at them go," Egg muttered half to himself as he squinted in the morning sun.

"Summer's pup has gotten huge!" I stated.

"Yeah, can you imagine what she would have done with such a big boy?" Egg responded. "He'd probably be half starved to death by now." Who's to know, I thought. Maybe she would have been good to the pup. Or maybe not. The pup was happy anyway, and well taken care of. It was obvious Egg loved his dogs very much.

He pulled a little pouch made of colorful patches of velvet from the pocket of his white cutoff jeans, then out of that he pulled an equally colorful glass pipe, hand blown and bulbous. "So, what's your names?" he asked our riders as he packed a pinch of fragrant buds into the bowl. Alexandra offered her name first and introduced her companion, Charles.

"Zed picked us up off the streets of Denver. Seems like ages ago already," she admitted. "We met these guys in the forest above Sedona and have been riding with them ever since."

"Well, this is a pretty kind place. I know a few tricks on how to get the most out of your time here." Egg added as he passed the pipe to Alexandra. "There's a drum circle tonight in fact, in a parking lot near the Ocean Amusement Park. Lots of heady kids roll out, lots of dank buds. They usually have a bonfire, and a few of us park overnight, provided the cops don't get called in."

"Sounds great!" she beamed.

Once we had a good buzzing high going, we hitched up the pups to their leashes once again and took a stroll down the beach to the Newport wall. Egg often had to return a greeting or wave from a distance from a number of beachy folk along the way. He seemed to know everybody, from lifeguards up on their high perches to tanned surfer chicks with their glossy boards under their arms to retirees out walking their dogs in the sand under the shade of their large-brimmed straw hats. He really seemed to be in his element here.

He walked us by a few of the shops down on the strip, pointing out the ones worth engaging with if we found we had a few extra dollars to spend, as well as the ones that would not be friendly to road kids like us on account of the sun-hardened, disheveled appearance we possessed. The beach had a lot of homeless folks, as is to be expected in a city situated in a climate so conducive to sleeping out of doors. And a good deal of the local population was not too cool with this fact. There were some bad actors on the streets, not surprisingly: tweakers, violent drunks, and those with unstable mental states lurked in numbers. The actions of these folks painted us all with a wide brush, he explained, so it would be in our best interest to recognize when we weren't welcome and when shit was going south around us so we could bounce out before the cops rolled up and swept us up in the action.

"Most everybody on the beach is friendly. Don't get me wrong. You just need to be smart, need to keep your eyes open. You do not want to spend a night in the lock up here, trust me."

We all split up for the afternoon. Egg had some business he had to attend to, and Jen was interested in looking to see what the apartments in the area looked like from the street. Her desire to settle back into a more mainstream way of life had been growing steadily, and now that OB had laid such a rosy first impression on us, she was already talking about finding work and getting a roof. I was on the fence with all that. This life on the road was working out pretty well for me so far. I was not ready to abandon it for a job and a rent bill to spend my paychecks on just yet.

I was on my own for most of the day, aimlessly wandering around the neighborhood, getting a feel for the place. I made a collect call home at a gas station pay phone and talked with my mom for a while, filling her in on my adventures, and got some reassurance that everything was ok back home. Towards the end of our conversation, she asked me if I thought I might be coming home soon, maybe for Christmas. I hadn't thought that far ahead and told her as much.

"But we might stick around here for a while," I assured her. "Maybe get an apartment, and jobs or something." That seemed to please her greatly, so I let her keep that feeling unmolested.

As the sunset approached, I found myself down on the shore between Newport and dog beach right under the path of the many thunderous commercial jet planes that passed over the neighborhood one after the other, reclining in the soft warm sand and stripped down to my stained and patched cargo pants. I had set myself up on a stretch of beach someone from my crew would surely pass on their way back to the car, so I felt no rush to go looking for them. The blazing orange disk had just touched the horizon when Charles plopped down next to me.

"Hey, brother," I greeted him. "How's it going?" He shrugged and sighed. I noticed then he was alone. "Where's everybody else?"

"Not sure. I went off with Alexandra after Pete and Jen started arguing about something. We went to some head shop sort of place, just looking around. On the way out some cops saw us and followed us on foot a few blocks. I got spooked and ducked around a corner, hid behind a dumpster while Alexandra led them away. That was a few hours ago now."

"Shit, man. Well, we're bound to catch up with them all soon."

"Yeah, I know," he responded gloomily. "I don't know how much more of this I can take, man. This shit's got me all wound up. I got half a mind to just turn myself in and be done with it. I'm not cut out for a life on the run."

I didn't know what to say. He had gotten himself into a serious mess, being AWOL and all. But what did I know about any of that? I was a homeless, jobless road kid far from where I started, but I could always go back. My mother made sure I knew that. But there was no real going home for him. We sat together in silence as the sun sank below the horizon with a tiny flash of green.

The two of us met up with the rest of the crew back at the car just as the streetlights were firing up. They were relieved to see us. Alexandra had not been able to find Charles after she had led the cops away and was terribly worried he had been caught. She gave him a big hug and a long kiss while we all stood awkwardly by.

"Come on, lovers," Pete finally interjected. "Let's go find that drum circle Egg was talking about."

We had a general idea of where it was supposed to be happening, back in a cul-de-sac of some large parking lot complex near the canal. We followed the directions as remembered and wound our way into what appeared to be the property of the oceanic-themed amusement park described to us earlier. Pete motored the car around a series of vast empty lots, looking for any sign of a gathering of drum beating kids among the tall palm trees and radiant municipal lights.

"Stop the car!" Charles blurted out suddenly. "Turn down the music. I think I hear them." We sat there for a moment, holding our breath. We could hear them too. Pete poked his head out the window to get a clear position on the low rumbling beats.

"That way!" he announced as he slid back into the car. We looped around an artificially forested divider island onto a little lane. Rows of parked cars, some with hippie-type stickers plastered all over their back sides, came into the view of our headlights. Then we saw some appropriately dressed kids stepping out from behind a van in a cloud of smoke. "Here we go," he muttered under his breath. "Hi guys!" he greeted to the kids as he rolled up beside them. "Where's the party at?"

"Hey, dude, bro," one replied. His eyes drooped into slits. "The party is everywhere, man."

Pete snagged a decent parking spot close to the end of the cul-de-sac and we all piled out, proceeding directly to a blazing pile of shipping pallets like moths to a light. A good dozen or more drums were in play off to the side of the bonfire, operated by an assortment of drummers, old and young alike, while around the ring of fire a group of kids, mostly hippie-looking girls, danced and swayed in their flowing skirts and beads. Not knowing exactly how I was supposed to engage with this vibrant scene in the sober state I was in, I chose to stand off to the side and watch. Alexandra joined in with the dancers right away, while Charles and Pete made their way over to the drums to get closer to the thunderous sound they were producing. Jen stood with me, and together we swayed to the beat.

"Hey, guys," a voice spoke from behind, almost drowned out by the drumming. "I see you found your way." We both turned simultaneously. It was Egg, grinning ear to ear. "Smoke a bowl?" he asked. As if we would ever turn that offer down.

"Man, there's a lot of kids at this thing," I said, pointing out the obvious. "How are they able to pull this thing off without the cops shutting it all down?"

"Somebody knows the right people," Egg replied flatly. "Most everyone here is a local; homeowners, business owners, the gainfully employed. They pay taxes, they steer the local government to some degree. They have been doing this down here for years. As long as the drumming stops by midnight and no one gets stupid, the cops leave us alone."

"And they do this every week?" Jen asked.

"Yup. Usually, it's on Saturday night. Unless it rains," he explained.

Charles had made his way onto a drum somehow and was pounding away with the group. I watched him as he played, his eyes closed, his body fluidly moving with the beat. He was good on that drum, better than some of the kids he was playing with. I was feeling the high of Egg's powerful bud strongly, perhaps intensified by the energy around me, so I had a seat right below where I had been standing and closed my eyes as well. The rumbling rhythm pulsed through my body, prompting me to sway with the motions of the sound involuntarily. I must have slipped into a sort of trance, for time sped rapidly by. Before I knew it, the drums had stopped. It was midnight, and the crowd was dispersing, heading home. Soon only the road kids and a few locals remained around the glowing embers of the fading fire. Charles and Alexandra had already wrapped themselves up in blankets just out of firelight, while Pete chatted with Egg and some locals.

"You and Pete wanna get the car tonight?" I asked Jen, leaning over to her. "I don't know if pitching a tent is cool here."

"Where will you stay?"

"I'll sleep out under the stars," I replied. "The weather is fine."

"But there are no stars here," she pointed out with a smirk.

I looked to the sky. I could just make out a few of the brighter points of light poking through the hazy orange glow of the canopy, polluted as it was by the omnipresent lights of the city. "Ha, yeah. Well, under the light pollution then."

It was quiet out there in the open and I slept well. The only real noise were those ubiquitous passenger jets flying low over the city on their approach to, or departure from, the municipal airport not far away. Those frequent flyovers were so constant they were beginning to pass unnoticed as part of the ever-present background noise of the city, but out where we were was far enough away from their standard flight path that the huge machines were not passing directly overhead like they did on the beach. Still, the dull roar of the jet engines colored my dreams and mingled with the echoes of the drumming still lingering in my mind.

Giant planes, impossibly large, flew together in great flocks across a sunless sky colored a soupy yellowish hue and roared together in thunderous harmony. I lay on a beach watching them pass over me. I was not alone. Someone else lay beside me, a girl.

She rolled over and whispered something in my ear. I couldn't hear it over the roar of the engines, though I could smell the sweet breath that carried her indiscernible words. I turned to look her in the face. She was radiant, glowing even. Like no girl I had ever seen. Her features were a composite of a multitude of pretty girls I had witnessed, but all the same, unlike any other.

She smiled and spoke again in a voice as angelic as it was foreign. I still could not understand what she was saying to me. She swung her leg over my torso, straddling me, her long curly hair spilling away from her round face. Was she blond? Brunette? Somehow her hair was every color and no color at once. She wore a robe of some sort, also of this same indescribable color. A low-cut robe that hung loose around her breasts. She laughed as she sat there upon me, the giant bird-like planes hovering around her head like a roaring metallic halo.

Then I felt her heat, a heat radiating into me from her crotch, warm and perfect. She spoke again, and again I understood nothing. She seemed to understand the futility of these attempts at communication, for she smiled again and leaned in for a kiss. Her mouth was warm and sweet and all encompassing. I lay there in ecstasy as her warmth washed over me in increasingly intense waves. Waves that matched the increasing intensity of the rumbling roar of the giant planes over us, now so low as to completely blot out the unnaturally colored sky. Suddenly she pulled back from me, straightening herself out. Now she was a giant, and the planes around her head were like a cloud of loud, dull-colored hummingbirds. She pulled her robes open wide before me, revealing her perfect womanhood in blinding light, and cried a single word, echoed by the cloud of loudly humming planes around her.

"Walk!"

The roar of a particularly low-flying jet broke the spell, and I opened my eyes to the murky gloom of dawn. I lay there in a sort of shock, the sensual energy of the dream slowly fading like the receding hum of the jet that awoke me. I could still taste the girl on my lips, could still feel her warmth on my torso. My God, she was beautiful! I closed my eyes again, trying to summon a vision of her form, but the memory was blurring already.

What did she mean by "walk"? I wondered. Of all the words she muttered, in all the strange indecipherable tongues she spoke, that was the only one I could understand. And her warmth, given to me so freely. Her glorious smile spent on me alone! Jesus Christ, I wanted her to be real! To be there beside me, sharing my sleeping bag, sharing my life. I felt so incredibly alone in that moment, lying on the bare dirt, my bedding covered in slimy beach city dew. More alone than I had ever felt before, due in part to the loss of something I had never even had and a fear that the only girls I might ever get to be with intimately were alive only in my dreams. No, there was a girl for me somewhere,

I just knew it. There had to be. Perhaps that's what the dream girl was telling me, I thought; to walk on, to keep searching.

I summoned again the fading image of her throwing open her robes, of her milk-white breasts, of her perfect soft belly, and reached down to touch myself, only to find I had already cum in my sleep.

CHAPTER 33

I spent the next few days idly kicking it on the beach for the most part. Jen was keen on making a go of it in this city, whether or not Zed and his crew ever showed up, and spent most of her days out applying for jobs and looking at apartments, with Pete reluctantly joining her. She had me half into the idea of it as well for a minute, and I filled out a few applications too; one down at the supermarket, one at a convenience store. I even inquired into a few restaurants about any openings washing dishes. But I ran into dead ends at every one. No one was interested in hiring a dirty road kid with no address to call home.

Apparently, my companions were running up against the same conundrum. No one would rent them an apartment without proof of a job, and no one would hire them without the permanent address of an apartment. I gave up after a few days and settled into a life of total sun-soaked slack, to the frustration of Jen. Pete noticed my lack of interest in what mainstream society was offering and was inspired to follow my lead. Though I'm sure he didn't need much prompting. This led to a few heated arguments between them, and since we were no longer cooped up in the car all the time, I often chose to leave the area whenever they got into it.

Charles and Alexandra did their own thing, and I didn't see them much those first few days. But I ran into the Egg Man every day down on dog beach. He would stroll down the raised walkway about mid to late morning with his dogs and his wide grin and meet me at the end of the rock jetty to smoke a few bowls. Sometimes he would bring a friend or two, sometimes we would meet random folk on the beach, and he would smoke them up. He also turned us on to several good places to overnight park around the area, so we wouldn't need to rely on fester island all the time. Pete and Jen had the car every night now since they couldn't pitch the tent out in the open. So I slept outside. Sometimes in the dunes of fester island, sometimes in the low bushes near these safe parking spots, and sometimes right on the sand of the beach, if the weather wasn't too misty.

After about a week of living like this, we all chipped in on a hotel room just off the freeway. It was another hook-up Egg turned us on to, and he in fact joined us there for the evening. He called the place "The Sleazy Eight" as a pun on its real name. It was a crusty old retro-looking, two-story motel built decades before and had never been updated. The manager knew damn well we were a group of homeless kids, but we had cash money which was all that mattered. He gave us a room apparently set aside for the likes of folks like us, all the way at the end of the complex on the bottom floor.

The room was beat to shit, its pastel colored walls smudged and colored with tobacco smoke, its dull orange carpet stained and matted, its twin beds drooping from the weight of ten thousand one-night stands and made up with blankets shot through with dozens of cigarette burn holes. One of the more striking features of the room was the large colorful sunset mural painted on the wall behind the headboards of the two beds. It was poorly done, apparently by someone not well versed in the art of painting, but had been marred all the more by roughly applied patches of spackle used to fill in what looked like fist-sized holes. And upon closer inspection, you could see that someone had drawn in a stick-figure couple doggy-style fucking in the palm trees with a black magic marker. It was a real classy joint, but it had a shower with hot water.

We got a bunch of beers and stayed up late knocking them back, watching shitty local television and taking turns at the shower. The couples got the two beds, and Egg slept in his van just outside the door. That left the dirty carpeted floor for me and my sleeping bag alone. Even Dylan got to sleep on a bed, but I didn't mind.

We all went our separate ways for the day again, after we were chased out by the cleaning guy. I had a pretty crusty hangover, enhanced significantly by a full body stiffness acquired from sleeping on the hard floor, so all I really wanted to do was to find a big bush over a sandy spot where I could sleep off the headache. I got a ride down to the beach with Egg, and he smoked me up right. We got to talking about where we came from originally and what our old friends would think of us if they could see us now.

"I don't think any of them would recognize me now," he stated. "Though I guess I don't look as wild as I did a few months ago," he added, rubbing his stubbly chin.

"I miss my friends back home, honestly," I admitted. "I wish they were here on the beach with us."

"Why don't you invite them?"

"Ha, I don't know. It'd take them weeks to get here, if they would even get up the courage to make the trip." I tried to picture my metal-head friends back home, dressed in black and boots on the sunny beach, hanging out with dirty hippies. "Yeah, I don't know," I laughed.

"Give 'em a call, see where they are at. You might be surprised."

"With what money, man?" I laughed. "I'm not made of quarters."

Egg chuckled to himself and pulled his bus over to the curb. He popped open the glove box and fished out a small black box about the size of a book of matches attached to a little chain and key ring. "Here, use this," he offered, handing the box to me. I looked the thing over. It had a little keypad like a phone. "Press this button," he said, pointing to the keypad. I did, and the device chirped a little warbling tone. "Recognize that sound? That's the sound a pay phone makes when you drop a quarter in it." A smile creeped across my face as I realized just what this thing was. "It's called a chinger," he explained. "Just dial the number you want to call, and when the robot-voiced operator asks you to deposit however much money it wants to complete the call, you hold the chinger up to the receiver and slowly add the required amount by pressing the button. The automated system the phone company uses to track how much coin is fed into the payphone can't tell the difference. You can call anywhere for free!"

"Holy shit, man! Where did you get this?"

"Never mind that. The important thing is that you don't key the thing too fast. Think how much time it would take to manually feed each coin into the machine and hit the button to match that speed. They have ways of telling if the chings come in faster then a human could physically feed in the quarters, and they'll cut off the call."

"I'm going to call everyone!" I laughed, high as fuck. "Thanks, man."

"I'll catch up with you on the beach later. Enjoy!"

I hopped out of his ride there where he had pulled over and started looking for a pay phone right away. I was excited to get the chance to talk to my friends back home, but more excited really to see how this tool worked. I spotted a standalone pay phone by a convenience store and gave it a shot. I knew the numbers of my friends' houses by heart (well, their parent's houses really since most of them were still in high school at the time) and dialed the first one without hesitation. The robot voice asked for a few dollars worth of coins, and I dutifully keyed the chinger. "Ring ring" It worked!

The first call went to an answering machine. I left a message and tried another. This time I got my friend's mom. She handed the phone off to her son who happened to be home, and we rapped for over an hour. He was completely dumbfounded by how I was able to make the long-distance call for free and was amazed by my story of life on the road and the places I'd been, the things I'd seen. We laughed together and reminisced about times past, and I tried to get him to consider hitting the road himself. But he wouldn't do it. He was well into his senior year of high school and was already looking at colleges, an activity I had recently engaged in myself but could now hardly fathom the concept of. He was in the middle of describing some raging beach party kegger he'd been to the weekend before when a man's voice broke in over him.

"Hey! I know the sound of a chinger when I hear it you little punk! You're gonna be in big trouble once the cops catch you!"

I slammed the receiver down on the cradle hook and jumped back from the phone. Shit, I thought; guess I went too fast on that last ching. I swung around and scanned the streets around the payphone, half expecting to see some cop determinedly striding up to me. But no one seemed to notice. I hoofed it away from there anyway just in case the operator had called the police. I wanted to find Egg and give him back his chinger before I had it forcibly taken from me.

I spent the rest of the day much like I had set out to do. I slacked off in the shade of a bush, scribbling in my road journal and snoozing the hours away. It was a good life at the time, and luckily I had the wherewithal to appreciate it in the moment. I knew hard times would find me eventually, so I felt justified in just kicking it as much as I damn well pleased, lying in store as much slack as I could for the coming trials, whatever they be. Fuck the future! All we have is the Now!

That night, we all reconvened at the parking lot drum circle, it being a Saturday night. The scene was much the same as before, except someone there was wealthy in shrooms and distributed them freely among everyone in attendance. I didn't get enough to trip hard, but I got a significant head change nonetheless. Again Alexandra danced and Charles drummed while I hung around with Pete and Egg on the periphery.

"Where's Jen?" I asked Pete after a time.

"Ah, she's pissed at me again," he replied, his voice muffled by the drums. "She wants me to find a job so we can get an apartment. I'm trying just like her; I'm out following leads and filling out applications and shit. Now she's all pissed because we're eating shrooms. She took Dylan to the car I guess."

"That's a bummer," Egg said.

"Fuck it, man. Fuck it," he muttered as he wandered off towards another group of people.

"Those two ain't long for each other, mark my words," Egg declared.

"I don't know," I replied. "They have been arguing off and on the whole trip."

"I'm telling you, man. They're breaking up. Sooner or later, they're breaking up."

I paused to think that possibility through, and what it would mean for me. I mean, was our road trip even a thing anymore? The feel of it had certainly changed. If they were looking to settle down here in OB then for all intents and purposes, we had arrived at our destination. But I wasn't ready to settle down. I wanted to keep traveling, I wanted to see more. Well, I thought, if the trip for them is over, that means I'm on my own.

From that night on I took to carrying my pack with me most of the time instead of leaving it in the trunk of the car. I loaded it with only the bare bones essentials. My sleeping bag, my sweatshirt, my journal, the strange book Zed had given me, the little stone figurine I swiped from the RV crew. By then the only clothes I had left I wore on my back, so my pack was light. The rest of the junk I had brought from home and had collected along the way I left in the car or dropped in a trash can.

The next morning, I found Charles and Alexandra engaged in a somber conversation when I went off towards the water's edge to have a morning piss. I couldn't hear what they were saying, but I could hear her softly crying. I hung back for a minute, wondering if I should engage with them or just leave them alone, but then he saw me and waved me over.

"Good morning, brother man," I greeted, squatting down beside them. "What's up?"

Alexandra gave a convulsive sob, and he reached over and embraced her. "I'm turning myself in," he replied. "I can't keep this up. I had a vision last night while drumming, an awful vision. I need to settle this account, or it will destroy me."

"But you're going to go to prison!" Alexandra moaned.

"It won't be that bad," he assured her. "It's not like I murdered anyone. Besides, the military courts are more lenient on AWOL soldiers who turn themselves in. Who knows, maybe they'll just slap me with a dishonorable discharge. I don't want to be in the army anymore anyway."

I knelt and put my hand on his shoulder. "You're a good guy, man. You sure you want to do this? Maybe wait till the shrooms totally wear off."

"Nah, I've made up my mind." And he stood up, his tall frame towering over our crouching forms. "Come on with me to the car. I need to offload my stuff."

Pete and Jen soon became aware of this turn of events and stood wide-eyed in shock for a moment before each attempting to change his mind. But he would have none of it. He offered his stuff to us all and picked out the most regular-looking clothes he had left from the pile. "Let's head to the beach. I need to find a cop."

We cruised back to the beach in silence, rolling into the dog beach parking lot at an idle. Far down at the other end of the lot, a police cruiser sat parked, its occupants sipping their morning coffees.

"Well, this is goodbye, my friends," he said soberly. Alexandra started sobbing again, and he gave her a big hug. "Don't cry, girl. It'll be alright."

We all gave him a hug and watched from the car as he strode off across the parking lot towards the cop's cruiser. We watched the cops exit their car, speak with him for a moment, then frisk and cuff him, before guiding him into the back seat. And then he was gone.

Alexandra was near inconsolable for a while after that and hung on Jen for support. The two of them strengthened their bond that day, and they began to spend more of their time together, while Pete began to hang with Egg and me more often.

A few days passed. There was still no sign of Zed and company, and Pete had all but given up on finding work. Jen was still at it though, assisted by Alexandra. The two of them were now hinting at going in as roommates on some place, which seemed to threaten Pete considerably. Despite Egg's assumptions, Pete was not ready to end their relationship yet.

We met other travelers on the beach during those days. Egg introduced us to an old bald guy called Thompson who lived in a little pickup-truck-nosed camper with two fat old black labs. His RV was made of fiberglass and was rounded to the extent that it looked like a bubble with a pickup truck nose coming out of it. So we called it the bubble house. Thompson was a Vietnam War vet with faded green tattoos on his forearms who had been following the Dead for decades and smoked weed like a chimney. We often found ourselves his guests in the bubble, hot boxing the shit out of his space and eating the vegetarian food he would make for us. We also met a young newlywed couple from Colorado, Don and Mary, who lived in a big red, flat-front, class A camper. They were on an open-ended honeymoon and had found their way to dog beach. They were older than most of us, late twenties I think, and often bought beers and wine for us. They also often opened their floor space for me, so I had a safe place to sleep every few nights.

One of those hazy afternoons, Pete met a couple guys, I'll call them "Dude Bros," down on the strip, who invited him and any girls he could find to a keg party at some place they were staying. From the start, the scene was off. We were the only dirty road kids there; everyone else looked like frat boy surfers and beach bunny chicks. But the beer was free, so I hit the keg hard, despite the side-eye shade I got from a number of the other dude bros in attendance. The dance music got louder as the night grew darker, and I soon found myself pretty well shitfaced. I was purposely shocking some clean, normal-looking chicks with stories of sleeping in the bushes when Jen grabbed my arm.

"You gotta help me!" she implored. "Alexandra is really fucked up; I don't think she can walk out of here on her own. I don't know where the hell Peter is. You have to help me get her out of here before one of these fucking frat boys drags her into a bedroom."

She led me over to a couch where Alexandra sat slumped over, her long curly blond locks obscuring her face. Already two dude bros lurked behind the couch like a couple of cats about to pounce on their prey. We tried to get her to snap out of her stupor, shook her by the shoulders and spoke close to her face. She was awake, sort of. She just laughed and mumbled incoherently.

"Pick her up, man!" Jen demanded. "Come on, fuck this shit, let's go!"

I summoned the power of my drunk, hoisted her up on my shoulders, and carried her towards the door. One of the dude bros who had invited Pete and by proxy the rest of us to the kegger stepped towards the door as I approached.

"Leaving so soon, man?" the guy asked me. "Maybe you should leave the girl here with us, so she can sleep it off. There's a quiet room in the back. I promise no one will disturb her."

"Hell fucking no!" Jen retorted, holding up her hand palm forward towards the guy. "She's coming with us."

I followed Jen down around the block, hauling Alexandra across my shoulders in a fireman's carry while she giggled and mumbled near my ear.

"God damn it, where is Peter!" Jen muttered more than once as we speed hiked our way the few blocks towards the shore. We made it to a grassy patch separating the streets from the beachside parking lots and stopped. "Here, put her here by these bushes, so the cops don't see us." I did as she asked, gently laying her down on the soft spongy turf. "Go back and find Peter, I'll stay with her."

I hoofed it back towards the party and ran into him on the lawn outside, chatting it up with a couple beach bunny chicks. He was pretty lit up too and laughed aloud when I filled him in on the latest happenings. "She'll be fine," he dismissed. "Come on in and have another beer with me."

"Nah, man. Come on," I pleaded. "Jen's like wicked pissed already. And Alexandra's gonna choke on her own vomit or something. We gotta take care of this."

We got back to the bushes to find Alexandra on her side, convulsing and puking unconsciously into the grass, with Jen attempting to keep her mop of hair out of the vomit. "Where the fuck were you, Peter?" she hissed at him in the dark as we approached. "Someone slipped some shit in her drink or something! This is not a beer drunk she's on!" He mumbled something about being outside, smoking a blunt. "Whatever!" she shot back. "Go to the car and get some blankets. We're staying here tonight."

I went with him to find the car, some number of blocks away in the other direction. "Jesus, what a fucking buzz kill!" he stated as we walked. "How'd she get so fucking hammered?"

"Maybe she did get roofied; those dudes were mad sketchy in there," I offered. "At least we got her out of there before some shit went down." Police sirens were now wailing away not far from us, over in the direction of the kegger. "Shit, hear that man? I think the cops are at that place now!" We got to the car, and Pete climbed into the driver's seat. "We're driving back? You ok to drive?" I asked.

"Of course I'm not ok to drive," he laughed as he started the engine. "I'm fucking hammered. Come on, get in. Let's go."

He piloted the Olds effortlessly back towards the little park and parallel parked a dozen or so yards away from where the girls were huddled. "Damn, dude," I chuckled. "You drive even better when you're drunk." He replied to my compliment with a crooked smile.

Alexandra was much better by then, sitting up and speaking somewhat coherently. Jen wrapped her up in a blanket right away, and she sat there shivering in her dirty cocoon. "His name was Anthony," She muttered after a time. "He's the one, I know it."

"He's the what?" Jen asked, her brow furrowed.

"He was coming on to me hard right from the start. He brought me my second beer."

"You only had two beers?" I asked. She shook her head yes.

"Fucking assholes!" Jen growled. "This is your fault, Peter!"

"How the fuck is it my fault?" he protested. "I didn't fucking roofie her!"

"Bah!" she responded dismissively. "I'm fucking done with this shit. Get some blankets for the rest of us."

We spent the rest of those early morning hours holed up around the bushes, wrapped in blankets and sleeping bags. Alexandra passed out quickly, as did Pete. I could tell he was out by his grumbling snore. But I didn't get much sleep. I kept hearing Jen lighting a cigarette seemingly every half hour, followed by the smell of it carried on the briny breeze. It was a shitty night under those bushes; the atmosphere cool and damp, the gentle sound of the surf frequently punctuated by the roar of a passing passenger jet overhead, or the wail of an ambulance somewhere nearby.

I found Jen sitting upright when dawn awoke me from my fitful sleep, looking out towards the ocean absently, an unlit cigarette dangling from her lips.

"You sleep at all?" I asked her. She shook her head no. It was quiet there in the early morning light, the sound of the pounding surf somehow muffled by the damp foggy air.

"What the hell are we doing out here?" she finally asked after those few minutes of silence, directing the question out towards the western horizon.

I didn't have an answer.

CHAPTER 34

The days passed easily there on the beach, and I often found myself wondering what Dustin might be doing. I'd be puffing a bowl with good folk, or some fun or funny thing would arise and I'd be suddenly taken with a strong desire to share it with him. I hoped he was doing ok, wherever he was. As for my companions, I only saw them once or twice around the beach. Jen had them hitting the pavement hard in search of work despite the bleak prospects of finding anything beyond collecting cans, which was an angle the local home bums had on lockdown.

I spent the days on my own, much as I had been doing, or hanging with Egg Man, helping him run his errands and smoke his pot. He had some frequent business with a gaunt, wiry-haired guy at a local flea market; a total spazz. The guy bought and sold electronics of all sorts and repaired them too. Each time we went to see the guy, Egg had random stereo components or some other electronic devices to sell, from who knows where. I would help him carry the stuff to the guy's storage unit/workshop or to his booth at the flea market. The two of them would then haggle back and forth over the selling price in cash or drugs of various sorts before invariably coming to a smiling arrangement.

One of these occasions, a deal was struck over a small guitar amp, a bag of weed, and two tickets to see the band Rush at the local arena that night. Egg was super stoked over this deal, as this band was one of his absolute favorite groups. He invited me to join him on the second ticket.

The show was in a large stadium not far from the beach, and our seats were up in the nosebleeds towards the back. But that worked out well for us, since the high perch gave us something of a bird's eye view of the show. I was not too familiar with the band at the time beyond the radio hits you couldn't help but frequently hear, since they came up on every classic rock station regularly. But the performance was great. Especially because of the shrooms we both ate on the way in. Between the group's wild laser light show timed to accompany the flow of their music and the hallucinatory effect of the fungus, the experience was enhanced considerably.

It was a great time, and I was grateful to have been included. Egg was becoming a good friend to me, someone I could look up to as a guide, someone I felt I could rely on to have my back, and someone who was generous in his road-kid wealth, always hooking me up in one way or another. I crashed in his van that night down by the interstate. It felt good to be included, to be accepted. But knew I was not really his equal, not his peer. He was a decade older than me, after all. No, I was just a wayward road kid with nothing tangible to offer, taking the days as they came and greedily snatching any hook up or handout that came my way.

Perhaps he saw some of himself in me, remembering how he started out on the road. Or perhaps not. Maybe he just saw me for what I was, inexperienced, gullible, and ripe for ripping off, and felt like I was worth a little worldly instruction. Or perhaps it was something more nefarious. Perhaps he was keeping me around because I was inexperienced and gullible, figuring he might one day have a use for me in the furthering of his aims and angles. Whatever it was, I was glad to have met him and glad he offered his van to me that night because for the first time since we had landed on that beach, it rained all night like a son of a bitch.

I bumped into Pete the next afternoon down on dog beach. He was alone with Dylan.

"Hey, man. Where you been these past few days? You get caught out in that rain last night?"

"Nah, crashed in Egg's bus," I replied, followed up by a brief recounting of the show I'd been to and what I'd been doing, including the deals with the wiry electronics guy at the flea market.

"No shit, eh?" he replied, stroking his chin. "Think he'd wanna buy that CB radio we got a while back? We could use the money." I couldn't see why not. "We're having no luck finding work at all. I've about given up."

"What're the girl's doin?" I asked, their absence uneasily significant.

"Oh, I don't know, out looking for work, I guess," he replied, averting my gaze. "Oh, look. Here comes Egg now."

We all shot the shit down at the end of the jetty over a few bowls, burning down the afternoon to cinders. Pete asked Egg about the prospect of his guy being interested in purchasing or trading for the CB.

"Yeah, I imagine he would," Egg assured him. "Gonna go see him again in a couple days. Come along with your radio, and we'll see what he says."

A few more days passed, and the slack life continued uninterrupted. I took a few meals with old Thompson in his bubble; I crashed a few nights on the floor of Don and Mary's mobile honeymoon suite, all the while continuing to whittle away the traveler's checks I still had left on malt liquor and rolled tacos. The weather was growing cooler now and damper too. I already felt like I was somehow cheating at this road kid life thing since I still had money to spend, and that I could still sleep outside in relative comfort so late in the year just added to that feeling. I knew it was well below freezing by now back home, or pretty much anywhere else in the country. But here I was, sleeping under bushes in the relative warmth of a Southern California winter, unsure of what day of the week it even was. I chuckled uneasily to myself, remembering how much weight I had up until recently put in the Lord's Day, in Sunday.

I hadn't performed the communion ritual in over a month now, nor hardly even prayed, but I still carried in my pack the little plastic bag of stale matzo crackers, a couple little cans of grape juice, and my beat-up little bible held together with duct tape. The ritual felt more pointless the more I thought of it. The whole of faith itself felt pointless now, really. Maybe that's why I couldn't let them go. To toss them in my wake would be to admit I had spent so much mental anguish racking myself in a sort of perpetual state of anxiety over nothing but fiction, beating myself up over Bronze Age-era platitudes no more fit to guide me in my daily walkings then any other ancient story from a dusty old book.

Saturday suddenly showed up completely unannounced and dragged the passage of time back into focus. The drum circle was again the place to go, for lack of anything else to do. It was a little brisk that evening down by the bay, and those who were not drumming or dancing were positioned a little closer to the fire then in times past. Egg was not around this time, only the four of us. Jen had made a few acquaintances with some of the locals there and was working a few angles towards getting a job, while Alexandra danced to the rolling beats of the drums. That left Pete and me to ourselves, so we kicked it by the fire, hoping to get caught up in the rotation of the next doobie, blunt or bowl.

Later, as midnight and the required ending of the drumming approached, Alexandra pulled me aside and asked for my advice.

"I met these guys. They invited me to a rave downtown after the drumming stops."

"What guys?" I asked.

"Those kids over there," she pointed. "Those raver kids." A few yards away a couple of clean and colorfully dressed guys in huge-legged jeans and hoodies danced and swayed to the drumming. "They said they have ecstasy and will share it with me." My eyes lit up. "But I don't want to go alone, not after what happened last time. Will you come with me?" Frankly, she had me at "ecstasy" and I readily agreed. "Ok, I'll see what they say."

Minutes later, she gave me thumbs up from across the fire, so I went to grab my pack from the Olds and tell Pete we were out. "Bring some back for me," he asked with a grin.

Before long, Alexandra and I were tucked into the back of the raver boy's open-top jeep, speeding along the freeway towards the twinkling lights of the downtown area. The roar of the freeway around us, and the uncompromising hardcore techno the kids had blasting from speakers on either side of our seats, made it impossible to communicate verbally, but I could tell by her wide smile and dilated pupils that she had already gotten her promised dose. I was looking forward to mine.

The highway let us off somewhere in the Gaslight Quarter down near the water. The whole area was a ghost town, all locked up for the night. Apart from a few random cars and a police cruiser or two, we were the only vehicle on the streets. The kid in the passenger seat cut the music down to background noise and turned as if to speak to us, but then just smiled a wide grin, and turned back forward as the driver scanned the street ahead intently. We came up on a tall, nondescript office building, and the driver steered the jeep down a ramp into the empty underground parking lot below the building.

"We're here," he said as he cut the engine. The silence of the garage was deafening after all that roaring noise it took to get us there. It was so quiet down in that subterranean space I could hear the overhead lights hum, punctuated by the snapping noise the Jeep's hot exhaust made as it cooled. "Follow us, the party is upstairs." I tried to picture what the rave would be like; flashing lights in the darkness, thundering techno beats, and anonymous drug-induced dancing with a crowd of like-minded kids till daylight. I was ready for anything.

The two kids shuffled forward towards a wide freight elevator, their huge pant legs dragging across the pale concrete floor. The "ding" noise of the landing lift echoed out across the vast empty parking lot behind us, and we followed them into the elevator. The silence continued as we ascended, with the two facing us, their faces split in wide smiles, their pupils as wide as saucers. An uneasy feeling began creeping up behind me. Perhaps Alexandra felt it too, for she grasped my hand and gripped it tight as the elevator came to a lurching stop. "Ding!" The wide doors slid open into gloomy darkness.

"Uhh… What's this?" I muttered quietly.

"Oh, shit," one of them responded. "Looks like a dud night."

"Sorry, guys," the other offered. "Come on, let's see who's home." And the two walked off towards the only faint light in the place.

I went to follow them, and Alexandra attempted to pull me back. "Come on, girl," I assured her. "I'm with you. I won't let anything happen to you. I wanna see if I can get some of that X you're rolling on."

The dim light was coming from a couple computer monitors hooked up to a bank of partially disassembled desktop computers tethered to a number of thick cables descending from the blackness above, a thin pasty fellow at the keyboard intently typing away, the rapid clapping of the keys chopping up the shadowy gloom. Around him several blown out old couches and overstuffed chairs positioned on a spacious oriental rug supplied accommodations to a few other reclining forms, their eyes glistening in the computer screen's greenish glow. Apart from this lone carpeted island of population, the entire floor, windows to windows, was empty. Even the ceiling tiles were missing, making the space feel as tall as it was wide.

The two raver boys strode up to the guy at the computer array and conversed quietly with him as the other folk watched us from their places of repose. "Please take your shoes off," a voice asked from one of the dimly lit recliners. We did as we were asked.

I couldn't help feeling totally bummed. I was really stoked at the prospect of getting into a rave, something I had wanted to do since my high school acid hook-up told me tales of the epic parties she was going to. But whatever this scene was, it certainly was not a rave. Alexandra still clutched my hand tightly. I could feel her energy, her anxiety radiating into me. I locked eyes with her and smiled. She smiled back and relaxed a bit. "Let's go look out the window," I said softly. She shook her head yes.

The view from those wide windows was striking. We were many stories up, higher than many of the other buildings around us, and those structures below twinkled and shone like diamond studded obelisks. "We can't stay here," she spoke softly. I knew she was right. I didn't know what the intention of those raver boys was, whether benign or villainous, but whatever it was would be mad sketchy. We walked back over to the electronically lit oasis. The pale guy at the computer briefly looked up from his screen at us with mild disgust in his sunken eyes. He cleared his throat and resumed his work on the keyboard.

"So…" I said aloud, the sound of my voice consumed by the vast darkness around us. "What's up?"

"You guys can crash here if you want, but there's no party tonight." One of the raver boys replied.

"Obviously," someone said from one of the darkened couches, followed by a strange high-pitched giggle from another.

"Can you give us a ride back to the beach?" Alexandra asked.

"No," the driver of the jeep abruptly replied,

"Are there any cabs running?" I asked, even though I knew we probably didn't have enough money to pay for one anyway.

"Not likely," the driver of the Jeep replied flatly, followed again by the high-pitched giggle from the dark. She grabbed my hand again.

"Then I guess we're walking," I said.

"Then there's the door," the pale guy at the computer replied without looking up.

Alexandra threw her arms around me once the elevator doors closed. "Oh my God, thank you for coming with me. Those people were monsters!"

"I don't know if they were monsters," I replied, lifting one eyebrow. "Assholes maybe." She laughed ecstatically and squeezed me hard. "I just wish I had gotten some of what you got." She pulled back from me, her smile as wide as ever.

"Here," she said, dipping her fingers into the front chest pocket of her corduroy overalls. "They gave me two. I only ate one."

She handed the little pill to me. Then I noticed that her feet were only in rainbow-colored socks. "Oh, shit! Where are your shoes?"

"I forgot them," she said coyly.

"We have to go back and get them," I decided, reaching for the stop button on the descending elevator.

"No!" she cried. "We're not going back in there. I don't care. Fuck my shoes, I'll find new ones."

Then we were back out on the empty streets below. Neither of us had a watch, but it had to be well past one in the morning by that point. It had taken at least ten minutes to drive there from the beach; who knows how long it would take us to walk back. I looked down at her shoe-less feet. Fuck it, I said to myself, and popped the pill in my mouth.

"I wonder which way we should go," she said aloud.

"Where you lookin' to get to?" a hoarse voice behind us asked. We both wheeled around to find a tall, thin wraith of a man standing behind us, dressed like a faded 1980s hair-metal rocker, his long curly graying black hair topped by a black cowboy hat with a silver band, his eyes sunken and bloodshot. "You kids lost?"

"How do we get back to OB?" Alexandra blurted out.

"Straight that way," he gurgled, pointing in the direction behind us with a long thin finger decorated by a couple of chunky silver rings. "You missed the last light rail trolley some time ago. You have a long walk ahead of you." And he chuckled a crooked laugh. "What brings two little chickens like you out to this God forsaken place at this God forsaken hour? Looking to score some crank?" And he put a hand on each of our shoulders. "I can make that happen if y'all got the cash."

"Nah," I replied, involuntarily wincing at his touch. "Just looking to get back to the beach."

"Ok, then. Safe travels, kids," he said as he released us. "Keep the highway on your right and the water on your left. You'll be there by daylight." And he turned and slowly walked away, his silver chains lightly jingling and his black cowboy boots knocking on the pavement with each step.

We followed the zombie rocker's directions, keeping the interstate within earshot until we could actually see it, then keeping abreast of its passing by means of a completely deserted industrial road down near the water. Past the airport we hiked, past the sleeping commercial businesses, and past the many rental car lots full of identical late-model sedans.

I was rolling on the pill pretty good by then, but I could tell it was dirty. I had been lucky enough to score real-deal MDMA a couple times in high school along with a good deal of dirty shit, stuff cut with heroin, or coke. These were cut with coke or some speed for sure because I didn't feel like nodding off on my feet. But I could tell it was wearing off for Alexandra, having taken hers at least two hours before me. Her pace slowed, no doubt exacerbated by her lack of footwear, but she never whispered a complaint.

After what seemed like hours of walking, she finally asked to stop. "I don't think I can go much further. I'm so tired."

I looked around the area where our progress had ground to a halt. We were right up against the highway now, an on-ramp sailing over us, with a series of low warehouses and parking lots on the other side of the street. Just up the embankment of the interstate, on the other side of a low fence, I saw a very large bush. "Come on; let's go see if we can get inside of that big bush over there." She smiled again, albeit weakly, and followed me as I clambered up the low concrete wall, over the knee-high fence and up the bank.

The surface of the bush was dense, but we found a small opening towards the bottom which we could crawl into on our hands and knees. Once inside, the space opened up like a tent, with a nice bowl-like depression in the middle, the glow of the streetlights barely penetrating the thick foliage. "This is perfect," she sighed. "It's like a little fairy house in here." I peeled open my pack and pulled out my sleeping bag.

"You can have my bag tonight," I offered.

"Of course not!" she exclaimed. "I can't hog the whole thing! We can share it. We'll both fit inside." A sudden rush of drug-addled butterflies mobbed my insides. Sensing my discomfort perhaps, she added, "It's ok, I feel safe with you." And she briefly placed her hand on my leg just above the knee. Her light touch hit me so hard that my balls ached from the impact. I was exhilarated. I was terrified. Is this a test? Has the devil made a wager with God over my sexual morals? I automatically asked myself, momentarily forgetting I had more or less abandoned my faith at that point, which made the plausibility of such a scenario ridiculous. My heart thumping, I rolled out the bag between us. She unzipped the long zipper down the side and slid in, clothes and all. Half of me was relieved; she wasn't expecting us to bone. The other half was crushed; she wasn't expecting us to bone. "Climb in," she instructed, holding the flap open. I dutifully obeyed.

Once inside, there was no other option but full-body-length contact. She positioned herself behind me, spooning me and wrapping her arms around my chest. I could feel her heartbeat, I could smell her sweet odor, I could feel my cock swelling uncontrollably despite my abject terror that she might brush it with her hand and be repulsed while simultaneously yearning for her deliberate touch. Good God, man. I told myself. This is your chance, if ever there was one. Turn and kiss her! I screamed silently to myself. Maybe she wants it. Maybe she's waiting for you to make the first move! Do it! But I was frozen. Rock hard frozen in place.

"Thank you for taking care of me," she whispered softly in my ear as my mind raced in place, sending tingles cascading down my body. "Thank you for keeping me safe." Like a switch thrown, my sexual angst began to ground out, shunted away from bristling desire. I had my answer.

So we lay there together inside of our bush beside the highway, like two little children lost in the forest. It felt good to be one she could trust, that she felt she could share my sleeping bag without having to pay for it bodily. I wanted it bad no doubt, but I couldn't do her like that, it didn't feel right. It wasn't fear of divine retribution anymore that stood between me and what might have been my first time, had I the gumption to ignore the unspoken and attempt a move. No, what I feared was rejection and shame. What if she rebuked me? What if she was disgusted by my advances? What if it shattered her opinion of me as one of the "good guys?" I loathed the thought of being lumped into the meathead dude bro camp. I had her at my mercy there in the urban darkness, and I felt that most guys would have snaked their way into her overall corduroys by then. I could hear the echo of their expectations mocking my virginity. But I couldn't bear the thought of taking advantage of her, of betraying her trust in me.

Wrapped there in her embrace, with my mind and guts in a twist, I accepted the truth of the moment and breathed deep of the Now as it was. This is a peak point, I realized. I was engaged with right action. I knew then that the memory of this brief connection of trust and acceptance would stay warm in my soul till I breathed my last, and that was enough.

We lingered there under that leafy enclosure till long after daybreak. I had slept remarkable well, considering the situation. You'd think my sexual anxiety and emotional wrestling would have kept me up all night. But her warm breath on my neck had a hypnotic effect on me that overpowered my monkey mind. Coming down from a chemical high probably helped too. It felt so good to be so close to a girl, even if it was platonic, that I was loath to be the one to end the embrace. But all things must come to an end, and an over-full bladder waits for no man, or woman for that matter.

"I have to pee pee," she finally whispered as she unwrapped herself from my body. A rush of cool, outside air quickly took her place, and I sighed at the loss. "No peeking," she added as she popped a squat at the edge of the soft dirt bowl we were nestled in. I could hear her urine tinkle as it left her body from that mysterious unknown place which wielded so much power over my thoughts. I closed my eyes and sighed again.

The day was bright and sunny without a cloud in the sky, causing the pale concrete skin of this place to shine blindingly. Even the ever-present ocean haze seemed thinner than normal. We traced the service road towards the beach, slowly making our way back to the familiar. An hour or so later, I began to recognize landmarks and buildings. "I think we're getting close," I assured her. Then, as we approached the outer blocks of the neighborhood we had been treading for weeks, the Olds pulled up abruptly beside us.

"Where the hell have you guys been? We've been looking everywhere for you two!" Jen asked in a desperate high-pitched tone, her head and shoulders protruding from the passenger side window. I caught Pete's eye from the driver's seat. He gave me a raised eyebrow and a knowing smirk from behind Jen, a "what have you two been up to all night" sort of look. I just smiled and rolled my eyes. "Alex, we have an interview today, remember? This is like the last chance we got of getting a job here!"

"Oh, yeah," she muttered. "I forgot."

"Holy shit, where are your shoes?" she added, even more desperate sounding than before. "Never mind, just get in the car! We only have an hour to clean you up." And she flung the door open, hopped out, and held the seat forward so Alexandra could climb in the back. "You coming?" she asked me sharply as we stood there. I shook my head no. She climbed back in, and they sped away, the car skirting through a yellow light as it changed to red. I was alone again.

CHAPTER 35

It was getting cold and lonely on the beach. I often found myself thinking of just walking away and seeing where the road took me. But I never did. Instead, I just wiled away the days down by the shore with my hoodie up, watching the waves break and waiting for the next distraction.

That came with the sudden arrest of old Thompson. Pete, Egg and I had just a pulled mess of bong rips with the guy in his bubble RV down at the dog beach parking lot while the girls were out looking for work and were just walking off across the parking lot to give the pups a run around in the sand, when two black and white municipal cruisers pulled up lights and sirens blazing, blocking in his funny shaped RV at both ends. We watched from a distance as the four cops took the four sides of the vehicle, their hands on their still holstered guns. The cop at the door knocked hard and ordered Thompson out, calling him by a different, unfamiliar name. The old man stepped out, hands on his head. The cop frisked him, cuffed him, and had him kneeling on the pavement when Egg lost his composure, left us, and strode up towards the scene. Pete and I stood there frozen, stoned as fuck. All I could think was what if those cops had rolled up minutes earlier when we were all still inside ripping bong loads. Probably kneeling on the pavement in cuffs beside him, no doubt.

We watched as Egg spoke with two of the cops quietly. The arresting officer asked Thompson something, and the old man shook his head yes. Then Egg stepped into the bubble briefly and emerged with the old man's two fat black labs. Some more words were spoken, and Egg returned to us.

"Fucking cops!" he cursed quietly, the two goofy gray muzzled dogs wagging their tails and butts behind him.

"Holy shit! What's going on?" Pete asked.

"Active warrant, parole violations, some other shit. He's going to the lock-up for a few days. I need to get his dogs to someone who will watch them for the duration."

"What about his bubble?" I asked, as I watched the two cruisers pull out of the parking lot, leaving the guy's camper unlocked and unattended, the side door still open to the world.

"Impounded," Egg replied. "Don't touch it; you'll get in big trouble if they catch you inside. The tow truck is already on the way." Just then a police flatbed truck pulled into the far end of the parking lot. "They'll need a warrant to search it, but they'll get one. They won't find this though," he added with a grin, half pulling a fat bag of Thompson's weed out from his front pocket.

We helped him secure a temporary home for the elderly dogs with some old hippie lady Egg knew. Pete and I were not allowed inside, so we waited on the curb. Once that job was complete, Egg offered to take Pete to meet the wiry-haired electronics guy at the flea market. We went back to the Olds, cut the wires tethering the device to the underside of the dash, and climbed into Egg's bus.

We found the guy in his storage unit, prodding at the insides of some ancient tube radio with a sizzling, smoking soldering iron. He welcomed us into his world of derelict electronics, and we consecrated the meeting with a few puffs off Egg's bowl.

The guy was interested in the CB radio. Apparently it was a top-of-the-line model, albeit a few years old. He offered Pete sixty bucks for it. "Or perhaps you would be interested in these," he added, rummaging around in a big cardboard box on the floor. He pulled out a sealed display case of pills in blister packs. "Mini thins; legal speed. There's well over a hundred bucks worth of pills here." And he handed the case to Pete.

He turned the box over in his hands a few times, scrunching up his face in internal thought. "What do you think?" he asked me. I just shrugged. "How about forty bucks and half this box?" he counter offered, handing the case back to the guy.

The guy moaned like we were breaking his balls, which made Egg laugh out loud. "Ok, ok. Forty and half the box," he agreed and ripped the top off the box of pill packs to divide the contents.

We spent the night on the smelly shore of Fester Island again, Pete, me, and the girls. We had a small fire going to ward off the damp chill and a jug of wine we were passing around, but nothing to eat. Jen was glum. Despite her concerted effort every job prospect she chased down had evaporated in her grasp. And now they were down to their last bit of cash. The two of them discussed their options.

"Alexandra has a friend in Florida. She spoke with her today," Jen explained. "She said she could get us work at some high-end restaurant she works at. I think we should go."

Pete was not convinced. "Florida? That fucking redneck state?"

"What other option do we have, Peter?" she shot back. "Freeze on the beach all winter like bums?"

"We'll think of something." he assured her. "We've traveled too far to just turn back east, to just go back to waiting tables and washing dishes."

"I'm done with this shit, Peter. I'm done sleeping in the car. I want an apartment with a bathroom."

We four sat in silence for a long while, the crackling of our meager fire providing the only conversation.

"You wanna snort some mini thins?" he asked finally, pulling the blister packs out of a knapsack he had next to him. "Might make you feel better."

"Mini thins? I haven't seen those things since high school. Where the hell did you find those?" she asked suspiciously.

"Traded that CB radio for 'em today. That and forty bucks."

"What the fuck, Pete? Only forty? And kiddie coke? What the hell are we going to do with that shit?"

"We can sell 'em, make some money."

"Sell them to who? High schoolers?" she asked exasperatedly. "Oh my God, Peter! What the fuck?"

"Fucking A!" he yelled. "Get off my back, already!" She glared at him from across the fire. "How 'bout you?" he turned and asked me, holding up a blister pack. "You wanna join me?"

"Fuck it," I said and followed him to the car.

I sat beside him on the front seat while he crushed a few pills into powder on a tape cassette case, cracking the plastic in the process.

"God damn it!" he growled. "She really knows how to push my fucking buttons." And he took a hard snort of one of the lines he'd cut with a half of a soda straw picked off the floor. "Here," he said, passing the case to me. I took the other line. "I don't know how much more I can take of this; she's driving me fucking crazy. Get a job, get a job, get an apartment. There are no fucking jobs in this town!" he yelled, and he punched the ceiling of the car. I looked out at the girls by the fire. I could see Jen in animated discourse with Alexandra, probably venting a similar frustration, but about Pete.

"What are you going to do?" I asked, snorting back a big chunky drip at the back of my throat.

"Like I said, I'll figure something out."

We spent the next hour in the car, crushing a few more pills, while he vented and moaned some more. I basically just listened. I didn't have any answers for him. Plus, I was so geeked my jaw was clamped shut anyway. Jen pulled the door open eventually in the middle of his latest tirade, stopping him mid-sentence.

"Get out of the car, Peter." she demanded through clenched teeth. He didn't move. "Get out of the God Damned car!" she yelled. Then he acquiesced. "You're sleeping in the dunes tonight."

"Fine!" he stormed, and he went around to the trunk, pulled out the tent, and slammed the lid.

"You too." she told me quietly. "Out of the car." I obeyed.

I helped him set up the tent in the dark as he grumbled and cursed. Egg's prophetic words rang in my ears. These two really aren't long for each other, I thought.

"You coming in?" he asked me once the tent was set up. I was so fucking spun sleep was a hundred miles from wherever the hell I was. I told him as such and stumbled off towards the shadowy interior of the island.

I stayed up most of the night, I think, but eventually nodded off on the sand. All I had was my hoodie; I had left my pack and sleeping bag in the car, so I didn't sleep long, if you could even call it sleep. By dawn I was shivering and strung out. I made my way back to the car and knocked on the window. "Can I come in for a while?" I asked. "I'm freezing." They let me in.

Jen then confided in me their plans. She was going with Alexandra to Florida, with or without Pete. And after last night, she was of the mind to go without him. She did not extend the offer to me. "Once Pete gets his ass up, he's driving us to the bus station." she declared. "We're leaving today."

It took a while before he emerged from the dunes, his eyes puffy and bloodshot. She hit him with the news right away, as soon as he was within earshot, and he took it without a word. She had packed up what she wanted while we had waited for him to wake up, so she was ready to go. Now.

I had them drop me off at the beach first, and we had our goodbyes. Jen gave me a hug but was a bit cold and distant. "Take care of yourself," she told me. "And don't be stupid."

Next Alexandra gave me a hug, a much warmer hug, as it were. "Come see us in Florida," She suggested, "I can get you a job washing dishes or something."

And then they were gone. I felt so incredibly empty, standing there in the parking lot, a cold damp breeze running up my back. I had really grown close to both of those girls and hated to see them go, especially like this. I walked to the end of that long pier at the end of Newport Ave, thinking about it all. Remembering the times we'd shared out on the road, the sights we'd seen, the experiences, the life. What would I do now? What would Pete do now?

I ran into Egg as I trekked back to dog beach.

"Jesus, man! You look like death!" I filled him in on the news. "I told you, man," he answered. What could I say?

Pete met up with us a short while later, a brooding darkness hanging over him like a cloud. "Well…" Egg stated matter of factly as we stood in the sparsely populated, windblown parking lot. "Now we're just three homeless guys with three homeless dogs." And he put an arm around each of us. "Come on; let's get some breakfast, on me."

On the walk down towards the strip, Egg told us what he was planning to do to make some money over the next few months and invited us to join him. "Christmas trees!" he cheerily declared. "It's almost December. I've got a friend up in L.A. that sells Christmas trees this time of year. He rents a few empty lots near the better neighborhoods, buys a few truckloads of cut trees from Canada, and sells 'em for good money. But he can't do it all by himself, of course. He hires folk to run the lots, like me! I've done this two years already; you can work with me on my lot." It sounded promising. "We'll talk details over breakfast. Funny, right? A Jew selling Christmas trees?" And he let out a hearty laugh.

As we approached the end of Newport Ave where it met the beach, I spotted a familiar-looking vehicle in the hot lot, where the cops are always on point. "Holy shit," I said quietly. "Is that Zed's RV?"

We made our way towards the beat-up white and mustard yellow striped camper from behind, and instantly recognized the dead-head stickers and the California license plate with tags expired by more than a year. It was the RV, and there, his back to us, was Aiden, wearing one of my t-shirts I had given him at the Quartzsite camp.

"Brother man!" I cried out. "You made it!" He turned and grinned from ear to ear when he recognized us.

"Oh my God, you don't know the half of it," he laughed as he embraced me. Tick poked his pock marked face out a side window, his teeth bared in a grin of sincerity with Barb peeking over his shoulder. We had a round of hugs with Aiden, as the others looked on from the window.

"Where's Zed?" Egg asked. Aiden just shook his head no, a frown stomping out his smile. "Ok, well we got to get you out of this parking lot with those expired tags. This is the hottest lot in all of OB. Six up is gonna ruin your day if they roll in here and spot those plates."

We all climbed in, and Tick took the wheel. Egg dropped into the passenger seat and started directing him towards a parking lot not far away, where there was less of a chance of running into the cops. They were rolling light, no riders. Just the three of them, with Zed noticeably absent. They explained as we drove.

After Quartzsite, they headed to Yuma for some deal Zed had to wrap up. It was only supposed to be an overnight thing, but the transmission quit just outside of the city. It took every penny they could scrounge to cover the tow and repair the RV.

While they were stranded in Yuma, they practiced their usual hustle; shoplifting, reselling to pawn shops and to other nefarious characters, and getting shitfaced on booze whenever they could get their hands on some. On one of their shop lifting excursions, Tick, Barb and Zed all finally got caught in the act and were thrown in jail. When they ran their fingerprints, Zed's came up bad, really bad. In fact, his name wasn't even really Zed, although we all kind of figured that. He was wanted on a murder charge from over a decade before. Apparently, he had run down his friend with his van during the throes of some drug induced mania, mutilating the guy's corpse in the process, and had been on the run ever since. Supposedly his case was even featured on one of those "most wanted" TV shows once. So he was pulled from the city lock-up they were in and taken to some federal prison. They didn't even get to say goodbye.

"At least now he'll get the medical care he needs for the lung cancer," Barb added halfheartedly.

Tick and Barb were released on their own recognizance after about forty-eight hours in the lock up, with a court date in Yuma a couple months later. They caught up with Aiden, who had hustled the RV from the repair shop with cash and trades from their stock of hot merchandise, but their riders had all split by then, finding their own way to wherever they were going. I asked what had happened to Dustin, if they knew where he was headed.

"No idea, bro." Aiden replied. "He split as soon we all found out Zed and them had got snagged by the cops, didn't say where he was going."

The three of them then trekked to OB and had only just rolled up when we found them.

Next it was our turn to fill them in on what had happened to our crew since we had last met, what we had been up to on the beach over the past month, and that we were now looking to move on to the next thing.

"So, what are you all going to do now?" Barb asked us. Egg explained his Christmas tree angle. "Yeah, we did that one year too. Decent cash. We're gonna have to settle down for a while too I guess, got to go back to Yuma next month, to court. We're gonna need cash for that."

"Curb painting," Tick chimed in. "Stupid easy money in that." We asked him to elaborate. "You go into these endless strip mall neighborhoods around L.A. and start knocking on doors, offering to paint their house number with stencils on the curb out front of their house. You can get like twenty bucks a pop in some hoods. That shit adds up fast."

"But first, we need to offload all this shit in here," Aiden added, gesticulating to the boxes and bags of stolen merchandise that cluttered the interior space of the camper. "You all got any connections for selling this shit?"

"Yeah, I think we can make something happen," Egg said. "Thanksgiving is in a couple days. I'm headed out to Escondido to feast fat with some friends of mine tomorrow night. We'll all go; they will probably pick up some of this stuff for their business."

And so a plan was made. We spent that night on Fester again, fueled by a few gallons of cheap wine, some snacks they lifted from the supermarket on the beach, and more of those speed pills crushed up into powdered lines. It was the perfect distraction for Pete and me, still reeling from the abrupt exit of the girls. Pete especially was hit hard by it, not surprisingly. He and Jen had been together for a few years, since college, and had been through a lot as a couple even before we all set off on this road trip. Now that she was gone, I could tell he was pretty fucked up by it. But that night we had enough intoxicating substances available that the reality of his situation was sufficiently distorted to keep him from descending into the black depression awaiting him.

There was also a group of four Swedish kids here on student visas camping in their rental car very close to us, and after we pulled them into our drunken circle, the distractions of communicating with them became even more encompassing. They had never met anyone like us in America, so in response we really cranked up the show. We taught them some American slang and swear phrases like "punk bitch" and "dip shit" and roared with laughter at their confusion. The Swedes were also very excited about our crushed up ephedrine pills, thinking it was real cocaine. Pete made some decent money off them that night.

The next day, Egg brought Tick and Aiden over to the electronics guy, and they offloaded every piece of electrical equipment they had in the camper; Walkman radios, speakers, car stereos, cameras, and who knows what else. That afternoon we all piled into the RV and shot out to Escondido.

Egg's buddies went by nicknames, Twig and Knot, and were about the same age as him. They had a nice clean house out in the suburbs with a couple citrus trees in the yard. The place looked good from the outside. Inside was another story. Black light posters, flags, and tie-dye tapestries over the windows, a cluttered low coffee table crowned with a big elaborate glass bong. It looked reminiscent of a college dorm room, but the place was clean.

The two welcomed us heartily, and we got to know each other around that big bong for a while. Twig, Knot and Egg had met on Dead tour almost a decade earlier, when they were all freshmen in college. They had traveled all around the country together, getting into and out of all sorts of trouble along the way. None of them were from Southern California originally, but out of all the places they had been they found that San Diego suited their needs best. They had girlfriends too, who were busy making the Thanksgiving feast in the kitchen, a point Tick did not miss.

"Keepin' 'em barefoot in the kitchen, eh?" he sneered.

The RV kids managed to sell a good portion of their more hippie themed stuff to these cats while we were there, and apparently at a good price because everyone seemed very pleased with the deals, whatever they were. Once the business was completed, it was time to eat.

The food was amazing. And there was so much of it. I hadn't been eating much since we got to OB and had lost a considerable amount of weight. But I think I gained it all back that night. We ate like kings and drank like them too. Only the best beers were available; dank British beers in tall, strangely shaped bottles that I had never even heard of before. And the weed! Jesus H Christ, by the time I passed out on the carpet I was so full, drunk and high I didn't know what to do.

Back in OB, we found Barb's grandparents had come down from L.A. with another Thanksgiving feast in the truck of their late model Cadillac. They had been waiting for us to show up on dog beach all morning apparently, so the food they brought had gone cold, but we didn't care. We gave thanks to their generosity and ate everything they had brought down to crumbs, grease, and bones. While we gorged on congealed mashed potatoes, turkey gravy and creamed string beans, they talked Barb into coming back with them and cleaning up her act ahead of her court date. We all wished her well, figuring we'd all run into each other sooner or later. I never saw her again.

Shortly after Barb left with her grandparents, as we reclined in the RV digesting and taking one-hitters, there was a knock on the door. "Hey guys!" a girl's voice sounded. "It's me, Summer. Open the door!"

She was dressed in the same beat-up, homemade hippie blouse and dress I last saw her in, months ago up in the hills above Ned. But she was much thinner now. Her cheek bones displayed prominently where once there was the softness of youth, her fair skin darkened by weeks out in the open. "Wow! I can't believe I found you guys!" she exclaimed, as she dumped her backpack down on the floor.

"Well, we're glad you're alright," Pete told her. "We ran into Sherri in Quartzsite." Summer's eyes widened. "She was with some super creepy old man."

"Fuck that son of a bitch!" she barked. "Do you know what he did to her? To me?"

"Yeah, we rescued her from the guy. She told us he threw you out on the side of the road in the middle of nowhere."

"Where is she? Is she alright?" she asked desperately.

"We lost her in Yuma," Aiden replied.

"Lost fucking everybody in Yuma," Tick added. "She went off with this other chick we picked up. What was her name?"

"Toni, I think," Aiden answered. "She was a nice chick. They were gonna head east."

"God, I was supposed to protect her," Summer moaned, plopping down on her pack. "I was supposed to keep her out of trouble, and I lost her."

"It's not your fault," I consoled. "The guy abducted you two, then forced you out of the truck." She looked up to me from her sitting position, tears welling up in her eyes. "But Pete saved her." She turned her attention then to him.

"Thank you, Pete. At least someone fucking helped her." She took a deep breath and composed herself. "You all got any water? I'm wicked thirsty." Aiden passed her a gallon jug three quarters full. "Thanks, man."

She then told us a little of the road that brought her to this parking lot on the shores of the Pacific. She had been hitching rides or just hoofing it for weeks, trying to get to OB because of what everyone had said of the place back in Ned. She figured she might find Sherri here, or some other friendly face. She had close calls with shady fuckers, and with cops, but she made it.

"And now we're a family again!" Tick declared sarcastically.

"Egg Man is in town too," I added.

"That fucking dog thief? He still have my pup?"

"He's not a pup anymore," Pete said. "He's almost as big as his other dog."

"I can't wait to give him a squeeze!" And for the first time since she stepped into the camper, she looked legitimately happy.

The next morning, I drove Pete out to the zoo. He had been in contact with his mom, and she was in L.A. on a business trip or something. She had rented a car for the day to come see her son. He wanted to be alone with her, away from all of our crusty action, so he suggested the zoo. Summer came along for the ride since she didn't get along well with Tick. "Because he's a fucking dick," she said.

On the ride back to the beach, we rapped about life on the road and how it had changed us from the kids we were when we left home. Her more so than me judging by her harrowing tales of close calls with dirty old rapists and nights spent out in the open desert as the coyote calls grew steadily closer.

There was a real freedom to living like this, but you often found yourself making compromises with your better judgment just to survive, little ones at first, just little ones. But before you knew it you catch a glimpse of yourself in a filthy restroom mirror, and you don't recognize the kid who's staring back.

When we rolled back into the parking lot of dog beach, we found Tick, Aiden and Egg Man standing in an empty parking space among a pile of duffle bags, overflowing cardboard boxes and back packs.

"They took the RV." Tick growled once we pulled up beside them.

"Who did?" I asked.

"Fucking six up! Who else?"

I remembered the expired tags. "Oh, shit." I muttered. "Can you get it back?"

"I doubt it," he replied gloomily. "It'd take a shit ton of money. Plus, we'd have to find the owner and get him to sign a bunch of papers."

"Owner?" I asked. "You mean Zed?"

"Ha! That wasn't Zed's camper. Zed was just borrowing it from some fucking creepy-ass nudist named Jimmy."

CHAPTER 36

We helped to sort and better pack the hot stock they had hastily removed from the RV before the flatbed took it away, and stuffed it all into Egg's bus. The three of them then went off to meet up with the wiry electronics guy in hopes that they could turn the loot into cash, or drugs. I chilled with Summer most of the day, walking around OB and shooting the shit about whatever while we waited for Pete's mom to drive him back to the beach.

I was really starting to dig this girl. She had a fiery pragmatism honed by her experiences on the road that I deeply admired. But in some other aspects she struck me as very cliquey, very scenester-y. I often came up against her arbitrary walls of opinions as we rapped, especially when it came to music. She held an almost religious reverence for the big name acts in the hippie jam band world and would suffer no disparaging remarks against her musical prophets. Despite my attempts to find a shared ground musically, she would give no audience to the "terrible noise" that coursed through my veins.

Though I enjoyed her company, and she seemingly enjoyed mine, I understood that I didn't fit the profile of a kid of her scene well enough for her to consider me dateable material, even though I was arguably just as filthy as her. But I didn't sweat it too much. Honestly, the only reason I was anywhere near this dead-head scene was because they were giving out the kicks for free, and I'm sure I was not the only one.

We were strolling down Newport together, despite our differences, when we ran into Judith, the rough and tumble mountain lady from the Ned camp. Except she wasn't so rough anymore. She was dressed in a long, flowing off-white linen dress cinched around her waist by a sort of belt/purse thing made of colorful woven wool and beads, her big buck knife absent. She had her long salt-and-pepper hair unbraided and spilling down her shoulders, and wore sandals instead of the chunky hiking boots I knew her in. She looked so different in fact that we both didn't recognize her at first. But she recognized us.

"Brother! Sister! It's so good to see you!" And she gave us a hug both at the same time, pulling us all together in a trio. "Are you two, like a couple now?" she asked with a wide grin.

"God, no!" Summer exclaimed as we all embraced. "Oh, sorry," she halfheartedly offered me when she realized the forcefulness of her rebuke. "You're just, like, not my type."

I just shrugged my shoulders. Girl, you're not really my type either, I thought.

Judith, aware of the awkward exchange she had inadvertently birthed, quickly moved to change the subject. "You guys on tour?" she asked. "Phish tour?" she added when she read the confusion on my face.

"Phish is coming to town?!" Summer asked excitedly.

"Yeah, they're coming here in a couple days. They're in Arizona now, I think. Gonna be a great show!"

Summer was ecstatic and seemed visibly annoyed when I didn't automatically react in the same way. It was all I could do to keep from rolling my eyes.

Over the coming days, the impending arrival of this band, and the lot kids who followed them began to dominate the atmosphere we were all in. This honestly was a welcome change from the dreary loneliness that had been creeping into our lives until then. First it was a trickle of grimy kids shuffling around Newport, but within twenty-four hours it was a deluge of ratty white-kid dreads, huge-legged corduroy pants, and crunchy smiles everywhere.

"Holy shit, look at all these fucking kids!" Tick swore as a few of us hung down by the wall. "I wish we had more of that loot from the RV. There's sure to be a hundred custys on the lot for this show. We'd be able to sell all that crap, make some dank coin."

"I know where the impound lot they took the camper to is," Egg mentioned. "It's not far. Maybe you could sneak in and grab some shit."

They all thought that was a fantastic idea, so we tucked into the Olds straight away to have a scout out mission and see what we were up against.

The place was not an official police lot, but a privately owned tow company lot with a city contract. It looked promising from the start. We walked the fence line up to the gate and ran into a driver opening up to drop a car off inside. Tick tried his luck right away without hesitation.

"Dude, you work here?" he asked the guy. He said he did. "That's our RV in there." He pointed. "We just need a couple things from inside."

"You gotta pay the fees first, bud," the guy stated blankly.

Tick looked to Aiden and smiled. "How about this. That camper is full of all sorts of merchandise, right. We don't want much, just a few of our things we couldn't get out before the tow truck took it away. Let us in, and you can loot the fuck out of that camper cuz we're never coming back for it."

The guy stood there a moment, pondering Tick's proposition. You could tell by his face he already knew damn well what was in that RV. "Hold on, lemme ask Slim." And he stepped to a little job site trailer office. A minute later, he emerged with a huge bald black guy made of solid muscle who had to duck to clear the door frame of the aluminum box of a trailer.

"So, what's your story?" the guy asked, his deep voice almost as imposing as his figure. Tick repeated his offer basically word for word. "What say I just loot that shit anyway? I know you gutter kids can't afford to bail out that camper."

"So, what if we can't?" Tick answered. "You know what's in there; we know what's in there. You can let us in, let us grab our shit, and we'll walk away. You can have the rest. Or we can get the cops involved. I recognize that fancy belt buckle over your driver's dick there. What else you two already clipped from our camper?"

The guy frowned even deeper than he already had been and shot a stabbing glance at the tow truck driver, who flinched in response as if a blow were imminent. "Ok. Deal," He growled. "But just you two." And he pointed two of his massive thick fingers at Tick and Aiden.

They set to work right away, tearing into the camper and stuffing trash bags, shopping bags, boxes, and anything else they could get their hands on and tossed them over the fence to us. The two tow lot guys joined them a minute or so later to slow them down before they emptied the whole camper out. Some words were said, and the window of opportunity was closed. Tick and Aiden joined us on the sidewalk as we loaded up the twice stolen loot into the Olds, while the lot guys surveyed their winnings inside. We were just pulling away when they stepped out of the RV, the tow truck driver now wearing Zed's black leather jacket. We waved, and they did not wave back.

That evening we met a load of kids in a dirt-smeared, red station wagon tagged with Colorado plates down on dog beach. There were seven or eight of them with their dogs and gear stuffed in that beat-up ride, and they had been on tour for months. The road grime-covered car looked like it had been through hell. The front grill was shattered, the passenger side headlights were knocked out, and a big spider web crack emanated from the upper right-hand side of the windshield. The captain of this interstate transport shuttle, a tall thin kid with his natty dreads wrapped up in a filthy tam, explained that one of his gas riders had passed out behind the wheel as they drove through the night to catch a show the next day. The car had dived off the road and torn through some rancher's fence as the occupants screamed for their young lives. He pointed out the deep gouges in the paint where the barbed wire had raked the hood and right fender and shrugged it off. "It was not our night to die," he stoically said.

We invited them to Fester Island for the night, and we all camped up in the dunes, leaving our cars unattended. Early the next morning before dawn our little tent city was visited by a police helicopter, hovering low. They stayed above us long enough to blow away any remnants of sleep any of us had, and we cleared out at first light, lest police officers of the terrestrial variety descend upon us.

The show was a day away now, and the beach was overrun with crusty lot kids. It was a blast. For once I felt we outnumbered the normal folks ten to one.   As evening approached, I met one kid called Wingnut, and the name was fitting. He was dread-less under his low-riding ball cap, which was unusual among these kids, since it seemed everyone had twisted their dirty locks into uneven misshaped dreads, including me by that point. But he wore the huge velvety patchwork corduroy pants and oversized colorful print t-shirt and flaunted the thick braided and beaded hemp necklaces like the rest of them.

He also had some nasty scars on his face, which he attributed to a bad car wreck a few years before. He had been driving a flat-nosed VW bus all tripped out of his head on ketamine with one of his buddies and slammed into a wall head on. The wreck killed his friend, and almost killed him. He had been in a coma for months and was not expected to ever wake up again, but he did wake up and live to party another day, albeit a little more twisted in the head. He was supposed to be on meds to keep his head straight, but he didn't like the way they made him feel; gave him a limp dick, he said. So he devised his own medication routine that included basically any drug he could get his hands on. He told me all of this within the first minute of meeting him, without any prompting whatsoever. He then offered me a fat pinch of shrooms and proceeded to make a techno -like music by pounding a beat on his chest and somehow mouthing two octaves of his voice simultaneously. It was mad trippy, and I hadn't even eaten the shrooms yet.

"You want a Q-tip?" he asked me as I munched the fungus. I thought he meant some kind of drug reference I hadn't yet been made aware of. Nope, he meant a real Q-tip, and pulled one out of a little box. "Clean your ears, man. It feels fucking great." I did as he suggested and found he was right. I hadn't cleaned my ears in months, and rolling that cotton swab around my ear canal wiping out the wax felt fucking awesome.

I stomped around with him most of the night, meeting all the many lot kids he knew who were rolling in, and generally tripping face about town.

The next morning, Pete and I, along with Tick and Aiden and as much loot to sell as we could fit in the car, made our way to the stadium where the show was to be held. We were early, and they hadn't opened the parking lot yet, so we just hung out in an adjacent parking lot with all other crusty kids and waited.

I watched as car after car, van after van of travelers rolled up and unloaded their unwashed cargo of kids. Weed was going around; someone passed me a jug of wine. Things were looking pretty good. Then they opened the gates. A rush of kids scrambled to get their cars parked so they could get down to the serious business of partying, hustling, and trying to get miracle tickets into the show.

The place was mad! It was like a carnival where there was only one ride, and everyone was on it. We set out our wares on the hood of the car and started raking in money from the clean custys who had cash to burn. Tick and Aiden had good taste in hippie-themed shit, it seemed because the stuff damn near sold itself. They also quickly amassed enough drugs to get us all lit up, plus a couple tickets to get the two of them into the show. High as fuck and bored with the hustle, they handed off whatever was left of their merchandise to Pete and me and wandered off into the crowds.

We played shopkeepers for a little while before it became apparent that the money on the lot had been spent and that no one was interested in the dregs. So we wrote "FREE" on a piece of cardboard and abandoned the rest. I had gotten ahold of a hit of acid and some ecstasy, which had me rolling hard. Pete was in a similar boat, and we lost each other in the melee almost immediately.

I spent hours cruising the lot, blazing up with random folk, dancing to drums, sucking on balloons full of nitrous, laughing with strangers, all while the actual show was raging away inside the stadium. It was an absolutely mind-altering experience, and I decided then and there I would follow this band too. Not so much because I liked the music, since I couldn't name one of their tunes if my life depended on it, but because of this crazy parking lot party. Shit, I would travel to the ends of the earth to keep up with a wild scene like that.

I don't really remember how it ended, being as lit up as I was, but it was well after dark when I realized most of the people had cleared out because the show was long over. The facility security ushered the last of the stragglers off the lot, including us, and we made our way to Fester Island, where the party continued with a few other car- and van-fulls of kids at a dull roar until dawn.

Pete and I got to talking as the sun rose and agreed we should follow this party to the next city, which was Las Vegas. Unfortunately, it would also be their last show of the tour. That kind of put me out, seeing as I had decided to follow this party to the ends of the earth. I didn't expect those ends to come so soon. Still, I was down to go all in and figured that since the Vegas show would be the last one on a multiple city, multiple month-long tour, it was sure to be an even bigger, wilder party than this last one. It was in Las fucking Vegas after all.

Aiden and Tick we're not into going, deciding to trek north to L.A. for the holidays instead and play their hustle there, painting curbs and whatever other scheme they came up with ahead of Tick's court date in Yuma. So we bid them farewell, figuring we'd all meet again sooner or later. I never saw either of those crazy kids again.

Egg was also not into going to Vegas, having had some bad experience there that repulsed him noticeably. He was off north as well to work a Christmas tree lot like he had described, and again invited us to join him. "Once the show is over, come find me on Venice Beach. We'll make some cash, then head further north after the New Year, smoke dank in Mendocino, welcome the spring in Cougar Hot Springs, up in Oregon. It will be good living." We thanked him for everything and agreed we might just take him up on his offer. I never saw him again either.

No, my path was in a different direction now. I didn't realize it yet, but I was at the apogee of my western arc and would soon succumb to the gravity of home.

Pete and I picked up Wingnut and some girl he had hooked up with, and we took off for that unnatural oasis in the desert where the party rages on forever. The directions were easy, get on interstate 15 and drive till you're there.

It was a long drive, and the sun set behind us long before we reached the state line, dropping curtains of darkness on the empty desert flying by around us. As we were coming down the mountain pass dividing the two states, we caught a glimpse of the city far in the distance, glimmering and shining in the absolute blackness of the high desert. Right over the border in Nevada we passed a little town lit up like a miniature Vegas for those travelers who just couldn't wait one more fucking minute to gamble. We blew through it in a blink.

The next half hour brought the glowing orb on the horizon closer and closer, until we realized we were inside the dome of light. Night was banished here, where the incandescent bulb was king. We wormed our way to the Vegas strip and marveled at the glittering obscenity around us. Pete landed a parking space on a side street near where the venue of tomorrow's show would be, and we spilled out onto the pavement.

What a place this strip was! The lights were overpowering, strung out looking normal folk in sensible shorts were stumbling around with hollowed-out eyes, and the hum of a million industrial grade air conditioners filled the space where the flashing lights couldn't tread. We found other groups of lot kids right away and hooked up with them. Wingnut knew all these kids, so Pete and I slid into the groups effortlessly. Someone got hold of a couple gallons of cheap wine and we kicked it on the strip road-kid style, drinking from used coffee and soda cups plucked from the trash and watching the mad, mad world roll by. Eventually we four headed back to the Olds and passed out sitting up in the seats.

In the morning, I treated my companions to one of those all-you-can-eat breakfast buffet places, breaking one of my last traveler's checks in the process. Wingnut, realizing I was not totally broke, asked me if I would be into going halves on a hotel room for the night. "I ain't got enough skrill to pay for the whole thing," he explained. "But together we can make it happen." I agreed, and after our mid-morning breakfast we found a low-budget, single-story motel further down the strip away from the big casinos. The guy at the front desk eyeballed us like the dirty road kids we were, but our money spoke for itself. We got a room secured for after the show.

As evening approached, we made our way to the venue, gradually hooking up with the other kids who were scattered about the strip until we had convened into a sizable mob. The parking lot was already filling up when we arrived. It was a smaller lot than the last one, sandwiched between a few tall buildings, and there seemed to be fewer vehicles too. There were only a few heads hocking their wares, and less of a jovial atmosphere in general. But the weed and wine flowed freely, and I even got another couple hits of acid to dose for free.

I lost track of Pete and the others early on in the evening and found myself wandering the lot alone, tripping pretty hard. The scene this time was much darker, much dirtier. I caught a lot of aggressive vibes from the clouds of kids I passed through, and it left me with an uneasy feeling.

As the show wrapped up and the venue disgorged its contents, there was a sudden rush of kids into the lot, and everywhere I looked there was disappointment and woe. This was the last show of the tour, the party was ending, and everyone was bumming out hard. People were hugging and crying like they might never see each other again, and some shirtless kid with blood on his face was having a bad trip melt down, yelling and freaking out. Security began pushing us out soon thereafter, forcibly in some cases. The lot security in San Diego had let us mill around for hours after the show. Las Vegas had no patience for any of that shit.

So everyone wound up wandering the strip aimlessly, taking on that same hollowed-out eye look I had noticed on the normal, mainstream society people the night before. Who were these shady kids I was following around? Who were these twisted hippie crooks whose tribe I had joined? I began to realize that almost everyone I had met on this whole trip, damn near every person I had crossed paths with was spiritually dirty and morally crooked and hopelessly flawed in some serious way. And I realized too that I had become just as dirty and crooked as everyone else. We were all total hypocrites, draping the robes of new-age spiritual righteousness on our soiled bodies only to stain the garments through with the filthy, greasy corruption of our true human natures, amplified as they were by the desperate measures we were called to engage in just to keep wine in the jug and weed in the bowl. I began to feel that I needed to get away from all of them and find my own way, whatever way that would be. I began to feel that I needed to walk.

I wandered alone through the casinos, the incessant ringing and dinging of the flashing slot machines washing over me at every turn. The carpets, acres long all carried insane geometric patterns that rose off the ground waist height, so I had to wade through the place like I was slogging through some sort of day-glow swamp. I was starting to bug out, and I had no idea where the door out of this madness was. It felt as if I had been wandering around inside of this glittering insanity for hours, days, my whole fucking life even.

Then I saw a vision of familiarity. A couple kids dressed in black, dirty black. Metal band t-shirts, stitched up zipped up jeans, ragged, overgrown Mohawks made of colored dreads, and boots, big dirty boots. I was outside somehow and back on the strip, who knows how, and there before me kicking it on the curb were a couple crusty road kids that looked more like me, like metal head punks. I stepped up to them, just to see if I was hallucinating or not, because I was tripping out of my head by now.

"Yo, man!" one of them asked, as I stood there before them leering like a maniac "You alright?"

"Look at his fucking eyes!" the other added. "He's tripping his fucking balls off."

"You roll in with all these fucking hippies?" the first one asked me. I shook my head yes, still unable to form words. "You don't look like a hippie."

"I don't know what the hell I am," I answered.

They laughed. "Here, have a drink." And one pulled out a can of cheap shwag beer from the remains of a twelve pack they were sharing. The beer tasted like magic. "You're on the road though, right? I mean, you're filthy as fuck."

"Just as filthy as you," I responded, as I sat down beside them. They laughed again.

We sat there and rapped for I don't know how long, but long enough that I was on my way down from the peak of the trip and regaining my grasp on reality by the time the beers were gone. They were gutter punks, crust punks, and they had come into town by hopping a freight train from out east. They were headed south, towards Arizona because it was warm there. I told them I was adrift, that I was looking to walk away on my own. "Head south," one of them suggested with a shrug. "Head south and see where the road takes you."

I made my way back to the hotel room I had partially paid for and found it populated by probably two dozen lot kids reclining on every available surface. There was even some kid lying in the bathtub. I took a few puffs from a doobie that was going around and lay out on the floor near a few other kids, their long dirty dreads smacking my face as they tossed and turned in their fitful sleep.

I dreamed that night I was running, running as fast as I could down a deserted city street. The world around me looked a lot like the city I had just spent the night wandering, but all the lights were out. It was totally dead. Only the moon cast any light on the pavement ahead of my frantic pace. Was I running away from something? Was I running to something? It didn't seem to matter; I just had to move, and now.

I woke early, having only slept a couple hours at most, and shook Pete awake. "Come to the car with me," I asked him. "I'm leaving."

He was a little alarmed by my intention to just walk away, not surprisingly. But he admitted he was looking to make a move himself. He missed Jen terribly and felt he had blown his only chance at true happiness by all the wrongs he had done to her. He was going to trek to Florida and try to find her. He was going to try and win her back. He gave me a long hug. "Take care of yourself, my friend. We will meet again." I then stooped and gave Dylan one last rub on the head. He had been a fantastic canine companion all down the road, and I was happy to have been able to travel with him.

And with that, I hoisted my pack up on my back and started walking south.

CHAPTER 37

My first day on foot, I strode along with my head held high, enjoying the self-inflicted solitude I suddenly found myself in. Who needs a car for transport when you could just walk? I arrogantly thought. I had this thing by the ass, and the world was mine for the taking. I refused to give doubt any audience.

About a week prior to this change in direction, I had bought a pair of beat-up old infantry boots of Vietnam Conflict vintage for a couple of bucks at the flea market to replace the sneakers I had left home with. My old kicks had become so blown out, it was the duct tape alone keeping the soles from walking off without me. I thought the boots were a pretty good score, considering they were my size and they were built for combat. But after a few miles of Vegas sidewalks, I began to reevaluate this conclusion. They fit well enough, but they offered no support whatsoever. It was like the soles were made of polished wood. But I refused to acknowledge the discomfort. I set my goal as getting one foot placed in front of the other, come what may. Besides, I thought, this dumpster country is awash in used shoes. I figured I'd find another pair before long better suited to my feet anyway.

By the afternoon, I was tracing the 515 freeway by way of a series of concrete wash troughs, tubes and walls covered in crooked, poorly applied local gang graffiti. I was definitely off the path of the average walker now. My only company out here were the speeding cars separated from me by tall fencing and the dusty garbage in the dry, artificial creek beds. At one point, my path took me into a long tunnel made for shunting the infrequent storm water runoff away from the streets of the living. Taking note of the high-water mark stains up near eye level, I imagined what this tunnel would be like full of a raging torrent of dirty, garbage-filled water. I would be washed away to my death instantly. I quickened my pace then and focused on the light at the end of the tunnel.

As evening approached, the concrete began to break up into sandy earth and dry plant life decorated with windblown shreds of plastic bags. The metro area was beginning to thin out. I found a shallow, human-sized depression under a rather large bush that looked as though it had been used as a sleeping place many times before and decided I should quit the day while I was ahead. I felt good about the distance I'd traveled, and since there was no particular destination I was aiming for, and certainly no timeframe on arriving wherever the hell that destination was, I felt I could justifiably stop and camp wherever the hell I damn well wanted to.

The sun slowly set on that no man's land between the city and the dry untamed wilds ahead, leaving me with a feeling of uneasy peace. I had made the jump, and there was no going back now.

I had fragmented, incoherent dreams all night to the tune of moving rushing water. The traverse through the storm drain tunnel and the constant sound of the nearby freeway probably colored my sleeping mind so aquatic.

In the morning, I awoke rested but uneasy. Little doubts began poking through my rosy screen. Where was I headed? How was I really going to get there? These thoughts came to me in the voice of my father, thousands of miles away. Was I making the right choice here by walking out of Vegas? I stuffed those questions into my pack along with my sleeping bag and pushed forward. I had made my choice, and now I needed to walk it off.

Keeping along the side of the highway without walking on the shoulder was proving very difficult. I often had to scramble up or down some concrete abutment or scale some chain link fence to keep moving in the direction I wanted to travel. At one point, I came up on a big cloverleaf cluster fuck of elevated freeway on ramps, off-ramps and overpasses. It took me damn near an hour just to thread my way through that pedestrian prohibitive environment. The one positive side of all that elevated concrete was the ample shade it afforded. It was hot out in the sun, and clouds didn't seem to exist on that part of the planet. Still I pressed on, shading my eyes from the sun or the glare of the concrete, or both.

The hours clicked away, and I was still tracing the freeway. I had the energy in my legs to go miles more, but my feet fucking hurt. Those boots were starting to take a toll on my step. And I was hungry too, so when the highway passed over a double set of train tracks, I scaled the fence and tucked in under the bridge to have a rest in the shade.

I pulled my boots off to air out my feet and found I had already contracted blisters. Nothing outrageous, but some had already popped. I dug around in my pack and bandaged them with some gauze and the only band aids I had as best I could. While I was in my pack, I rummaged around for anything superfluous, so as to lighten the load. I gathered a little bindle's worth of trinkets and keepsakes I had saved, including my duct-taped bible, and tucked them up in the beams of the bridge above me, chuckling to myself that the odds of ever returning to retrieve them had to be damn near zero. Once I had rested myself sufficiently, I crossed the tracks, tossed my pack over the next fence and, climbed over after it.

By late afternoon, the southbound interstate highway I paralleled had reduced itself to a four lane US route, making it much easier to trace. I was in the position now where I could start waving my thumb at the passing cars for a ride, but I wasn't ready yet. I was walking on principle. I felt that to accept a ride this early in the game would be cheating somehow. No, I had to clear the city on my own two feet.

The afternoon sun was intense, and I lamented my lack of a brimmed hat. But still, I would not stick out the thumb. Not that anyone would have readily given me a ride. Everyone who passed me did so at upwards of seventy miles an hour, so even if they did notice me, clad as I was in filthy road-kid clothes, they would most likely choose to pass up on the opportunity of smelling me in their nice clean cars. I was running low on water now too. But I figured I had to come up on a gas station sooner or later; I was still within city limits after all.

Hours later, and nearing nightfall I still had not come up on any semblance of store whatsoever, let alone a service station stocked with stacks of cold clear water in gallon jugs. The doubts begin poking larger holes in my screen, and rightfully so. In response I stuck out my thumb. But much as I anticipated, no one even slowed down as they passed me.

As the sun began to fade, I spotted a partially built complex just off the road at the base of a low, dark, craggy hill and trekked out to it. Maybe some construction workers had left something behind I could steal and drink. But when I got to the site, I could tell that whoever was running this job had run out of money. The site sat unfinished, and judging by the windblown dust inside, had sat that way for quite some time. I considered bedding down there for the night since my feet were screaming by then. But the place gave me the creeps terribly, and my thirst egged me on in hopes of quenching it.

Soon after nightfall, I caught sight of a pulsing glow on the hilly horizon ahead, a sort of flash of color in the sky reminiscent of the background radiation of the Vegas strip. As I came around a bend and up over the rise, I realized what it was. A small casino/hotel/gas station combo loomed out of the surrounding darkness like a beacon of life, calling out to me with promises of water and rest. I hiked straight up to the restaurant and dropped down into a booth. The waitress looked me up and down disparagingly, obviously unhappy with the prospect of serving a vagrant and the possibility of payment issues once the bill came due. But my money was good, what little I had left of it. I placed my last two traveler's checks on the table along with the few bills of cash I had in hopes of calming her fears that the cops might need to be called once the meal was through, and she responded well to the signal.

I drank a pitcher and a half of water before my food even came out, and a few more pints after that, filling up till my guts hurt. I asked my waitress what lay on the road ahead. "Nothing," she curtly replied. "Just miles and miles of empty desert." Undaunted, I restocked on bottled water and food at the gas station and trekked on a little south of the outpost, out into the open scrub of the surrounding desert. There I found an old, discarded couch with no cushions and bedded down for the night.

The ruined and abandoned piece of furniture proved incredibly comfortable, considering. But to be fair, I had not slept on anything but the back seats of cars, hotel room floors, and the bare hard ground for months, so even a cushion-less wreck of a couch out in the open desert was like a feather bed to me.

As I drifted off, with my view of the night sky above switching between an intermittently wide swath of twinkling cosmos and a multicolored milky fog of light from the flashing casino sign nearby I was reminded of that last real bed I had slept in, seemingly a lifetime ago.

Jen's aunt. That odd, non-stop talking woman. That sad, sad woman, alone in that big house of hers. I had slept in her son's bed, in her son's bedroom. But there had been no son living in that room. There was no one living in that house but her and her madness. God damn what a long, strange trip this has been.

I rubbed my face at the thought of it all, replaying other random snippets of memory now from various points along the way. Making artistic sculptures out of the colorful wave-tossed plastics on the rocky shore of Lake Erie, partying with those high school kids up by the radio towers outside of Rapid City, meeting and being welcomed by the RV kids in the forest up above Ned, Dustin's kiss on my cheek as he bid me farewell out in the desert. And that old mountain man traveler I met in a supermarket parking lot in Sedona, the one who gave me the carved owl pendant.

I touched the talisman through my shirt and felt the joy and happiness of all those memories, of all those experiences, of all those souls I had grown close to in my travels. But all too soon those warm feeling cooled into loneliness. Those amazing experiences were all behind me now, and all those people I had grown to love, dirty crooked flaws and all, were all far from me and my ruined couch, cast aside at the edge of civilization. Maybe this was a mistake, walking away alone. I began to worry I was leaving behind something I could never retrieve, much like the bindle of things I stashed under the railroad bridge, who knows how many miles now behind me. And I began to worry that whatever I was trekking towards would ultimately destroy my youthful dreams and would cause the life I had previously enjoyed to be forever beyond my reach. With mournful foreboding wrapping my consciousness, I drifted to sleep.

The sun woke me at dawn, there being no shade to hide me from its searching gaze. I turned for one last look back towards the city of sin, the taste of crusted salty sweat on my lips, and set out on my way. Very soon I came to a southerly route and broke right on US 95. Before long, all sign of civilization beyond the sun-bleached, garbage-strewn road was gone. My feet carried on now in a sort of dull burn, and my face felt taught and dry from the sun. I stuck my thumb out early, fishing for a lift to no avail. It was as if I was invisible out there on the side of the road. I walked myself into a trance, and the hours ticked away as the sun trekked across the clear blue sky.

Near midday I came upon a sort of crossroads, a rough-hewn wooden post at each corner. The sight was striking; for it reminded me of a dream I had had months earlier. I rubbed my eyes, expecting to see a child-size owl perched on a post, staring me down. But there was nothing but dry rocks and broken bottles. Minutes later, I got my first ride.

A little beat-up mid-size pickup truck with a cap over the bed abruptly pulled over ahead of me in a cloud of dust. I jogged on aching feet to catch up to where it came to rest.

"Hello, son," the withered old man at the wheel croaked, his sun-stained skin offsetting the silver whiteness of his wispy overgrown hair and stubbly beard. "Toss your pack in the pack and hop in up front with me."

I lifted the rear window above the tailgate and dumped my pack on what looked like the guy's bed. There were clothes and blankets and beat-up paperback books and dirty cookware all strewn about the covered bed of the truck. It was the old guy's nest; he was living in there. That realization lightened my spirits momentarily, for I thought I might be crossing paths with someone with whom I could relate. Those lightened spirits did not last long.

It got weird the moment I shut the passenger side door. "Boy, I'm sure glad I found you." The old man smiled and placed his hand midway up my thigh and squeezed. "And I bet you're glad I picked you up, eh?"   I could not deny that. My feet were vibrating in waves of burning pain, as was my back, and my legs and, well, all of my body. "Where ya headed, son?"

"Don't really have a destination in mind," I admitted. "South ways, I guess."

"Ah, good, good," the man muttered. "Then you're headed my way." He then asked me my story and cut me off in the first sentence of my response. "I did some traveling once, back when I was younger, back before the war. You know the war, son?" he asked me. I assumed he meant World War Two, but he didn't look like he was old enough to be a veteran of that global conflict. "That's right. I was just out of engineering school and had drawn up a set of plans for an aircraft that would be more efficient than anything they had in the air at the time. In fact a few tweaks and it'd be more efficient than anything they're flying even now, commercial or military," he crowed, beaming with pride.

"Then came the war. Being a proud American, I felt obliged to offer my services to the government, even though I felt that Hitler feller had some good ideas and was on to something big.

You know who Hitler was, son?" he asked me, placing his hand above my knee again. Of course I fucking knew who Hitler was, alarm bells ringing now loudly in my head. "I was just checking. Kids these days don't know their ass from their elbow."

He rambled on then for a good while about how kids these days don't value hard work, and don't know the value of a dollar, and wouldn't know the meaning of the word value if it smacked them in the balls. I hadn't said much more than ten words to this guy yet, and the way he was going in I'd be lucky to get in another five.

"Where was I? Oh, yeah! So, I traveled to Washington DC so I could deliver my aviation plans to the president, German spies trailing my every move. I couldn't get to the president himself, of course. They don't just let anybody in off the street, you know, no matter how well qualified he might be, but I did speak with some of his closest advisors. They saw the merits in my design right away and promised to take me on board. Then do you know what the bastards did?" he asked me, his hands clenched to the steering wheel so tight I thought his veins were going to blow out of his white knuckles. "They stole my design!" he yelled. "The god damned bastards stole my designs and left me with the bill!"

I looked at the road ahead, and the dry desolate landscape flying by, not a sign of life for miles. I was glad I was not on foot out here, though the price for the privilege was steadily climbing. Beside me the old man was now raging away about the government and how they had screwed him out of his future and ruined his life. The guy wasn't even really addressing me anymore; he spoke as if he had been rehearsing this speech for years, decades even. I'll just have to stick it out, I thought. I need this ride.

"So I took my plans to the private sector, laid them out right on the desk of the captains of industry," he continued, his pitch slowly rising. "Here's how you're going to beat the government at their own game, I told them. Here's how you're going to win the war for your country. Well, they took my plans, alright. They took my plans, and then the god damned Jews threw me out!"

I looked over to him in increasing unease, as he was now intently staring at me. "You still got your foreskin, son?" he asked point blank. Startled by the directness of the question, I admitted that I in fact still did, and his face brightened considerably. "Real red-blooded Americans like us need to stick together, you know?" He said, his hand again placed above my knee, squeezing my mid-thigh. "Those God damn Jews will ruin us all. They already have the ni**ers at our throats!"

I was speechless, and more than a little afraid. He had been accelerating his little four-cylinder pickup during that whole last tirade and had the little truck up near eighty miles per hour by now. The whole vehicle was vibrating under the strain, rattling and shaking like it was about to fly to pieces. "You know what I mean, son?" he asked, his eyes again locked intently with mine and not on the road ahead. "You know what I mean?"

"Uh, yeah, man," I stuttered. "Sure."

"Once I get these plans to Washington, I'll be a shoe-in for the Nobel Prize," he continued, turning his gaze back to the road and rapidly decelerating the shuddering little truck. "The lives they will be able to save with my designs, son. I will be a hero; I will be a household name!"

He continued on with his madness, his shrill voice rising and falling with anxious passion but I was no longer paying attention. I was picturing myself hundreds of miles away, back on dog beach, torching a fat bowl of dank nugs with Egg Man, when suddenly the old man spotted something off on the salt flats in the distance. "Lookit there!" he exclaimed, shooting his pointing hand close past my face towards the perceived action. "Model planes are up! Come on, let's go have a look!" And he steered the truck off the pavement and onto the earthen flats at speed.

A couple hundred yards off the road, a group of half a dozen cars and trucks were parked, their occupants standing about with big chunky control boxes in their hands, their necks craned skyward. The old man stopped his truck and hopped out with all the youthful vigor of a schoolboy, whipping around to my side of the truck and pulling the door open.

Come on, son," he pleaded, attempting to take me by the hand. "I want to show you the wonders of mechanical flight!"

Circling above, dozens of buzzing, whining model airplanes tore about, burping smoke. He raced around, his neck bent unnaturally back attempting to track their progress across the sky and gesticulating wildly as he attempted to engage me in his treatise on mechanical aviation. I looked to the hobbyists piloting these loud little birds and registered their expressions: some bewildered, some amused, some annoyed. The old man went on like they were not even there, and so did the operators. I got the feeling that this was not the first time this old man had run up on their activities.

Embarrassed, annoyed and more than a little nervous of what that guy might do next, I took this opportunity to collect my bag from the back of the guy's truck while he had his attention towards the heavens. I was just hitching it up on my back when he realized I was not there hanging on his every word and ran back to stop me.

"No, no, son! You can't leave!" And he grabbed me by the arm. "We're a hundred miles from anywhere. Let me give you a ride." He had me in a tight spot. I did need a ride off these salt flats. I agreed, and he squeezed my shoulder with joy. "Excellent, son, excellent."

I rode with my pack between my legs from then on. I figured if I had to bail out, if I had to tuck and roll out of that guy's insanity, I better have my gear handy. It was getting late in the afternoon now, and the shadows of the passing signposts were growing long. The old man was not speaking much anymore. He would only mutter from time to time under his breath or point out some rock formation or other feature in the distance as if to convince me we were very far away from anything. His silence was almost as unnerving as his earlier tirades, but it gave me pause to think. I needed this ride, but I also needed to get out of this ride alive.

"So, can you take me towards civilization?" I finally asked him.

"Oh, I'm taking you to my home," he said matter of factly. I took another look behind me through the back window and into the bed of the truck. This was his fucking home; we were riding in it. What the fuck does he mean by that? "You can have a shower, and I'll make you dinner. Breakfast too." And he placed his hand on my upper thigh again. My skin crawled at his touch.

He slowed down at an intersection in the road, where a minor route led away from the other minor route we had been traveling on. "Actually, man. Just drop me off here. I'm not going your way."

He hit the brakes hard, throwing me forward. "No, son. You can't get out here. There's nothing out here for you. Come to my home with me, son. I will take care of you. You will like it in my home." And he reached to touch my leg again.

"Nah, man," I responded, brushing his hand away. "I'll take my chances here."

"You ungrateful little cunt!" he growled, his face contorting into a fearful grimace. "You're going to die out here!"

I hopped out in hurry, and he hit the gas before the door was even closed, showering me with gravel. I sat there on the side of the road where I landed as he accelerated away, thanking God I was off that crazy ride. But the ride was not over yet, and there was no God out there on that sun-blasted pavement to hear my thanks.

CHAPTER 38

The sun was setting as I crossed the state line back into California. If it had not been for the big metal sign welcoming my arrival, I'd have never known the difference. Everything out there looked the same. Dry, flat and scrubby, framed by dark jagged hills on the horizon. I had no idea where I was in relation to that sign though, so the fact that I was crossing a border meant nothing. I was still many miles from anything at all, and I was low on water. I figured I was still heading south. At least more south than if I turned around and walked the other direction, so I carried on into the night.

It was very dark out there in the open desert, broken only by the infrequent passing of a car or semi-truck thundering by. The stars were gorgeous, but their beauty was lost on me. I was spooked now. The reality of the choice I had made to walk out of Vegas was beginning to land squarely on me. I stuck my thumb out at every vehicle that passed now, even though the next ride might be as insane as the last. I had to take that chance. I had to get a ride back to civilization, or this desert might just kill me.

I walked in the dark for a couple hours before another little pickup truck with a cap on the bed pulled over ahead of me. At first I thought it was the brilliant aviation engineer come back around to hunt me down and finish me off, but I quickly realized not only was the truck a different make and model, it was also a different color. Another old man and a huge shaggy dog welcomed me into the front seat.

"Where ya headed?" he asked with a noticeable drawl.

"Civilization," I answered. "Or anywhere where I can get water."

We drove on through the night for well over an hour. I nodded off a few times, my exhaustion overcoming my desire to remain alert, but his big dog licked my face every time my head dropped. Eventually we came up onto a large, brightly lit, yet deserted service station. He pulled in and put it in park.

"Here you are. Stay safe, young man."

I thanked him and stumbled into the store. The place was so brightly lit it damn near burned my eyes out of their sockets. But once I became accustomed to the overpowering lighting, I spotted the prize I was looking for. Water! I grabbed a few bottles and some food and made my way to the counter. There I found myself face to face with a grumpy looking, potbellied sheriff with deep pockmarks all over his face. He had been chatting with the guy at the register, an equally unsavory-looking character. The both of them stared me down silently and sized me up. I was obviously on foot; they must have seen my ride drive away. I hastily made my purchase with the little bit of cash I had and retreated from the reach of the fluorescent lights and their malicious eyes, deep into the scrub across from the station. I'd rather spend the night out in the open then in a county lock up. Lord knows what that sheriff might throw at me if he had a mind to, I reasoned.

I found myself a nice bush and rolled out. It was still sort of warm out, too warm to zip up all the way in the bag, so I lay on top for a while and looked at the stars above. A faint mist seemed to muddy the view somehow, and I attributed it to my thirsty fatigued eyes. But soon I realized what I was actually seeing.

Clouds. A cold pinprick smacked my face, and then another, and then two more. It was rain! I was in the dry desert, a place that gets rain like once a fucking year, out in the open with no tent, and it starts to rain! Of all the fucking things! Waves of woe washed over me, and I begin to weep. My whole body hurt, I was dehydrated, and I was alone, all while getting rained on in the fucking desert.

The sweet oblivion of sleep took me then, and for a time brought me home. I dreamed it was Christmas Eve, and I was with my parents in their house. The sweet smell of the holiday tree and the aroma of good food permeated my being. All was right and good in the world. But it was not real. I was but watching the scene on a screen from a great distance, many, many miles away. It was like a drive-in movie, only there were no cars lined up before the massive screen, many stories tall. There was only me, alone in an empty dark wasteland watching the screen from an unfathomable distance away. But somehow I could still smell the wonderful smells of the holiday meal, even across space and time. I held on to that signal, held on with all my strength. If I could use that scent as a lifeline, a rope to pull myself closer, then maybe I could get home.

I had a new direction when I awoke, damp, sandy and sore. I wanted, no, needed to go home. I wanted to spend the holidays with my mom and dad more than I had ever wanted anything in my life. I didn't care anymore about the self perceived shame of returning home again, I didn't care if the world called me a failure for returning to where I started. But I had a long road ahead, all the more long now that there was an actual goal at the end of it. I packed up my gear and trudged back to the gas station. I had noticed a large map on the wall the night before. I needed to get my bearings, figure out which way to go.

I stood before the map and felt my heart sink as I realized just where I was, and where I had been only hours earlier. The nearest city of any size where I was sure to find a bus station was Needles, California, many miles away from me. But if I were still at that spot on the road where my last ride had picked me up, It'd be about a dozen-mile walk, less probably. I slammed my fist on the map in frustration.

"Hey, punk!" the guy behind the counter yelled. "Buy something or I'm calling the cops."

I bought some snacks with the change in my pocket, not wanting to break the last traveler's check I had till I could spend it on a bus ticket, and filled up the two big empty bottles I had bought the night before at the sink in the restroom. Then I set out, backtracking towards where I had been as the sun set on the previous day. Near as I could tell, I had a good twenty-five miles or more ahead of me before I got to US95 and a shot at Needles. Twenty five miles through a trackless desert unnervingly close to an area labeled "Dead Mountain Wilderness." Jesus Christ, I thought, I had really fucked up.

I had a good couple hours of decent hiking before the sun really cranked up the heat. I put my thumb out to every car that passed, hoping I'd get swooped before sun had its way with me. But my thumb dangled in the dry desert air to no avail. Again, every car that passed me did so at damn near eighty miles an hour. No one was stopping for me. No one gave a shit. Undaunted, I trekked on.

By mid-morning, I came upon what on the gas station wall map had been listed as a "town." There was no town there. Only a cluster of empty boarded-up buildings where the road crossed some train tracks two sets wide. There was a payphone there, though. And amazingly it had a dial tone. I made a calling card call home, knowing full well there would be nothing my folks could do for me to get me out of the situation I had put myself in. I just wanted to talk to someone sane, someone who loved me and whom I loved. I wanted to talk to my mother just to hear her voice. But no one was home. I left a message on the machine, probably the saddest most desperate message I had ever left them.

Once this last ruined outpost of humanity was behind me, the fear really set in. The sun was climbing high now, and its glare was punishing. My feet, four days into almost constant hiking, were wailing with a degree of pain that could only be managed if I just kept walking, if I didn't stop. I tried to ration my water supplies but soon found I had consumed one whole jug, and I knew from my memory of the map that I was not even close to halfway there. But what could I do but push on? So I did.

Both sides of the road, as it stretched away to the horizon, were glittering with discarded glass beer and soda bottles, millions of them. The sun would catch the greens and browns of the glass as I progressed which caused a shimmering, rippling effect that at times was strangely beautiful. As for the rest of the landscape, desolation is really the only word that does it justice. Far off in the distance, dark peaks of mountains could be seen, and perhaps three quarters of a mile or more off to my left those freight rail tracks I had crossed earlier ran parallel to the road I traveled. There were often incredibly long trains following these rails in either direction, often moving at a good clip, but sometimes they would pass relatively slowly. I began to wonder if the slow trains were traveling slowly enough that I could hop on and catch a lift out of my poor decisions. But they were so far away from the road. I did not know if I would have the energy to make it all the way out to the tracks, and still make it back to the road if I couldn't match the speed of the train on my ruined feet. I was also afraid of collapsing out there in the scrub where no one but the vultures would find me. At least if I crumpled in a heap on the side of the road, I stood a better chance of getting picked up before I expired.

Maybe that's how I can get a ride, I laughed to myself, my parched lip splitting in the process of smiling. I could collapse as a car drove by, and they would stop. I gave it a try three times, and three times they never even slowed down. I didn't attempt a fourth time. Righting myself and pack from the ground after a controlled fall proved surprisingly energy intensive. I need to conserve my resources now. I couldn't afford to fuck around.

It must have been near midday, being that the sun was nearly overhead, when I noticed something coming towards me on the road: a small speck of an object, tracing the yellow lines out where they converged. I strained to see what it was, and as it drew closer I could just make it out. It was a man, and he looked like he was dancing or something. Swaying back and forth rhythmically. Closer still and I realized his odd movements were caused by his mode of transportation. He was on roller skates, roller blades to be exact. He was a skinny white guy, black hair slickly parted with a well-groomed black mustache and dressed in loudly colored spandex shorts and matching tank top. I nodded to him as he rolled past, and he nodded back with a smile.

I wish I had some skates, I thought. I could really make some distance in a hurry on those. If only I knew how to ride skates without busting my tired broke ass all over the blisteringly hot pavement. Then I saw something else coming towards me, something much bigger. I thought it was a camper truck or a van, but it was moving too slowly. Gradually it drew close enough for me to figure out what I was seeing.

It was an old-timey covered wagon, being pulled by a single brown horse. It had heavy-duty truck tires on old rusty steel rims instead of wagon wheels, and painted on the side of the canvas top in drippy red paint was the phrase "From Russia with love." At the reins of this strange vehicle another man steered, a man who looked identical to the guy on the skates, except without the day glow spandex outfit. This other guy on the wagon was dressed as a cowboy in a red-checkered buffalo print button-up shirt, bright blue dungarees, and cowboy boots with pointy tips. The cart lumbered by, hanging pots and pans clanging against each other as it progressed. I nodded to the driver, and he nodded back with a smile.

A few moments later, a sharp piercing bolt of pain shot through my foot, and I crumpled to the ground involuntarily. Wincing in misery, I pulled off my boot and found my sock no longer the grimy brown I had come to know but red with blood. I peeled off the sock and surveyed my ruined foot. Huge blisters, raw with gore, oozed in the sunlight. I leaned back against my pack and cursed those boots. If only I still had my old sneakers, duct tape and all, I'd give damn near anything for them now, I thought.

I pulled the last bottle of water from my pack and took a swig. There was only a half quart or so left. Why didn't I ask those weird Russian twins for water, I asked myself? They would have surely spared some life-giving liquid for a fellow traveler, maybe even given me a ride out of this place on their crazy wagon. I turned to look back down the road, hoping I could call out to them since they had only just passed me moments ago.

But there was nothing. I could see down the direction from which I had come for miles behind, clear to the vanishing point. No Russian twins, no covered wagon. It was all a hallucination. They were not real. Sweet Jesus, I'm losing my mind, I realized, a sob bursting from the deepest part of my soul. I'm going to die out here on this desert road. I wish I had gone to L.A. and found the Egg Man and his Christmas trees; I wish I had ridden with Pete to Florida, I wish I had done any other fucking thing than walk out of Fucking Las Vegas! I silently shouted.

This is because you have forsaken your God, a punishing voice in my head answered me. You knew Jesus, and you turned from him! Now you are going to die and suffer the eternal punishment you deserve! Now you will know Hell!

No! The logical, newly liberated pragmatist fired back. There is no Hell but the one we make for ourselves. Heaven and Hell exist here alone, on this earth; death is but a release back into nothingness, only a return to dust!

But who formed the dust? Who formed you from the earth and gave you life? Who imparted upon you a soul?

There is no soul! Life is nothing but a chemical reaction! An improbable grouping of atoms! An emergent phenomenon! Life is right now, only Now; nothing more, nothing less!

My head was swimming, full body pains rippling through my form, spinning sparkles of light floating before my eyes. "Eloi Eloi Lama Sabachthanai!" I croaked aloud to no one as I lost consciousness. You know God damn well why, you worthless worm! Because you have forsaken him!

All was black before me, and I was alone. I was conscious of the fact that I was unconscious somehow. I knew I was still lying on the ground on the side of some God forsaken road in the middle of nowhere, but I also knew I didn't have to wake up if I didn't want to. I could call it quits right there; I could choose death. It was very comfortable in the blackness. There was no pain, and I was no longer troubled by thirst. There was nothing there, absolutely nothing. But instead of sheer terror in the presence of the void, I felt, well, nothing.

Is this a preview of Hell? I wondered lucidly. It's certainly not the flame and brimstone, and fire pokers up the ass I was led to believe it would be. But then again, this isn't quite what I was told Heaven would be either. Maybe it's neither Heaven nor Hell, but only the inside of my mind, the back side of my eyelids. Maybe this void I now stand before, this black nothing is all there was to death. Game over, done, that's it. That would mean there really is no Heaven or Hell, no God or Devil, no anything beyond the very moment you find yourself in. The right Now. And right now, this black nothing is kind of hitting the spot, I admitted. But should I stay here? Should I take this easy ride away from pain and suffering? I was pretty sure I wasn't dead, not yet anyway. Shit, I was trying to get home for Christmas, remember?

Ugh, but there is still so far yet to go, I thought, still so many sun-baked miles ahead, still so much thirst and pain. I really already am in Hell, right now. A Hell of my own making, and I am damned to walk through it. And if I am damned, if I am forsaken, If I am truly alone in this Now then it is up to me to live. It is up to me to survive this self-inflicted trial. It is up to me to walk out of here.

CHAPTER 39

I opened my eyes upon a dazzling punch of light, as if my face were within inches of a ten-thousand-watt crystal chandelier. I was alive, and it fucking hurt. I sat up and took in my surroundings. It was still a desolate forbidding world around me, but I no longer felt so despondent. I could do this. I had to do this.

My bare, wounded feet had dried somewhat in the sun, the sweaty blood now crusting into scabs. I rummaged around in what was left in my pack and found the last pair of socks I had, a pair of thick winter socks made of a wool blend, stiff with filth. I had no more band-aids to apply, not that a little band-aid would do much for my issues, so the thick socks would have to serve the function of bandages. They were dirty, but at least they weren't bloody. I struggled to pull my boots back on, laced them up tight, and got to my feet despite the protest my flesh waged against me. I had a new energy in me, or at least some reserve of energy I had found I could tap. I now needed to put that energy to use by putting one foot in front of the other.

I pressed on into the afternoon, using my flagging water reserves to wet my tongue only, and covered a good distance before that newfound energy was all but spent. It was very difficult to determine distances out there, where all the landmarks were so far away that their positions never seemed to move, but I was sure I was past the halfway point towards where this sun-blasted, two-lane blacktop met US route 95, and eventually, Needles. I had to be.

The train tracks were passing closer to the road now, and again I considered attempting to hop on one of the slower moving train cars. But where were they going? I was basically out of water by now, having one mouthful of warm water left sloshing hollowly in the plastic bottle. If I spent the last fumes of energy I had running down a freight train, and then that train stayed away from civilization for days, then that'd be it. Game over. No, I had to stay on this god damned road and keep walking, even if my feet told me I was treading on red hot embers. There was no other option.

At one point, I noticed that far ahead of me one of the impossibly long freight trains had stopped on the tracks. I had seen them roll by slowly before, but never completely stopped. The engines were well over a mile away, but I could just make out a figure of a person walking away from the head units through the open desert separating the tracks from the road. I wonder what that guy is doing, I asked myself, half thinking it may all be just another dehydrated hallucination. A short while later, I could see the figure trekking back towards the engines of the train. Then some puffs of black diesel smoke rose against the empty sky as the train began rolling along once more. I tried to imagine why what I just witnessed had happened, but my weary mind could make no sense of it. I was succumbing to a growing delirium and was unsure of the truth of anything I was experiencing by then. I kept catching movement out of the corner of my eyes, as if something were behind me, kept hearing scuffles like the steps of some light-footed entity keeping pace with my labored progress. This set me to laugh out loud madly more than once, for it felt like this unseen Other was playing with me, staying just out of sight no matter how swift I turned to catch sight of it.

Thirst alone dominated my thoughts now, driving away everything else. I tipped the empty bottle to the unrelenting sky to catch the last drop on my tongue. And then it was gone. I began scanning the discarded bottles on the side of my path for any swill that might still be inside, anything that resembled water. But there was nothing. My feet were screaming again, but I was afraid to stop, fearing I might not be able to get up once I sat down. And still the landmarks on the horizon did not move. It was as though I were walking on a treadmill, pushing forward and getting nowhere. Despair began to overtake me once again, and I was too weak to stay ahead of it. I began to wonder if they would ship my body home, or if my parents would have to fly out here and retrieve it. I hated to think I'd have to inconvenience them so. Maybe if I left the road, walked out into the brush and let the vultures take me, then they could just ship my bones home in a box. That would only weigh a couple pounds, so it couldn't cost that much, right? I stopped and looked out into the trackless waste stretching away from the roadside, seriously considering that plan for a moment before coming to my senses and shaking it off. No, I'm not dead yet. I must keep walking.

Then I saw something on the ground ahead where the pavement met the dirt, something out of place among the sun-bleached roadside trash and sand. I continued walking slowly towards it, unable to quicken my pace. It was a group of short plastic bottles sitting upright. They were aqua blue, had no labels, and were attached together with a plastic six-pack ring. And, for the love of all that is holy, they were full.

I dropped to my knees before them, unsure if what I was seeing was real. They were like no other bottles I had ever seen for sale anywhere; strangely shaped and unmarked. I touched them, and they were wet with condensation. They had been in the cold but a short time ago.

The guy from the train! He must have seen me walking out here under the blazing sun and taken pity on me. He must have stopped his train and hiked these bottles of railroad company-issued water out to the side of the road where I would surely find them. A sob climbed up my throat and choked on my swollen tongue. Someone does give a shit! I twisted the top off greedily and upended the bottle to my split lips. Never in my life had anything tasted so good. I peeled another bottle off the six-pack ring and slid it into my cargo pants pocket. I then stuffed the remaining four in my pack and climbed back to my feet. I had enough water now to last me another day. I had enough to get me out of this fucking desert alive.

I started walking again, now with renewed hope. The sun was much lower in the sky now, its heat less intense. I figured I still had three or four more hours of daylight left ahead of me. Surely I would make it to US 95 by dark. But even if I didn't make it by nightfall, I would make it in the morning, of that I was certain.

I pushed ahead for maybe another hour before I caught a flash of sparkle and color moving perpendicularly across the horizon far ahead of me, then another, and another. I strained my eyes to see what could be causing these sights. Was it a mirage caused by the heat of the afternoon sun on some road sign in the distance; was it another hallucination?

No, they were vehicles! Vehicles traveling along a road running perpendicular to this God forsaken stretch of pavement I was on; it was US 95! I was almost there! A swelling of emotions welled up inside of me, and I began laughing uncontrollably. A song popped into my head then, an old gospel hymn I used to sing in church. I found myself singing it aloud, belting it out with all my soul. I was heading home; I was going to live! But that crossroad was still over a mile away. That's the thing about long flat expanses. Just because you can see your goal ahead doesn't mean you're going to reach it any time soon.

The sun had set by the time I reached the intersection of Goffs Road and US 95, and I was absolutely spent. I had nothing left in me, barely enough power even to drag my body off the side of the road. In the dark of the starlit night, I rolled out my bag in the bushes within shouting distance of the intersection and laid my ass down. My head had barely hit the ground when sleep dropped on me like a pile of bricks.

I dreamed I was much older. Older, but not yet old. I had a wife and a child. I had a job and a house. I had a life, a normal sort of life, and it was good. I dreamed I was playing in soft green grass with this child, the sun mildly shining. Together we were running and laughing and rolling around without a care in the world. And my wife, standing a way off watching; she was beautiful, she was radiant, and she loved me. It was the most peaceful, wonderful dream, and it all seemed so real. The dream shifted then, changed perspective. I was in a forest of my youth, back on my island town, walking a well known path through the trees. Someone was with me, an older woman of faint green skin covered in simple line tattoos of animals and symbols, clad in burlap, with leaves in place of hair that rustled as she moved like a breeze through the trees. She stopped me at a large and ancient oak, silently drawing my attention to the branches, the pale green skin of her arms writhing in ink-drawn snakes. I watched the branch tips bud, grow into young fresh leaves, harden into dark green, fade into autumn colors and finally into brown. I looked at her again then as the dead leaves fell, swirling around us on their decent, and watched a tear spill from her eye and fall to the ground. She smiled and again called my attention again to the tree before us, where fresh buds were already beginning to emerge anew. I knew then that I was a part of this seasonal cycle of birth, life, death, rebirth, unending. That I had always been, that all of life was of this cycle, that there was never an end, only a change, a constant change. One manifestation giving way to the next for as long as life animated this world. I felt so silly in the presence of this truth that I wept, and the green woman embraced me. She smelled of soil and flowers and hummed a low warbling tone. A whispered word rose from the hum then as I buried my head into her burlap breast in joy and sorrow. I pulled back then and looked again into her eyes, and with the face of my mother she spoke clear as a ringing bell.

Walk.

I awoke before dawn, driven to consciousness by the many aches and pains that wracked my body, aggravated even more by the hard ground. I got my shit together by feel in the dark and stumbled out of the bush and into the headlights of the road. US 95 was ten times busier than the last desolate stretch I had journeyed on, so much so that I never had much chance to put my thumb-wielding arm down.

I had walked east maybe a mile when the light of dawn found me. Shortly thereafter, a truck pulled over, responding to my outstretched thumb. It was a mid-size flatbed truck, with the name of a local wrecking yard painted on the door and the road-worn rear axle of another truck lashed down to the bed with bright yellow straps.

"I can take you as far as Needles," the grease-stained, blue-collared driver told me frankly over the country music on his radio.

"Thank you, sir," I answered, my voice shaking with gratitude. "Thank you so much."

The man smiled uncomfortably. "Ok, kid. Hop in then."

ABOUT THE AUTHOR

Toby Dunne is a commercial equipment mechanic based in New York's Hudson Valley who would rather be painting and writing and walking in the woods.